A Bennet of Royal Blood
A Pride & Prejudice Reimagining

By Shana Granderson, A Lady

CONTENTS

DEDICATION

This book, like all that I write, is dedicated to the love of life, the holder of my heart. You are my one and only and you complete me. You make it all worthwhile and my world revolves around you. Until we reconnected I had stopped believing in miracles, now I do, you are my miracle.

ACKNOWLEDGEMENT

First and foremost, thank you E.C.S. for standing by me while I dedicate many hours to my craft. You are my shining light and my one and only.

I want to thank my Alpha, Will Jamison and my Betas Caroline Piediscalzi Lippert and Kimbelle Pease. A special thanks to Kimbelle for her forthright and on point editing. To both Gayle Surrette and Carol M. for taking on the roles of proof-readers and additional editing, a huge thank you to both of you. All of you who have assisted me please know that your assistance is most appreciated.

My undying love and appreciation to Jane Austen for her incredible literary masterpieces is more than can be expressed adequately here. I also thank all of the JAFF readers who make writing these stories a pleasure.

INTRODUCTION

This story starts with one of King George III's sons marrying the love of his life secretly. The woman is a daughter of an Earl. After more than a year of marriage, all of the time with his beloved wife spent at her estate of Netherfield Park in Hertfordshire, the Prince reveals his marriage to his father hoping the elapsed time will protect them. The King orders his son to leave the lady and plans to have the marriage annulled. The King was at least convinced by his son not to annul the marriage, so instead he orders a speedy divorce.

The reason was **NOT** that the lady was unsuitable, the opposite was true, but for political reasons, the King has promised his son's hand to a European princess to strengthen alliances for England. It saddens the King to do so, especially as this son is one he is very close to, knowing he is breaking his son's heart the King forces the divorce as the other country in question is one England sorely needs as an ally.

In the meanwhile, the lady had become best of friends with Mrs. Francine Bennet of Longbourn. They met a few months after Jane was born, shortly after the lady moved into Netherfield Park. When her devastated husband informs her of the forced divorce, his wife does not inform him she is with child to try not hurt him more. It so happens Fanny Bennet is also pregnant with her second child.

Due to the ignominy of divorce and worried about the social ramifications coupled with making assumptions about what the royals would expect of them, the lady's family cut ties with her when she needs her parents more than ever. The only one she feels she has left is Fanny Bennet. A few other friends write but the broken-hearted lady is not ready to accept their overtures and respond yet. As both ladies near their confinements Thomas Bennet is called away—for what he tells his wife—is to assist his good friend from Cambridge the Earl of Holder in Staffordshire. He is actually investigating ways to break the entail on Longbourn.

Fanny moves into Netherfield to be with her best friend during their confinements along with 2-year-old Jane. Before the final confinement, her brothers, Phillips, the solicitor, and Gardiner, the man of business are summoned. Phillips draws up a will for the lady and Gardiner is given management of her fortune.

Just in case the worst happens, the lady writes a number of letters, among them one to her child, one to the Prince, one to Bennet, and one to her parents as she has a plan in the event of her death.

The best friends go into labour within hours of each other. Fanny delivers a still born son and some hours later, her friend delivers a healthy baby girl, who is the legitimate daughter of a Prince, making her a Princess of the United Kingdom of Great Britain and Ireland. The friend has complications of birth and will not survive long. She implores her best friend—her sister of the heart—to take her daughter and raise her as her own and she will claim the dead baby son. Fanny cannot deny her friend her dying wish.

The Lady names her baby Elizabeth after her maternal grandmother. She charges Fanny with waiting until Fanny feels Elizabeth is ready, to reveal her birth right to her explaining her reasons for waiting. Other than a few small bequests to some, the lady's will bequeaths her child all of her worldly possessions, including an enormous fortune and Netherfield Park on reaching her majority of 21 or being married. When Bennet returns he is introduced to, and falls in love with, *his* second daughter. Jane and Lizzy are the loved equally by their parents.

The story looks at how the Bennets' lives are different with a much different Fanny than canon. Also how will Elizabeth and the world around her react to the news when she finds out her true heritage. The Bennets meet the Darcys and Fitzwilliams much earlier than in Miss Austen's masterpiece.

PROLOGUE

His Royal Highness, Prince Frederick Augustus, Duke of York and Albany, Earl of Ulster, had just returned to London—he hoped permanently—after having lived abroad, primarily in Hanover, since 1781. The Prince was the second son born to King George III and Queen Charlotte of the United Kingdom of Great Britain and Ireland in 1763.

His father the King had decided early on that his second son would pursue an army career and had him gazetted a Colonel in 1780. The Prince was appointed Colonel of the Second Horse Grenadier Guards in 1782, then was promoted to Major-General in November of that same year. He was next promoted to Lieutenant General in October 1784 and was appointed Colonel of the Coldstream Guards that same month.

His title, Duke of York and Albany, Earl of Ulster, was created in November 1784, and he became a member of the Privy Council at that time. On his return to Great Britain, the Duke took his seat in the House of Lords, where, on fifteen December 1788 during the Regency crisis, he opposed William Pitt's Regency Bill in full-throated support of his father, which caused the bill to fail. The bill had been tacitly supported by his older brother and heir to the throne, George, Prince of Wales.

In November of 1787, the Duke of York met a lady who took his breath away and quickly captured his heart. Lady Priscilla De Melville was almost twenty and the eldest daughter of Lord Cyril and Lady Sarah De Melville, the Earl and Countess of Jersey. She was petite with wavy dark mahogany tresses, and the greenest eyes he had seen. The next daughter, Marie, was more than ten years her sister's junior, and their son Wesley, Viscount Westmore, was only three at the time.

By early 1788, the two were ardently in love. Lady Priscilla turned one and twenty in April of that year when, despite warnings from her parents—mainly her father—to think better of it without royal sanction, Lady Priscilla married her Prince in a quiet ceremony in Essex during May 1788.

The Duke had demanded there be no announcements in the papers. He was fairly certain his father would attempt to arrange a marriage for him just as he had for many of his sons and daughters. Given that their new son-in-law was a son of the King, Priscilla's father begrudgingly agreed, although he warned his daughter no good would come of the subterfuge.

Shortly after the wedding, the couple moved to Lady Priscilla's estate of Netherfield Park in Hertfordshire. Her maternal grandmother, Beth, had willed the estate to her eldest granddaughter; it was to become hers upon her reaching her majority—which it did the day Priscilla turned one and twenty.

Because the Duke was sure some of his servants at Oatlands Park, his estate near Weybridge in Surrey, reported to his father, residing there was not an option for the couple. For their limited contacts with neighbours in the area where Netherfield Park was situated, Frederick introduced them as Mr. and Mrs. Oatland.

A Mr. Bennet visited to introduce himself, and not long after they moved in. Soon after Lady Priscilla made the acquaintance of Mrs. Francine Bennet, called Fanny, and her daughter Jane, who was yet an infant. The two ladies were drawn to each other and soon were calling one another Priscilla, or Cilla, and Fanny. Their husbands were friendly as well, but not near to the same level of intimacy as their wives. In the early days, Priscilla did not disclose the truth of who they were to any in the neighbourhood, not even Fanny.

The Prince would be gone for lengthy periods as he attended to his military and Privy Council duties, and to his parents from time to time. When he was home, he spent as much time with his beloved wife as he could. While in residence, Bennet, the only man he was close to in the neighbourhood, would join him in a game of chess and drinks after dinner now and again.

Their wives, on the other hand, were to be found in one another's company almost daily. An unintended, if welcome, consequence of their friendship was the amendment of Fanny Bennet's behaviour.

Fanny was the youngest daughter of a local solicitor, Mr. Elias Gardiner, and her looks and vivacity had attracted the prime catch in the neighbourhood—the heir of Longbourn—Thomas Bennet. He was blinded by her beauty, and in the first throes of love did not see that they seemed intellectually incompatible.

Fanny was not lacking in intelligence, but her late mother had drummed into her head men were not interested in or looking for intelligence in a woman. The result was both of her daughters, Hattie, the older, and Fanny, became more interested in fashion and gossip and repressed their innate intelligence.

Too late, Bennet realised that she seemed to be of mean understanding, spending her time talking of fashion and inconsequential gossip. He decided there was naught he could do to change things, so he never let her know how much he would have appreciated intelligence in his wife. Things continued in this vein until Fanny met and became friendly with Mrs. Priscilla Oatland. As their friendship deepened, Fanny clearly saw the deficiency in her own behaviour as she observed that of her friend. She noted in the interactions between her friend and her husband how much—in direct contradiction of what her mother taught her daughter—he appreciated and respected Priscilla's intelligence.

One day, not long after the two had decided to use familiar names to address one another, Fanny took a deep breath, "Cilla, I have a request," Fanny told her friend nervously.

"Fanny, you may ask anything; and if I am able, I will grant it," Priscilla averred.

"As you know, I was not raised as a gentlewoman. I have been following the teachings of my late mother which I now see were completely wrongheaded. Observing you, I have begun to see the deficiencies in my behaviour." Fanny raised her hand to kill the protest her friend was about to make. "My husband probably believes that I am of mean understanding, for that is the consequence hiding my intelligence. I am not deficient of mind, but the way I was taught to behave has led Thomas to believe so. What I hope is that you, my friend, will teach me how to behave as a gentlewoman should. Please say you will assist me in this, Cilla," Fanny beseeched.

"Fanny, it will be my absolute pleasure to help you in every way that I am able," Priscilla had returned emphatically, inwardly relieved that Fanny had asked.

And so, it began. Between observing how her friend behaved and instruction, within six months no trace remained of the wife Thomas Bennet thought to be crass, vulgar, and of mean understanding—very much to his delight. She had become a gentlewoman in every sense of the word and allowed him to see the intelligence she had been hiding from him.

There was no more gossip; she read and discussed books with him insightfully; she spoke calmly, hardly ever raising her voice as she had been wont to do in the past; and her nerves, which had begun to trouble her soon after their marriage, were never in evidence again. Never again did she ask the housekeeper at Longbourn, Mrs. Hill, to come running with the salts.

An unintended and welcome consequence of Fanny's changed behaviour was that her sister, Hattie Phillips, changed in her behaviour as well, as Fanny convinced her of the falsity of their mother's teachings. Hattie was married to Frank Phillips, who had taken over the Gardiner law practice when Mr. Elias Gardiner had passed soon after his youngest daughter's wedding to the heir of Longbourn.

Hattie had always followed her younger sister's lead, and when she saw the way her sister had changed, and accepted what Fanny told her about their mother's lessons as nothing but the truth, she emulated the behaviour, much to her husband's pleasure. No more gossip was heard from the former Gardiner girls again, which had an additional and beneficial effect of increasing their local circle of friends.

Many of the ladies in Hertfordshire had avoided Fanny initially, as she tended to boast relentlessly after her marriage. It took the ladies of the neighbourhood some time to trust the changes in Fanny and Hattie were real when they first became evident. It did not take long for them to see the changes were permanent, which led to Fanny quietly becoming one of the leading voices in the area.

The middle Gardiner son, Edward, had no interest in the law. He worked first in another's import-export concern; when he felt he had garnered enough experience, he struck out on his own. He founded Gardiner and Associates with the money he had saved plus about a fifth of the needed funds which had been invested by his brother Bennet.

~~~~~~~/~~~~~~~

The Prince and his beloved Cilla had been married a for a little more than a year in September 1789, when Frederick made the agonising decision that he had no choice but to inform his father—the King—of his marriage. He hoped, because his marriage was of more than a year's duration, his father would not separate him from his wife like he had with his older brother, the Prince of Wales. He knew that without royal sanction his father could declare his marriage invalid, but he hoped he could convince his father not to do that and sanction his marriage.

Lady Priscilla believed she was with child—she had missed three months of courses—but she did not share her suspicion with her husband before he departed for London to see the King. Fanny, too, had recently shared with her friend the belief she was carrying her second child.

It was early September when Frederick was preparing for his journey to Town. "Do not worry, my love; all will be well," he stated more out of hope than conviction. "I waited beyond a year on purpose, so there would be no question whether or not the wedding was consummated, making it harder for my father to order an annulment."

"Freddy, I am afraid," Priscilla worried. "What if my parents were correct and we were doomed from the start?"

"All will be well; you will see, my love. Do not forget that you are a Princess of the United Kingdom of Great Britain and Ireland." Frederick kissed his wife, and with a final wave of farewell, he was off to Buckingham House to see his father.

Later that day, Fanny and her daughter Jane were visiting Netherfield. It was a balm to Priscilla's troubled soul to see her friend and her serene, beautiful blond, blue-eyed daughter. "Cilla, you look troubled; can I be of any assistance or otherwise ease your burden?" Fanny asked hopefully, concerned at the worry she saw clouding her friend's eyes. "Your husband often travels, but I have never seen you thusly before. You know you can tell me anything, and mayhap sharing will relieve your distress."

"If only this was like his former travels, but he is on his way to see his father—the *King*!" Priscilla owned. She had wanted to tell her best friend the truth for so long, and in her troubled frame-of-mind it all rushed out.

Fanny quietly rang for Netherfield's housekeeper, requesting that she take Jane to the nursery for a nap before she reacted to the incredible news her friend had shared. "My goodness, Cilla, you are a *princess*. Your husband is the second son of the Monarch!" Fanny reiterated as she assimilated all of the information she had been told. "Is this the reason we have never met your parents, their opposition to your marriage?"

"It is, Fanny. They are too afraid of the possible backlash from the King, so they have kept their distance. They are worried what others will think. We write to one another occasionally, but no more than that," Priscilla shared sadly. "If that was not enough, I too suspect I am with child." As worry overwhelmed her, Priscilla began to cry.

Fanny held her friend, offering what comfort she could until she had cried herself out. "Let us pray all will be well, Cilla. Until we know if there is aught to worry about, nothing is to be done. Just know I will be here to support you, no matter what," Fanny assured her best friend in the world—her sister of the heart.

In the time since Lady Priscilla befriended her, Fanny and her husband had become as close as a married couple could be. That day, when she returned from visiting her friend, Bennet could tell his wife was troubled. He would not force a confidence, and knew if Fanny had something to tell him, she would, but hoped that whatever it was that she, and likely Priscilla, was concerned about would turn out well.

As Priscilla had given her leave to do so, Fanny told her husband the truth of who their neighbours were. Bennet was not as surprised as she would have thought as he had seen a drawing of Prince Frederick in *The Times of London* and Mr. Oatland looked like he was a twin of the Prince.

~~~~~~~/~~~~~~~

Frederick held his breath as he was shown into the receiving chamber at St. James where he greeted his father, mother, and brother George, the Prince of Wales and heir to the throne of the Kingdom.

"Frederick, we welcome you, son. It has been too long since we have seen you. What news do you have for us?" the King asked.

Frederick paused for a few beats but knew the moment had finally come. "Father, Mother, George, I need to inform you that I have been married for more than a year to the former Lady Priscilla De Melville," he managed to say before he his father cut him off.

"How could you marry without our permission?" the King thundered. The Queen placed a hand on the King's arm to calm him. "We negotiated a betrothal for you with Princess

Frederica Charlotte of Prussia some years ago! You will marry in 1791 when she is eighteen," the King stated firmly.

"But father, I am already married!" Frederick objected.

"As the head of the Church of England, I will have the wedding annulled as you did not obtain royal sanction," the King returned.

"Father, think about what you are saying. I have been married to her for over a year, the marriage is fully consummated, and no one, not even the Archbishop, should issue an annulment," Frederick pleaded.

"Our brother is correct, father," the Prince of Wales intoned thinking of his own situation.

The King looked to his wife who shook her head. "In that case, we will seek a divorce effective immediately and allow the marriage to stand until the divorce," the King decided.

"Please father, no! I love my Cilla, *Princess* Priscilla, more than life itself. I beg you not to do this. I have always been the one to stand by you," Frederick begged as he looked at his brother pointedly.

The King too looked at his eldest, who had the decency to look away in embarrassment for his attempt to gain the regency in 1788. "Son, your support has always been invaluable. Your wife is worthy, but this *must* be done. To those who much has been given, much is demanded. It was not a whim, but an alliance with Prussia, one that England desperately needs. We understand you love your wife, but this will be done for the good of the country. This is one of those times where obligation and duty trump all other concerns. If it were not for the future security of our nation, we, I would not take this action." The King attempted to dull the blow as much as he was able. It killed him to see the depths of his favourite son's despair, but he had no choice in the matter.

The King summoned the Lord Chamberlain and instructed him to have the Prime Minister, Mr. William Pitt the Younger, attend him forthwith. In a matter of hours, with quick approval by the commons, it was done. Frederick was divorced from the love of his life, and his heart was shattered in millions of tiny pieces.

He knew his wife would be well financially; he had settled two hundred fifty thousand pounds on her to go along with her dowry of fifty thousand pounds. The King had agreed his former daughter-in-law would receive everything enumerated in the settlement. The King also agreed his son could inform his former wife before the notice was published in the papers.

~~~~~~~/~~~~~~~

As soon as Priscilla saw the abject dejection on her husband's face, she knew the worst had happened. "Tell me, Freddy," Priscilla requested as soon as he sat beside her on the settee.

He explained all; it was the first time she had ever seen her husband cry. The strain in his voice when he said that as of yesterday, they were divorced, helped her find her deepest strength. He apologised over and over again for what had happened, and for putting the love of his life in such straits.

Once he had calmed, Priscilla took his face in her hands and looked deeply into the blue eyes she loved so. "We always knew there was a possibility this would happen, my love," Priscilla said with far more strength than she felt. She had long realised that should this come to pass, she would have to have enough outward strength for the both of them. "You told me the King does not object to me as being unsuitable for you as a wife, but this is a matter of duty and for the security of our nation, did he not?"

"Yes, my darling Cilla, that is what he claimed. I cannot be certain, but I believe it was not easy for him to cause me—us— the pain he did," Frederick averred dejectedly.

It was then that Priscilla decided she could not add to her beloved's pain by telling him she thought herself with child. "My parents warned me this could happen, yet I allowed my heart to rule, so I own as much fault in this as you. You must know, surely you must know, that I will love you until the day that I die, even beyond the grave; there will never be another."

"No one else will ever claim my heart, Cilla, for it is yours alone until I draw my last breath. I care not what the decree says, you will always be my wife in my heart. When I marry Princess Frederica Charlotte, in my heart my vows will be to you, not to her." Frederick rubbed his former wife's hands with his thumbs. He was nearly desperate to kiss her, but he restrained himself, for it was hard enough on her already, and he knew one kiss would never be enough. "The only news which I do not despise having to share is that my father has honoured our settlement to the letter. Here is a record showing three hundred thousand pounds deposited in your name in the bank of England."

"You must also know that is the last thing which concerns me at this time," Priscilla stated quietly as she fought to keep her composure.

There was a cough from the door, reminding his Highness it was time to depart. With a last longing look at the only woman he would ever let himself love, His Royal Highness Prince Frederick, Duke of York and Albany, Earl of Ulster, took his leave.

Once she heard the coach begin to move outside, the dam broke, and Priscilla cried, giving vent to her broken heart as she lay curled up in a ball on the settee which still held her beloved's scent.

An hour or more later, Priscilla regained some composure and wrote a note to her best friend, requesting her immediate presence at Netherfield Park. Fanny did not miss the tear stains on the note, immediately surmising that the worst had happened.

"Thomas, I must go to Priscilla; I may be there for some days' duration," Fanny stated after her husband had invited her into his study. Seeing her husband's look of concern she added, "Thomas, it seems the King has dissolved Priscilla marriage. I must go to her; I can only imagine the pain she is in. Jane will be well taken care of by her nursemaid."

"I will not delay you before you leave, Fanny," Bennet

offered his understanding, for she would not make such a request were it unnecessary.

Bennet kissed his wife and saw her to the Bennet carriage which would carry her to Netherfield Park, promising he would have a trunk sent should she request it.

~~~~~~~/~~~~~~~

As soon as Fanny was shown into Cilla's private sitting room, the latter collapsed into her arms with a fresh bout of tears. Each time Priscilla thought she could cry no more, devastation would overwhelm her, and more tears would flow.

Fanny said not a word. She held her friend and rocked her gently in an attempt to soothe her intense pain. It was more than an hour before Priscilla regained the ability to speak coherently. She told Fanny all, what the King had done and why.

"It is not fair, Cilla. As much as I feel your pain, in matters of state, I can see why the King did not hesitate to take the action he did. You were his wife for a little more than a year, and in that time your heart knew the purest version of love. I know what I am telling you may sound like empty words at this moment, but in time you will move past the pain and be comforted by the memories," Fanny opined. Priscilla gave her friend a watery nod, beginning to comprehend what she said.

When the London papers were delivered the next day to Netherfield Park and Longbourn, they contained the divorce decree. At Longbourn, Bennet nodded to himself; when the time was right she would relate any additional pertinent information to him. It would be a tale of both love and woe.

At Netherfield Park, Fanny ordered Mrs. Nichols to dispose of the papers. There was nothing to be gained by Priscilla seeing the decree; it would not change anything. Slowly but surely, over the course of a sennight, Fanny began to draw her friend out. All progress was lost when a curt letter arrived from Lady Jersey.

September 18, 1789
Broadhurst, Essex

Lady Priscilla,

As you have brought the scandal of divorce down on our family, we have no choice but to break with you to protect the reputation of the family, most especially that of Marie and Wesley.

May God bless you,

Lady Sarah De Melville

Although Priscilla expected this, but it did not stop the added infliction of pain on her already frail emotions. Fanny stayed with her friend for almost a month complete, supporting Priscilla until her friend was able to get through a whole day without spontaneously bursting into tears.

It was during Fanny's stay at Netherfield that both her and Priscilla's state were confirmed. They would both give birth in February or March of the coming year. Before she departed, Fanny received her friend's permission to tell Mr. Bennet all she had not already shared.

What Priscilla was unaware of was that the decision to cut ties with her came from her father who was very conscious of his position in society, and what the *Ton* thought of him. Her mother had pleaded, begged, and cajoled, none of which had moved him. She had taken a vow to obey him—as much as she would like to ignore her vows, she could not as her husband made sure she would not go against him putting measure in place to keep her in check.

CHAPTER 1

February 1790

"Fanny, you remember my telling you about my good friend from Cambridge, the Earl of Holder, Lord Paul Carrington?" Bennet asked as he sat as his desk with a letter from the man.

"I do, Thomas," a heavily *enceinte* Fanny replied. "Why do you ask?"

"A letter arrived today; he begs my presence to help him with some matters about which we have been corresponding. I pledged to help him if he ever needed it for the service he provided me at Cambridge, protecting me from those vicious lordlings. He has never expected anything in return, but I feel honour bound to assist him now that he has need," Bennet explained. "I will allow you to make the decision, Fanny, as I am not able to promise I will return by the time you enter your final confinement." Bennet did not inform his wife that a large part of his reason for travelling to his friend was to see if there was a way to break the entail on Longbourn, for he did not want to get her hopes up if it came to naught.

"You should go, Thomas. I will join Priscilla at Netherfield Park until you return so we will not be alone. Miss Jones and Jane will accompany me," Fanny agreed.

"Only if you are sure," Bennet verified again, more to reassure himself she was accepting of his leaving at such a time as this.

"I am. I will be with Priscilla and I am able to call on Hattie, Sarah Lucas, or any number of other friends, if needs be. Do not forget the midwife, Mrs. Sherman, is experienced and will be there with us," Fanny assured her husband.

"From my observations, Priscilla has never fully re-covered from her heartbreak. I believe it is part of the reason why she had been ill far more than her wont since that terrible day," Bennet opined.

"She is as well as can be expected," Fanny replied protect-ively.

In the neighbourhood, other than the Bennets, only her sister Hattie and brother-in-law Frank knew the truth of Priscilla's situation. Telling them had been necessary because Frank Phillips drew up a new will for Priscilla. Most in the area did not read the London papers; those who did had not made Priscilla's acquaintance, so none were aware the divorce decree referred to her.

The Gardiners were also aware, because Edward Gardiner had been entrusted with managing Priscilla's massive fortune; he was able to produce returns around ten percent per annum. Of the approximately thirty thousand per annum income, a quarter was used to fund various charities, with a small por-tion kept for Priscilla's personal needs. As Netherfield's profits were in excess of four thousand pounds per annum, of the bal-ance was reinvested as principal.

The following morning, the Bennet carriage departed for Holder Heights in Staffordshire, just before the Netherfield coach arrived to transport Fanny, her daughter, a nursemaid, and the governess to Priscilla's estate.

~~~~~~~/~~~~~~~

March 5, 1790

"Priscilla, are you sure you do not want me to notify his Royal Highness?" Fanny asked the morning both of them woke with the beginning stages of labour pains.

"No, Fanny. I do not want him contacted; of that I am sure. It was too painful when he informed me of his father's decision and actions. It will do nothing but occasion him more regrets, and now that his betrothal to Princess Frederica

Charlotte has been announced publicly, I choose not to be the reason he is pained again," Priscilla averred.

"I will respect your wishes, my sister," Fanny indicated her understanding as she squeezed her friend's hand.

"Have you heard from Thomas lately?" Priscilla asked.

"There was a letter two days ago. You know what a poor correspondent my husband is." Fanny laughed around a wince and Priscilla nodded that she knew it to be true. "He should be home in a fortnight."

"Then you will be able to introduce him to his new son or daughter. I am sure he will be delighted with either," Priscilla opined. "Our children will grow up as best of friends—cousins."

"Are you sure you want to be so generous to me and my future daughters in your will, Cilla? You know I never wanted anything in return for my friendship, do you not?" Fanny asked.

"If I had believed otherwise for a moment, I would never have written my will as I did. My parents have cut me from their lives and that of my siblings, but I have a family, Fanny. It is you, and our bonds are stronger than any blood ties could have made them," Priscilla stated adamantly.

When Mr. Phillips had written her will, Priscilla had added a clause to provide for Fanny and any of her daughters, starting with Jane. If Bennet predeceased her, Fanny would receive two thousand pounds a year for life. It was written in such a way that even if she remarried, her husband would never have control of the funds. In addition to that, each daughter would receive a dowry of twelve thousand pounds.

Fanny had objected vociferously, just as Priscilla had anticipated. She had used the argument that Fanny and Jane, who called Priscilla 'Aunty Cilla,' were her only remaining family. She also pointed out that the amounts she was bequeathing to Fanny, Jane, and any subsequent daughters were but a drop out of the bucket that represented her annual earnings from her invested wealth and Netherfield Park's income, not to mention the principal.

It took some cajoling, but eventually Priscilla convinced her friend to accept the bequest graciously. Both hoped it would be many years before either Cilla or Thomas were called home to God. For Fanny, it meant she never had to worry about the entail to the male line that dictated Longbourn—if she never delivered a son—would pass to some distant cousin. The relief such knowledge offered was as if a large stone had been lifted from her. She had not carried the burden on her shoulders alone, but deep in her soul fear for her, and more importantly, her children's future had taken root.

About three hours later, Fanny entered the final stage of her confinement. Mrs. Sherman attended her, while receiving regular updates on her Ladyship's progress who, as yet, was not as far along as Mrs. Bennet.

Half an hour later, Fanny Bennet's babe was born into the world. Fanny began to panic when she did not hear the tell-tale crying she had experienced with Jane's birth. "It pains me to tell ya' Missus, but your son were born dead. 'is chord were wrapped around 'is neck," Mrs. Sherman informed Mrs. Bennet.

"Let me hold him, please," Fanny asked, quietly crying for her dead son who she had loved from the day she had learned he was inside of her. After the silent body was cleaned and swaddled so his face was visible, he was passed into his mother's arms.

Just then, the midwife was called away to attend Lady Priscilla. An hour later, the lusty cries of a new-born were heard, and Fanny cried for joy knowing her best friend had not suffered the same fate as her. She had Jane and a husband she loved; she was sure she would have more children in the future, but she knew this had been Priscilla's only chance to bear a child. Because it was her beloved's babe, it was a most precious gift. Her friend could never love another and would never marry again.

What Fanny did not know just then was that her friend

was suffering a side effect too many women experienced and was haemorrhaging blood in enormous amounts. It took much, much longer than was healthy to stem the flow. When Fanny heard of the problem, she forced herself out of her bed and went to her friend's side.

She stifled a gasp when she spied Priscilla. Her pallor was as white as the sheets she lay on. As weak as she was, Priscilla requested the chambers be cleared of all but her and Fanny. "Fanny, I am so sorry; I was informed your son was stillborn." Fanny was about to interject, but Priscilla stilled her with a weak squeeze to the hand. "You are my sister of the heart, and you will do *anything* for me, will you not, Fanny?" Priscilla asked. Fanny nodded as the tears streamed down her cheeks. "Swear to me, Fanny, swear you will do whatever I ask of you."

"You have my solemn word, but you need to conserve your strength to get better for all of us who love you, for your daughter most especially, Cilla," Fanny pleaded.

"Fanny, you are too intelligent to not see what is before your eyes. By tomorrow I will be no more. My baby girl, I want her named Elizabeth Sarah for my grandmother Beth and my mother. Yes, even if Mother has rejected me, I have not rejected her," Priscilla paused as she drew on the reserve of strength left in her body. "This is the hardest thing you will ever be asked, but have your son brought to me, and I want you to take Elizbeth and raise her as your own. I promise to care for him above in heaven as you will care for my Elizabeth here on earth until you join us a great many years from now. We will have many stories to share then, Fanny, a great many." Seeing her friend was about to protest, Priscilla curtailed her. "Fanny, you swore you would do as I asked!"

"I did, and I will. But what of the two maids, Mrs. Nichols, and Mrs. Sherman? They all know the truth," Fanny asked carefully, trying to determine the best path to accomplish all that was being asked of her.

"First, I leave it to you Fanny to tell Elizabeth the truth of her birth when she is eighteen, or you feel she is ready, that she is a Princess of the United Kingdom of Great Britain and Ireland, and more than likely high in the line of succession to the throne. How she proceeds will be up to her at that point.

"To help you in this, I have written some letters, two that you will post for me after you have told her. I wrote just in case the worst happened. The most important of them all is for my —our—daughter. You will know when to give it her if you need to before she is eighteen.

One is for my Freddy; it is the top one on the escritoire in the corner. Please fill in her name and gender where I have left spaces in his letter. As far as her birthfather goes; what, if any, relationship she has with him will be her choice alone."

Priscilla went silent for a minute or two and Fanny was worried she had passed until she saw her chest still rising and falling—barely. "Priscilla, conserve your strength," Fanny beseeched.

"No, I must complete this now. One is for Thomas to thank him for raising my child as his own. Will you be able to keep this from him until Elizabeth is eighteen?" Fanny nodded —she had given her oath. "I need you to understand, Thomas will not allow the truth of Elizabeth's birth to be concealed from her birthfather, and you know why I believe it is imperative to keep this from him do you not? I do not want her being raised in a loveless gilded cage as the royals are wont to do." Fanny nodded her understanding.

"The fourth one is my goodbye to my parents. If they try to contact me before that time—only if they are looking to make amends and not for selfish reasons—you may inform them of my passing, otherwise, the letter will suffice." Priscilla paused to gird her strength and recover some breath. "I need to dictate a letter to you in case you ever meet any of my friends— the few who have remained true to me—and they suspect the truth. Fanny brought paper and wrote what her friend dictated and then with some of the little strength Cilla had left, she signed the letter shakily.

"Lastly, please summon the midwife, maids, and Nichols

back in, but have one of them bring your son. Did you name him, Fanny?" Fanny shook her head. "We will name him Frederick, as that will allay suspicion when his gravestone is seen."

With effort, Fanny reached the door and conveyed the mistress's orders. As soon as the four women entered, one maid was told to transfer little Elizabeth to the cot in Mrs. Bennet's room and the other maid was told to place Fanny's stillborn boy in Priscilla's daughter's cot.

With supreme effort, Priscilla swore the maids to silence and had Fanny write out a note that awarded each two thousand pounds. Next, Mrs. Nichols and Mrs. Sherman were sworn to silence, and awarded five thousand pounds each. Mrs. Nichols told her ailing mistress she would do it for nothing, but Priscilla insisted, telling her to gift the money to her children for their future if she did not want it for herself.

Once the two of them were alone again, Priscilla had the breath to speak to Fanny one last time. "You, my sister, were the reason I did not give up after I lost my Frederick. I love you, Fanny." After her final speech, her breathing became nearly undetectable, until she breathed her last and her last exhale slowly escaped.

Priscilla had clung to life to make sure her wishes were known and had let go once she knew all was in order. Fanny sat crying, holding her best friend's hand for more than an hour after she ceased to breathe and only slowly made her way back to her chambers when she was told her daughter needed to be fed.

It was then that Mrs. Nichols sent a footman to summon Mr. Jones, the local doctor and apothecary. He pronounced both mother and son dead. He examined Mrs. Bennet and her daughter and exclaimed that both seemed to be doing as well as could be expected in these first hours.

Fanny looked at her daughter, discovering she had a great deal of hair on her head already; it was the same mahogany colour as Priscilla's. Her eyes were blue, but Fanny was aware her eye colour could change as much as six to eight months after birth.

'I will love your Elizabeth, your Lizzy, as if she were born of my body, Priscilla, just as I will always love you. I will do all you have asked of me, and as difficult as it will be to keep this from my husband, I will not tell Thomas about the swap of our babies until the time you have decreed. I will miss you every minute of every day I have left in the mortal world, but I will have a small part of you with me at Longbourn. Farwell, my friend; may God bless you and watch over both you and baby Fredrick for me.' Fanny intoned to herself—her eyes lifted to the heavens—as Elizabeth suckled hungrily.

~~~~~~~/~~~~~~~

The day before Priscilla and baby Frederick's funeral, the Prince arrived at Netherfield. After he spent time crying over the body of his former wife and his late son, he sought Fanny Bennet out. "Why did she not tell me she was with child, Mrs. Bennet?" Frederick asked.

"You know why, your Highness. She loved you so very much, and she did not want to make a terrible situation harder than it already was. She intended to tell you after you were married to ensure you would not dishonour your father's wishes," Fanny explained.

"Thank you for not letting her pass away alone, Mrs. Bennet. She may not be with us anymore, but she will always reside in my heart," Frederick stated solemnly.

The Prince admired Mrs. Bennet's baby daughter, who Jane was watching over as Elizabeth slept in her cot. He saw her hair colour was similar to Priscilla's, and when the babe woke and opened her large eyes he noted her deep blue eyes which looked like Fanny's eye colour. He may have been a Prince, Duke, and a General, but he had no idea that eye colour could change, as Elizabeth was the first babe he had seen so soon after birth.

His Royal Highness, the Duke of York and Albany, Earl of Ulster, remained until after the funeral, then, with his heart breaking all over again, he departed back to Town.

~~~~~~~/~~~~~~~

Less than a week after Priscilla's passing, Thomas Bennet returned to Longbourn. Once informed by the Hills where his wife and daughters were, he went directly to Netherfield Park without stopping to change or wash.

Bennet had started his journey merely hours after receiving the missive from Fanny telling him that both Priscilla and her son had passed. He was sure his wife was devastated, understanding well how strong the bonds of sisterhood were between the two.

On his arrival at Netherfield Park, he was shown to the chambers his wife was in. On seeing her husband, the well of emotions Fanny had been holding back burst open as she fell into her husband's arms, crying with wracking sobs that tore at his heart. Bennet had no reason to believe she was crying for anything but Priscilla and her son. He, too, lamented; they would have gladly taken him into their hearts and home had he survived. It would have given his wife the solace of assisting her Cilla during all of her years to come.

Fanny's resolve to honour her late friend's wishes by not informing her husband of Elizabeth's true parentage almost failed her as she cried in his arms, and he comforted her with soothing words. Just as she was about to tell him all, her pledge to her dear Cilla replayed in her head and she remained silent on the subject.

"How I will miss her, Thomas. To lose both her and her son in the same day almost killed me, but I knew I needed to remain strong for our daughters," Fanny told her husband once she was able to talk again.

"I know how close you were, Fanny, and it is understandable you will mourn her and her son. Take as long as you need to grieve her, for we will face this as a family," Bennet promised gently as he kissed her wet cheeks.

"Thomas, there is much I need to tell you," Fanny stated as her husband dried her tears with his handkerchief. "A month ago, or perhaps it is now longer, Priscilla made a new last will and testament. She dowered each of our daughters we have or will have with twelve thousand pounds each, except for Elizabeth," she nodded in understanding at his confusion. "I will explain all of that soon, Thomas, but please know that if you predecease me, I will have two thousand a year, making the entail immaterial if we are never blessed with a son."

"My goodness, Fanny, such generosity! I am speechless," a flabbergasted Bennet stated. "You do know we have money invested with Edward do you not?" Fanny shook her head. "I will add to Jane and our future daughters' dowries, and to your portion as well from the dividends your brother earns for us."

"Thomas, Cilla was enormously wealthy. I have trouble comprehending the size of her wealth, and she argued when I tried to refuse her gifts that it was a mere pittance in the grand scheme of things. Now, to Lizzy. I do not know if Cilla had a premonition, but she said she took it as a sign from God we were with child at the same time. In her last will and testament, *everything* not willed specifically to another would have been for her child had he survived. She added a clause that in the case both she and her child passed away, everything else would go to our second child," Fanny told her husband the well-rehearsed story.

"Good Lord! Just how wealthy is our new daughter, Fanny?" Bennet asked in shock.

"In addition to Netherfield, Cilla had over three hundred thousand pounds invested for her; it is being managed by Edward. We are allowed up to five thousand per annum from the dividends to use as we see fit." Fanny paused as her husband assimilated the size of the enormous fortune his second daughter had been gifted. "Our brother Phillips is the executor of the will, and there is a stipulation that her wealth is to be carefully hidden from the world and herself until she is betrothed or until her eighteenth birthday. Lizzy is to be informed then, and everything becomes hers when she attains her majority three years later or if she marries prior to turning one and twenty."

"We will use a good part of that annual allowance to

increase the portions of Jane and any subsequent children we have in addition to the money we earn from my investment with Gardiner. I will have our brother draw up documents that will safeguard our daughters from fortune hunters, and I cannot but approve that Elizabeth's wealth must not be known until she is ready to make that decision for herself," Bennet agreed.

Fanny told him of the heart-breaking scene when Prince Frederick came to say his farewells to Cilla and his son. She then led her husband into the adjoining room where Jane was sitting and watching as a nursemaid bounced the gurgling babe on her lap.

"Papa, do you see my Lizzy," Jane enthused as she ran into her father's outstretched arms.

"I do, my little Janie, but let me get a closer look at your new sister," Bennet said as he accepted the babe from the nursemaid. Out of her swaddling the biggest blue-green eyes stared back at him, and Bennet was lost in that instant. Unlike Jane, she had mahogany coloured hair similar to Bennet's late mother's, and he was immediately under her spell.

Two days later, the Bennets moved back to Longbourn.

CHAPTER 2

March 1795

For the previous five years, the Bennets had been living at Netherfield Park. There had been many days of debate before they agreed to move to the estate after Fanny had returned home with her two daughters. It was not the larger size or the prestige of living at the premier estate in the area that drove the decision. It was because Fanny felt her best friend's presence at Netherfield, and it was, in a way, a balm to her soul to reside in the house Cilla had lived in for almost two years. Bennet understood his wife's feelings, and so had agreed to the move, understanding that she seemed more at peace in their Priscilla's space.

In January of 1792, Mary Rose Bennet entered the world; she was followed about a year and a half later by Katherine, who was called Kitty by her family. The current babe of the family, not yet one, was Lydia, who was born in October 1794.

The fact they had no son—yet—did not concern the Bennets. Bennet knew the future of his wife and daughters, especially Elizabeth's, had been secured by the unbelievable generosity of the late Lady Priscilla.

Fanny loved all five of her daughters and although she did not to show it, Lizzy was her favourite. Fanny sometimes called her 'princess' knowing the only one in the house who understood the reference was Mrs. Nichols, who, unlike the two maids and Mrs. Sherman, had not retired after they had received their settlements.

Mrs. Nichols' husband, the butler at Netherfield, had exclaimed his amazement at her Ladyship leaving them five thousand pounds in her will. As had been suggested to her by her late mistress, Shirley Nichols proposed they use the bulk of the money to better the lives of their three children. Peter, her husband, had accepted his wife's wisdom; they had invested one thousand pounds for their retirement with Mr. Edward Gardiner, based on Mrs. Bennet's suggestion.

Miss Anita Jones, who had been Jane's nursemaid, became the girls' governess. She was the sister of Mr. Jones, the local doctor and apothecary. They had been raised on a tiny estate in Bedfordshire with little wealth. However, their late father had saved to educate his three sons and only daughter. After her parents passed, her eldest brother would willingly allow her to continue to live at the estate, but she did not want to be a burden, so she had left of her own accord and made her way in the world.

She was invited to reside with her brother in Meryton and had accepted the position of nursemaid to Jane Bennet with the understanding that when Jane was of an appropriate age, Miss Anita Jones would become her governess. She was now content as she was the governess of the three older Bennet girls and would have Kitty join her for lessons within a year. All three were intelligent, well-behaved young ladies; however, the second Bennet daughter, Elizabeth, was more so than her older and younger sisters.

In the afternoons, Fanny always took time to join her daughters in the nursery. Jane and Kitty had their mother's blond hair and blue eyes and were a little taller than most girls of their age. Taking after the Bennet side of the family, Mary had dark hair and hazel eyes; she was tall for her age as well. All three of her daughters of her body were beautiful, but Fanny made it a point not to emphasise beauty as an accomplishment.

Then there was Elizabeth. Fanny saw a miniature Priscilla in the girl she called *Princess* as an endearment now and again. She had the identical mahogany-coloured wavy hair her mother had and was petite, as Cilla had been. Most striking were her eyes. They were definitely Priscilla's green eyes. As Miss Jones had noted, Elizabeth was as smart as a whip, and more advanced than an almost five-year-old should be. Then there was her radiant beauty. As pretty as her three sisters were, Elizabeth was perhaps a bit more so.

When Bennet remarked on the coincidence of their second daughter having eyes similar to those of the late Priscilla, Fanny pointed out that green eyes were not unheard of, given their other daughters had blue and hazel eyes. Seeing the logic in his wife's statement, Bennet had never remarked on the similarity again.

The Bennets did not lord it over their neighbours because of their good fortune. When the Lucases, Longs, and Gouldings, their closest friends, asked how they had ended up owning Netherfield, they told a story as close to the truth as possible.

Their friends were informed that as an afterthought, Lady Priscilla Oatland had added a clause to her will, almost as a joke, what to do in the event she died without another heir. It was due to the tragedy that took both the lady and her son that Netherfield Park had unexpectedly become the property of the Bennets. As their friends had no idea of the massive wealth the lady had possessed, no more questions were asked, nor was any further information volunteered.

The only friend who knew the truth—well, the truth as Bennet knew it—was his good friend, Lord Paul Carrington, the Earl of Holder. He was very happy for his friend, as it relieved the stress over the entail Bennet had discussed with him during his visit to Holder Heights in 1790. The two men had examined the entail documents, as Paul Carrington specialised in the laws the Court of Chancery dealt with, but they had found no loophole to end the entail. The only way in the current generation was for Bennet and the heir presumptive— as long as he was one and twenty or older—to agree to break the entail. Knowing his miserly, mean spirited, and illiterate Cousin Collins, Bennet knew there was no chance of that outcome. Once Fanny had shared the information about Priscilla's gift to her and any daughters, securing their future, Bennet shared the information he had learnt from his friend with his wife.

Masters were hired to teach the girls, supplementing the lessons that Miss Jones gave them. The most prominent Master was *Signore* Alberto da Funti, the music master who also taught singing up to a certain level; he was widely acknowledged as the best master available in the field of playing music. Luckily for the Bennets, they lived close enough to London for him to be willing to travel to their home.

Shortly after the move to Netherfield, Bennet leased Longbourn and the home farm out to a family. The Hills and their servants remained with the estate to make sure things were run correctly. Mr. Hill was promoted to steward, and, under Bennet's close supervision, made sure Longbourn's tenants were happy, well looked after, and productive.

There were two servants who had made the move with the Bennets, Sarah, the upstairs maid who became Fanny's personal maid, and the cook, Mrs. Lucinda Mills, known as Lucy. Netherfield's cook had decided to retire just prior to that tragic day in March of 1790, which led to Lucy Mills being installed in a larger and more modern kitchen.

~~~~~~~/~~~~~~~

Prince Frederick, Duke of York and Albany, Earl of Ulster, did his duty to King and country in November 1791 by marrying Princess Frederica Charlotte of Prussia. The King expressed urgency for an heir and some spares to be produced since his own heir, George, Prince of Wales, was not legally married to Maria Fitzherbert and did not think he needed to be bothered by dynastic concerns.

By 1794, no children were forthcoming, and Frederick believed it was God's punishment for the forced divorce and subsequent demise of his Cilla and their son. His relationship with Frederica Charlotte was amicable, but Frederick was unable to hide his heartbreak or his devoted love for his late Cilla from his wife.

After it became clear there would be no children and that theirs was a marriage in name only, Princess Frederica Charlotte, the Duchess of York and Albany, Countess of Ulster, and Frederick separated without rancour. She retired to Surrey to live a completely separate life permanently at Oatlands Park, near Weybridge, where she lived in peace for the rest of her days.

One day, some months after the separation, Frederick angrily informed his father that his true wife and son had passed away, and that had the King not forced the divorce there would have been a much-needed heir. It was the one of the times King George III openly regretted his decision and subsequent actions.

The Duke of York and Albany, Earl of Ulster, turned to the arms of mistresses and started to live a dissipated life, unlike the life he led before. He would gamble and carouse, earning himself the reputation of being quite the rake.

The truth was he was not a rake, but he looked for any distractions which would take his mind off all he lost after he was torn from his first wife. Not a night went by that the Prince did not dream about his beloved Cilla. He honoured his late ex-wife's wish, which had been forwarded by Mrs. Bennet, that he not inform Cilla's family of her passing unless they asked about her themselves first. To date they had not.

~~~~~~~/~~~~~~~

Charlotte Lucas, who was Jane's senior by five years, was friends with the two eldest Bennet daughters. One would have thought the not yet five-year-old Elizabeth was too young to be her friend as Charlotte approached the *ripe old age* of twelve, but Eliza's intelligence ameliorated the age difference. Charlotte and her family, Sir William and Lady Sarah Lucas, and her brothers Franklin and John, were the only ones Elizabeth allowed to call her Eliza. The Lucas baby, Mariah, was between Kitty and Lydia in age.

The group of close friends was rounded out by Jenny

Goulding, who was between Jane and Elizabeth in age, and the five-year-old Mandy Long. Mandy and her sister Cara, two, had been adopted by Jonathan and Cheryl Long when their parents, Mr. Long's brother and sister-in-law, succumbed to a bad bout of influenza. Thankfully, their young daughters had been visiting their aunt and uncle in Meryton when the outbreak swept through their late parent's neighbourhood.

The parents of the various friends were beyond happy when the Bennets invited their daughters to take lessons with the Bennet daughters, including with the masters. With so many to teach, *Signore* da Funti spent two days a week at Netherfield to accommodate all of his students. Bennet requested the master instruct only his two oldest daughters in his native tongue, after it had become evident that they had an ear for languages when they quickly picked up Italian from the *Signore*.

After more than a year of conversing with *Signore* da Funti, Jane and Elizabeth were fluent in Italian and had mastered the accent to perfection. Mary was beginning to learn as she had started music lessons in the last few months. It seemed that at their young age, the children were able to assimilate languages much more easily than older children. After Lizzy's upcoming fifth birthday, Bennet and Fanny planned to hire masters in Latin, Greek, French, Russian, and Spanish. Their girls had a thirst for learning, and their parents were wise enough to quench it.

One afternoon, Bennet joined his wife in the west drawing room after his day of making sure everything was running smoothly at both estates. "Fanny, who is your letter from?" Bennet asked as he sat down after kissing his wife's cheek.

"It is from Edward. He is betrothed. While he was travelling for work, he was stuck in the town of Lambton in Derbyshire for three days while a new wheel was being fabricated for his carriage. There he met the pastor's daughter, according to his letter, a Miss Madeline Lambert. Now he is betrothed to her, and they will marry from Lambton the first Friday of the month in June. He would love us to attend, Thomas. He has written to Hattie and Frank, too. We can journey there, can we not?" Fanny asked hopefully.

"I see no reason why not. It does not hurt that we have access to Lizzy's, I mean *our* coaches which came with this estate. If Hattie and Frank want to join us, they may use one of our conveyances," Bennet agreed. "I will contact Holder to see if he is willing to host us either on the way there or the way back, as Holder Heights is no more than four hours from Lambton, if memory serves."

"Lydia will be more than one, so there should be no issue with her travelling with us; I am not of a mind to be separated from our children for very long," Fanny stated firmly.

"We are of one mind in that, Fanny," Bennet confirmed. Just then their three oldest girls joined them as their lessons were completed for the day. It had become a tradition that they take tea with their Mama and Papa every day after lessons.

The three were excited when they heard Uncle Edward was to marry. "Will our new aunt like us?" Jane asked innocently.

"I am sure she will love you, Janie, all five of you. One would have to travel far to find such well-behaved daughters as you and your sisters," Fanny assured her eldest.

"Where is Lambton?" Elizabeth asked. She loved to find places on maps.

"In Derbyshire, Lizzy," Bennet averred. "The town is in the southwest of the county, a few miles from the border with Staffordshire. We hope to visit Uncle Paul and Aunt Edith while we are in the area."

"Will I come too?" Mary asked apprehensively, worried she was too young for the journey.

"Of course you will come with us, Mary. Kitty and Lyddie with also be with us, and before you ask, yes, Miss Jones and the nursemaids too," Fanny told her middle daughter indulgently.

Less than two hours later, Hattie Phillips arrived to discuss travel to their brother's wedding with her younger sister. As her husband had agreed they would be at the wedding, Hattie accepted the use of one of her sister's family's coaches, as even the Bennets' small vehicle was far larger and more comfortable than their own.

A few days later, a letter was received from Holder Heights with an invitation to stay after the wedding for as long as the Bennets and Phillips chose. A letter of thanks was posted accepting the kind invitation and informing their hosts they would impose on the Carrington's hospitality, possibly until the end of June.

CHAPTER 3

June 1795

The Bennet and Phillips families arrived at the Big Bull Inn in Lambton on the second day of June. All of the rooms in the inn had been reserved for their four-day stay; they intended to depart for Holder Heights on the following Saturday morning.

The families were in awe of the splendours which nature in the area; they had a good view of some of the peaks from Lambton. On Wednesday morning, Bennet asked the landlord what sights were nearby, and he was told the estate of Pemberley, one of the largest in Derbyshire, was often visited when people travelled through the area. As far as the landlord knew, the family was away from home and the house was open to visitors.

Fanny Bennet remembered that one of Cilla's friends, who did not abandon her, lived at an estate in Derbyshire. She had not thought about the name for some time—Lady Anne Darcy. Pemberley sounded correct, but she was not sure.

The Phillipses had no children to entertain, so they chose to spend the morning with Gardiner and his betrothed at the parsonage. Kitty and Lydia were left at the inn with their nurse and Miss Jones, and the largest travelling coach containing the other five Bennets commenced the five-mile journey to the estate.

The gates were open, and the gatehouse keeper doffed his cap to them without stopping the conveyance. Bennet surmised the man was intimidated by the two huge footmen on the back of the coach. For added security, Bennet had hired extra footmen/guards, led by the two with them this day, former sergeants in the army, Biggs and Johns.

The Bennets travelled through a few miles of thick forest on either side of a gravel drive. As the forest receded, the drive turned to the left and there was an incline. At the crest, Bennet struck the roof, and the family exited the coach to wonder at the sight before them.

Below them was a valley with the Derwent River meandering through it, and what seemed like a man-made channel that diverted some of the water to a lake in front of the largest house either Bennet parent had ever beheld. The house was built on rising ground on the opposite side of the valley glowed with a golden hue in the early morning sunshine reflected from the Derbyshire stone used in this part of the country.

Up the side of the hill they could see, over the roof of what appeared to be at least a five-story structure, a forest. In front were formal gardens, but it was easy to see they were not overly manicured. In the centre of the gardens was a large rose garden laid out around a gazebo.

There was a large expanse of grass which led to the lake, then the forest was allowed to be free from the awkward attempts of man to tame it. "Never have I seen a place for which nature did more and where the awkward tastes of man have not been employed to counteract it," Fanny marvelled. She was, after all, a gardening enthusiast.

"Why would anyone need such a huge home?" Elizabeth asked innocently.

"Princess, it is not the size that makes it a home, but the people who live in it. I will wager the housekeeper will tell us that the structure was erected some generations ago. Do not forget, to some the houses at Longbourn and Netherfield Park would look palatial; it is just a question of perspective," Fanny explained.

They were met at the door by a kindly looking lady with greying hair protruding from her cap and wearing a housekeeper's chatelain; she introduced herself as Mrs. Reynolds. As the master and mistress were away from the house and it was open to visitors, she conducted the tour.

During the tour, she pointed out portraits of the master and mistress, Mr. Robert and Lady Anne Darcy. It was then Fanny realised she was correct about this being Cilla's friend's house.

The tour of the house ended with the music room. All three Bennet girls, including Mary who was just three, marvelled at the grand pianoforte in the room, for it was a Broadwood grand.

"The young misses seem enamoured with the music room; do they play?" Mrs. Reynolds asked, thinking to indulge the young girls who likely had but rudimentary skills.

"Mary has just started to learn," Mrs. Bennet stated, pointing to her youngest present, "but Jane and Lizzy have been working with a master for some time now."

"Would one of the young misses like to indulge us with a tune?" Mrs. Reynolds asked, believing at best they would be able to play scales, but it would be a pleasant change to her afternoon to hear them from one so young.

"May I really play?" Elizabeth asked gleefully. "I have not been able to do so since we left home." Based on the petite, but strikingly beautiful girl's size, Mrs. Reynolds guessed she was three, mayhap four.

"Go ahead, Miss," Mrs. Reynolds indulged the child who looked at her mother and only climbed up on the stool once she received a nod from that lady.

~~~~~~~/~~~~~~~

At eleven, Fitzwilliam Darcy was the only Darcy child so far and the heir to Pemberley. He and his cousin Richard, thirteen, the second son of the Earl and Countess of Matlock, were exiting their chambers when they heard what sounded like an expertly played Hayden sonata ringing through the halls of Pemberley.

"Wills, I thought Aunt Anne and Uncle Robert are visiting Snowhaven," Richard stated.

"That is what I was told, Rich. Come, let us go greet my parents; hopefully the riffraff visiting my home have left already," young Master Darcy sneered.

"Wills, how did you become such a snob?" Richard asked as he shook his head. He knew his cousin behaved as he should in front of his parents and could not understand where his arrogant attitude came from—although he suspected their Aunt, Lady Catherine de Bourgh, had a hand in it.

When the two entered the music room, rather than Mr. Robert and Lady Anne Darcy, they saw an unknown couple with two girls watching a little girl playing at a level many adults had not reached, and Mrs. Reynolds looking on open mouthed.

"Who gave you permission to touch my mother's instrument riffraff?" young Darcy demanded. The playing stopped in an instant, and the frightened girl began to cry. "I will recommend to my parents that they not allow such lowborn people as you into our house anymore."

Richard Fitzwilliam tried to silence his cousin. He did not miss that the clothing the visitors were wearing was as good as anything they and their families wore, and neither did he miss the thundercloud that passed over the man's countenance.

"Are you insensible, boy?" Bennet thundered as he hugged his frightened daughter to his side. Fitzwilliam Darcy shrank back in fear. Never had anyone, except on occasion his father, asked him to account for his words or actions in such a way before. "Do you not see your housekeeper standing right there?" Bennet pointed at a quaking Mrs. Reynolds. "Did you think us some paupers who entered your house uninvited and sat down to use the instrument without permission?"

"Who are you to yell at my little sister?" Jane demanded with asperity. Jane portrayed a picture of serenity until you hurt one she loved, then she could be most fierce in her protection of a loved one. Mary stood on Elizabeth's other side holding her sister's hand tightly, also angry at the rude boy.

"I...er...um..." young Darcy stammered, belatedly realising he may have erred.

"Master William," Mrs. Reynold regained her composure, "it is *I* who gave the young miss permission to play." She turned to the Bennets, not missing the anger still written on the parents' faces as they hugged their daughters to them. "Your daughter's playing is what I would expect from one three or four times her age. I apologise for the misunderstanding. Master William thought you were here uninvited." Mrs. Reynolds tried to defend the young master.

"Unless the *boy* has no eyes in his head, he saw you when he entered the room, yet still decided he needed to assert his authority in a vulgar and unacceptable manner. You said the master of this estate is Mr. Robert Darcy, did you not?" Bennet asked.

"Yes sir," Richard responded. "My Uncle Robert Darcy is master here.

"In a few days, I will be visiting my *good friend* Lord Paul Carrington; I believe he knows Mr. Darcy well. He will hear all, and I will request he pass it on to this whelp's father," Bennet pointed an accusing finger at the Darcy son, "so he may hear what sort of *gentleman* he is raising." With that, the Bennet parents shepherded their daughters out to the waiting carriage.

"Wills, I have warned you to control your superior urges. Do you have any idea what your father will do when he hears of your behaviour today?" Richard asked.

A dejected and deflated young William nodded his head even as he hung it in shame. Why had he yelled at a little girl, and one who could play so well? He considered their clothing for the first time and started to realise how great an error he had made. Richard and William walked to the main doors in time to see a large coach, comparable to the best his parents owned, pull away; it was drawn by six matched horses with the biggest footmen either boy had seen on the back bench.

"Wills, are not your parents and mine to visit Holder Heights next week?" Richard asked. and William nodded. "It seems the gentleman may be able to convey his message directly to your father. Are you not friendly with Jamey?" James Carrington was the twelve-year-old Holder heir.

"Yes, what of it?" William asked dejectedly.

"Think, man! You will have to get yourself invited to join your parents. No matter what happens, you need to apologise to those people," Richard stated emphatically. "What has gotten into you to make you such an insufferable snob lately?"

"Has not Aunt Catherine lectured you about maintaining the distinctions of rank? I thought I was behaving as I should. Father has always told me to uphold the Darcy name and to be proud of it," William tried to justify his attitude.

"Aunt Cat! Have you not noticed how no one in the family pays her nonsensical ramblings any heed? Do not tell me you also believe her codswallop about being betrothed to Anne. You need to talk to your parents, William. I suggest you tell them what happened today when they return home this evening—before they hear about it from anyone else. It may save you a much-deserved thrashing," Richard told his younger cousin who was thoroughly chagrined.

"Have I really become an insufferable and arrogant snob, Rich?" William asked, wincing when his cousin nodded vigorously.

~~~~~~~/~~~~~~~

"Lizzy, my Princess, you know you did naught wrong, do you not? You had permission to play, and may I say you played beautifully today," Fanny soothed her still upset daughter.

"But why did that awful boy shout at me?" Elizabeth asked as her tears again flowed down her wet cheeks.

"He made an assumption and did not stop to verify the facts before he acted," Fanny explained. "Now do you girls understand why your father and I tell you never to make assumptions? As Lizzy was hurt today, it can hurt people if we assume our opinions are facts and act on them."

"You had permission from both the housekeeper and Mama to play, so you did no wrong, my girl," Bennet assured his second daughter. "Come, let us forget this unpleasantness, and after a rest we will join the Lamberts at the parsonage and meet your soon-to-be aunt.

The prospect of the visit succeeded in diverting the girls' attention. Two hours later, the Bennets made their way to the parsonage across the green in the centre of the town, past an enormous chestnut tree in the middle of said green.

~~~~~~~/~~~~~~~

When Robert and Lady Anne Darcy arrived home from Snowhaven, they did not miss the troubled look on Mrs. Reynolds face nor the agitation of their son. Their nephew was the only one who seemed his normal, affable self. The parents went to the master suite to change, then summoned the three to the master's study.

"What is it? What has happened?" Robert Darcy asked as he sat on a sofa in the study with his beloved wife next to him.

"There were visitors today, sir," Mrs. Reynolds started.

"Not an uncommon occurrence for people to come view the house, Mrs. Reynolds," Lady Anne stated questioningly.

"They were what looked to me, sir and madame, a very well to do family, parents and three delightful daughters." The Darcy parents did not miss how their son blanched as the housekeeper said the last. "On the tour, as is normal, we ended in the music room. I saw the three girls, who I now know are seven, five, and three, looking longingly at your pianoforte, my Lady. I thought to indulge them and half-jokingly asked if one of them would like to play a tune, not truly thinking either able."

"Richard and I left our chambers and we heard playing; it was a Hayden sonata, Mother. We thought it was you playing," William related.

"Wait! A seven-year-old girl was playing a Hayden piece and made you think it was me at the instrument?" asked the astounded Lady Anne.

"It was the girl of five years, Mistress," Mrs. Reynold corrected, "and she played from memory." Lady Anne was gobsmacked; a musical prodigy, possibly more than one, had been in her home, and she had missed it.

"William, tell us what you did!" Mr. Darcy demanded, getting a sinking feeling the arrogance he had started to note in William—no matter how much his son tried to hide it from his parents—had been exercised. He had meant to talk to his son about it; if what he suspected had come to pass, now it seemed imperative.

William Darcy hung his head again as he related his actions and the reaction of the little girl and the girl's father fully, with no prevarication. "Oh William, how could you?" Lady Anne asked sadly.

"Did you say they will be at Holder Heights next week, William?" Robert Darcy asked. William nodded. "After you have accepted the punishment I intend to mete out to you, you will accompany us and make a full and sincere apology. Do I make myself clear?"

"Yes, sir," William looked anywhere except at his angry father.

"William, I love you as much as any mother could love her son, but how on earth is it that you have come to act like my sister Catherine? How could you show such disrespect and disdain for visitors to our home? You called them riffraff? William, we taught you better," Lady Anne stated sadly.

Richard shot his cousin an 'I told you so' look. "Richard, you could not restrain your younger cousin before he placed his boot in his mouth so effectively?" Robert Darcy asked.

"Unfortunately not, Uncle Robert. William went off halfcocked before Mrs. Reynolds or I could utter a word. The gentleman took him to task for the rude words most effectively. Other than by you, I have never seen William taken aback in that way before. To me it looked like the visitor had to restrain himself not to turn William over his knee there and then. The gentleman certainly put William in his place," Richard replied.

"Good! It was no less than you deserved, William. I will

not whip you, but you will learn humility. You will join young George Wickham mucking out the stalls in the stables each day until I tell you differently," Mr. Darcy stated decisively.

~~~~~~~/~~~~~~~

George Wickham was the son of the honourable and loyal steward of the estate. Mr. Darcy had been amenable to stand as the young man's godfather until some vicious behaviour was reported to him by various servants. The boy was a year younger than the heir to Pemberley, but had been acting as if he was, in fact, the heir.

He had been barred from the manor house, and his father was made to understand the master's reasoning for withdrawing all support for his son. Young George had learnt bad behaviour from his late mother who was a spendthrift, gambler, and had been unfaithful to her husband on many occasions. Lucas Wickham discovered the latter only after her death, thus calling into question George's parentage.

Regardless of his suspicions, the steward did not treat George any differently, but he agreed that unless the boy was corrected at the age of ten, he would surely follow his mother's ruinous course.

Unfortunately, George Wickham was determined he would make his fortune without working for it, as he had believed what his mother had told him about it being his due. He hated the degradation of working in the stables, but knew he needed to bide his time. He was sure he would be able to charm Mr. Darcy into becoming his godfather again, and bestowing largess on him as was his right and due.

~~~~~~~/~~~~~~~

"I will do as you have instructed, Father. I am sorry I brought dishonour to the Darcy name today," William replied contritely.

"William, the stablemaster will be your manager, and you will follow his orders to the letter. Do not let me hear of any arrogance directed to any of the grooms, stable hands, or any other. It is time for you to learn some humility, my son,"

Robert Darcy told his heir.

After the boys and the housekeeper were dismissed, Lady Anne turned to her husband. "We need to formalise a document that refutes my sister's nonsense about a betrothal between William and Anne. Also, as much as it pains me to say this about my sister, we need to severely limit contact between her and our son and any future children we may be blessed with." Lady Anne wistfully rubbed her belly. She suspected she was with child again, but with so many failures between William's birth and the present, she would not say anything to her husband until she felt the quickening—if it got that far this time.

"You have the right of it, Anne, my darling wife; I could not agree with you more. Ever since Lewis drowned fishing, she has become unbearable, so we will keep our distance. I will not miss her pontificating on subjects of which she has no knowledge. I intend to suggest to Reggie he exercise his prerogative as Anne's guardian, as I do not believe Catherine will put anyone's interests ahead of her own selfish, avaricious ones," Robert Darcy said resignedly.

~~~~~~~/~~~~~~~

"William, you got off lightly. I was convinced your father would whip you," Richard stated as he mock wiped sweat of his brow after they reached their suite.

"**Lightly!**" William shouted in a high pitch which his voice changed to when he was upset. "I have to work as a common servant, I am to be…"

"Shut up, William! Have you learnt nothing from your folly today?" Richard asked as he shook his head in wonder as his cousin seemed to miss the point of his upcoming lessons. "You can be such an arrogant arse at times. You need to make a decision. Will you follow the insensible ravings of Aunt Cat, or your parents?"

"But Aunt *Catherine* was so adamant she was right," William protested, even though he was not as sure of himself as he was before.

"So, according to you, he who makes the most noise is right? Do you not know empty barrels make the most noise? And here I thought you intelligent, Wills," Richard responded.

His younger cousin felt the gut punch as he started to question his own beliefs in earnest, something he had not been willing to do before. As he examined his memories, he realised that the rest of the family only tolerated his Aunt Catherine, and no one paid her pronouncements any heed, except for himself.

"It could be I was mistaken in my beliefs," William owned sheepishly after almost twenty minutes in serious contemplation.

"Could be?" Richard challenged with raised eyebrows.

"Was mistaken, alright, Rich? I see now I was wrongheaded. I need to accept my punishment graciously, do I not?" William realised.

"Finally, some words of sense out of your mouth today, Wills. There may be hope for you yet." Richard slapped his cousin on the back and changed the subject to one they both loved: horses.

CHAPTER 4

"Fanny, Bennet, and my beautiful nieces, I am so happy to see all of you," Edward Gardiner said to the Bennets as they arrived at the parsonage. They were welcomed by Reverend Lambert for a family dinner to meet his daughter and her siblings.

"Will you introduce us to your new family please, Gardiner?" Bennet requested.

Gardiner proudly introduced his betrothed Madeline, called Maddie; her father, the Reverend Arthur Lambert; Harry, the eldest Lambert offspring, and his wife Amanda; and the middle sibling, Grant.

"Edward told me you girls are very advanced in your musical and language studies," Madeline Lambert told her soon-to-be nieces, hoping to put them at ease. "Where are your other three sisters?"

"Mary was tired from our excursions today, so she is with Kitty and Lydia at the inn," Fanny explained.

"Oh, yes," Hattie Phillips interjected, "Fanny's girls are more accomplished than many older girls." Hattie no longer gossiped, but she was proud of her nieces, for it was on them she and her husband poured their attention and time to make up for the sad fact she and Frank had not been blessed with children of their own.

"*Quam operor vos facere,* Miss Jane?" Reverend Lambert asked Jane how she was in Latin, sure girls so young might know a word or two, but no more.

"*Ego sum etiam valde gratias ago tibi, domine. Quid agis hodie?*" Jane responded in his selected language, saying she was well and asking the clergyman how he was with perfect elocution. Just when he believed he could not be more shocked, the younger girl introduced as Lizzy spoke.

"*Domine dominus noster Latina didicit ex nostra bene Lectiones sumus.*" Elizabeth offered proudly, telling him that they had learnt Latin well from their masters.

"Good lord!" Mr. Lambert exclaimed.

"Would you rather converse in Greek, French, or Italian, sir?" Elizabeth asked innocently. After the shock wore off, there was laughter in the room as everyone assimilated the knowledge that Hattie Phillips had not made an empty boast.

After a very enjoyable dinner, Maddie led the ladies and the two eldest Bennet sisters to the drawing room while the men sat and drank their port or brandy at the table. "Lambert, do you know the Darcys?" Bennet asked.

"Quite well. They are the nicest of people, always willing to help, and not just with money. Why do you ask? Do you know them?" Lambert senior asked.

Bennet relayed the happenings at Pemberley that morning. He had to calm his daughters' uncles down; both wanted to ride to that estate to whip the insolent whelp. "There is no need, because his father will hear of it and punish him," Lambert senior opined. "Trust me when I tell you that Robert Darcy does not believe in sparing the rod and spoiling the child. Lady Anne loves all things musical and is an extremely proficient player of the pianoforte and harp, so I am sure she would have loved to have heard your Lizzy play."

The statement from Lambert calmed the uncles considerably and placated Bennet to a certain degree. No one spoke to any member of his family thus, no matter who they were in their circle of society or whatever their rank.

When the men joined the ladies, Jane entertained them on the upright pianoforte in the drawing room. It was the second time that night that Hattie Phillips' pronouncement had been proven as honest as it had been unbelievable.

"My goodness, first Lizzy and now Jane. How is it you are so proficient at such young ages?" Madeline asked.

"Have you heard of *Signore* Alberto da Funti, the most sought-after music master in London?" Fanny asked playfully, and both Maddie and her sister-in-law Mandy agreed they had. "He has been with us for two days a week for more than three years now, teaching our girls and others from our neighbourhood."

"Even so, your girls must have innate ability to be as advanced as they are at such young ages, regardless of the quality of their masters," Amanda Lambert opined. She was pregnant with her and her husband's first and could only pray her child would have a small measure of the intelligence and talent she saw in the Bennet sisters, not to mention the striking beauty of the two present.

"The reason we started bringing in language masters was the way Jane and Lizzy, and later Mary, picked up Italian from the *Signore*. He has been working with the older two for over two years but has had only a few months with Mary. Jane and Lizzy speak Italian like a native, and Mary is just beginning and catching on nicely. It seems my girls have an aptitude for languages," Fanny offered by way of an explanation. It was not a boast, just a statement of fact.

Not long after, the Bennet, Gardiner, and Phillips families returned to the Big Bull Inn to turn in for the night.

~~~~~~~/~~~~~~~

Two days later, on a warm and clear Friday morning, Edward Gardiner and Madeline Lambert were joined in holy wedlock at St. Crispin's church in Lambton. As he preferred to walk his daughter up the aisle to her betrothed, Mr. Lambert's good friend and the pastor of the Pemberley church had the pleasure of performing the marriage rites in his friend's stead.

The wedding breakfast had been organised by a committee of ladies from the parish and was celebrated in the hall where the bi-monthly local assemblies were held in Lambton. Given the Lamberts' popularity, especially their goodhearted Madeline's, practically everyone in the small market town wanted to wish them well.

Many of the ladies in the town had provided dishes, so there was enough food to feed all those who attended—twice over. It was a boisterous affair, and only quieted for an instant when the master and mistress of Pemberley stopped by.

Mr. Robert and Lady Anne Darcy made a brief visit to wish the bride and her groom happy. They scanned the crowd, quickly finding the well-dressed couple with the three beautiful and impeccably behaved girls, correctly guessing they were the family to whom William had been so rude.

When the little girl with the mahogany hair turned around, Lady Anne gasped, blinking slowly because she was certain she was wrong, despite what she thought she had seen. Growing up, her dearest of friends was Priscilla De Melville. The two had been introduced when Priscilla was five and Anne Fitzwilliam, as she was then, eight. From that point on, they had spent as much time together as their respective parents would allow.

Lady Anne knew all about Priscilla's marriage to Prince Frederick and had written to her friend on a regular basis. After the King had forced the two apart, Lady Anne's letters were not answered again, and she suspected it had something to do with Priscilla's parents breaking with her. It had hurt Anne Darcy to lose touch with her friend, but she had respected her friend's wishes.

Lady Anne could not believe her eyes; before her she saw Priscilla as she was at age five when they first met. She gracefully rubbed her eyes to make sure she was not seeing things, but it did not change the picture before her. The same hair, height, and the eyes. The brightest green eyes, so stunning, which Lady Anne would never forget. Realising that she was staring, she took her husband's hand as they paid their respects to Reverend Lambert and departed.

"Anne, are you well?" Robert Darcy asked with concern. His wife suffered from indifferent health at best. "You look as if you have seen a ghost."

"Robert, I should not have stared, but the family, the one

William abused, their one daughter? It gave me chills up and down my spine when I saw her," Lady Anne shared with her worried husband.

"What about the girl perturbed you, my sweet?" Robert asked his wife, concerned at her feeling so very unsettled when they were discussing none but a child. "I will cancel our acceptance of Holder's invitation if you are too disconcerted by being in company with that family."

"NO! That is not what I want, in fact I want the very *opposite*. You remember my friend—my dearest friend—Lady Priscilla De Melville as was?" Lady Anne asked.

"I do. She was a Princess of the United Kingdom of Great Britain and Ireland, the Duchess of York and Albany until the King ordered a divorce," Robert remembered.

"You know she was my very close friend since we were little girls, do you not?" Robert Darcy nodded. "What flustered me today was seeing one of those gorgeous girls, the one with the mahogany-coloured hair and green eyes," Lady Anne explained.

"I saw all three, but did not note individual features," Robert owned.

"I felt as if I were eight again; I would have sworn I had gone back in time to the day I met Priscilla at five, because that girl did not just look similar to her, she looked *exactly* like my friend," Lady Anne insisted.

"How can that be, unless the family is somehow related to the De Melvilles," Darcy surmised.

"Which is why it is imperative we keep to the visit with the Carringtons next week. I need to see her close up to be sure it was not a trick of the light or my imagination, as I have been missing Priscilla these almost six years with no news of her," Lady Anne stated emphatically.

"You know I would deny you nothing it is in my power to grant you, Anne. I will not change the plans. I did receive a note from Holder, and William is welcome. In fact, Jamey is excited to have the company of another boy his own age," Darcy shared.

Lady Anne hoped Priscilla did not think she had cut her as her parents and many others had. If only she had some way of contacting her friend again!

~~~~~~~/~~~~~~~

"Mama, why was the tall, pretty, blond lady staring at me at the wedding breakfast?" Elizabeth asked as the family walked back to the Black Bull.

"You were not the only who noted that, Lizzy, so did I. I have no idea why, but I doubt we will ever see the lady again," Fanny responded. She would not admit it—could not admit it—but Fanny felt she knew exactly why Lady Anne Darcy had started at Lizzy. She might have need of the fifth letter she carried with her.

"How long will it take us to reach Uncle Paul and Aunt Edith on the morrow?" Jane asked.

"It is about four hours," Bennet averred. "Do you have somewhere you need to be tomorrow that you worry about the time it will take us?"

"No, silly Papa; I just wanted to know," Jane returned through a big smile.

"You have the right of it, Janie. Your Papa can be silly, can he not?" Fanny responded playfully to her now giggling daughters.

"Do not be silly, Papa," Mary told her father in between giggles.

Bennet gave a mock-stern look which caused his three daughters to giggle all the harder, a sound he could never hear enough times in a day. "If I see that mean boy again, I will kick him," Elizabeth insisted. It was true she had been upset, but at some point that had turned to anger. William, that was his name, the housekeeper had called him William. Insufferable William!

"If that rude boy shows his face again, Uncle Phillips and your father will protect you," Hattie stated with conviction. She would have loved to have given the boy a piece of her mind, for no one frightened her nieces and got off scot-free!

"If I see him, I will box his ears," Jane insisted, her arms akimbo, "No one talks to my sister in that fashion!"

"If I were the rude boy, I would keep far away from you, Jane," Fanny stated with amusement.

"Will you box his ears if he apologises?" Bennet asked, trying to hide his grin from his almost eight-year-old.

"Mayhap not if it is a sincere apology," Jane replied thoughtfully. "I may hold off punishing him for now," Jane related perfectly seriously.

"Do not forget, daughters," Fanny stated as they entered their suite of rooms, "we must always allow those who trespass against us the chance to own their error and beg the aggrieved party's pardon first."

"Yes, Mama," all three girls chorused.

~~~~~~~/~~~~~~~

That evening at the inn, as their servants packed for their departure to Holder Heights, another group of servants were packing for the master, mistress, the young master, and their nephew, young master Fitzwilliam.

Like the Bennets and Phillipses, the Darcys planned to depart for the Carrington's estate early the next morning. The Earl and Countess of Matlock, Lord Reginald and Lady Elaine Fitzwilliam, and their older son and heir, Andrew Fitzwilliam, Viscount Hilldale, would arrive at Holder Heights early in the afternoon that Saturday, if all went as planned.

CHAPTER 5

As the Bennet and Phillips families were disembarking from their coaches, another coach arrived behind theirs. It was the largest of the Darcy travelling carriages. Elizabeth recognised the adults from the wedding breakfast, and it seemed the lady was staring at her again. She became self-conscious, wondering if she had dirt on her person or outfit.

She was about to move to where Uncle Paul and Aunt Edith were greeting her parents when she saw *him*. Without thinking, she forgot what her mother had said regarding allowing an apology first and marched up to the frozen lad and kicked his shin. As she was wearing slippers and not half boots, it was not painful, just surprising.

"Why did you follow me to Uncle Paul's?" Elizabeth demanded. "Did you come to be rude and hateful to me again?" When her parents reached her, her mother gently drew Elizabeth to her.

Robert Darcy and Richard Fitzwilliam both guffawed, and Lady Anne just stared at Elizabeth, as from close up there was no question in her mind the girl looked exactly like Priscilla. Not only that, but she also sounded like her friend.

"Lizzy, a young lady does not kick anyone, regardless how much he deserves it," Fanny admonished her daughter, though she was fighting the urge to smile, then looked directly at William Darcy, who did not know where to look.

"Your daughter has my blessing to kick William anytime he behaves as he did to you the other day at Pemberley," Robert Darcy assured Fanny Bennet when he managed to control his laughter.

"Should we all repair to the drawing room and I can effect introductions and hear why William deserves to be kicked by our little Lizzy?" Lord Holder asked.

The Darcys were the last group heading indoors. "You are right, my dear. I only met Priscilla after I started to court you, but my goodness, the one they call Lizzy could be her daughter," Darcy said softly to his wife so no one else could hear him, and Lady Anne simply nodded.

Her emotions were in turmoil; how could it be that the daughter of one she never met look so much like her friend? Hopefully, she would glean some answers during the sennight the Darcys were to be at Holder Heights.

In the drawing room, the Earl introduced the arriving parties one to the other. The two youngest Bennets were taken up to the nursery. Before any could talk, William cleared his throat. "Mr. and Mrs. Bennet, Miss Bennet, Miss Elizabeth, and Miss Mary, please allow me to proffer my most sincere apologies for my unconscionable rudeness to you at Pemberley the day you were touring the house. My presumptions were arrogant and based on assumptions with no facts to support them." He turned and addressed Elizabeth directly. "Miss Elizabeth, you are correct. I was rude and hateful, and even worse, I did not behave like a gentleman. Your kick was well deserved. Please know that I deeply regret my actions and beg your, and your family's, forgiveness."

Elizabeth looked to her mother and father, both of whom nodded. "In that case, Master William, you are forgiven," Elizabeth allowed.

"Miss Elizabeth," Lady Anne addressed Elizabeth, "any time you happen to be at Pemberley, you and your sisters are more than welcome to play any of the instruments you see." Lady Anne bent down and made like she was whispering conspiratorially to Elizabeth. "I too love to play the pianoforte and I heard you are an extremely good pianist. Will we hear you play while we are here?"

Elizabeth felt a strange pull to the kind and pretty lady. "If

Mama and Papa allow me, then yes, Lady Anne, I will play for you. Jane is even better than I, and *Signore* da Funti is teaching her the harp as well," Elizabeth informed Lady Anne.

Lady Anne looked at the Bennet parents with surprise. "Your daughter's music master is *Signore* Alberto da Funti?"

"Yes, your Ladyship," Fanny replied and then told Lady Anne about the *Signore's* teaching schedule.

"I was happy your kind housekeeper asked if I wanted to play your pianoforte, Lady Anne. It is the same as the one we have at Netherfield Park. Longbourn only has an upright," Elizabeth reported. Lady Anne froze as she had when she first caught sight of Miss Elizabeth. Netherfield Park! That was her Priscilla's estate!

Fanny knew Lady Anne was one of Pricilla's friends who had tried to correspond with her after the divorce. Priscilla had meant to start writing to her friend again but had been taken before she was able to follow through on her intent. Fanny knew she might not be keeping to the spirit of her promise to Priscilla, but she had to talk to Lady Anne—alone.

Lady Edith suggested everyone go wash and change, as her housekeeper was ready to show them to their chambers. As they walked up the stairs, Fanny touched Lady Anne's arm and held her back a little, waiting until the others were ahead of them and out of earshot. Both husbands were relieved, as it seemed their wives would handle whatever it was that caused them both tension.

"You have questions about Priscilla, do you not?" Fanny asked quietly. Lady Anne did not trust herself to speak at that moment, so she just nodded. "Meet me in our private sitting room in an hour." Lady Anne nodded again, and they proceeded up the stairs.

When Robert Darcy saw the look on his wife's face as she entered their suite, he was concerned. "Anne, what is it?"

"Did you not hear what Miss Elizabeth said when she named one of their estates, Robert?" Lady Anne asked. "She mentioned Netherfield Park. She did not mention the shire, but I have a feeling it is Priscilla's Netherfield Park. There is no evidence to support my conjecture, but I pray the Bennets have not imposed on my kind-hearted friend when she was at her lowest after the King ripped her soulmate from her."

"Do not make the same mistake William made, my love. Find out the facts before you jump to conclusions," Robert Darcy calmed his wife. "Do not let your worry for your friend cloud your judgement; try to speak to the Bennets. If you do not get enough information from her, I will ask Mr. Bennet to talk to me, for he seems to be an honourable gentleman. He would not be a close friend of Holder's if he were anything but."

"Mrs. Bennet invited me to come talk about Priscilla; she saw my worry in the drawing room," Lady Anne informed her husband.

"There you go, Anne. Ask as many questions as you need to so you can feel at ease, just try not to be accusatory," Darcy suggested.

~~~~~~~/~~~~~~~

"Your judgement is sound in talking to Lady Anne, for you know she was a true friend to Priscilla who did not drop the connection after the divorce. I suggest both her husband and I should be present for the disclosure of Priscilla's death," Bennet opined. "It has been more than five years, and you are about to inform her that her friend is dead."

"Your suggestion is logical, Thomas; I agree with you," Fanny stated. "Will you go and ask Mr. Darcy to join us for the first part of the discussion?"

"With pleasure, my wife," Bennet replied. He kissed his wife then made the short walk to the Darcys' suite and knocked on the door. It was opened by Robert Darcy.

"Mr. Bennet, how may I be of assistance?" Darcy asked.

"First, as we will be together in company from time to time, please call me Bennet. Second, will you please join your wife, at least for the first part of the discussion our wives need to have?" Bennet requested.

"Yes to both, and please call me Darcy," he replied easily, grateful he would be there to support and temper his wife.

"We will see you at the top of the hour, Darcy. Thank you for your understanding," Bennet extended his hand, and the men shook.

~~~~~~~/~~~~~~~

"You did not, Wills!" Jamey Carrington had tears streaming down his cheeks from laughter after William and Richard explained the kick that necessitated the apology William had made in the drawing room.

"He most certainly did," Richard confirmed with much mirth.

"And you will be working in the stables, mucking out stalls?" Jamey declared. William nodded sullenly. "I cannot say you do not deserve it, William. You were getting far too haughty and presumptive, just like..."

"My Aunt Catherine," William cut his friend off. "Thank you, Jamey. That has been pointed out to me *once or twice* lately. The truth is, I did not see I was becoming like her, but now that I know and can see the error of my ways, I will be correcting my behaviour, and hopefully Father will not leave me to languish in the stables too long."

"It will build character—and muscles," Richard informed his cousin.

"Do you still want to join the army when you graduate Cambridge, Richard?" Jamey asked affably.

"I do. Some of us have to work for our daily bread as we do not have the luck of being born first sons like you two fortunate sods," Richard ribbed his friend and cousin.

"Hopefully, you will learn to follow orders before you join the army, cousin of mine," William stated.

"You begin at Eton in September do you not, Richard?" Jamie asked.

"I will be in my first year, and Andy will be in his final one. You will join me the next year, and William will join us the year after," Richard pointed out.

Soon the three were talking about one of their horses—but not before Lady Cassandra Carrington, who was almost seven and called Cassie, invaded her brother's chambers wanting to play, and had to be evicted. She had been bored and impatient, as a girl of her age was wont to be, waiting for her friends to wash and change.

~~~~~~~/~~~~~~~

There was a knock on the Bennets' sitting room door and the Darcys were welcomed inside. They were not wholly surprised to see their host and hostess present as well. There was a tea service on the table, and Lady Edith poured for everyone. There was silence except for the sounds of teacups on saucers until all six had drained their cups.

"First, Lady Anne, in her letters to you, did Priscilla mention her sister of the heart who lived at a neighbouring estate?" Fanny opened.

Lady Anne nodded her head, as she remembered how often her friend wrote of her best friend she had made in Hertfordshire, Francine. "Fanny—you are that same Francine, are you not?" Lady Anne asked softly. As she now recognised who Fanny was, she knew from what Priscilla had written before the divorce, that the lady opposite her would have done anything for her friend. The relief of knowing she was with Priscilla's true friend was nearly overwhelming, and any thoughts of Priscilla being ill-used by the Bennets were expelled from her consciousness. "Why did Priscilla stop writing to me? I never cut her, unlike others did, including her own family."

"You will understand shortly, and please call me Fanny." Fanny proceeded to tell Lady Anne how their mutual friend had been with child when the King tore her apart from her Freddy, how they had entered their confinements together, and that each given birth, Priscilla a stillborn son she named Frederick after his father, and Lizzy born to herself. "Now, Lady Anne..."

"Please call me, Anne," Lady Anne requested softly as she dried her cheeks, the news immediately overwhelming her with sadness.

"Now, Anne, we come to the hardest part I need to tell you, which will explain why she never wrote to you again," Fanny began again, trying to find the gentlest way to tell the lady sitting opposite her.

"She is no more, is she?" Lady Anne asked quietly, wilting into the arms of her husband when she saw the answer in Fanny's eyes, grateful she had his arms around her and knowing that her friend had been denied such comfort when her Fredrick had been torn asunder from her life.

"I am so sorry." Fanny herself fell into tears as she had finally met someone who loved her friend as much as she had and who would grieve with her. "She went home to God only hours after she had given birth. I sat with her and held her hand until she left the mortal world," Fanny informed Lady Anne gently.

It took about ten minutes for Lady Anne to recover some equanimity. "I am well now, Robert; I think I suspected she was gone, but I hoped I was wrong. Do her parents not know?"

"No, they do not, and that is per Priscilla's wishes. She told me, made me swear to her on her deathbed, that I could only inform those who asked. I understand now you were honouring what you thought were Priscilla's wishes when she did not respond to your letters, but based on my vow, I could not inform anyone who did not reach out first. For that, I am sorry, but I trust you are able to understand why I could not," Fanny stated evenly.

"It speaks very well of you that you are as good a friend to her in death as you were to her in life. Yes, I completely understand," Lady Anne returned.

"Given the news you just learnt, do you want us to continue our conversation as we planned, Anne, or would you like to do so at a later time or date?" Fanny enquired.

"No, Fanny, I am willing to continue now if you are." Lady Anne averred.

"Are you sure, Anne?" Darcy asked his wife, his concern

for her touchingly obvious.

"Yes, Robert. I am sure. I have regained my composure and would very much like to hear about Priscilla's life after she married the Duke—the Prince," Lady Anne assured her husband.

With that, the other four exited the sitting room and the door was closed. The two ladies moved to sit next to one another on the settee. Lady Anne took Fanny's hand in hers, the bond created in their mutual admiration of Priscilla one that would be for life, and already made them friends, and more, in under an hour's time.

"If you have questions, please ask them, Anne," Fanny allowed.

"How is it you have Netherfield?" Lady Anne asked.

"We live there, but do not own it. Priscilla added a clause to her will, one she never thought would be needed, but did so in the event the worst happening. Other than some small bequests, she willed everything to my Lizzy because we had been with child together," Fanny related the same explanation she had told her husband to Lady Anne.

"Tell me honestly, it was your son who died, was it not? Elizabeth is Priscilla's daughter, is she not?" Lady Anne asked with surety.

"How did you know?" Fanny enquired, already knowing the answer as it was in her daughter's green eyes, should anyone be looking to find it.

"When I met Priscilla for the first time, she was Lizzy's age. When I first saw Lizzy at the wedding breakfast, I thought I was hallucinating—seeing Priscilla as she was when we met. Then when I saw her from close up, I could see Priscilla looking back at me. Not only that, but Lizzy also sounds just like her mother," Lady Anne stated. "Her father does not know he has a daughter, does he? Does anyone know she is a Princess of the United Kingdom of Great Britain and Ireland?"

"No, the Prince is unaware. Let me retrieve something for you. Priscilla wrote four letters before her final confinement. At Priscilla's behest, I wrote the name and gender where needed in the letter for her birthfather; it is to be given to him when Lizzy receives hers, on her eighteenth birthday or when I feel it is needed beforehand. There is one to my Thomas, and one to her parents, all to be given to or posted to the recipients when Lizzy is informed.

"She made me swear I would honour her wishes before she told me what it was she wanted. It was her wish that we switch the babies and for me to raise Lizzy as my own. I made the vow; I could do no less. What I am about to retrieve is a fifth letter she had me write for her before she let go, which she signed herself." Fanny stood and retrieved the letter she always kept close and handed it to Lady Anne who opened it and began to read.

5 March 1790
Netherfield Park, Hertfordshire

If my sister Fanny Bennet has handed you this letter then you are someone who was very close to me, and I can only think of two, Anne Darcy and Elaine Fitzwilliam, who might see my daughter and guess she is of my body and not Fanny's child by blood.

I am weak of body, but not of mind. Before I told her what she was promising to do, I convinced Fanny to promise me she would obey my wishes to the letter as I have asked of her. Who better to raise my daughter than the woman who has been at my side through these recent times, good and bad? The same lady whose daughter Jane is my niece in all ways but blood.

Yes, Elizabeth Sarah, named for my beloved late Grandmother Beth and my mother is my daughter. Even after she cut me, I have honoured my mother with my daughter's middle name. No matter her actions, she is still my mother and I will always love her.

I have made some small bequests, but everything else, including the money Frederick settled on me, will be Elizabeth's. Other than Fanny, and now you, the only others who know the full truth are the solicitor, Mr. Frank Phillips, and my man of business, Mr. Edward Gardiner.

Not being here to have you give me your vow as I requested Fanny make, I beseech you to honour my wishes. When Elizabeth is eighteen, she will know the truth, as will her birthfather, my parents, and Thomas Bennet. I ask that you not share the truth of Elizabeth's parentage, even with your husbands. As I dictate the last, I am sure it is something you will not be able to do.

Anne or Elaine, if it is you, I understand if you need to tell Robert or Reggie all. I know you do not keep secrets from your husbands under any circumstances. Before you do so, please have them promise they will not inform anyone until Elizabeth's existence becomes common knowledge.

Mr. Phillips has the true page of the register, the one witnessed by the midwife and others if there is ever a question of her paternity. As I was with child before the divorce, Elizabeth will never be tainted with the stain of illegitimacy. Given she was born less than six months after Frederick was torn from me, there will be no question who the father is. The law states that a child born up to ten months after separation is the child of the previous husband. Thus there is no legal or moral question of my daughter's paternity.

I support Fanny in keeping her true fortune from becoming common knowledge as it would draw every fortune hunter in the known world to her.

Please know how much I value those like you who did not abandon me. I meant to write and reopen correspondence, but it was not to be. If the reader is either Anne or Elaine, know how much your friendship meant to me.

God bless you,

Cilla

"I am so happy she had you with her Fanny; what a burden you have shouldered these five years." Lady Anne repeatedly wiped away her tears, her shoulder resting against Fanny's as she was grateful to share her grief with someone so connected to Priscilla, who had been her support and comfort until she breathed her last. "Mr. Bennet does not know Lizzy is not his daughter by blood?" Lady Anne asked after she composed herself.

"No, he does not. He commented once on Lizzy's green eyes, but never anything since. If he asked me directly I would tell him, but I cannot break my promise to Cilla," Fanny averred.

"Where is she buried?" Lady Anne asked.

"At St. Alfred's in Meryton. It is the church closest to Netherfield Park," Fanny replied.

"You live at Netherfield now, correct?" Lady Anne asked, her mind starting to race now that she had more from Mrs. Bennet than she had ever imagined she might gain during this visit, and within but three hours of their meeting.

"Yes, we lease out our estate, Longbourn. When Lizzy gains her majority, she will receive control of her inheritance, including Netherfield Park. I still feel Cilla's presence in the house, which is why I asked Thomas to allow us to live there." Fanny smiled sadly, understanding the look of longing in Lady Anne's expression. "When you travel to Town for the season—I assume you do?" Lady Anne nodded. "If we are home—and the chances are we will be as Thomas eschews Town—you will be welcome to visit Netherfield Park. It is as Cilla decorated it; I am sure you will feel her presence there as well," Fanny suggested.

"Fanny, may I take the letter to show Robert when I tell him? Priscilla knew me well; as she herself asked you to write, we do not keep secrets, and I did not make that vow to her, but Robert will be the only one I share the information with, as she asked of me," Lady Anne requested. "You should know that my sister Elaine will not keep secrets from her husband—my bother—either."

~~~~~~~/~~~~~~~

After his wife told him all and allowed him to read the letter, Robert Darcy was silent for some minutes. "So William insulted a Princess of the United Kingdom of Great Britain and Ireland, one who has more wealth on her own than we do. And unless she tells him, or there is an announcement from the royals after she turns eighteen, he will not know."

"You know we are about to become close connections of the Bennets do you not, my love?" Lady Anne asked.

"No doubt, Anne; I had no doubt when the two of you started crying together." He soothed her as he held her hand a little tighter in appreciation of her finding some relief after being sad so long because she had no word from her friend. "It does not hurt that Bennet seems to be exactly the kind of man I would like to know. What about Elaine and Reggie?" Darcy asked.

"If Elaine draws the same conclusions I did, Fanny will tell her and allow her to read the letter. Whether or not my sister then tells my brother will be up to her. I am sure Elaine would not keep secrets from Reggie," Lady Anne opined.

Lady Anne returned the precious letter to her new friend. An hour later, the Matlock coaches arrived at Holder heights.

CHAPTER 6

The Fitzwilliams went directly to their chambers to wash and change. Andrew, who was fifteen, went to join his brother, cousin, and Jamey, while the Earl and Countess of Matlock joined the rest of the adults in the drawing room for afternoon tea and were introduced to the Bennets.

The Bennet sisters were in the nursery playing dolls with Cassie. The latter normally only had Jamey as a playmate, and he never wanted to play dolls with her—just as she had no interest in playing with his toy soldiers.

As much as it was killing Lady Anne not to mention anything regarding Priscilla to Elaine, she bit her tongue and honoured her friend's dying wishes, just as Fanny did. If Elaine said anything about Priscilla, or noticed anything about Elizabeth, then she would ask Fanny to join them for an enlightening talk.

When Lady Elaine learned that the Bennets lived in Hertfordshire, she asked if they had ever met Priscilla, and was truly surprised when she realised the Bennets had been introduced as being from Netherfield Park, and that Mr. and Mrs. Phillips were from the same shire. "Is that not the estate of Priscilla De Melville, so named before marrying the Duke of York and Albany—Prince Frederick?" Lady Elaine asked, not missing the small, sad smile that passed between her sister Anne and Mrs. Bennet. "How is Priscilla, and can you tell me why she stopped communicating with those of us who refused to cut her because of a divorce in which she had no say?"

"Elaine, our friend passed in childbirth some five years ago," Lady Anne said gently as she took her sister's hands in her own. "Her son was stillborn."

"No! How can that be? She was so healthy and vibrant. What happened to her? And why are the Bennets living at her estate?" Lady Elaine asked, feeling the shock of the news washing over her.

"Your Ladyship, you may know my name as Francine from Cilla's letters. For her own reasons, she always used my formal name when writing about me to her friends," Fanny shared.

"You are the one she had a sisterly bond with?" Fanny nodded. "Please tell me all," Lady Elaine asked as her husband replaced his sister sitting next to his wife and held her hands in his to ease her obvious distress. He needed to understand if there were actions which should be taken on behalf of his wife for their friend, as this was had makings of a scandal if there ever was one.

"Bad business, that whole forced divorce and the way the De Melvilles cut her to try and protect their place in society, very badly done," Lord Matlock opined, watching the Bennets carefully, and confused as to why neither of the Darcys seemed angry; he intended to follow their lead until given cause to act otherwise.

"It pained Cilla no end that her parents cut her and kept her sister and brother from having a relationship with her, your Lordship. Through it all she loved her parents until she drew her final breath," Fanny informed the Fitzwilliams.

"Please, Mrs. Bennet, share what you are able," Lady Elaine beseeched. She quietly cried, accepting her husband's handkerchief to dry her eyes.

"As you know, Cilla and I became the closest of friends..." Then Fanny told all, right up to and including the devastated Prince attending his beloved's and son's funerals. She explained how, as an *afterthought*, the clause had been added to the will in case Priscilla passed with no heir. When she was done, silence encompassed the room for a few moments.

"So, you are telling me that when she reaches her majority at one and twenty, your second daughter will be the wealthiest person in the land outside of the Royals?" Lord Matlock asked in wonder.

"Yes, Matlock," Lord Holder confirmed, "which is why Lady Priscilla exacted the promise of secrecy regarding Lizzy's wealth. Could you imagine the line of fortune hunters if they had any inkling of it?" Lord Holder looked to his friend and his friend's brother. "Bennet and Phillips, you have things structured to protect Lizzy from any such horror, have you not?"

"Very much so, Carrington. Not only that, but when Lizzy chooses a husband, the marriage settlement will be ironclad, leaving control of her fortune in her own hands," Bennet confirmed.

"At least I know she did not want to cut our friendship," Lady Elaine stated softly.

"As sorry as I was when Fanny told me about her death, I was relieved to know Priscilla was surrounded by love when she left this world. It helped when Fanny told me Priscilla fully intended to establish communication with those of us who had remained true to her after her child was born," Lady Anne added.

"You two do not yet know what happened at Pemberley last week," Darcy told his brother and sister-in-law.

"What happened; is everything well?" Lord Matlock frowned, certain that whatever it was, this was not the time to discuss it during such a conversation as they were having.

"The Bennets were, by chance, touring the house the day Anne and I were with you at Snowhaven. William heard the pianoforte and assumed it was his mother..." Darcy told the story fully.

"He called them riffraff?" Lord Matlock asked in surprise and was met with multiple amused nods.

"Wait, your five-year-old daughter plays so well that William thought my sister was home and playing the instrument?" Lady Elaine enquired in disbelief.

"The Bennets' music master is none other than *Signore*

Alberto da Funti," Lady Anne informed her sister.

"Gracious me, when will we hear this prodigy play?" Lady Elaine wanted to know.

"*Prodigies*, Elaine," Lady Edith interjected. "The older sister Jane, who is a whole seven years of age, or is it eight now Fanny?"

"She will be eight in September, Edith," Fanny confirmed.

"Jane is as good, if not better than Lizzy on the pianoforte, and well on her way to becoming a virtuoso on the harp. The youngest daughter here with the Bennets, Mary, who is three, has just begun to take lessons from the *Signore*. Am I still correct, Fanny?" Lady Edith informed her friends.

"Yes, Edith, that is still all true. Mary has started catching on so fast that the *Signore* feels she may exceed her two older sisters in musical talent," Fanny offered calmly, used to the astonishment such words brought, so she allowed them some time to grasp it.

"Will I meet these wonders who are your daughters, Mrs. Bennet?" Lady Elaine asked hopefully.

"I was about to go see how they are doing in the nursery playing with Cassie. You are welcome to join me, your Ladyship," Fanny offered.

"It is Elaine if you please, Mrs. Bennet," the Countess allowed.

"Then please call me Fanny," she replied, seeing easily why her Cilla had so loved these ladies and missed their company.

"May I join you two?" Lady Anne asked, knowing she needed to be present when Elaine saw Elizabeth for the first time.

"Of course, Anne. Edith, gentlemen, please excuse us," Fanny intoned as the three ladies stood and started up to the nursery.

~~~~~~~/~~~~~~~

When the three ladies entered the nursery, the girls were having a tea party with their respective dolls. Mary and Jane were facing the doorway; Elizabeth and Cassie had their backs facing that direction. Kitty and Lydia were being entertained by their nursemaid.

"Girls, there is someone here who would like to meet you," Fanny said, claiming the older girls' attention. After making sure their dolls were seated securely, all four girls stood and lined up in order of age. "My oldest is Jane." Jane gave a most creditable curtsey. "You know Cassie, I am sure?" Elaine nodded. "Next is my Lizzy, the one from the tale at Pemberley."

Lady Elaine had been looking at Fanny when she said the last; as she turned, the petite girl with mahogany tresses was in a curtsey, and then stood and looked at the Countess with the greenest eyes—eyes that green and large she had only seen once before, on Priscilla De Melville.

"Last," Fanny carried on as if she had not seen the reaction to Lizzy, "this is Mary, who is but three years old. Over with the nursemaid are Kitty, who is two, and Lydia, not yet one."

"Your daughters are very pretty," Lady Elaine offered, but her eyes were locked onto Elizabeth. It was as if she were looking at Priscilla at a young age.

"Girls, it is my pleasure to introduce you to Lady Elaine Fitzwilliam, Countess of Matlock," Fanny completed the introductions.

Lady Elaine turned to Fanny. "Elizabeth is *your* daughter, a daughter of your body?" she asked quietly.

"Come, Elaine; you need to join Fanny and me for a talk," Lady Anne suggested in such a tone that let her sister know it was not a request.

~~~~~~~/~~~~~~~

As soon as the door to the sitting room was closed, Lady Elaine turned to the other two ladies. "Elizabeth is not your daughter by blood, is she?"

"She is not. Let us sit. Read this first and then I—we—will answer any questions you have." Fanny handed Elaine the letter. Both she and Anne sat in silence while Elaine read the letter twice over.

"Goodness gracious. Elizabeth is Priscilla's and the Prince's legitimate daughter. She is a Princess. Why did Priscilla not want her to be raised by the royals?" Lady Elaine asked.

"Because Cilla's dying wish was for Elizabeth to be raised in a regular family with love. She was afraid if her existence as a Princess was known earlier than eighteen, her daughter would have been taken from her and cloistered in some palace or country house belonging to the monarchs and raised by governesses, nursemaids, and fawning attendants. She wanted Elizabeth to know the love of a mother and father, unconditional love." Fanny sat back and allowed the Countess to assimilate the information.

"What if she is seen in society?" Lady Elaine asked.

"She will not be, not for many years, at least. My Thomas has no time for the hypocrisy and debauchery of many in the *Ton*, so until Elizabeth is much older, there is no worry on that front. I know your families are members of the *Ton*, so I am sorry if my words offend," Fanny stated contritely.

"No apologies are needed; we happen to agree with you. It is that hypocrisy which caused Priscilla's family to cut her and lose contact with their granddaughter," Lady Anne stated emphatically.

"You know I will not be able to keep this from Reggie, as Anne was not able to keep the news from Robert," Lady Elaine explained. "I have a suggestion Fanny." Lady Elaine took Fanny's hand.

"What is it, Elaine?" Fanny asked although she felt she knew what was coming.

"Is it not unfair to your husband not to know the truth of his daughter's parentage? Do you worry he will love Elizabeth less if he knows the truth?" Lady Elaine asked softly as she looked at Fanny.

"No, I cannot see anything that would cause Thomas to love her any less. But I promised Cilla." Fanny was conflicted between her vow and the knowledge Elaine was correct.

"You have honoured Priscilla's wishes more than any other would have; I am sure that if she were here, she would be the first one to tell you she understood the need to be completely honest with your husband. Do not forget he has been denied the right of mourning his son," Lady Anne soothed.

"You are both correct. I will inform him when we return to Longbourn, as Priscilla's letter is there. I want to be able to have him read it when I make the full disclosure to him. Thank you; this will lift a great weight I have been carrying." Fanny felt relief now that Cilla's friends had allowed her fears and concerns to be discussed, and she could finally tell her Thomas all of the truth.

~~~~~~~/~~~~~~~

Lord Reginald Fitzwilliam was very seldom—if ever—so at a loss for words as he was after his wife told him the truth about Priscilla's daughter and gave him the letter to read.

"She is not the wealthiest non-royal, she *is* a royal! She is a Princess of the United Kingdom of Great Britain and Ireland, Elaine," Lord Matlock stated as he emerged from his stupor.

"That she is, Reggie, and we *will* honour Priscilla's wishes and allow Elizabeth to be raised with love and family," Lady Elaine stated not brooking any opposition.

"You have my word, Elaine; I will not breathe a word of this to anyone," Lord Matlock raised his hands in mock surrender. He would honour Priscilla's wishes anyway, but he also would not gainsay his wife. "Your suggestion that Mrs. Bennet inform Bennet is a good one. Did you see his pride and love for them when she and her older sister exhibited for us after dinner?"

"It was hard to miss. There was no exaggeration of those girls' musical talent," Elaine averred. "I loved the story of how Elizabeth kicked William's shin. It pleases me that our brother is making him learn humility; one Catherine in the family is more than enough, thank you very much."

"We must do anything we can to assist the Bennets if

they ever need it. Mayhap one of our boys will have the good sense to fall in love with Elizabeth," Lord Matlock stated. "Do not look at me so, Elaine; I will not interfere. I want our sons to marry for love as their father did."

"Can you remember ever seeing more strikingly beautiful girls? All the Bennet sisters are gorgeous in their own way. I wonder if the two youngest will have the musical and language talents of their older sisters," Elaine wondered.

"Given the talent of the two older daughters by blood, I would assume it will be so," Lord Matlock opined.

Lady Elaine returned the letter to Fanny. On her return to her chambers, Lady Elaine felt drained from the day of disclosures, so fairly soon after that she and her husband climbed into bed.

The time at Holder Heights flew by, and before each family departed to their own estate, invitations were proffered and accepted. The Darcys and Fitzwilliams would stop at Netherfield on their way to Town after Andrew and Richard were dropped off at Eton.

CHAPTER 7

On arriving back at Netherfield Park, Fanny's first order of business was to make sure all household issues were addressed; she met with Mrs. Nichols to hear if there were any urgent issues.

After Fanny washed and changed, she knew she could no longer put off the task before her. She retrieved the letter Cilla had written to Thomas, then made her way to the study, where he was going over the ledgers with Netherfield's steward.

"Enter," Bennet called when he heard a knock.

"Mr. Bennet, we need to talk. Is now a good time or would you prefer to finish your meeting with Mr. Harrelson first?" Fanny asked, almost hoping for the reprieve of more time. She prayed Thomas would not be angry with her.

"No, Mrs. Bennet; Harrelson and I had just completed our meeting, and we have scheduled to spend the whole of the day together on the morrow when we meet with Mr. Hill at Longbourn as well," Bennet indicated the chair the steward just vacated. The man bowed to the master and mistress and took his leave.

"Thomas, what I have to tell you may shake the very foundation of our marriage, but I trust you will understand and not be too angry with me for not telling you the whole truth. Before I say more, I have a letter—from Cilla—I need you to read. After that, we can discuss all," Fanny stated as she sat on the settee and patted the cushion next to her. As Bennet sat, she handed him the letter.

27 February 1790
Netherfield Park

Thomas,

If you are reading this letter then the worst has come to pass, and I am no longer with you and my dearest friend—my sister—in the mortal world. Let me start by begging you not to be angry with Fanny for not telling you all, as I have made her swear to honour my wishes.

I am aware that since the King tore Frederick and me asunder I have not been the same. I knew I was with child before my beloved went to his father and did not mention it to him just in case what I feared happened. To my everlasting sorrow, it did.

My will has been made over with the help of your brother Phillips. I am sure Fanny would have told you about the bequests to her, Jane, and any future daughters. She fought me valiantly on my bequeathing her and your children anything, but in the end I prevailed.

This letter signifies that not only am I dead, but that Fanny agreed to take my child as her own, and by extension your own. I am not sure Fanny will be able to wait until my son or daughter is eighteen to tell you, but that is what I intend to ask of her.

My reason for not telling Frederick he has a child is that the son or daughter will be fourth in line in succession to the throne, and I want our child to grow up with loving parents rather than being a piece of furniture forgotten at some country estate of the royals. Not telling you connects to not telling Frederick as I am sure you will insist he is informed soon after you know the truth.

I want my child to be raised by you and Fanny who, will love the child with all of your hearts—in other words, just what I have seen in you and Fanny and how you have so far raised our Jane. My ardent belief is that it is the same way you and Fanny will love all of your children, including the one I have asked you to take into your home and love as your own. I know not if you are reading this on my child's eighteenth birthday or before then, but I do know this: I could not for ask better parents to love my child than you and Fanny.

As we will enter our confinements close to one another's time,

I will ask Fanny to tell you she bore twins—so I hope she does not, in fact, bear twins; that would make three babies a harder tale to tell —if I do not survive. I thank you both for whatever you have done for my son or daughter, and reiterate that if you are upset, it is me to whom your ire should be directed.

Both of your brothers know of these arrangements; Mr. Phillips will take care of all legal aspects, including holding the genuine page of the register that recorded the birth, and Mr. Gardiner, who will manage my heir's fortune.

Until my child reaches his or her majority, Netherfield is yours, so use it as you see fit. All I can do is apologise from beyond the grave to you for this subterfuge and pray it does not diminish the love you feel for our dear Fanny or for the child you now know is not yours by blood.

My eternal thanks, and may God bless you and your family,
Cilla

"Lizzy," Thomas whispered as he put the letter down.

"Yes, Thomas. Lizzy is Cilla and Prince Frederick's daughter," Fanny admitted with her head bowed as her tears flowed freely.

"Little Frederick buried next to Priscilla?" Bennet asked, already knowing the answer.

"Our stillborn son. It was her dying wish, Thomas. How was I to refuse her?" Fanny asked forlornly.

"Fanny, look at me," Bennet requested as he gently lifted his wife's head applying gentle pressure to her chin. "I am not angry. I understand you were sworn to secrecy, and should our son have survived, any child Priscilla left to us would be living in our household, as he or she would need us. Why inform me now?"

Fanny related the happenings at Holder Heights, and Bennet then understood why both Ladies Anne and Elaine had been fixated on Elizabeth. She explained that Lady Matlock had suggested she reveal the truth to him; her logic was needed as until then Fanny had had not known any person with permission to know the truth with whom she could discuss her burden. Without Lady Matlock's advice, she would have waited until Lizzy was eighteen, just as Priscilla had requested.

"For me, Lizzy is as much my daughter as any of the other four. You will not push her away now will you, Thomas?" Fanny worried.

"Fanny, how could you even think that a possibility? Like you, I love her as a father should love his daughter, but there is something we must do, regardless of Priscilla's wishes. As she knew I would, I must contact the Prince." Bennet held up his hand to stem the protest forming in Fanny's throat. "Lizzy is a royal, not a cousin, but a Princess! If we wait until she is eighteen as Priscilla wanted and the Prince is angry with us, we could be charged with treason. This *must* be done. We will have to rely on his love for Priscilla to induce him to follow her wishes. That way we are covered legally, and we will have the Prince's royal sanction."

"But what if he takes her away, Thomas?" Fanny asked in a panic at the thought of losing Lizzy.

"It is a chance we must take, Fanny. Surely you can see that we cannot risk the welfare of all of us, including our four daughters of your body, if we do not do this," Bennet asserted.

"As much as I hate to own it, Thomas, you have the right of it. How will you go about it?" Fanny asked. Her insides were roiling at the possibility of losing Lizzy, but she understood it was the only course open to them.

"I will write to him at York House. From bits I have read in *The Times*, I believe that is his primary residence. You know they separated, do you not?" Bennet asked and Fanny nodded. As Bennet picked up his quill and pulled a fresh sheet of parchment from the stack on the corner of his desk, Fanny went to seek her daughters, for she felt an uncontrollable urge to hug Elizabeth. After her long hug, Fanny sat down and wrote letters to both Elaine Fitzwilliam and Anne Darcy.

After his letter had been dispatched by express to York House, Bennet rode to the cemetery at St. Alfred's to visit his son and offer a prayer for his eternal salvation.

~~~~~~~/~~~~~~~

As it happened, the Duke of York and Albany, Earl of Ulster, was on the continent in negotiations for a treaty for the King when the letter from Thomas Bennet arrived at York House on St. James Square in London.

He arrived at his town house a fortnight later. On the following day he sat in his study with his private secretary sorting through correspondence. His secretary asked his master if he knew a Thomas Bennet, and at first the Duke demurred, but just before the man threw the missive into the fire the Duke grabbed his arm.

He remembered, just in time, the man was the husband of his Cilla's best friend and correctly surmised there must be a good reason for the man to be writing to him out of the blue. It might have something to do with Priscilla.

That very morning, the Duke ordered his coach be made ready, and along with a contingent of the royal guard, he departed for Netherfield Park.

~~~~~~~/~~~~~~~

Both Anne and Elaine responded to Fanny's letters and asked if she needed their company. Fanny had thanked them from the bottom of her heart but had refused their offer, saying that as yet they had no response from the Prince. There was no telling when, or even if, they would hear from him.

She was about to hie to the study to ask her husband if mayhap he should seek a personal audience with the Prince when she heard the sound of riders and a coach in the drive. Her husband heard it as well and joined her at the entrance to the house.

There was no mistaking the royal guards' uniforms or the royal standard on the coach's door. Biggs placed a step, opened the coach door, then stood to the side, his back ramrod straight as the Prince alighted from the conveyance.

"Welcome to Netherfield, your Royal Highness," Bennet intoned as he and his wife bowed and curtsied deeply.

"Come now, Bennet, you used to call me Oatland; there is no need for formality," Frederick said amiably.

"That is before I was aware you were the King's second son," Bennet retorted.

"As it is my prerogative, please call me York," the Prince commanded.

"Please follow me into the study," Bennet invited.

Once the three were ensconced within, the Prince refused refreshment, impatient to know the reason for the urgent request he attend the Bennets at Netherfield. He was not surprised to have surmised that his generous Cilla would have bequeathed the estate to the Bennets.

"I am about to give you a letter from Priscilla written before she died. She wanted it to wait for another thirteen years, but when I found out the facts of the matter the day I posted my letter to you, I decided you must be made aware of the facts now," Bennet stated as he handed the confused prince a letter from his late former wife.

For a while, the Prince simply held the letter, staring at the penmanship which could be none other than written in his late wife's hand, trying to feel her presence. When he felt ready, he broke the seal and started to read.

27 February 1790
Netherfield Park

My one and only, Frederick,

Let me open this letter by telling you how ardently I love you, and that even in death it will never change. If you are reading this, Frederick, then the worst has happened, and I am no longer living in this world without you. Know that when God brings you home to His kingdom, I will be waiting to be reunited with you.

If you are being handed this letter, then our daughter, Elizabeth Sarah, is now eighteen. Yes, we have a child. Before you become angry with the Bennets, I ask you in the name of the infinite love we shared to listen to my reasons. I am confident that you will agree with my decision once I give you my reasoning.

"I have a daughter?" The Prince asked wondrously, returning to his reading when they both nodded that he did.

The reason my sister Fanny will not have contacted you about your daughter before she is eighteen is that I intend that Fanny vow to me she will honour my wishes for the following reasons: First, you told me how you and your brothers and sisters were raised, and second, how many times did we comment that Fanny and Thomas were the best of parents?

Do you remember, my love, how you told me how lonely your upbringing was—placed in a country house with nursemaids, governesses, and tutors, seeing your parents only once in a great while? You told me how your parents were almost strangers to you until you were older and could be used for their advantage? Is that what you want for our Elizabeth? Do you want her to grow up not knowing a parent's love?

I can hear you, Freddy, you are saying you would love her, but if you are honest, you also know as soon as she is known to your parents it will be out of your hands. We made a pledge, one to the other, do you remember, my love?

"Yes, I remember Cilla, I remember," the prince said aloud, tears trailing down his cheeks. He was not ashamed of his emotional display, for the Bennets had loved his wife too; he knew that if any would understand it would be them.

You know in your heart that Fanny and Thomas will raise our child with love, compassion, and caring, and that she will have a real chance to be the best version of herself possible.

If, as I suspect she may, Fanny tells Thomas about our child before she is eighteen, I know Thomas will do his duty to inform you, and I beg you, Freddy, allow Elizabeth to remain with the Bennets. Work out a way to be part of her life without anyone else knowing you are her father.

In case you are wondering why Fanny's script appears in places, it is because I will ask her to fill in certain words if I am unable to myself.

I ask this in the name of all that is holy and the love we

shared, the love I hope we still share.
Yours in this life and forevermore,
Cilla

The Prince read the letter over twice more before he was willing to speak. "Like you, Fanny, I made Cilla a promise, and I will not break it now. Elizabeth will remain with you. Is your brother Phillips available?" the Prince asked.

"He is, York; I will have him summoned for you," Bennet stated. He stood and called the nearest footman in the hall, dispatching him to summon Mr. Phillips.

"If you assumed the house is ours, it is not..." Fanny went on to explain all about Priscilla's will. She also explained to the Prince that it was her son who lay in eternal slumber next to Priscilla.

"It is as it should be. The only difference is that when she is older and whether she allows me to acknowledge her or not, she will be my heir," the Prince informed the Bennets. "I see some very large footmen in your employ, Bennet; would you allow me to supplement them with some of the royal guard, who will be incognito as footmen, coachmen, and outriders? Also, I would like to place a doctor at Netherfield who will go wherever my daughter does."

"Of course. We will accept whatever you feel is needed to protect your daughter. I assume you would like to meet our children; it has been many years since you saw our Jane," Bennet suggested with a twinkle in his eye.

"How will I know...I am guessing I will know her when I see her. I assume she has some of my Cilla in her?" the prince asked. "Before we go, do the De Melvilles know about Elizabeth, or even about Priscilla's death?

"No, they do not. While I have bent a few of Cilla's wishes, I will follow them exactly in this matter, and tell them their daughter died only if and when they contact me. Otherwise, they will receive a letter when Elizabeth is eighteen or if we feel we need to inform her before that age," Fanny stated flatly, unwilling to be moved in this, as she had never forgiven them for disowning their daughter when Cilla needed them most. "Let us repair to the west drawing room; the three oldest girls will be there waiting for us." Now that she knew the Prince would not remove his daughter and intended to honour Priscilla's wishes, Fanny felt as if a millstone had been lifted from her shoulders.

The moment the Prince walked into the drawing room and three inquisitive girls looked up at him, he knew, for he was staring into his Cilla's eyes. Not only that, but his daughter looked like a miniature version of his beloved, based on a miniature of her as a young girl he always kept on his person. She had Cilla's complexion and her mahogany curls, which Frederick had so loved winding around his finger. She seemed to have her mother's looks; to Frederic, she was the prettiest little girl he had ever beheld. He believed she would break many hearts when she was older and thought he might have to assign an entire regiment of royal guards to protect her once she came out into society.

"Jane, Lizzy, and Mary, you remember all of the stories I told you about your Aunt Cilla who gifted us this house?" All three nodded vigorously. "This is Uncle Frederick; he was Aunt Cilla's husband."

"Uncle Frederick is a big mouthful is it not?" the Prince asked the three sisters as he sat near them.

"Uncle," Jane exclaimed as she ran to him and accepted a hug. "I have missed you."

"And I you. You are even more beautiful than I remember," the Prince stated as Jane beamed with pleasure.

"It is, Uncle Fred-rick," Mary responded seriously.

"Well, in that case you may call me what Aunt Cilla used to, I will be Uncle Freddy," the Prince told the girls, who agreed it was a much easier name to say.

"Would you like to accompany us to the music room, Frederick, to hear Jane and Lizzy play?" Fanny asked. "Yes, they can play—quite well," Fanny told the Prince after seeing his quizzical look.

When Jane played the pianoforte followed by his daughter, he thought he was dreaming. They played better than most debutantes he had heard. If that were not enough, the two played a duet with Jane on the harp.

Frederick remained for the midday meal, and before he left, he met with the Bennet parents and Phillips, who had just arrived, in the study. Now that the girls accepted he was another uncle, the Prince agreed it was the role he would fill and that he would visit when his duties allowed and was convenient for the Bennets. He went over the legal protections for his daughter's inheritance with Phillips and signed a document placing custody of his daughter with the Bennets. Once he was satisfied with all that had been done, he returned to where the Bennet daughters were.

When Frederik departed Netherfield Park that day, there was a new spring in his step. For some reason the *Ton* would not comprehend, his days of being a rake were behind him. There was no more excessive drinking, carousing, gambling, or even a hint of foolishness. Furthermore, no one could fathom what had changed to lift the veil of sadness which had descended on the Prince since his forced divorce, but all agreed it could not but bode well for the country.

CHAPTER 8

March 1800

Lady Catherine de Bourgh, née Fitzwilliam was seriously displeased. She was isolated from her family, and five years earlier the executor of her husband's will and her daughter Anne's legal guardian, her brother, the Earl of Matlock, had done the unthinkable and removed her daughter from her care.

The self-styled great lady was never happy with what she had; she was always more interested in what she did not have —what others had. Growing up, she had been jealous of the attention her brother and heir to the Matlock Earldom had received, as well as the love showered on her younger sister only because she was more pleasant.

She had been launched into society when she was eighteen, supremely confident she would capture no less than a Duke—but it never happened. She had been certain that all she needed to attract a man of such exalted rank was her dowry of five and twenty thousand pounds and the fact her father was an Earl.

It was quickly evident to the men searching for a wife that the woman with strident opinions, few of which were correct, was a harridan, hoyden, and termagant all rolled into one unpleasant package. No first sons would approach her; a few second and third sons made the attempt, only to be spurned as not good enough for Lady Catherine Fitzwilliam's inflated opinion of herself.

By her fifth season, her father had enough and brokered a marriage for his older daughter with Sir Lewis de Bourgh, a lowly baronet. Lady Catherine had harangued her parents about the degradation of marrying so far below her expected station, even if the man was wealthy and had a large estate in Kent.

It was all for naught; she had been married to Sir Lewis and had begrudgingly allowed him into her chambers to claim his marital rights. After their daughter Anne was born, Lady Catherine locked her door to her husband permanently.

Sir Lewis did not repine the loss of congress with his shrew of a wife and met his needs in the arms of a mistress. He doted on his daughter. When he drew up his last will and testament, he made sure that Anne inherited all when she reached her majority. Knowing his wife well, he put the protections in place to make sure if he passed before she did, she would not be able to drain the estate accounts with her extravagances and penchant for filling their home with overpriced gaudy décor and uncomfortable furniture.

When Anne was six, she had suffered from a mild case of scarlet fever, but recovered. It was not long after that illness that Sir Lewis drowned while on a fishing trip. As Anne would inherit Rosings Park when she attained her majority at one and twenty, Lady Catherine determined to keep her weak so she would be able to control her. She used her position as mother and used Anne's illness and made it seem that her daughter had been much sicker than she actually had been.

This, too, had been thwarted. No manner of ranting, raving, or cajoling had weakened her brother's resolve to remove Anne from her care. To make matters worse, her traitorous younger sister Anne had supported her brother's actions. All of her life, Lady Catherine believed she could get what she wanted by sheer force of will, and when that failed, by vociferous haranguing until she achieved the desired result. The fact it was not true was an inconvenient fact she ignored.

No matter how much she had vented her spleen, her brother would not be moved. Anne had been removed and was being educated, becoming known to the *Ton* away from Rosings Park, and, worst of all, was in perfect health.

At the same time, after her sister and brother-in-law had refused to announce a betrothal between Anne and her nephew Fitzwilliam—she refused to call him William as it was such a common a name—she had started to work on the boy, and it had seemed to bear fruit. He had accepted her advice on maintaining the distinction of rank.

Once she had the boy agreeing with her, she planned to manipulate him into agreeing to marry Anne. When he did, he would take Anne away to the north and leave her at Rosings Park, which is what she wanted. If she was successful in that, a request to manage the estate funds would surely be a small hurdle. As he would be so grateful to her, he might even offer up the accounts of his own accord.

She knew not what, but about five years ago, before her brother took Anne from her care, something had changed. She stopped receiving any positive responses to invitations to Rosings Park from both the Darcys and the Fitzwilliams, and from that time forward there were no invitations issued for her to visit them.

How could she continue working on her nephew if she never saw him? On two occasions she had shown up uninvited at Pemberley, and both times without so much as a by your leave she had been sent away unceremoniously. The second wasted journey, she had not been allowed to pass the gates to the estate! Lady Catherine could not understand why she could no longer get what she wanted. She had also been barred from her brother Reggie's estate. It was unconscionable!

When her sister Anne delivered a baby girl who they named Georgiana, there had been no invitation to the christening, never mind a request to stand as a godmother.

To rub salt in the wound, her brother, the Earl, had blocked her access to all estate accounts belonging to Rosings Park; he went even further by even restricting her access to funds her late husband's will had given her. For her personal needs she had only the interest from her dowry, which amounted to a little more than one thousand pounds per annum. Her brother had taken away her power to hire or discharge servants—much to the delight of Rosings Park's servants; he vested that power, and the ability to pay them, with the steward.

She knew she had to bide her time, as her brother had made it clear if he perceived that she misbehaved, she would be relegated to the dower house—or worse, a pensioner's cottage.

~~~~~~~/~~~~~~~

Lady Anne Darcy would have loved to have had more than two children, but she was more than pleased with the two she had. Since the incident at Pemberley and the now infamous *shin kicking* incident, all influence her sister Catherine had attempted to exert over William was banished.

The Bennet, Darcy, and Fitzwilliam families had become close friends over the five years since that first meeting at Holder Heights. All three families had been close to the Carringtons before that particular visit, but now they all felt like one large extended family. After the Prince was notified of his daughter's existence, Paul and Edith Carrington had been brought into the tight circle of those who knew the truth of Elizabeth's heritage, because it was likely someone would slip up and they were too often in company for them not to surmise there was something different in how they all looked at and treated Lizzy.

William was still wary around Elizabeth, as she was with him. There was an uneasy truce between them. Although the two seemed to tolerate one another, they always seemed to find points to disagree on in books and other subjects. They would debate vigorously—neither willing to concede to the other.

In April of 1796, Robert and Anne Darcy were blessed with the safe delivery of Georgiana Imelda Darcy. Her middle name honoured Anne's late mother. It was not long before she was called Gigi by friends and family alike.

As she grew, the bond between Gigi and the two youngest

Bennet sisters became stronger and stronger. Kitty and Lydia Bennet were a little older than Gigi and looked on her as a younger sister.

The Darcys, Carringtons and Fitzwilliams would often spend time with the Bennets at Netherfield Park on their journeys south for the season and little season, sometimes around Easter, as well as a month in the summer. The Bennets were frequent visitors to Pemberley, Snowhaven, and Holder Heights.

Both the Darcy and Fitzwilliam parents had lauded the Bennets' decision to inform Prince Frederick of the truth about his daughter. Just as he had for the Bennet children, the Prince became known as *Uncle Freddy* to the Fitzwilliam, Carrington, and Darcy children. At the same time, the adults in the three families had become close and trusted friends of the Prince.

If anyone asked about the relationship between the families and His Royal Highness, they were told the friendship had germinated during the time he was married to his former wife, which was essentially true. They had a bond even stronger than blood—their joint love for the late Priscilla.

The few times the Darcys were in company with the De Melvilles, it was no hardship not to mention anything to them, as they neither mentioned nor asked about their daughter.

When Georgiana was three, Lady Anne began to teach her to play the pianoforte. Gigi had an aptitude for the instrument, not quite at the level of the three oldest Bennet sisters, but on a par with her friends Kitty and Lydia Bennet. As *Signore* da Funti would not travel too far from London, Gigi would begin lessons with the *maestro* during the upcoming visit to Netherfield Park to celebrate Elizabeth's tenth birthday. She would have lessons with him whenever the Darcys were in London or at Netherfield Park.

~~~~~~~/~~~~~~~

Prince Frederick, Duke of York and Albany, Earl of Ulster, had not felt so happy since before the King forced his divorce from his beloved Priscilla. He still missed her every day, but a large part of the grief and misery had been soothed by learning of their daughter's existence.

He could never refuse Priscilla anything in life, and it was the same after her death. He understood her reasoning for protecting their daughter from the same loveless and lonely existence in which he had been raised. By watching her closeness with her sisters, he could not but agree it would have been nice to have had a chance to be his brother's brother.

Frederick performed all of his official duties with aplomb, so his absence from London every now and then raised no question. If he had neglected his duties, such would not have been the case.

A smallish estate had come up for sale near Longbourn and just over two miles from Netherfield Park. The Purvis family decided to take advantage of the cheap cost of land in the Canadas and offered their estate, Purvis Lodge, for sale. The Prince had been notified by Bennet; he bought it sight unseen in 1796, and had the house fully renovated before he resided there.

For the time being, he decided not to change the name of the estate. When the King and Queen asked what the attraction of Hertfordshire was, he did not lie. He told them it was a good place to relax, and that it was close enough to London in case he was needed. More importantly, it was where the love of his life had lived with him and died alone, and he had good friends in the neighbourhood.

The King, who still felt guilt over what he had had to do, asked no further questions. So long as his second son performed all of his royal duties, he would not interfere in his second son's life again. As parents, the monarchs were pleased that he was living his life in the same manner as he had before the death of his former wife and stillborn son.

Over the five years since he became aware of his daughter's existence, the Prince had become the much-loved Uncle Freddy to all *six* Bennet children. As he watched his daughter grow older and more accomplished, she began to look even more like his beloved Priscilla than she had when he first met her.

Seeing the carefree and loved little girl reaffirmed his commitment to allow her to be raised as a normal young lady. Frederick made sure he never usurped the Bennets' role as parents, and every day he prayed that when she found out the truth on her eighteenth birthday she would not be angry with those who loved her for not telling her the truth.

~~~~~~~/~~~~~~~

"Girls, where is Tommy?" Fanny Bennet asked. It was Saturday morning, the first day of March. The Darcys, Carringtons, and Fitzwilliams would arrive that afternoon from Town for a sennight to help celebrate Elizabeth's tenth birthday. The Prince had been in residence at Purvis Lodge since Wednesday. He had not missed any of the Bennet children's birthdays if he could help it since he had found out about his daughter.

On the second day of December 1796, the Bennets had been blessed with a son and heir, Thomas Henry Bennet Junior, called Tommy. Fanny had opined to her husband after having been gifted with their son that since she was no longer concerned with the entail, as soon as she stopped worrying about birthing a son they had been blessed with one.

Tommy was a little imp, with wavy, sandy blond hair and blue-green eyes. For his third birthday, Uncle Freddy gifted him a pony. So his sisters would not feel left out, the Prince gifted the youngest three with their own ponies, and cobs for Jane and Elizabeth. Miss Jones was teaching Kitty, Lydia, and Tommy. When he got a little older, his father planned to hire tutors for his heir.

"Tommy is at the stables talking to Scottie," Lydia, now five, informed her mother. "Papa is with him, Mama."

Fanny was relieved. As hard as it was with a boy that age who loved to run free, he was not allowed out of the house alone after they had received an abusive letter from Ned Collins, the displaced heir presumptive of Longbourn. They hoped the man was not that insane, but they would not take any chance with the security of Tommy, nor that of their other children.

Once he was shown the letter, the Prince sent some of his men to Wiltshire to keep an eye on Collins. When Bennet objected and said it was his responsibility, the Prince had trumped him by telling him he was just making sure that the man was never able to approach his daughter.

~~~~~~~/~~~~~~~

When notice of Tommy's birth was sent to the illiterate Ned Collins, and once he had his own son read the missive to him, he had gone into a rage. Until this birth, he had been the heir presumptive of Longbourn. He had gone so far as engaging a solicitor to challenge the parentage of the Bennet son, but he found no one daft enough to take his case.

From that day on, he attempted to drum into his son's head that his inheritance had been stolen from him by those artful Bennets, promising his own son they would find a way to right the wrong one day. While his son William could read, it was often said that he had no more sense than his father. The truth was William was not deficient of intellect but he did not want to show his father up as he knew how cruel the man could be.

Even though he was a miser, he set money aside for his son to attend school, and William Collins, at sixteen, was at a local school for boys in Wiltshire. He was in his final year, and his father planned to send the boy to a seminary to receive a degree in divinity. When he graduated, hopefully he would take orders.

~~~~~~~/~~~~~~~

"Mary, Kitty, Lydia, have you finished with all of your lessons and chores?" Fanny asked her three youngest daughters. Mary was eight and Kitty almost seven.

"Yes, Mama," they choroused. Fanny looked to Miss Jones, who smiled and nodded in agreement that they had indeed.

The Bennets' wealth had grown over the last five years.

Each of their four daughters by blood had dowries in excess of twenty thousand pounds. Nevertheless, Fanny and Thomas did not want *any* of their children—including Elizabeth—to take things for granted, so they were assigned certain chores each week. While they were often indulged by their extended family, they were far from spoilt.

Kitty and Lydia were learning French and Italian well, but they did not seem to have the same ear for languages as their older sisters. Kitty had a talent for art, and even before she started to work with a local art master she could sketch well indeed. Lydia was intelligent and well behaved like her sisters, but as yet she did not excel in any particular discipline. She was, however, well rounded and was becoming more proficient on the pianoforte and especially with her singing. Given her age, Fanny and Bennet did not want to push too much as that might make her give up before she learned what it was she loved to do.

The Bennet children had been looking forward to the guests' arrival that afternoon. The girls especially were excited to welcome Anne, Cassie, and Gigi. Charlotte and Mariah Lucas, who were seventeen and almost six, respectively, had been invited to spend a fortnight at Netherfield Park with their friends.

The four teenaged boys would all be at school. William was in his final year at Eton; Elizabeth was not sorry for his absence. Andrew, Richard, and Jamey were at Cambridge.

Tommy was not happy they were away, but at least Nick Lucas, who was four, would be with them some of the time. Lady Lucas had not yet decided if Nick would be allowed to stay for the full fortnight with his sisters. What Tommy did not know was that Uncle and Aunt Gardiner were coming, bringing Eddy with them, who had been born but a month after Tommy. Lilly, almost one, would accompany her family for the first time.

Bennet was in his study meeting with the Longbourn and Netherfield Park stewards. The yields of both had increased under his management. When the income from leasing Longbourn, from the estate—excluding the home farm—were added up, the profits were over four thousand pounds per annum.

Finding Jane and Elizabeth practicing in the music room, Jane on the harp and Elizabeth on the pianoforte, Fanny was satisfied all her daughters were occupied. She sought out Mrs. Nichols to make sure all the required chambers were prepared for the arriving guests. Being her usual efficient self, Mrs. Nichols had everything well in hand.

It was a little after two that afternoon when the Bennets were notified the first coach had entered the park.

CHAPTER 9

At almost fifteen, George Wickham was more jealous and resentful of the Darcys and their friends than ever. He had ended up working in the stables for over a year and, even after that degrading task, had never been allowed at the manor house again, nor was he admitted to William's or his cousins' company to play with them.

The few times he had made the mistake of inviting himself to the manor house had not ended well. The first time, Douglas, the butler, had sent him on his way with a flea in his ear informing him he was not welcome without a specific invitation, which was bad enough. The next had been far worse, he had been physically thrown out by two burly footmen.

To add insult to injury, his father had been summoned before the master of the estate, and on his return, young Wickham did not miss the thunderous look on his mien. Adding to the indignity of being thrown out of the great house, his father had taken his belt to his son.

Mr. Wickham told George in no uncertain terms he was not allowed into the park around the house, never mind the house itself, and as soon as he was old enough he would be apprenticed out, and that was only possible if someone who had not heard of his reputation was willing to take the young reprobate on.

About six months after his last unsuccessful attempt to enter the manor house, he noted the arrival of the Fitzwilliams and two families he did not know. He had heard one family was the Carringtons, the father an Earl, and the other the Bennets from somewhere in the south.

One day, young Wickham spied William, Andrew, and

Richard riding the estate escorting a cart with eight young girls and a boy in their company. He subsequently learned that five of those girls were Bennets, one a de Bourgh, one a Carrington, and the last was the little mouse Miss Darcy. The boy he cared not who he belonged to. He would have approached, but the group was escorted by a number of grooms and footmen; two of them were the biggest men he ever remembered seeing.

One girl, she must have been around eight, was willowy, blond, and very pretty, with the bluest of eyes. On that day, he marked all friends of the Darcys and Fitzwilliams as enemies, for the crime of being included where he was excluded.

Over the years he had seen some or all of these friends visit Pemberley and had marvelled at how the blond one grew more attractive each time he saw her. On her last trip, when he guessed she was about thirteen, she had begun to develop womanly curves, and young Wickham had felt stirrings in his loins as he leered at her from afar.

He did not know how, but he would have his angel one day.

~~~~~~~/~~~~~~~

The Bingleys of Scarborough were well-off tradesmen. The older brother, Arthur Bingley, was married to Martha. His younger brother and a partner in the Bingley Carriage Works, Paul Bingley, was married to Henrietta. For the most part, the Bingleys were happy with their lot in life.

The exception was Arthur Bingley's wife Martha, who felt they should raise themselves above their roots in trade. She and her husband had three children, Louisa was going on fifteen, their son and heir Charles was almost thirteen, and their youngest, Caroline, had just turned eleven.

Paul and Henrietta Bingley had a six-year-old daughter, Maude, and a three-year-old son, Paul Junior. The brothers were close—or had been—until Arthur's wife began her social climbing and put on airs and graces, looking down on anyone in trade even though it was money from trade that put food on her table and kept a roof over her head.

The two older children were not interested in their mother's constant harping on raising the family's status in society, but in her youngest daughter she found fertile soil and her ideas took root. Her husband was always busy running the business, so he left the rearing of his daughters to his wife.

Charles had already begun to learn about the profitable enterprise from his father and uncle. It was clear from a young age that the boy had a head for business. Not only that, but young Charles also loved working in the business in any role his father and uncle assigned him, from physical labour to meeting with customers for sales and design discussions.

His mother and sister Caroline did not like that he enjoyed putting his energies into trade as much as he did. Eventually, Martha wore her husband down and Arthur agreed to send Charles to Harrow the following year, then to Cambridge after that, so at least Charles would have a gentleman's education. In his father's mind, this would open up greater choices for his son than he had been gifted with.

Louisa was asked if she wanted to attend the fancy seminary in London that her mother was pushing for the following year, but she demurred, telling her father she wanted to attend school locally, with her friends. He granted her wish, and no amount of haranguing from his wife could change his mind.

He had planned to dower each daughter with ten thousand pounds and was close to having the needed principal to reach that goal. He invested some of his money with a man he had met in London, Mr. Edward Gardiner, the founder and owner of Gardiner and Associates.

~~~~~~~/~~~~~~~

"Welcome Anne, Robert, and Gigi," the mistress of Netherfield stated happily as she and Bennet met the arriving guests at the base of the stone steps leading to the entrance to the manor house.

"Aunty Anne, Uncle Robert, and Gigi," Kitty exclaimed excitedly. As much as she liked her adopted Aunt and Uncle, it was Georgiana for whom she and Lydia were waiting patiently. Of the two youngest Bennet daughters, Kitty was the clear leader. It was not just that she was the older of the two, she guided those with her carefully and with encouragement, making her a natural leader.

"It is so good to see the two of you," Georgiana returned breathlessly with the innate excitement one would expect from a girl of four years. "It has been forever since we were all at Snowhaven together."

"Elaine and Reggie, Edith and Paul, you are all most welcome. My, Miss Cassie, you look so grown up," Fannie greeted the rest of the arrivals. "Welcome, Miss de Bourgh; it is good to see you again." As all of the younger guests were females, Fanny did not miss the dejected look her son was sporting at the lack of young male company.

"It is good to see you again, Fanny," Lord Matlock bestowed his hostess with a kiss on her cheek, "and you, Bennet." The two shook hands. "I hope you are ready for me to challenge you to a game of chess, my friend."

"When will the children's Uncle Freddy be arriving?" Lady Elaine asked.

"His note stated he would join us at Netherfield by Monday afternoon," Bennet related.

Tommy was looking down the drive forlornly when he spied the Gardiner coach making its way up the drive. "Mama! Papa!" Tommy exclaimed as he jumped up and down excitedly when he noticed his cousin Eddy's head in the coach's window. "You surprised me. I will not be the only boy here after all!"

"Did you forget Nick will arrive on Monday, Tommy?" Bennet asked his exuberant son.

"I know, Papa, but now I will have someone to play with until Nick joins us," Tommy explained with some exasperation, for in the logic of a boy of four, he could not grasp how his parents had not understood what he meant.

"Welcome, Brother and Sister," Fanny embraced her brother and his wife, and kissed her niece Lilly, who would be one in April, tucked safely in the arms of her nursemaid.

"Your girls are even prettier than when we saw them last. My goodness what a little lady Jane is, Fanny," Madeline Gardiner stated as she looked at her nieces. "Is everyone who is visiting now returning from Town to spend Easter with you this year? You remember we will not be able to join you, do you not?"

"Yes, Maddie, I am aware; the Fitzwilliams and Darcys will return for the holiday, but not the Carringtons. The Carringtons are invited to Edith's parents' estate in Suffolk so they will depart London by the end of March," Fanny averred. "If any of you do not remember where your chambers are, Mrs. Nichols is available to assist you," Fanny stated when she and the Gardiners joined the rest of the arrivals in the entrance hall. "Water for washing will be ready for you by now." The Darcys, Fitzwilliams, and Carringtons would return to Town the day after Elizabeth's tenth birthday, and then the former two families would return with their sons who would be on term break from their various schools at the end of March.

Elizabeth could not wait for her tenth birthday, not because she anticipated any special gifts, but because she would move out of the nursery to join Jane in the family wing and share a suite with her. It had been a long two and a half years of missing Jane without her in the nursery.

On the other hand, she was sad as she would miss sleeping in the nursery with Mary, Kitty, Lydia, and Tommy. As her parents pointed out, just like she had been allowed to have the occasional time to sleep with Jane in her bedchamber, so would her sisters and brother be allowed from time to time, so long as it was what both sides wanted.

Fanny and Bennet would not play favourites or give any of their children that which all would not receive, though there was no denying in just over eight years all their lives would change, Lizzy's most significantly.

Jane was excited that Anne de Bourgh was present. Over the years since Anne had come to live with the Fitzwilliams, the two had grown very close. During her visits to Hertford-shire, Anne had become close to Charlotte Lucas as well, and while she was visiting the Bennets she too would take lessons from the masters.

The Bennets were adamant they would treat Lizzy the same as their other children. The blow to the younger Bennet children, who would miss Lizzy in the nursery, would be miti-gated temporarily; they would have Gigi, Cassie, Mariah, Nick, and Eddy with them in the nursery after Lizzy moved out. To everyone's joy, Georgiana was to remain at Netherfield when her parents returned to London until their return for Easter.

Recently, Bennet had added two new science and maths masters. The science master was Mr. Brian May. He had come to Bennet's notice though a mutual acquaintance who, like Bennet and Mr. May, loved astronomy.

The maths master was a Mr. John Deacon. He seemed to be a little shy but was a good teacher and was very know-ledgeable in his area. There was now a doctor resident at Netherfield. He travelled with the family any time they left their home, at the insistence of the Prince, to make sure his daughter had access to medical care if and when needed. Doc-tor Roger Taylor had graduated from the prestigious medical school in Edinburgh.

There was one more master, recommended by *Signore* da Funti, a voice master by the name of Mr. Fred Mercury. He seemed to have too many top teeth in his mouth, but per the *Signore,* the man could sing better than many could imagine. Mr. Mercury claimed the extra teeth gave him a greater range when singing.

The Bennet parents suspected that the music and singing masters had a far closer relationship than mere friends, but they believed in love above all. Gratified the two had found one another under their roof, they respected the men's privacy, and the men were grateful for not being persecuted for the way they were created.

The five Bennet sisters loved their singing lessons with

Mr. Mercury; there had been a marked improvement in their singing since he was hired as their voice master. Every now and then in their free time, the science and maths masters would join the doctor and the singing master, and they would entertain everyone, playing and singing together.

A family member had gifted Mr. May with a guitar from Spain, which he played almost as well as he taught science. Mr. Deacon played a bass cello, and Doctor Taylor played along on a snare and a long drum quite well for a physician. Mr. Mercury was accomplished on the pianoforte, and his voice would swell with song. At times, *Signore* da Funti would play and sing with them when he was in residence.

An hour later, all the guests met the Bennets in the drawing room, after the younger children had been settled in the nursery under the watchful eyes of their governesses and nursemaids. "My goodness, Fanny," Lady Anne spoke softly to her friend as the two sat away from the rest, "All of your children look so well. In a few more years, you will have Jane's come out. If nobody has volunteered to sponsor her yet, I would like to be the one to do so."

"Thank you, Anne; we will let you know," Fanny replied appreciatively. "As Edith is one of her godmothers, I would have to see if she wants to sponsor Jane, but as there will be three after her, I am sure I will be calling on you."

"I understand why our friend decided to reveal Lizzy's true birth at eighteen. As a Royal Princess, Lizzy's presentation will be vastly different from that of regular debutantes," Lady Anne opined.

"She is technically fourth in line for the throne, but Frederick explained even though she is legitimate, the King will ask parliament to remove her from the line of succession as she was born after he and Cilla were divorced," Fanny explained to Ladies Anne, Elaine, and Edith softly. The latter two had joined them as they sat off to one side of the drawing room. "The Prince also opined that even though the King and Queen might choose not to recognise Elizabeth, if she chooses to make her

A BENNET OF ROYAL BLOOD

true status known, they will not do that as the King still feels guilt over forcing the divorce on Frederick and Cilla."

"It has been more than ten years since the divorce, yet Sarah de Melville has never attempted to contact Priscilla, is that not true?" Lady Elaine asked.

Fanny confirmed it was so. "I have honoured Cilla's wishes regarding her family, and barring any unforeseen circumstance, I will post the letter to them when Lizzy turns eighteen, which is also as she requested."

"Could you imagine one of us throwing off one of our children for some arbitrary societal rule?" Lady Anne asked with obvious distaste at the idea.

"I am sure I speak for all of us," Lady Edith stated firmly, "I would never even consider such a thing."

"In a way, I feel sorry for the De Melvilles," Fanny informed her friends. "To be so willing to elevate the perceptions of society above the love of your own flesh and blood—it is a life which cannot bring happiness, as society never perceives the same things as important from one month to the next. It must be exhausting to force yourself to live by their ever-changing mores and predilections." After a moment of reflective silence, Fanny continued. "Enough about them; how are your sons doing at their schools?"

"William is lonely at Eton now that Jamey has joined Andrew and Richard at Cambridge," Lady Anne shared.

"Jamey is enjoying his time at Trinity College," Lady Edith informed the group.

"As are my boys," Lady Elaine added. "Do you ever think William and Lizzy will allow themselves to become friends?"

"Hopefully, yes," Fanny replied. "I have asked Lizzy why they are constantly at odds since she had stated that she fully forgave William the day he apologized at Holder Heights. She said she is not sure why, but she does love to debate with him."

"That is not news," Lady Anne smiled. She was happy with the young man her son had become; there was no trace evident of the arrogant and haughty boy he was five years previously. "I asked William the same with regard to Lizzy, why he is standoffish with her. He had no good answer."

~~~~~~~/~~~~~~~

The men were amusing themselves in the game room. Gardiner, Darcy, and Holder were playing billiards, while Matlock and Bennet were locked in a chess battle. They were evenly matched, so no matter how many games they played between them, no one ever had a large advantage over the other.

Robert Darcy would routinely roundly beat both of them, but was looking forward to Monday, as the Prince was one of a handful of men who were able to best him at chess.

CHAPTER 10

Wednesday the fifth day of March dawned as a cloudless spring day. The light breeze made the leaves on the trees wave gently. Elizabeth woke not long after the sun was up, knowing it was a big day for her. Yes, it was her tenth birthday, and she was looking forward to it, but much more importantly, she had just slept her final night in the nursery.

The nursemaid on duty that morning helped Elizabeth dress in clothes that were laid out and ready for her. The rest of her clothing had been moved to her new bedchamber the previous day, and once she left the nursery that morning, the remainder of her possessions would be moved to her new chambers. Not wanting to disturb her sleeping siblings—at least she assumed they were sleeping—Elizabeth slipped out of the nursery and made for her new chambers.

Jane had a maid, Miss Antoinette de Chambé, who had started with her when she turned twelve. Until Elizabeth turned twelve, de Chambé would assist her when needed, but only after she had seen to Jane's needs.

Prince Frederick wanted to gift his daughter with her own maid as soon as she moved, but he had been soundly overruled by both Fanny and Bennet, pointing out how important it was that his daughter not be treated differently than her sisters. Seeing the truth in their assertions, Frederick withdrew from that particular fight.

Elizabeth did not see anyone on her way to her new chambers and entered the sitting room she and Jane would share until one of them eventually left the house This was her first stop because her mother had given her permission to ask de Chambé to style her hair for her special day.

Elizabeth found the maid waiting for her in her new dressing room and was somewhat disappointed Jane was not up to wish her happy birthday, but she would not disturb her sister.

After her hair was done in an elegant updo—a special treat for her birthday even if she was a little young for such a coiffure—Elizabeth made her way to the breakfast parlour, intending to start her day off with a cup of chocolate. She then planned to take a walk in the park as she did most mornings until returning to break her fast with the family. On her way to the parlour, she stopped at her father's study to wish him good morning, but there was no answering call to enter. Disappointed, Elizabeth turned toward the direction of her waiting morning drink.

The doors to the parlour were closed, but as she approached, Biggs and Johns—almost cracking smiles—pushed the doors open for her. "**Happy Birthday**!" came the combined chorus of everyone resident in the house. Elizabeth stopped and gaped, but soon sported her biggest smile as she realised why she had not seen anyone from the time she got up until now.

Nearest to her was Jane, who opened her arms for her younger sister. "Were you surprised, Lizzy?" Jane asked as she hugged her sister. "It was so hard for me not to be there when you went to have de Chambé do your hair, but it was worth seeing the look on your face."

"Uncle Freddy!" Elizabeth exclaimed when she saw her uncle, who she loved dearly, and who was closest to her and Jane. "What time did you arrive from Purvis Lodge? As always, I am very happy to see you."

Prince Frederick almost melted at his daughter's words of affection. He hugged her in for a long moment, holding the living, breathing part of Priscilla which remained in the mortal world. "You are ten today, Lizzy. You are becoming an old lady, and you will soon be on the shelf," he teased.

"Very funny, Uncle," Elizabeth said with a smile. She loved all of her uncles, but for some reason she could not fathom, she felt a level of comfort around Uncle Freddy that was different than her other uncles.

Elizabeth knew he was a Prince, that he was in fact second in line for the throne of England after his older brother. Based on her uncle, she assumed all royals were friendly and as approachable as he. Frederick had been in her life for almost five years now, and he was wont to shower all six Bennet children with gifts. Jane and her cobs, Avery and Juniper, were only one such example. If that were not enough, he had gifted the rest of the Bennet children with ponies. She was sure Uncle Freddy had some extravagant present for her birthday, but she cared not as long as he was with her in person.

After Uncle Freddy, she was hugged tightly by her Mama and Papa, who both wished her happy and congratulated her on reaching the milestone of her own bedchamber. Elizabeth shared an opinion common to all six Bennet children that they had the best parents anyone could have.

Elizabeth was then surrounded by the rest of her sisters —Charlotte, Anne, Cassie, Gigi, and Mariah, as well as those that bore the Bennet name. Once she made her way through the wishes of that group, Tommy approached her with a baleful look on his face.

"Tommy, why do you look sad?" Elizabeth asked.

"You are leaving the nursery, and I will miss you," Tommy owned.

"You will not see me less during the day, Tommy," Elizabeth assured the pouting boy of three. Elizabeth put her mouth next to his ear. "Would you like to come visit my chambers later? After our guests leave, you will be invited to spend the night like we did in Janie's chambers sometimes," Elizabeth asked quietly.

The reaction was immediate. Tommy's look went from sad to beaming with happiness. For reasons known only to him, he felt closer to Elizabeth than to his other sisters—who he loved deeply—so her offer put him at ease. Eddy and Nick wished her happy too; each was rewarded with a hug from the birthday girl.

After she received hugs from her Gardiner, Phillips, Darcy, Carrington, and Fitzwilliam aunts and uncles, everyone was seated and enjoyed the celebratory breaking of their fasts. As was her wont on her birthday, Elizabeth was treated to a second cup of chocolate at the end of the meal.

From the dining parlour, all proceeded to the east drawing room, the largest at Netherfield Park, for presentation of her presents. For once, Frederick had not gifted his daughter with an over-the-top gift. His gift, as were most of the others, was clothing, in his case a sable pelisse.

When Fanny saw the material the pelisse had been made from, she looked at the sheepish Prince with arched eyebrow. "It is a pelisse, which is as you asked, Fanny," Frederick said quietly near Fanny's ear as his defence, and Bennet smirked, his 'I told you so' look making his wife sigh with exasperation.

"But sable, Frederick! I suppose it is my fault when I told you she needed a pelisse that I did not specify you should not be extravagant in the material," Fanny shook her head at the incorrigible Prince, who looked well satisfied with himself.

In the end, Elizabeth found her wardrobe well supplemented with day dresses, gloves, half boots for walking, and two riding habits. As happy as she was with the presents— and what girl of ten would not be—the thing she enjoyed more than anything was having their extended family with her on this special day.

It was true that the whole of the extended family tried to be present when any of their children had a significant birthday, so this occasion was not the first such meeting to celebrate a birthday, and neither would it be the last.

"Who would like to go for a ride?" Bennet asked once all the gifts had been revealed, the givers thanked most sincerely by Elizabeth, and two maids had removed them to go place them in the little miss's dressing room.

As would be expected, most replies were in the affirmative. Everyone decided to join the riding party save for Fanny, Madeline, and Ladies Anne, Elaine, and Edith. "Mama, may I wear one of my new riding habits?" Elizabeth asked excitedly.

"Yes, Lizzy, of course you may. Which one will you choose?" Fanny asked.

"The green one from Aunt Anne," Elizabeth averred and then turned to Lady Edith. "I will wear the one you gifted me the next time we ride, Aunt Edith." After being ensured her aunt felt no slight at the one from the Darcys being worn first, Elizabeth made for her new chambers.

~~~~~~~/~~~~~~~

It was a large party that rode out from Netherfield. Luckily for their guests who did not bring their own mounts, Netherfield's stables had more than enough horses and ponies available for everyone.

Even though there were several men in the party, there was still a full complement of escorts with them, especially as the Prince was one of their number. The guards did not know they were protecting a Princess as well, but that would not have changed their vigilance, which was always high.

The party made their way to Oakham Mount, which was just past the north-western border of Longbourn. Once they crossed from Netherfield Park's fields to those of Longbourn, those who were comfortable galloping gave their horses their heads. Although Tommy would have loved to gallop his pony, he knew he was not allowed above a canter, so he and the rest of the children on ponies brought up the rear.

When they arrived at the base of Oakham Mount—in reality a hill—everyone dismounted, and the party made their way on foot up to the flattened summit of the Mount. From the top, there was a clear view of the area. Bennet acted as guide and pointed out Netherfield Park to the east, Longbourn below them, and Purvis Lodge in between the two. It was easy to see Lucas Lodge, as it was the estate between Longbourn and the market town of Meryton.

"Lizzy, the habit the Darcys gifted you looks very well on you," Jane stated as the group of older girls stood under the big oak on the summit.

"Thank you, Janie," Elizabeth responded, "it fits me just so."

"Do you know that when I used to live with my mother she would not allow me to learn to ride, or learn anything else for that matter," Anne told her friends.

"Was your mother really that bad, Anne?" Charlotte asked.

"Worse!" Anne stated emphatically. "Until Uncle Reggie and Aunt Elaine took me into their household, I was not living, only existing."

"If it were not too unladylike, I would kick her shins like..." Elizabeth went quiet with embarrassment as she recalled her actions from five years in the past.

"Like when you kicked William?" Anne smiled. Elizabeth nodded. "That and lessons in humility from Uncle and Aunt Darcy changed William much for the better. He was on his way to becoming more like my mother than his. Even so, I would not recommend walking around kicking everyone who offends you, but that day it was well deserved and delivered. You also had the excuse you were but five at the time."

The group of girls giggled and talked among themselves while the three boys climbed into the branches of the oak tree. Biggs and Johns were the only men from the group of escorts who walked up with the family, and they stood beneath the tree, ready in case one of the boys missed his footing and fell.

"It is a nice view, Bennet," Lord Matlock allowed, "but I prefer the wilds of Derbyshire with the Peaks in the background."

"It is not surprising that either you or Darcy over there," Bennet inclined his head to where Robert Darcy was standing, "would favour Derbyshire over all other shires."

"If it were only our home county," Darcy stated, "that would be one thing, but even you must admit, Bennet, that there are few views that match the one from the lookout towards the Peaks at the end of the bridle path at Pemberley."

"You are not incorrect," Bennet conceded. "There are few vistas I have seen on this island of ours that rival that one."

"You can see the Peaks from Snowhaven as well," Lord Matlock defended.

"As you can from Holder Heights," Holder added. "However, I will not deny you do not see a view of the Peaks as spectacular as the one from Pemberley from my estate—or yours for that matter, Matlock." Lord Matlock admitted the truth of Holder's statement.

Once the debate about views in their home shires was completed, and the monkeys had descended from the tree, the party made their way back down the hill to where the horses were being minded by their escorts. Mindful of their mounts, there was no galloping on the return ride to Netherfield Park.

~~~~~~~/~~~~~~~

Lady Catherine de Bourgh felt the diminution of her power most keenly. The servants were no longer afraid of her, and if she was rude to them they simply ignored her. In her mind, she had excoriated her brother for imposing these limits on her, and on her late husband for not changing his will as she had demanded many times over.

She heard little snippets about how her family, both the Fitzwilliams and Darcys, had become a close connection of Prince Frederick. Lady Catherine could only imagine how her status would have been enhanced had she been allowed into the royal's company, but she had not seen any of her family since the infamous day Reggie had removed Anne from her authority.

Her brother had even removed her right to appoint a new clergyman to the living at Hunsford if it became vacant. The incumbent had always bent to her will, until the great day of change had occurred. She used to go so far as to write the man's sermons for him and had them often include a lesson about the importance of maintaining the distinction of rank.

Much to her annoyance, the Earl of Matlock had made sure the man understood Lady Catherine had no authority over him, and if he should ever allow her to write another sermon or shared with her what was told to him in confidence by his parishioners, the Earl would report him to the Bishop of Kent and have him defrocked.

The man used to bow and scrape before her, but this too was a thing five years past. She once attempted to deliver a sermon to the man, and then attempted to provide, in her opinion, necessary added instruction on the running of his household, but that, like so many other things since that fateful day, had not gone as she expected.

The sermon she wrote was consigned to the fire without a glance, and the parson—her parson—had told her in no uncertain terms that she was not welcome in his house to direct the way it was run. When she tried to ask if the parishioners had told him anything of import, he told her that he would never discuss anything with her regarding his flock unless they specifically requested him to do so.

Her world truly had come crashing in on her. How could she, the exalted Lady Catherine de Bourgh, the daughter of an *Earl*, be treated thusly? She decided soon after that she would gain her revenge for the degradation she was suffering. She did not yet know how or when, but she swore that her day would come.

~~~~~~~/~~~~~~~

The Friday after Elizabeth's birthday the Prince, the Darcys—minus Gigi, the Fitzwilliams, Gardiners, and Carringtons all departed for Town. "Why do we never go to London, Mama?" Elizabeth asked as she walked back into the house with her mother after farewelling their extended family.

"You know your father detests London, do you not, Lizzy?" Fanny reminded her daughter. In eight years, Elizabeth would be told why they could not go to London, but not now. Although it was not the whole truth, what Fanny told her—Priscilla's—daughter was at least half of the truth and not an outright lie.

The night before, the adults all met in the Bennet parents' private sitting room. Fanny could still hear the conversation in her head verbatim.

"We thought at some point, even at the end of the season, that taking Lizzy to Town would be safe," Fanny had said, *"it seems there is disagreement among you?"*

"As much as I would like to have Lizzy and all of you visit me at York house, she looks too much like my Cilla to take the chance. I move in the same circles as the Jerseys, as do the Matlocks, Holders, and the Darcys." The Prince said thoughtfully.

"The Prince has the right of it, Fanny and Bennet," Robert Darcy stated. *"There are too many in society who will recognise Priscilla in Lizzy, especially now. It will only become all the more obvious as she gets older."*

"When we are all together at one of our estates, we are able to control who visits and who does not," Lady Anne agreed. *"How would we explain to Lizzy, if she did go to London, that she would not be allowed to venture out in society? She, Jane, and Mary would see through the ruse and know there was something else at play. We may be able to fool your younger three, but certainly not the older sisters."*

"It seems that my aversion to London will have to persist. What of when Jane comes out in five years? How will we tell Lizzy she is not allowed to attend Jane in London for her festivities around her come out?" Bennet asked.

"Jane does not have to be in London for anything but her curtsy to the Queen," Lady Edith suggested. *"Using your dislike of Town, we can have her ball at one of the country estates, say Holder Heights, as we are her godparents. Just like we do now, we can make sure that we only invite those who would not have known Priscilla."*

"Not to mention as Lizzy will not be out yet; she will have minimal contact with those attending," Fanny stated.

"If Jane asks why she is not to have a London season, we will have to tell her," Fanny Bennet pointed out.

"*At eighteen, or there abouts, I have no fear she will not understand. It will be a surprise, but I am sure she will love Lizzy as she always has once she learns the truth,*" Fanny opined. "*At least we have five years before we have to confront that particular issue.*"

The meeting ended soon after with the consensus of their plan.

Having heard her father pontificate on his dislike for London and the *Ton* many times, Elizabeth accepted what her mother told her. She would go to London at some point, of that she was certain.

CHAPTER 11

"**D**o we have to go visit the Bennets for Easter, Mother?" William Darcy asked almost petulantly the day after he returned from Eton.

"Yes, we are going, William. When will this nonsense of you not wanting to be around Elizabeth end?" Robert Darcy asked pointedly.

"You are sixteen, William, not a little boy any longer. What you did five years ago has been forgotten by everyone except the two of you," Lady Anne told her son.

"You seem to enjoy your debates with her, Son," Darcy pointed out.

"She is intelligent, far more so than I would expect from a little girl, but she does not like me," William complained.

"Have you allowed her to know you the way we do? For whatever reason, when you are around her, some of your old arrogance and hauteur makes an appearance. It is like you wear a mask in her presence." Lady Anne looked at her son quizzically. "The rest of us know the month you spent in the stables after we returned from Holder Heights in 1795 chased the last of your improper pride from you, so why can you not relax around Lizzy?"

"I am not sure, Mother," William answered honestly. "Mayhap it is because she makes me nervous, and I do not know why."

"You will need to get over it, William," Darcy instructed. "We will be there for three weeks complete. You have not yet met the science and maths masters, Mr. May and Mr. Deacon, have you, William?"

"No Father, I have not," William owned.

"You like astronomy, do you not?" William nodded. "So does Lizzy, and other than your Uncle Thomas, I have yet to meet one more knowledgeable than Mr. May. That may be a good way for the two of you to at least call a truce and become more relaxed one with the other," Darcy suggested.

"You are good with maths, William, so there is another area of commonality you have with Lizzy. I am sure you will learn from Mr. Deacon while we are at Netherfield Park," Lady Anne told her son.

"Then there is the love of books you share," Darcy added.

"It is true, she does love the library at Pemberley," William allowed.

"You two have far more in common than not," Lady Anne pointed out. "The only problem is you are two of the most hard-headed people I have ever had the pleasure to meet. You both have an element of pride which holds you back from letting go of the past."

When William Darcy thought about the situation between himself and Elizabeth Bennet, he had to admit that there was no real reason for the distance between them other than neither was willing to give a inch to the other. Mayhap it was time to change that dynamic. As he was the older and the one who inflicted the first blow, he decided he needed make the first overture to Elizabeth.

~~~~~~~/~~~~~~~

"Will Uncle Freddy be with us for Easter, Mama?" Lydia asked as the family was breaking their fasts.

"No, Lyddie, I am afraid not. He has to spend it with his family in London," Fanny shared.

"You mean with the King, Queen, and the other princes and princesses?" Elizabeth asked.

"That would be his family, Lizzy," Fanny agreed.

"I will miss Uncle Freddy too, Lyddie," Elizabeth informed her younger sister. "He is always fun to be around, is he not?" None of her sisters or brother disagreed with her.

"The Darcys and Fitzwilliam arrive this afternoon, so we

will not be alone for Easter," Fanny related. "Uncle Edward and Aunt Maddie will not be able to join us, but Uncle Frank and Aunt Hattie will, as well as the Lucas, Goulding, and Long families on Easter Day." Fanny looked at her son, "You may go to Nick or have him here as much as you want, so you have another boy to play with."

As the children departed the breakfast parlour, Fanny put a restraining hand on Elizabeth's arm. "Please remain, Lizzy. Papa and I want to talk to you."

"How many years has it been since William was rude to you—all of us—at Pemberley?" Fanny asked once the other children had departed.

"About five years," Elizabeth owned.

"Then for what reason are you still standoffish with him?" Bennet asked. "He has not been rude to you since, has he?"

"No, he has not," Elizabeth confirmed.

"Then what is it, Lizzy?" Fanny pushed.

"He...he always thinks he is right about everything," Elizabeth got out. She was not happy with her parents, who laughed at her response. "What is so funny about that?"

"Do you know who you have just described, Lizzy?" Bennett asked through his laughter.

"Yes, William Darcy!" Elizabeth insisted indignantly.

"Mayhap, but also another. Do you know who that would be?" Bennet asked as he wiped tears of mirth from his eyes.

"I am sure I know not who you mean, Papa." Elizabeth gave a sniff and would not look directly at either of her parents. Neither of her parents were fooled; they were fully aware she knew exactly to whom her father was referring.

"Lizzy, if you gaze in the looking glass, you will see one who dislikes being told she is wrong as much as—if not more than—William," Fanny said gently as she took her daughter's hand. "You are both stubborn to a fault."

"Neither of you are right all the time, and neither wrong all the time. The truth is, if you would both listen to what the other is saying more closely, you would both benefit from learning together," Bennet told his daughter. "You know that William sometimes has a valid point when you are debating, do you not?" Elizabeth nodded. "Just as I am sure he recognises the same in you."

"Even when he disagrees with you, does William ever dismiss your opinions because you are a *silly* little girl?" Fanny asked.

Elizabeth searched her memories and could not find one instance William had been dismissive of her. "No Mama, I do not believe he has ever done so," Elizabeth owned.

"Is it not a sign of respect of your intellect that he who is six years your senior is willing to debate seriously with you? Would he do so if he felt your points were nonsensical?" Fanny pushed her daughter to look at the situation with a new perspective.

"There is nothing I can say to refute your points, Mama," Elizabeth deduced.

"If you two would move past your stubbornness, then I believe you would enjoy each other's company," Fanny opined.

"You have my word, Mama and Papa. I will try to be more open to William's points of view," Elizabeth allowed.

~~~~~~~/~~~~~~~

Georgiana was bouncing on the balls of her feet in excitement when she saw the Darcy coach coming to a halt in front of the entrance to the manor house at Netherfield Park. She loved being with the Bennets, but in these three weeks at Netherfield without them, she had missed her family.

As her father exited the carriage, and before he had a chance to hand out his wife, his daughter launched herself into his arms, her blond ringlets flying as she hugged him tightly. William helped his mother out of the conveyance, and as soon as Lady Anne was on solid ground, Gigi was in her arms, and William was not overlooked for one of her hugs.

"Only a few more months and it is off to Cambridge,

Wills," Georgiana stated. "I have missed you."

"And I you, Sprite," William said as he hugged his sister to himself again.

"How many years has it been since you saw Wills, Gigi?" Andrew Fitzwilliam asked after he, his brother, and parents greeted their hosts.

"I last saw him when he was home for the Christmastide break, Andy," Georgiana informed her cousin.

"And you did not miss Rich and me?" Andrew teased his young cousin.

"If Gigi did not miss you, we did," Mary informed Andrew.

"You were missed as well, Andy and Rich," Georgiana stated firmly, "I just missed William more!"

"You cut me to the quick, Gigi," Richard said with fake hurt as he dramatically placed his hand over his heart, his antics earning him a punch on the arm from both Andrew and William.

After he greeted the rest of the Bennets, William turned to Elizabeth. "Hello Elizabeth," William said as he gave her a half bow.

"William," Elizabeth returned his bow with a half curtsy.

"It is my understanding that there are new masters who teach science and maths," William saw no reason to delay his attempts at friendliness and engage Elizabeth in conversation, regardless of the audience they both knew were watching.

"Yes, Mr. May is very knowledgeable in the sciences, but especially astronomy," Elizabeth replied pleasantly. "Mr. Deacon used to teach at Oxford and is very skilled in his field."

William did not miss the knowing looks between their parents who knew that it would not be hard for them to converse about mutual interests. "From what I hear, you have a physician on staff now as well." William stated.

"We do, Mr. Taylor. Mama told me it is because Uncle Freddy is here so often," Elizabeth told William innocently.

William wondered why the doctor stayed at Netherfield

when the Prince was not in the area, but decided not to ask, understanding it would not be one of the Bennet children who would know the reason—if there was one beyond what Elizabeth had told him.

"And the new singing master?" William asked. "Do you enjoy your lessons with him?"

"I, we all, do," Elizabeth told William. The questions were so pointedly asked that her replies were more genuinely warm when given. "Mr. Mercury has one of the best voices I have heard. *Signore* da Funti introduced him to Mama and Papa." Elizbeth paused and added, "Sometimes, the masters and the doctor get together and play music. It is ever so good to hear them play, especially when the *Signore* plays the pianoforte with the rest of them."

As they followed the rest indoors, both William and Elizabeth accepted their parents had been correct; it would not be hard to become friends and enjoy conversation with one another when they were in each other's company.

~~~~~~~/~~~~~~~

After his son George turned fifteen, Mr. Lucas Wickham told him that he was to be sent to a carpenter just outside of York to be apprenticed. George had begged and pleaded for his father not to send him away.

"George, how do you think you will support yourself if you do not learn a trade?" Mr. Wickham asked.

"Mr. Darcy will take care of me," George replied, his tone surly.

"How many years has it been since Mr. Darcy has not allowed you into the park, never mind at the manor house?" Mr. Wickham asked and George turned away. "No matter how much I have tried to counteract the lies your mother told you, you have refused to heed my words, and it ruined your chances of a gentleman's education which Mr. Darcy would have provided for you. Before you start blaming one and all for your lot in life, for once in your life be honest with yourself. Your choices alone have set you on the path you are on."

"How can you say that about my mother, she was..." George began to say when his father cut him off.

"She was delusional, George. Not only that, but she was also a liar, a gambler, and a spendthrift. Do not become like her, always wanting what others have and not willing to work to gain that which you desire. If you become covetous like your mother was, it will lead to nothing but ruin for you," Mr. Wickham told his son, who was getting angrier by the minute.

"You lie! My mother told me you would never allow her to have an allowance; that is why she had to gamble to make some money," George spat back at his father.

Lucas Wickham stood and pulled a ledger from a pile on his desk. He handed it to his son without a word. It was titled 'Helen Wickham – Allowance' on the cover. George opened it and there he saw each and every month his mother's allowance recorded with her signature next to each one.

"Why would she lie to me?" George asked quietly, his confusion sudden and overwhelming.

"I am afraid your mother did not tell the truth about much, Son," Mr. Wickham replied gently. "If I had not had to cover so many debts she ran up in Lambton and Kympton, as well as her gambling debts, I would have had the money to send you to school and university without Mr. Darcy. Your mother's profligate habits all but destroyed my savings. In the years since her death, I have tried to rebuild my savings, but I am still far from what I used to have. If I am lucky, I will have enough to leave you a small legacy one day."

George Wickham felt as though his whole world was crashing down around his ears. If his mother lied about this, what else did she lie about. "How did mother die? You did not tell me at the time."

"In childbirth," Wickham senior shared. He hoped his son would not ask more as he did not want to disparage his late wife any more in his son's eyes than had been done already.

"I would have had a brother or sister, and you another son or daughter?" George asked.

"You would have, I would not," his father averred. Lucas Wickham could not lie to his son any more about the mother the boy had too long idealised.

"What do you mean, Father?" George demanded.

"George, you are an intelligent young man. If you want me to say it I will, but I think you know well what I mean," Mr. Wickham replied sadly.

"How do you know she was unfaithful to you?" George asked.

"Things had not been well between your mother and me for a long time, so she had refused to do her duty to me for more than a year before she passed," Mr. Wickham informed his son. He was mortified to admit such, but if it helped break the grip his late wife held on their son from beyond the grave, he would not shy away from doing so. "When she became with child, she tried to convince me we had been together, but that I was in my cups and did not remember. Although I knew it was not true, I chose not to provoke a confrontation. Have you ever seen me in my cups, even once, in the whole of your life, George?"

"No Father, I have not," George admitted quietly.

"On her death bed, your mother took pleasure in telling me she had been sharing her favours almost from the beginning of our marriage," Mr. Wickham shared the fundamental truth of his late wife with his shocked son.

"D-does that mean I may not be your son?" George asked the question he was petrified to hear the answer to.

"No Son, it means you *may not* be my blood son; however you are, and always will be, my son. Whatever your mother did or did not do was not your fault, and I love you now as much as I did before she made her dying declaration to me." After he avowed his love of his son staunchly, Lucas Wickham stood and pulled his son, who was in a stupor, into his arms for a hug, something he had not done since he was a small boy. George Wickham cried into his father's chest, also something he had not done since he was a small boy. His father handed him his handkerchief to dry his eyes when the tears ceased.

"It seems I have a lot to consider," George stated stoically. "I will accept my apprenticeship with good grace, Father. Carpentry may not be for me, but I will try to see if it is a trade I will enjoy."

"Will you commit to stay with it until you are eighteen?" Wickham senior asked and George nodded his agreement. "What you have learnt here today could have broken a lesser person, George. I am very proud of you," Mr. Wickham told his son sincerely. "The direction of your life is your choice, Son. Just remember, you and you alone are responsible for the choices you make. Lastly, there are consequences to every decision we make; whether they are good or bad depends on those decisions."

~~~~~~~/~~~~~~~

"It is good to see that the coldness between your Lizzy and our William seems to have been set aside," Lady Anne observed one evening when the three sets of parents were seated together in the drawing room after dinner.

"We spoke to Lizzy before you arrived," Fanny shared with her friend, which caused both Lady Anne and Robert Darcy to smile widely.

"It seems we had the same idea, for we spoke to William before we departed London," Lady Anne informed the group.

"In my opinion, you both showed sagacity, as those two would have not corrected things on their own; they both like to think themselves correct too much," Lady Elaine opined.

"Fanny, have you decided what to do about Jane's coming out and London?" Lady Anne asked. "Does she object to waiting a year so she can have her come out with Cassie?"

"Not yet, Anne, although I am leaning towards Edith's suggestion we have her ball at Holder Heights as they are her godparents," Fanny averred. "Also, Jane has no objection to waiting for Cassie, especially with the close relationship she has with Anne and the three having decided they would like to celebrate together."

"Do you think the three girls will object to their ball not being held in London? What will you tell Jane if she asks why the ball will be out of Town?" Lady Elaine asked.

"The other two will be happy no matter where their ball is and I do not believe that is in Jane's character to complain about the location. She is well aware how much Thomas eschews the *Ton*—present company excepted—and Town," Fanny explained.

"It seems my aversion to society in London is very useful," Bennet drawled with jocularity.

No one disagreed with his statement. "What if Jane asks why the ball cannot be in Town?" Darcy asked.

"Then I will explain the true reason to her," Fanny replied without hesitation. "She will be nineteen, and I do not believe it will change how she feels towards Lizzy one whit. Even now, Jane is like a steel trap when one shares a confidence with her that she is asked not to share."

"Given how protective she has always felt towards Lizzy and her siblings, I dare say you are correct in your estimation, Fanny," Lady Elaine stated.

The conversation halted as they were joined by their children. It was pleasant to see Elizabeth and William enter the drawing room deep in conversation and seemingly enjoying the company of one another with ease. There was no more trace of the moue of distaste which had been seen in past interactions between them; for all intents and purposes, it was banished.

CHAPTER 12

June 1803

I f there was one thing George Wickham was sure of, it was that after more than three years, he did not want to be a carpenter. Recently turned eighteen, George was certain he was meant for greater things, regardless of the truth about his mother.

For the first few months of his apprenticeship George had applied himself, as he had decided he needed to strive to be a better man, one more like his father, and to forget the lies his mother had told him.

His new attitude survived about six months. The hard work was not something he enjoyed so George tried to charm his father into taking him back into his home so at least he could be at his leisure. However, his father had pointed to the unwise agreement his son had made before he departed Pemberley for York.

Still reeling from all of the information he was trying to absorb, his father had proposed, and George had agreed, to give it until at least his eighteenth birthday. His wish had been for his father to have forgotten about his acquiescence to the agreement and welcome him home. In that he had been disappointed.

It was unfair that his father intended to hold him to what he had said, just because he promised to abide by his word. Were promises not made to be broken? Every day as he toiled, his resentment against his father for holding him to his agreement had grown exponentially.

Ignoring the concept of being responsible for his own actions, George also blamed Robert Darcy for his lot in life and, by extension, his family. He gambled with the little money he earned and, not being very good at it, lost more than he earned.

This meant that he had no money for anything else, excepting the pittance of an allowance his father sent him each quarter. Unfortunately for him, he was known in the area so none of the merchants, shopkeepers, or brothel owners would extend credit to anyone below his majority who was unable to pay his debts.

In the back of his mind, George remembered his father pontificating on good and bad consequences, but he ignored the warning in his head. It was most inconvenient that he often heard in his father's voice in his dreams but he was determined to chart his own course. After being badly beaten for not being able to pay a relatively small gambling debt, none of the hells allowed him to play unless he had ready funds to cover his losses.

To supplement his meagre income, George had taken to biting the hand that fed him—stealing small amounts from the carpenter's cashbox from time to time. Unbeknownst to him, his employer and supposed-to-be teacher was aware of the thefts and had written to Mr. Wickham before he called the magistrate.

The day after his eighteenth birthday, George was dressing with glee as it was the day he intended to leave the hell he had been living since he arrived in York. The door to his small chamber was pushed open and, to his horror, standing in the portal was his father, who looked none too pleased with his son.

"D-did you c-come to wish me well on my birthday?" George managed unsteadily.

"Have you forgotten what I told you about consequences before you departed my house, George?" Lucas Wickham asked with asperity. "Do you imagine me ignorant of your behaviour —the gambling, drinking, and theft! How could you?"

"I know not what you mean; I am not a common thief,"

George tried to bluster.

It was then George noticed his employer standing just behind his father. His face lost its colour as he only then realised he had not been as stealthy as he believed when lifting the money from the cashbox.

"Ya' 'ave stolen from me three times! It is just over ten pounds now!" the carpenter stated angrily.

"Do you know for an amount such as that, if Mr. Jones called the magistrate, you would hang, George? What were you thinking?" Mr. Wickham turned to the carpenter. "Mr. Jones, I will pay you fifteen pounds; will that suffice?"

"Aye, it will. But 'ave that thief out'a me 'ouse today!" Jones demanded.

"Thank you, Father," George started to say.

"Do not thank me yet, George. The money will come out of the legacy I was saving to will to you on my death. In the three years since your departure, I managed to save one hundred and fifty pounds for your future. I will give it to you now, minus the fifteen pounds to Mr. Jones, and you will shift for yourself." Mr. Wickham held up his hand as his son started to complain. "I spoke to Mr. Darcy before I came here, he has decreed he will not allow you on any of his properties, and I understand that."

"How can you stand by and allow me to be treated thusly?" George spat out.

"You are the one who determined your course. I know it all, George. I do not know why, but even after you found out the truth of your mother's character, rather than try to amend yours, you have adopted the worst elements of hers," Mr. Wickham stated resignedly. "If you are able to change your ways, and I do not mean for days but for a good length of time, then we may revisit things. Only then will I reconsider, so until then I will not assist you again."

"How am I to live?" George demanded fearfully.

"You will need to find honest work. Hopefully when you understand how hard the world is and that no one will hand you what you want just because you desire it, you will learn to behave in a more honourable fashion." Mr. Wickham handed his son the funds, and, with a heavy heart, departed York after his son vacated the Jones's premises.

~~~~~~~/~~~~~~~

At sixteen—in about three months—Jane Bennet would be allowed to be out in a limited way, only locally. Jane had grown into what—according to the *Ton*—was a classical beauty. She was tall, willowy, blond, and had the deepest cerulean eyes.

Elizabeth, at thirteen, was a striking beauty as well, but being petite with wavy mahogany tresses and green eyes, she would not have been classed at the same level of beauty as Jane by the denizens of the *Ton*. Mary, at eleven, was taller than Elizabeth, but not as tall as Jane. Mary was extremely pretty but, like Elizabeth, she would have been discounted by the arbiters of beauty in the *Ton*, who self-anointed themselves as the deciders of fashion because she had a fuller figure and was not a blue-eyed blond.

Kitty, who would be ten in a fortnight, looked just like Jane had at the same age. She was as tall as Elizabeth, despite the almost four-year age difference. Lydia, like Tommy, had dirty blond hair with green-brown eyes. The former would be nine in October, while the latter had attained the ripe old age of seven.

Seventeen-year-old Anne de Bourg and Jane were as close as sisters. Anne was close with all of the Bennet siblings, but the bond she shared with Jane was special, which explained her desire to come out with Jane, not caring she would be almost twenty.

Anne was anything but uneducated as her mother had intended her to be. She had learnt to play the pianoforte well, so no one would again be able to say if she had learned, she would have been a proficient—which had been her mother's favourite refrain about herself to explain her lack of accomplishments. Anne also had an aptitude for drawing, one she shared with both Kitty and Gigi.

She had not missed her mother in the eight years since her uncle had rescued her from that lady's lack of care. Where her mother had used intimidation and kept her sickly, she was surrounded by love and was as healthy of any of the children in her extended family—blood or adopted.

The Bennets were at Pemberley for the month of June, then would move to Snowhaven for July, and finally spend part of August at Holder Heights. Uncle Freddy intended to be with them while they were at Pemberley, and for a fortnight with the Fitzwilliams before his duties would necessitate his departure.

William Darcy would be starting his final year at Cambridge when he returned to the university at the end of August. At almost twenty, he was two to three inches taller than his father, and due to the physical labour he chose to assist with at Pemberley, he had grown into a fine specimen of a man. He had always been handsome; now he had a fit body to go with his handsome face and rider's legs.

At eight—having celebrated her birthday in April past, Gigi, as tall as Kitty, was a younger copy of her beloved mother, with the blue eyes common to the Fitzwilliams. Everyone hoped she had a stronger constitution than Lady Anne, who was suffering from an undiagnosed malady which had weakened her considerably during the last year.

If Fanny and Ladies Edith and Elaine were worried about their friend Anne, her husband who loved her to distraction was at his wit's end. Robert Darcy brought in some of the most prominent doctors in the land to no avail, for after much prodding and poking none could tell him what ailed his wife; one even nonsensically claimed she was with child.

When the Bennets and the Prince arrived from the south with Doctor Taylor in tow, Darcy asked if the physician would examine his wife. Dr. Taylor had taken his time, asking many questions of Lady Anne while he conducted his comprehensive examination. Unlike the men who had done so before him, he actually listened to the answers she proffered.

A little more than an hour later, Mr. Taylor met with Robert Darcy in his study. "As much as I would like to be able to give you better news, Mr. Darcy, I believe your wife has a cancer. You told me one of my colleagues who examined her opined she may be with child as he felt a firmness in her belly. I do not like to disparage one who is not here to defend himself, but I would question the man's medical knowledge based on where the mass is. It is above and to the right of her belly. In my opinion it is where part of her reproductive system sits," the doctor explained.

"Is my Anne going to die?" Darcy asked the question he must, but also the one he most dreaded hearing an answer to.

"Yes, I am afraid so, Sir," Mr. Taylor replied directly. "Not much is known about cancers; what causes them, how they grow, and even less—in fact almost nothing—about the treatment of them. I wish I had better news for you, Sir, but based on the yellow I see in her eyes, I would say she does not have too long. In my experience, when the whites of the eyes go yellow, the infection has reached other organs, I believe the liver in particular."

"Does my precious Anne suffer in pain," a defeated Darcy asked as he sat back in his chair, his shoulders slumped.

"From what I could glean from her answers, not much at this point. I would recommend you have a supply of laudanum on hand. Under normal circumstances, I do not like to have patients take too much of it due to the addictive property of the drug, but that is not a concern in this case." Mr. Taylor waited to see if Mr. Darcy had any further questions. "If that will be all, I will leave you."

"Thank you, Mr. Taylor. I appreciate having someone give me actual information rather than nonsense about bleeding her and taking waters," Darcy stated in dismissal.

~~~~~~~/~~~~~~~

"Did Mr. Taylor tell you, my loving husband?" Lady Anne asked gently, unable to miss the look of distress on the man she had been married to for close to a quarter of a century.

"He did, Anne. How will I carry on without you?" Robert Darcy asked with tears in his eyes.

"Robert Darcy, you look at me." Lady Anne demanded as she summoned all her reserves of strength. "Like Priscilla demanded of Fanny when she knew the end was near, I need you to make a vow to me."

"Anything, my darling Anne, for you know I can never deny you that which you deign to ask of me," Darcy stated as he took his wife's hands and kissed each one in turn.

"You are not allowed to give up or wallow in your mourning after I am gone. William will be twenty soon, but our Gigi is just eight and she will need you. You, my Robert, not a shell of yourself. Do not forget that in the Bennets and Carringtons, who have become our extended family, and in my brother and Elaine you will have support and the help you need, all you need do is request it.

"Mourn me for a year as is the custom, but then move on with your life, even if that means marrying again," Lady Anne said as firmly as she could under the circumstances.

"Anne, I could never replace you in my heart; that would be too much to ask of me, even from you, my love," Darcy averred.

"It is not to replace me in your heart, Robert. I believe that particular organ has unlimited capacity to love. Besides which, if you ever loved another as much or more than me, I would haunt you for the rest of your days," Lady Anne teased. "In all seriousness, Robert, as long as you do not wallow in your grief for the rest of your days, I will not make remarrying part of the vow I am requiring that you make, but I ask you not to be blind to the possibility, even open to it. Gigi is still so very young, and she will suffer without a mother, but with Elaine, Fanny, and Edith, not nearly as much as she would without them."

"That is nothing but the truth, my love. I swear to you, on our love, I will honour your wishes. I will not allow myself to withdraw from our children, and I will accept the help of our extended family when I need it," Darcy vowed.

"Your promise lifts a great weight from my shoulders, Robert. Make sure that she knows you are not sending her away, but you may want to have Gigi stay with the Bennets after the three months of deep mourning is complete for our children. She loves Jane, Elizabeth, and Mary but the bond between her and the two youngest Bennet daughters is a special one, a bond of sisterhood," Lady Anne told her husband.

"Do you want us to inform William and Gigi together, or would you like to talk to them alone, Anne?" Darcy asked.

"Together, it must be together. This is another thing; knowledge is power. Please do not keep pertinent information from our children, including Gigi, as without it they may be open to manipulation. Without knowledge, they would not be armed to protect themselves," Lady Anne insisted.

"It will be so, Anne." Robert Darcy leaned toward his wife and captured her lips. "Let me have William and Gigi summoned."

"After our children, I want to speak to my three sisters while you speak to their husbands and Frederick. One more thing, Robert. I am sure you will not, but do not allow my sister Catherine to revive her lies of an accord between us to try and claim some promises I never made. In fact, ask my maid to bring me my escritoire. I will write a letter to be read to her if she attempts to cause havoc after my death, as I suspect she will," Lady Anne requested. "I will leave it with the other letters I will be writing."

Darcy passed his wife's instruction to her maid and told her he would return in an hour with their children.

~~~~~~~/~~~~~~~

"Mama, Papa said you both wanted to talk to us," Georgiana stated as she sat on her mother's bed where lady Anne patted. "Will you be well soon? Did Doctor Taylor find a cure for your malady?"

"Slow down, Gigi, we will answer all questions soon enough," Darcy told his daughter.

William did not miss how sad his father looked, and he suspected the news they were about to hear was the opposite of his sister's youthful, hopeful exuberance. He sat on the bed where his mother indicated, then his father sat next to his mother and took her hands.

"I wish the news we had for you was what Gigi hoped…" Lady Anne told them what she and their father knew. It was not long before both children were in tears. Georgiana was weeping openly, while William's tears were rolling down his cheeks in silence. "This is the hardest thing I have ever had to tell you, my dear children. I could not love either of you more if I tried, and other than the love I have for your father, none has ever come close to that which I feel for you. Do you have any questions?"

"Whyyyyy, Mama," Georgiana wailed plaintively. "Why would God allow you to get sick like this? It is not fair! I thought He is the God of love."

"Gigi, we mere mortals have no idea what His plan is. Do not be angry with Him. In time, your anger will dissipate, and you will see. You will still have Papa, William, and a large extended family, any one of whom will do anything they are able to in order to help and support you, William, and your father. Remember, my dearest daughter, while you will not see me, I will always be here," Lady Anne reached forward and placed her hand gently over her daughter's heart. "It will not be the same, and we will miss one another, but when you close your eyes you will see me, and if you listen really carefully you will hear me in your head. One day, we will be together in heaven, though my hope for all three of you is that will be many decades from now."

"Mother, I will miss you terribly," William owned after his tears had ceased.

"I know you will, William. My charge to you, my son, is to be open to others. Do not prejudge them and remember that sometimes you will be convinced of a certain thing only to be proved wholly wrong, as you discovered when you were eleven in this very house," Lady Anne took her son's hand. "Allow your heart to direct you, and it will not lead you astray. Please never allow my sister to manipulate you again. She is my sister, and as such I will always love Catherine, but I am not blind to the fact she is only interested in that which she feels benefits her own selfish aims. It has been some years since she tried to influence you. Remember her behaviour as an example of how *not* to behave; do not emulate it." Lady Anne turned to her husband sitting next to her on the bed. "I am in need of rest. Please inform my friends I would like to see them when I awake."

"Come, William and Gigi, we need to allow your mother a respite. As hard as it will be, please do not discuss your mother's illness with anyone until she and I have talked to those who need to know," Robert Darcy told his children as he shepherded them out of their mother's chambers.

~~~~~~~/~~~~~~~

"Anne, Robert told us you wished to see us," Lady Elaine verified as she led the other two ladies into her sister's chambers.

"Yes, I need to talk to you three together," Lady Anne averred as she indicated the three ladies should sit. "Elaine, you are my sister; Fanny and Edith, you have become sisters. As you know, Mr. Taylor gave me a lengthy examination today..." As Lady Anne told them all, the three ladies became more and more distressed. "Mr. Taylor informed Robert and me that when I get close to the end the pain will be acute and I will need to be dosed with laudanum, which is why I needed to talk to you three now before that point is reached."

"Oh, Anne, your poor children, to have to be told such news by their mother," Elaine stated through her tears. "William is older, but Gigi is only eight."

"She is young, but she got to know me, Elaine, and we have had eight good years together. Imagine if I had passed just after her birth so all she would have had were stories others might tell her about me. Thankfully, she will have her own real memories." Lady Anne turned to Fanny. "Fanny, I told Robert and I want to ask you to consider this. With the bond between all of your daughters—especially your two youngest—and Gigi, after my children have mourned for three months, will you take her into your home for a while? She loves all of your children dearly, and it will be a balm to her. Rather than sitting around and allowing her grief to overpower her, she will be with girls who she counts as sisters and with the masters, especially *Signore* da Funti and Mr. Mercury, to help her with her music and singing. In addition, Tommy makes her laugh as well."

"Anne, you know we will do anything for you," Fanny stated emphatically, "and to have Gigi with us, for as long as your husband desires, will be our absolute pleasure. Robert knows he and William would be welcome at any time. I would suggest to him that he come and see her as often as he is able while she stays with us. That way, she will not feel as if she is being sent away."

"That is true for us as well, Anne. We will do anything we are able to in order to assist when requested," Lady Edith stated as she dried her eyes.

"It goes without saying for us, Anne," Lady Elaine added.

~~~~~~~/~~~~~~~

"Darcy, I am so very sorry to hear about Anne," the Prince stated.

"Your wife, my baby sister," Lord Matlock managed, his voice gruff with emotion.

"Darcy, you know that Gigi will be welcome for as long as you desire, and as I am sure Fanny is informing your wife, you should feel free to visit or stay at Netherfield Park any time you desire," Bennet stated sympathetically.

"Anything you need," Lord Holder told his friend.

"Do we have any idea how much longer Anne will be with us?" Lord Matlock asked as he regained his composure.

"Mr. Taylor told me there is no way to know. He opined, based on the length of time my Anne had been feeling poorly and the size of the thing growing inside her, that it will not be very much longer, mayhap weeks or a few months at the most. Once she starts to suffer with too much pain, we will use the laudanum. Until then, we will spend as much time together as we are able," Darcy averred.

"We are all family here, Darcy," the Prince spoke for the group, "and we will be with you and help in any way you decide you need. You are not alone in this, so do not try to carry the burden alone, let us share the load with you, just as we also love her as a friend or sister." The Prince's words were seconded by the other three men. Darcy thanked them sincerely for their statements of support.

CHAPTER 13

Plans to leave Pemberley for Snowhaven and Holder Heights were cancelled forthwith. The Prince sent an express to Windsor Castle, where the royals were for the summer months, to notify the King and Queen he would be in Derbyshire for longer than expected.

Between the other four men, Darcy's duties were covered, which allowed him as much time with his wife as possible. The ladies worked with Mrs. Reynolds to make sure anything that required input by the mistress was done.

Jamie, Andrew, and Richard kept William distracted when he was not with his mother. William found that debates with Elizabeth would take his mind off worries about his mother for a time. It was during this time that the last bricks in the wall between the two were forever destroyed.

Georgiana would spend time with her mother and would often be joined by some of the other girls as an upright pianoforte and a harp had been moved in Lady Anne's chambers at her husband's behest. Knowing how much her mother loved music, Georgiana would play if her mother was awake during her visits. When their Aunt Anne requested it, Elizabeth or Mary would play the pianoforte and Jane would accompany them on the harp. Every now and again, a group of the girls would sing for the ailing mistress of Pemberley.

The four Darcy's took their midday meal together in the bedchamber—even if Lady Anne hardly ate anything. Dinner would see the family together, and when Lady Anne felt she was able, one or two of the other adults would join the family for dinner in her chambers.

Mr. Taylor would check in on Lady Anne at least daily.

Each day he found evidence of the correctitude of his diagnosis, for the tumour was getting much larger and the whites of her eyes were now a very distinct yellow.

~~~~~~~/~~~~~~~

Towards the end of June, Robert Darcy had a meeting with his steward, Mr. Wickham. It was a meeting he felt he needed to have himself rather than leaving it to one of the men who were assisting him, for the subject was Mr. Wickham's errant son.

"I am afraid the news is not good," Wickham reported sadly. "After I revealed the truth of his mother, I thought—hoped—he had been reached. For whatever reason, it was not many months before he reverted to his old ways."

"You know what they say, you can lead a horse to water, but you cannot force him to drink," the master stated stoically. "There are some who are, unfortunately, intrinsically bad. It could be your George is not so but will need to fall lower before he wakes up. You did everything you were able to put him on the correct path, but it takes his desire to lead an honest and honourable life. By his theft—the ones which are known—he clearly demonstrated which path he has chosen—for now at least. We can only pray he still has the capacity for change inside of him."

"He departed York for parts unknown, though if I were to hazard a guess he is for London. It seems he shares the vice of gambling with his mother, and like her, he is not accomplished at the art," Wickham informed his employer.

"Using the miniature we have of him, I will have his picture made and circulated among my footmen, outriders, and coachmen so if he shows up in the area, even under an assumed name, we will know of it. I will also pass information to the other families with us, as it was noted how your son used to leer at the oldest Bennet daughter," Darcy stated with purpose.

"That kind of behaviour was one of the reasons I sought a position for him in York. I will not provide him more funds, even though as his father I love and worry for him," Wickham stated dejectedly.

"It is sad, but as you told me, you warned him well about consequences. He is no longer a young boy and has been forced to strike out on his own. We can only pray that he will be well and safe, but that will depend on his behaviour," Darcy opined.

"All I can do now is to keep my son in my prayers. Thank you for your time today, Mr. Darcy, for I know you would much rather be at your wife's side." Mr. Wickham stood. "Your wife is in my daily prayers, Sir. Please inform her that I asked after her."

"Your sentiments are appreciated; I will pass them onto my wife." Darcy gave a nod of dismissal, and the steward gave a bow and departed the master's study.

~~~~~~~/~~~~~~~

By early July, the situation the doctor had warned about was upon Lady Anne. She was wracked with pain throughout her emaciated body. She knew the end was very near, and that there was no choice but to start using healthy doses of laudanum. Before she could let go, she needed to make sure everything was in place for after her passing.

"Please, Robert, before the dose, I want to see my children. You know as well as I do there is a better than good chance I will never wake again." Lady Anne saw the look of abject anguish on her husband's mien through her pain. "Please be strong for me and our children, Robert." Darcy nodded and told the maid to summon his children.

Once William and Georgiana entered her chambers, their mother indicated they should sit as close to her as possible. "A mother could not have wished for better children than the two of you. I have been as brave as I can, but the pain is now to the point I must take the medicine to help me, which means I will no longer be awake for more than a few minutes at a time," Lady Anne told her stricken children as gently as she could.

"Noooooo, Mama," Georgiana wailed. "I do not want you to leave us."

"Gigi, my darling girl, I do not *want* to leave you, William, or your father either, but it is my time. Remember what I told you, Gigi, I will *always* be with you," Lady Anne stated as she tried to hide a wince from the pain that was wracking her body.

"Y-you w-will a-always b-b-be h-here," Georgiana managed between sobs as she put her hand over her heart, and Lady Anne nodded.

Lady Anne turned to her son, who was quietly crying in a demonstration of his deepening grief which was only evident in his eyes. "William, I will need you to help your father. Having a love like we share is a double-edged sword, my son. Do not mistake me, there is far more good than bad. You have seen the good in our love for one another each day of your life," Lady Anne paused as a wave of pain almost made her cry out. "The bad is that your father is going to be very sad, and that is why he will need your strength, my darling son."

"If love can cause that kind of pain, then I never want to be in love," William countered angrily. His internal fury was not directed at his mother, but at the fact he knew it was hours or days at best before she would be taken away from them forever.

"No, William, that is *not* the lesson I want you to take from what I said. A life without love is an empty one. When you are in London society, look around the *Ton* at all the marriages of convenience and you will see the true misery of many," Lady Anne paused again, slowly breathing through a particularly sharp pain which stole her senses. "That is not what I want for either of you. You have both seen the joy that loving one another and our extended family has brought to us. Promise me, both of you, that you will not harden your hearts to love. Do not allow status, wealth, or connections to influence you. I charge you both to listen to your hearts, and when you find your one and only true love, as I found in your father, never let them go. True love is worth fighting for. One minute with your father is of more value to me than having multiple lifetimes with a man I did not love."

"You have my word, Mother," William vowed as his anger released him.

"M-me too, Mama," Georgiana promised.

"Kiss your mother and say your goodbyes; she needs her medicine," Robert Darcy said gently, barely holding back the tears that threatened to fall from his eyes.

"Mama, I will listen for you in my head every day," Georgiana swore as she hugged her mother gently and then kissed her.

"Mother, I will miss you for the rest of my life," William stated as the tears still ran freely.

"William, do not close yourself off or retreat behind that mask you wear at times. Do not dishonour my life by using my death as an excuse to withdraw from all who love you," Lady Anne charged her son.

"It will be as you desire, Mother." William leaned forward and kissed his mother's cheeks. He was alarmed at how clammy she felt, but he held his peace. He stood and held his sister to him as he led her out of his mother's chambers.

Once the door was closed, Lady Anne allowed herself to let out a cry of pain. "You need to take the laudanum, my love," her husband pleaded as the dam broke and his tears started to spill.

"Soon Robert, my dear husband, soon," Lady Anne managed. "You have been my life, Robert; promise me again after you have mourned me you will live again. Do not let me go to meet God worrying about you."

"My promises to you will be kept, Anne, I swear on my life and on our children's lives that no matter how hard it will be for me to follow your directives, it will be done. I will live for both of us," Robert Darcy told his wife as he kissed her lips which had captivated him from the first day he had met her during her first season.

"Just as my beloved Cilla did, there are letters in my dresser for my sisters, our children, you, and for the inevitable visit my sister Catherine will make. Please make sure they receive them after I am gone. The children's letters have notes telling you when to give them theirs. Never forget, Robert, it is not just you and the children; we have gained a large extended family who need you as you need them." As Lady Anne said the last, a peace settled over her as if now that she had received the assurances she needed from her husband and children, she could leave the mortal world and the pain she had been experiencing behind.

Robert was holding his wife's hands as she seemed to smile and then her chest rose a final time, there was a long exhale as her life's breath escaped her body and then there was no more movement.

Those waiting in the suite's sitting room knew the end had come for Anne Darcy when they heard the terrible wailing of her husband. Luckily, William had led his sister out of the master suite and had joined the rest of the younger group so neither was present to hear their father's lamentations as his wife left the mortal world.

The doctor slipped into the bedchamber, and he knew before he tried to find a pulse that she was gone. Without disturbing her grieving husband, Mr. Taylor joined the three couples and the Prince waiting in the sitting room. All he needed to do was nod to confirm what they already knew; Anne was gone.

None in the sitting room had a dry eye. "My little sister," Lord Matlock stated poignantly as he hugged his wife to him.

"Who will inform William and Gigi?" Lord Holder asked.

"No one, unless Darcy asks us to," Bennet stated as held his wife close to his chest as she cried quietly. "It should be he who tells them."

No one disagreed with Bennet. They decided they would stay where they were until Darcy chose to join them. If not, his brother-in-law would approach him in a few hours to ask about informing William and Gigi.

~~~~~~~/~~~~~~~

When William and Gigi joined the group in the game room, there was no mistaking their anguished looks. Kitty, Cassie, and Lydia immediately moved to sit with and comfort Georgiana. They simply sat and hugged her, allowing her to cry as much as she needed.

William looked as if he were in a stupor. Andrew, Jamey, and Lieutenant Richard Fitzwilliam tried to distract him, but nothing worked. He was lost in a world of his own making as he tried to accept the inevitable.

~~~~~~~/~~~~~~~

On graduating Cambridge, Richard had followed through with his desire to join the regulars. Even though his father had been willing to purchase him a captaincy or even a higher rank, Richard had accepted only a lieutenant's commission in the Royal Dragoons under the leadership of Colonel Atherton. If he were to progress up the ranks, he wanted it to be because of his own merit. After his initial training, he had been granted some leave to join the family, and once his Aunt Anne's diagnosis had been confirmed, he requested—and was granted—extended compassionate leave.

Andrew returned from his grand tour in April, a month before the newly self-appointed Emperor of France started his war. He was especially hard hit by his Aunt's illness, as he had always been very close to her.

~~~~~~~/~~~~~~~

"William, do I need to kick your shin again to gain your attention?" Elizabeth asked in an attempt to snap him out of the obviously dark thoughts he was having, and her question elicited a ghost of a smile.

"I dare say at thirteen your kick will be harder than it was at five. Also, you are wearing half boots now, when then you wore slippers," William responded. He was not unhappy Elizabeth had managed to pull him out of the spiral of despair. Her intervention also reminded him of the vows he made to his mother.

"Do not forget, William," Richard, who had always been

more brother than cousin, stated, "Aunt Anne is in pain now, but when God calls she will be at peace after a well-fought battle so that we could have her with us longer."

After seeing the grimaces his mother tried to hide from them over the last weeks, William knew Richard had the right of it. He could not be selfish and hope his mother would hold on only for her to suffer immeasurable pain. Between Elizabeth snapping him out of his thoughts and Richard's timely reminder of his mother's finding peace being freed from pain, William was able to accept what was about to happen with a little equanimity.

He would miss his mother more than words could describe. However, accepting that her passing would end her suffering allowed him to feel an inner peace he had not thought possible. It was three hours later when Douglas entered the room and told Master William and Miss Darcy their father wished to see them in their mother's chambers.

<center>~~~~~~~/~~~~~~~</center>

As soon as the two entered the sitting room, they suspected what had occurred by the way their aunts and uncles looked at them with both compassion and great sadness on their countenances. When they walked into their mother's bedchamber, their father's tears were evident and there was no missing their mother was not moving at all.

"Mama is gone, is she not?" Georgiana asked as her tears started to flow freely again.

"Yes, Gigi, your mother is with the angels. She is in pain no longer," Robert stated as evenly as he was able under the circumstances.

"When?" William asked simply, not trying to hold back his tears. He would not see his mother again, but he held onto the fact she was not suffering any longer.

"About fifteen minutes after you and Gigi departed her chambers. I think she was holding on to make sure we would be reminded of her hopes for us after she left us to care for each other and our family without her guidance," their father informed his children as he pulled them both into a hug. "Once she received our assurances, she was able to let go. I will never forget the peaceful look that came over her just before her spirit left her body."

"Papa, may I kiss Mama?" Georgiana asked nervously.

"Of course you may, Gigi," Darcy replied encouragingly.

Georgiana placed a kiss on her mother's cold cheek and was followed in the same by her brother. The three remaining members of the Darcy family stood and hugged for a long while.

Once the children entered his late sister's bedchamber, Lord Matlock notified the butler and housekeeper of the mistress's passing. Douglas, who normally betrayed no emotion, did not attempt to brush off the tear which ran down his cheek as Mrs. Reynolds openly wept. The housekeeper had been especially close to Lady Anne, much closer than a regular mistress-housekeeper relationship. She had served in her post since Master William was but four, and in lesser posts for some years before that. Once the two recovered their equanimity, they started the process of notifying all of the servants and preparing the house for mourning.

When those in the game room heard some maids crying, they knew what had occurred. They knew William and Gigi would need them more than ever now and were determined to do anything needed to comfort their cousins and friends. They sat quietly comforting one another, as they waited to hear from their parents, for Aunt Anne had been loved by all present.

~~~~~~~/~~~~~~~

Bennet knew the last thing his wife wanted was to take any focus off the Darcys, but he also knew how she must be suffering from losing another sister of her heart. There was no doubt his wife would recover her spirits, as her protective instincts kicked in for William and Gigi as they had for Lizzy after Cilla passed away those thirteen years past.

Unlike with Priscilla, he was relieved Fanny would be able

to openly mourn her friend this time and that she was surrounded by friends who would share the burden, grateful for
them all that there were no life-altering secrets to protect.

The moment he saw the steely look of determination on
his wife's mien and the call for a small repast for the children to
be made and tea served to all, he knew her desire to protect and
help had come to the fore. There would be no fiercer protector
of the Darcy son and daughter than Fanny Bennet, of that her
husband was certain.

CHAPTER 14

Lady Anne Darcy was laid to rest on the fourteenth day of July, three days after her death. It was warm already—not as bad as London and the south —and her husband had no desire to keep his wife in the ice-house.

As she was his late wife's sister, Darcy had sent a notification of her death to his wayward sister-in-law the day before the funeral, making sure that if, as he and Lord Matlock suspected, she would make for Pemberley to try and renew some of her fantasies, there would be no one but their close extended family present to see the scene she was sure to create.

The Prince had filled a dual role; he had represented a close family friend, one considered family, as well as being the royal presence at the funeral. The Darcys were not titled— although the Royals had attempted to offer them a dukedom over the years—but they were considered one of the foremost families in the realm.

In order to keep the De Melvilles away, a letter had been sent from Lady Elaine, informing them they were not welcome as Lady Anne had decried their treatment of their friend, a sentiment that Lady Matlock and her husband supported whole-heartedly. Rather than cause a scene and always cognisant of what society thought of them, the De Melvilles did not attend the funeral.

While many members of the *Ton* were present, those not out in society were kept out of sight. Gigi had been asked to spend an hour with some of the ladies who knew her mother, though she stayed close to her Aunt Elaine and her Aunt Edith. Andrew, Jamie, Richard, and William attended the interment and spent time with those who called afterward to convey their sympathy.

By the day after Lady Anne Darcy was laid to rest in her grave, only the Prince and the three families were left with the Darcys at Pemberley. The next day, the expected arrival of Lady Catherine de Bourgh came to pass.

"Where is my brother; I am come to take charge of his house," Lady Catherine's voice reverberated around the entrance hall. "Are my daughter and her betrothed here? Where are they? Bring them to me now!" Her voice was accompanied by the click-clack of her cane on the entrance hall's marble floor.

"Catherine, what an unpleasant surprise; while we expected your arrival, you are most unwelcome," Darcy stated as he descended the stairs.

Her brother-in-law was followed by a group of people Lady Catherine did not recognise save her brother and hated sister-in-law, who would never bend to her will. "Come Robert, we cannot discuss private family business in front of strangers. Who are these hangers-on? Trying to take advantage of you in your grief, no doubt." Lady Catherine was sure she would be able to manipulate her late sister's husband, just so long as she could get him alone. The fool had been weak enough to love her sister, so she would exploit his love to get that which she desired.

"The *only* reason you were allowed past the gatehouse was because my Anne, your sister, passed," Darcy growled at Lady Catherine, who was taken aback at the vehemence of his response. "In that, I gave you too much credit. You never cared for either Anne—my wife or your daughter. The only one you care about is yourself."

"Darcy, let us take this into the drawing room," Lord Matlock suggested.

Darcy indicated Lady Catherine should precede him into the drawing room. She thought they would be alone, and she would be able to recover her perceived advantage. She was proven wrong—again!

"Why must these who are nobody to *our* dear Anne accompany us?" Lady Catherine gave an imperious sniff as she looked down her nose at the five individuals she did not know in the drawing room.

The Prince, the Carringtons, and the Bennets chose to remain silent—for the moment—and to allow the woman to dig herself a deeper hole.

"Why are you here, Cathy?" Lord Matlock asked. "It is certainly not to mourn Anne or condole with the Darcys."

"Our brother is in mourning; he needs someone to run his house, and I intend to honour my sister by formalising the betrothal between Fitzwilliam and Anne," Lady Catherine prevaricated.

"Are you out of your senses, woman?" Robert Darcy thundered. "It shows your total want of feelings for anyone that you would dare to come try and perpetrate that old lie of yours just days after my wife's death. If you were the last woman in the world, I would not trust you to run my household. Anne wrote a number of letters before she became unable to do so, one of which is addressed to you as she foresaw your very despicable actions."

"Let me see my letter," Lady Catherine demanded. She did not, however, miss the looks of derision and disdain being directed her way by everyone else in the room. "Do not look so at your betters," she hissed at the five she did not know.

"I will read it so you cannot consign it to the fire and then lie about the contents," Darcy stated firmly.

Lady Catherine was none too happy, for she had intended to do just that.

20 June 1803

Catherine:

If my Robert is reading this letter to you, then you have done what I was sure you would do; you have arrived at my home full of bluster and demands, repeating the lie I refuted more times than I care to remember.

First, not once did I ever agree to your ridiculous demand of a betrothal between William and Anne. Second, it is only my Robert who may make an agreement on our side, and our brother, Reggie, who may do so on yours. You, Sister, are not Anne's guardian; he is.

You have been under the misapprehension of two salient points for so long. One, the love Robert and I share somehow makes us weak and susceptible to your machinations. Two, the more times you repeat a lie, the more others believe it.

You, Catherine, are a disgrace to our family. You never took the time to be educated, yet you try and pontificate on all things without any knowledge. Anne's estate, yes, and I repeat, Anne's estate, would be bankrupt under your rule had you been granted any power over it in Lewis's will or by our brother, who is the executor.

Now it is time for a little surprise of my own since you decided to come and surprise us all, sister dearest, and I am sure you were rude and dismissive to our friends who are with Robert and the Fitzwilliams—more than likely you insulted them. Do you know what the penalty for insulting a Prince of the United Kingdom of Great Britain and Ireland is?

No? Well, you are about to find out, Catherine.

Anne

Lady Catherine was slack-jawed. She knew that Prince Frederick was one of the Darcys' close connections, but she was sure she would recognise the superior breeding inherent in a royal and would know how to act, for he would be in the centre of the room directing all according to his whim. She now slowly turned to the five people who were unknown to her, and though she scanned them all again, she was unable to identify His Royal Highness. "Why did no one introduce me?" she squeaked.

"When did you give us an opportunity to do so?" Lady Elaine asked evenly. "You were too busy trying to demonstrate your superiority and were quite intent on insulting those you thought below you."

"Will you introduce the rest of us to this person please, Elaine," the Prince requested.

"You all know who the *lady* is do you not?" Lady Elaine asked, not even bothering to wait for the five of them to nod. "His Royal Highness, Prince Frederick, Duke of York and Albany, Earl of Ulster." The prince inclined his head. "Lord Paul and Lady Edith Carrington, the Earl and Countess of Holder." The Carringtons barely acknowledged Lady Catherine. "And last but not least, Mr. and Mrs. Bennet of Netherfield Park *and* Longbourn in Hertfordshire. These are the people who you chose to insult."

"As I am the member of the Royal Family who was insulted; the punishment is my choice," the Prince stated. "Tell me how is it that you became so high in the instep?"

"I-it is not m-my fault, your Highness," Lady Catherine tried to obfuscate her responsibility. "I did not ask to be introduced."

"So, you are above me and would request the introduction?" the Prince demanded. Lady Catherine withered under his stare. "Yours is naught but a courtesy title. Lady is given far too freely, especially to those like you who do not deserve the appellation, as you neither behave like a lady nor do you deserve the title. I am recommending that my father strip you of the courtesy title. Within a few days, the Lord Chamberlain will be notified by the King and there will be a royal decree in the papers in case you try to lie about this like you did about a non-existent agreement with your late sister about Miss Anne and Master Darcy." The Prince paused and looked at the soon-to-be Mrs. de Bourgh with the disdain she deserved. "Begone from my company, *Mrs.* de Bourgh."

The soon to be former Lady Catherine's machinations had failed in the past, but there was no comparison to the level of this failure, nor the consequences she was now facing. Douglas was summoned and asked to place Mrs. de Bourgh in a parlour with two footmen to watch her so that she could not cause any more mischief.

SHANA GRANDERSON A LADY

Two footmen entered the drawing room and escorted the catatonic woman out. Lady Catherine was escorted to the parlour to the right of the drawing room they were in, and two footmen remained with her after the door had been closed.

'How did all of my meticulous planning go so wrong?' Lady Catherine asked herself. *'Not only did my late weak-willed sister anticipate what I would do, she denounced me without so much as a goodbye! And as I was so angry, I insulted the second in line to the throne of the realm. What will I do now? I will be without title, and it is obvious my family will not lift a finger to assist me. Could it be that I miscalculated?'* she asked herself.

Not being one who believed in introspection, she sat and stewed in the parlour. She started to imagine scenarios of revenge, but then it dawned on her it was her desire for such which had ended with her being reduced to being a nobody.

~~~~~~~~/~~~~~~~~

"What will you do with her, Matlock?" the Prince asked after the drawing room door closed behind the footmen who removed the termagant from their presence.

"She needs to learn humility. I will lease a cottage in Hunsford for her and place her on a strict budget which will afford her one maid of all work and nothing else. The townsfolk will be made aware she had lost her courtesy title and that she has no authority over them. Either she will learn, or she will have a very unhappy life—unhappier than she is now." Lord Matlock shook his head. He hoped his sister would learn her lesson, but he had no confidence in her ability to change.

"Will you inform our niece of her mother's presence?" Darcy asked.

"Unless Anne is deaf, I think she is well aware of who has arrived," Bennet opined.

"It will be Anne's choice; I will not substitute my judgment for hers," Lord Matlock informed the group of men.

When Douglas was queried as to where Miss de Bourgh was, he informed the gentlemen she was in the music room with older Bennets. At first, no one wanted to play and disrespect the state of mourning at Pemberley, but the master of the estate told them to play as often as they were willing; it would honour his late wife, being one of her truest joys and favourite activities.

Lord Matlock and Darcy entered the music room. Anne was practicing her scales, her back to the door while Jane and Elizabeth were sitting with her to keep her company. Anne ceased her playing as she heard the click of the door closing.

"Uncles Reggie and Robert, was my playing disturbing you?" Was the question from a concerned Anne.

"No Anne, we could hardly hear you, especially with the level of noise being made before," Lord Matlock reassured his niece and ward.

"You mean Lady Catherine's screeching?" Anne noted. "We heard her caterwauling quite clearly even inside this room." Jane and Elizabeth nodded their agreement.

"She will soon no longer be Lady Catherine, just Mrs. de Bourgh..." Anne's guardian explained all that had happened leading up to and including the Prince's intention to recommend that the King strip Anne's mother of her honorific.

"Goodness me, she will not be happy," Anne smiled sweetly at the thought of how that would upset her former mother. "Her whole identity was wrapped up in her feeling of superiority stemming from her title. She imagined herself a peer of the realm and was never happy if anyone reminded her about hers being a courtesy title only. What will happen now?"

The two uncles explained what was to be done. "Anne, before we send her on her way with an escort to make sure she behaves, would you like to see her?" Lord Matlock asked.

"No," Anne replied flatly, then paused as she reconsidered. "Yes, actually, I will see her, Uncle Reggie. Please have her brought in here. I want her to see her failure with regard to myself."

Not many minutes later, the door opened, and Anne's mother was escorted into the music room. She saw two of the most beautiful girls she had ever seen on a settee and a third girl playing the pianoforte well, with her back to the door.

"Why is my time being wasted? I was told my wayward daughter was waiting to greet me as is my due as her mother," Lady Catherine sniffed imperiously, still not reconciled to her soon-to-be lowly place in the social order.

"Do you not recognise your own daughter because she can play the pianoforte, or is it because I am as healthy as any of my age?" Anne asked after she ceased playing and turned around.

For the second time that day Catherine de Bourgh was robbed of the faculty of speech. "A-Anne, is that truly you?" the gobsmacked women managed.

"Yes, *Mrs.* de Bourgh. It is amazing how quickly my health improved as soon as Aunt Elaine and Uncle Reggie started treating me as I should be treated—a normal and *healthy* young lady. Did you think that if you kept me sickly with the poison your quack was giving me that somehow Uncle Reggie would have allowed you access to my inheritance?" Anne asked pointedly. Jane and Elizabeth stood either side of their friend for support, each taking one of Anne's hands.

"Y-you were too sick to learn to play!" the stupefied woman exclaimed.

"No, other than when I had a *mild* case of scarlet fever, I was *never* sick. It was the tinctures your so-called doctor prescribed for me which made me seem sick. Either you were complicit, or you are clueless. I am not sure which is worse," Anne excoriated her mother. "And yes, imagine that, as soon as I started receiving lessons, I learnt all sorts of things—things you claimed to know about, but about which you had boundlessly mistaken and no *knowledge*—and I have never looked back.

"I have good friends who like me for who I am, like Jane and Lizzy here. Your schemes for me failed, and I will never repine the day Uncle Reggie removed me from your influence," Anne drove the dagger home.

With a nod from Anne, the three girls exited the music

room without a look back for the wilting woman still rooted to the same spot. When the footmen escorted Lady Catherine back to the parlour where her brother and sister-in-law were waiting for her, she uttered not a word of protest.

While his sister was in the music room, Lord Matlock dispatched an express to Rosings Park via one of the Darcy couriers with instructions to have all of the former mistress's belongings packed up and all jewellery to be locked in the safe. It was her property, but a clause in his late brother's will granted the Earl complete authority over his sister Catherine. She would be on a very strict budget, and her brother did not intend to let her sell the jewellery to escape her punishment.

The Earl and Countess told the soon-to-be Mrs. de Bourgh to sit as they explained what her future was to hold. Both had expected vociferous argument from her, but she sat and listened without response. Anne's speech had affected her deeply and taken all of the fight out of her. When she was told she would not be allowed onto Rosings Park's lands or in the town house in London, all she did was nod slightly.

The de Bourgh carriage she used to travel to Pemberley would convey her to her new home in Hunsford, and it would be the last time she would be allowed to use it. Until her brother decided otherwise, she would have no access to her daughter's vehicles.

Rather than allowing her to remain at Pemberley, she began the return journey that afternoon. She would sleep at the Big Bull Inn for the night and be on her way at first light. None of the residents of Pemberley asked after her, most particularly not Anne de Bourgh.

CHAPTER 15

By sixteen, Charles Bingley had completed his third year of Harrow. He would turn seventeen before beginning at Cambridge near the end of August. Charles had enjoyed his education, but not the bullying he had received because his father was actively in trade.

Bingley hid the truth of his experience from his father, who had been pleased he was able to provide his son with the gentleman's education he himself had not had the option to attain. Whenever his father expressed pleasure at his son's academic achievements, Charles presented a picture of affability to the outside world while inside he hid his misery occasioned by the cruelty of others.

Not all of his experiences were bad. He had made a true friend in Stuart Jamison. Stuart's parents, Will and Yvette, owned a small estate in Bedfordshire called Ashford Dale. Stuart had only one sibling, Karen, who was thirteen.

Charles was grateful his friend would attend Cambridge with him rather than Oxford, and they planned to share a space in the first year's accommodations. Jamison was not picked on at Harrow like Charles Bingley had been, but he was not accepted by the haughty members of the *Ton* due to his lack of wealth, connections, and the size of the family's estate.

When Charles Bingley became friendly with Jamison, he thought his social climbing mother and younger sister would have been happy, for the Jamisons had been on their land for some generations, but they had reacted just the opposite. They saw Mr. Jamison as an insignificant country squire with a small estate and no useful connections. Luckily, his father and Louisa, then eighteen, encouraged the friendship because they knew it was true and wanted the best for him.

It was deeply frustrating to Martha Bingley and her youngest, Caroline, then fourteen, that they were the only two in the family who cared about raising the Bingleys from their roots in trade.

Louisa had completed her two years at the local school and did not have a second's regret for her choice rather than bend to her mother's will and attend the seminary in London.

One day, while Louisa had been working with her father and uncle in their office at the carriage works, a Mr. Hurst and his son Harold had an appointment to look at options for a new carriage. The family had a medium to small estate, Winsdale, a little southeast of Scarborough near the market town of Scampston.

There seemed to be an immediate connection between Miss Bingley and young Mr. Hurst. He was five and twenty and, from what Louisa could tell from her brief encounter, he seemed to be a good man. In the coming weeks, the younger Mr. Hurst contrived many reasons to visit the carriage works. A month after meeting her, he asked if he could call on her. Not many weeks later they were in a formal courtship.

One evening, Martha Bingley complained to her husband about the Hursts only being members of the lower second circles, not high enough to help them in society. Arthur let his wife know in no uncertain terms that she would not interfere in their daughter's courtship unless she wished to risk of permanent loss of her allowance. With bad grace, Martha Bingley kept her opinions to herself, and was almost pleasant to the Hursts when the families met and dined together after Louisa accepted a proposal from her suitor.

The wedding was set for August of 1803.

~~~~~~~/~~~~~~~

The day after Anne died, Robert Darcy presented his late wife's best friends and sisters with their letters. There were three letters he held in reserve. His wife had written one to each of her children to be presented to them on the day they wed. She had written two to be held in case her children had not married before they turned thirty. The other was for her sister Catherine if, as expected, she arrived at Pemberley spouting some of her well-worn lies.

The three ladies who received letters from Anne Darcy decided they would only open them after the funeral. The day after the former Lady Catherine had been removed from Pemberley was the day Fanny Bennet opened her letter. Her friends Elaine and Edith opened theirs at the same time.

June 20, 1803

To my dear friend and sister, Fanny,

What am I able to say to one to whom I have become so close over the last eight years? I love you as a sister, just as our Priscilla did. I will, however, not ask you to keep any life-defining secrets for me, my friend.

All I ask is that you, Thomas, and your children be there for Robert, William, and Gigi. You know my wishes for Gigi to spend some time with you and your family after her three months of mourning is completed.

If she is dead set against it and does not want to leave Pemberley, that is her prerogative. I want my darling daughter to be able to choose and have her choices respected, but I am confident she will want to be with Kitty and Lydia, not to mention the rest of your wonderful children. When you and Robert give her the option, you will know if I am correct or not.

William will need help, too. I intend to extract a promise from him that he will not withdraw into himself. I am sure he will deny me nothing, but he may need some prodding, or a kick from Lizzy.

Am I insane to think that one day they would be perfect for one another? Although Lizzy is still five years away from her come out, the revelations at that time will surely send shockwaves through her life. By then, William will have finished at Cambridge and will be able to help her through that transition. I swear I see something there.

'*You may have the right of it, Anne,*' Fanny shook her head as she read Anne's prognostication. William and Lizzy had become very close, but there was a long way between that and the notion of romantic feelings.

The answer to my above speculation is one you will have in the future. As much as I would love to be there to witness it for myself, it is not to be. I will have to find a way to send you a message from beyond when, as I suspect I will be, I am proved correct.

I want to thank you for your unwavering friendship, not only for me, but for our Priscilla. She gave you a herculean task, and you accepted without a second's hesitation. If that is not the purest form of love between friends—sisters—that exists, then I know of it not.

The one thing I am looking forward to is being reunited with Priscilla in heaven. What stories I will have to tell her. Do not take this the wrong way Fanny, but my prayer is that it will be many, many years before you join us.

It was my privilege to be accepted as a close friend by you, Fanny. You do nothing by halves, and it was—is—the same in our friendship. Because of the support my three sisters will give Robert, William, and Gigi, when my time comes, I will be able to enter my eternal slumber in peace.

I very much desired to be there for all of the coming outs from Jane on down. You will have to help represent me at Gigi's coming out, which I am also asking of Elaine and Edith. I will not be there with my daughter when she joins society, but I am confident in the three surrogate mothers who will be there in my stead.

I intend to have Robert promise he will not give up and stop living. William and Gigi will need him more than ever. I will not try to take away from his year of mourning, but after that, I want him to begin to live fully again. All of you, including Frederick, will be integral to making sure my Robert carries on with life with a view to not letting it pass him by.

Let me close by thanking you for gifting me your friendship, your loyalty, and most of all the love of a sister.

Farewell Fanny,
Anne

By the time Fanny completed Anne's letter, the tears were streaming down her cheeks. "Oh Anne, how I miss you," Fanny lamented aloud. The bond she had shared with Cilla had been deep, and she had never thought she would ever find such a bond with another friend. She was wrong, she had—with all three of her best friends.

~~~~~~~/~~~~~~~

After a subdued dinner night, the three ladies who had read their letters from the late Anne Darcy sat on one settee in the drawing room. No one spoke for a time. "Anne has charged us with looking after her family, and by goodness, that is what we will do," Lady Elaine stated quietly so only her two friends could hear.

"That she has, Elaine. I agree that it will be best for Gigi to be with the Bennets after the initial three-month mourning period is over," Lady Edith opined. "Fanny, if Cassie wants to, would you allow her to spend some time at Netherfield with Gigi? Cassie is not as close as Kitty and Lydia are to her, but even though she is closer to Jane's age, she counts Gigi among her best friends."

"Edith, surely you know there is no need to even ask," Fanny returned as she took and patted Lady Edith's hand. "With or without Gigi's presence, Cassie is welcome anytime we are home, as are any of you. Between the science, maths, music, and singing masters, we will keep all our children occupied, and the more the merrier. Mr. Mercury has said many times that with a few more voices and he will be able to form a choir from his students."

"If Robert is not up to travelling yet, Reggie and I will transport Gigi to Netherfield. If you prefer, Edith, we will collect Cassie on the way," Lady Elaine ventured.

"That would be perfect, Elaine," Lady Edith responded.

"We must have our husbands talk to Robert," Fanny remembered. "Anne did not want Gigi to feel abandoned by her father, so even during his year of mourning, it will be important for him to be present at Netherfield from time to time."

"We can always have Frederick issue a royal decree," Lady Elaine jested.

"It will be important for William to visit on his term breaks and holidays while Gigi is with us," Fanny pointed out. "Now that there is no longer tension between him and Lizzy, I feel he will enjoy coming to our home to visit Gigi as often as he is able."

The ladies allowed one another to read their letters from Anne as she had not asked them to keep what she wrote confidential. Not a few tears fell among them. They could each hear Anne's voice in their heads as they each read each other's letters.

~~~~~~~/~~~~~~~

The five fathers, along with Andrew, Jamey, Richard, and William were in the dining parlour still, each with a snifter of brandy, except Bennet who preferred his port. He would drink brandy or cognac if there was no choice, but when there was, it was port for him.

"I know it has been but a few days, but I still hear my Anne's voice echoing in the house; I can smell her lavender scent in our chambers," Robert Darcy stated reflectively as he swirled the golden-brown liquid in the snifter he held.

"It has been thirteen years since my beloved Priscilla died," the Prince stated pensively, "and I still imagine I see and hear her, and it is not only because of my daught..." At that moment Prince remembered there were four younger men present who had no idea about his daughter. He saw four pairs of eyes staring at him in question, and four others who shook their heads almost imperceptibly.

"Do you have a daughter, Uncle Freddy?" Richard asked as he gave the Prince a questioning look.

"Do you know of a daughter of mine, Richard?" Frederick deflected. "I have often dreamed of my Cilla still being alive along with the son who was buried next to her. In my dreams we have a daughter too, one who looks and sounds just like my late wife. In my melancholy, as I thought of my beloved, I misspoke."

"No Uncle, I know of no daughter of yours," Richard answered, but his suspicion was aroused. Andrew, Jamey, and William thought nothing of it, but Richard knew what he heard, and the Prince's explanation just did not add up.

"We are returning to the drawing room," Andrew stated as he led the other two young men out of the dining parlour. Lord Holder and Robert Darcy followed the younger men and closed the door behind them.

"Your Highness, who is your daughter?" Richard suspected who it was. He remembered the way his Aunt Anne and his mother both had stared at...Lizzy! By their bearing and professionalism, he recognised men from the royal guard imbedded in the footmen and outriders the Bennets employed. He looked at the Prince, his father, and Mr. Bennet all watching him as his mind wrestled with the problem.

"Do you have a question you need to ask, son?" Lord Matlock asked.

"Mr. Bennet, Lizzy is not your daughter is she? She is the daughter of His Royal Highness from his first marriage. Oh good Lord, William called a princess 'riffraff!'" Richard concluded.

"Lizzy does not know," Bennet owned. "We need you to swear under pain of death you will not disclose what you have stumbled on to *anyone* until she is told when we feel she is ready."

"Is it not treason so keep a royal in your household, Mr. Bennet?" Richard worried.

"No, Richard, it is not, as I have given the Bennets royal indemnification to keep and raise my daughter..." Frederick gave Richard an abbreviated explanation of why Lizzy was being raised by the Bennets.

"So Mr. Taylor is there to make sure Lizzy is healthy, not to see to you when you visit?" Richard asked.

"That would be correct, except he would take care of me as well, were I to fall ill when at Purvis Lodge or Netherfield Park," the Prince cleared up.

"Aunt Anne, may she rest in peace, and Mother found out eight years ago at Holder Heights. They would never keep secrets from you and Uncle Robert, so you have known since then, have you not Father?" Richard puzzled out.

"Yes, Son, but you understand why it is imperative to keep this knowledge to yourself?" Lord Matlock asked his son. "You cannot act any differently than you always have around Lizzy. This knowledge is a burden you will have to bear on your own for the next five years, and, as you know, you are now one of Lizzy's protectors."

"Netherfield Park was Lady Priscilla's, was it not?" Richard asked.

"Yes, and now it belongs to Lizzy, or it will when she turns one and twenty," Bennet explained. "That is another thing which is kept secret, Lizzy's wealth—which is vast—for obvious reasons."

Richard was almost sorry he pushed the point, for he was quickly seeing that the knowledge was a burden. He could not talk to Andrew, Jamey, or William about it; no one outside of the small circle who already knew. Lizzy, a Princess of the United Kingdom of Great Britain and Ireland. Richard just shook his head, wishing it would shake the knowledge back out of his consciousness.

"When we have absolute privacy you may talk to any of us, including your Uncle Robert and Lord Holder," the Prince assured Richard. "Swear to me, Richard Fitzwilliam, swear to me as your Prince that you will not reveal what you have learnt to another; we have five years to get through before it is to become known."

"On my life, I give you my vow of secrecy," Richard swore.

"Think of this as good practice for the army, Lieutenant," Frederick stated.

"Yes Sir, Field Marshal, Sir," Richard snapped off a smart salute. He often forgot Uncle Freddy was one of the highest-ranking military officers in the realm, and now he had sworn his oath to both personas as well as his trusted uncle, and it was a vow he would keep.

CHAPTER 16

August 1806

H is Royal Highness Prince Frederick, Duke of York and Albany, Earl of Ulster, marvelled at his daughter's beauty. In the last three years, she had matured into a refined young gentlewoman. She had always looked like her mother—the holder of his heart—but never more so than now that she was almost fully grown. In the last year, he had been bestowed with an additional honour from his father, the King.

In 1801, the Prince had been vocal in his support of the establishment of the Royal Military College, Sandhurst, which promoted the professional, merit-based training of future commissioned officers. He had opined that in order for the army to have the best, then the officers needed training, professional training, and not just the ability to purchase a rank.

The King had been so impressed with the quality of the officers being produced at Sandhurst, he made Frederick the honorary Warden of Windsor Forest in September 1805. As much as he appreciated the honour from his father, Frederick would have preferred that the wife of his heart was still alive to share his life and honours with him.

As he looked at his daughter, the Prince offered thanks to on high for being able to be part of her life. He was concerned that in two years when the truth was revealed to her she could be very angry at all of those who had withheld the information from her. Elizabeth prized honesty above all else, but he was willing to risk her possible ire to protect her for two more years.

He was at least sure about what the King would do if Elizabeth agreed to meet her royal grandparents. One day he had been visiting Buckingham House and he posited a hypothetical to his father, asking what he would have done had the dead boy lived, as far as succession went.

The King had given his son's question consideration and then had replied although the child would have been recognised as a legitimate son, and a Prince of the United Kingdom of Great Britain and Ireland, the King would not have angered the spiritual leaders of the Church of England by having a child born after divorce so close in succession to the throne. He would have the prime minister bring an act to the commons to remove the boy from the line of succession.

It was one of the few times in Frederick's life his father had expressed remorse for forcing the divorce. It did not repair the heartbreak that had been caused, but Frederick treasured the fact his father was willing to acknowledge such to him.

What the King did not admit to was that he knew he had made two women unhappy along with his son. Princess Frederica Charlotte lived in seclusion at his son's estate of Oatlands Park near Weybridge in Surrey. Although he acknowledged the pain his actions had caused to three, the King knew what he had done had been done for good reason, as now Prussia was an ally in the fight against the little tyrant and his wars in Europe.

The prince was returned to the present as he watched his daughter and some of her sisters talking quietly in the drawing room. Priscilla had left him the most special of gifts in the form of Elizabeth.

~~~~~~~/~~~~~~~

At one and twenty, George Wickham was an unhappy and resentful man. He was living in Seven Dials, the bowels of London. The money his father had given him was all but gone. He had lost most of it at the tables but had the good sense to keep a very little for living expenses. None of his schemes to make his fortune in the last three years had ever panned out as planned, instead costing him rather than producing the result he needed.

Since the day his father had given him the funds, George had not tried to contact the man. He was determined to make his fortune the way he saw fit, to show his father how wrong his estimation of his son was. To George's chagrin, so far the only thing he had proven was that his father's warnings had been true.

Almost three years in the past, in a little town in Staffordshire, he had claimed to be a Darcy—the one and only time he dared—and gained credit after he charmed the merchants into believing his claim. The problem was the village was close to Holder Heights, and when Lord Holder had heard of this mysterious George Darcy, he had a good idea who the man was.

Lord Holder sent an express to Robert Darcy, informing him what his steward's son was up to, sullying of the Darcy name. Unluckily for George Wickham, the Bennets were still with the Darcys as it was not quite three months after the death of Lady Anne.

Biggs and Johns were dispatched to give the wastrel a *gentle* warning. On the same day the two footmen arrived, Lord Holder had his steward canvass the business owners to get a list of the debts Wickham had run up. All of the vowels—a little more than fifty pounds worth—were purchased for his friend to be held until needed and the merchants were told it was the last time someone would cover them if they chose to extend credit to one unknown without an effort being made to verify his tale.

Meanwhile, the two huge men found Wickham in the local inn, drinking and spreading lies about the grand estate he would inherit. "An 'ow would the son of a steward in'erit Mr. Darcy's estate, *Wickham?*" Biggs growled.

George Wickham slowly turned and saw the two mountainous men with scowls behind him, all colour drained from his face. "'Ey," one of the locals who had been conned into buying drinks for the libertine spoke up. "Ya sayin' 'e's not a

SHANA GRANDERSON A LADY

Darcy?"

"No, 'e be a liar, thief, an' a cheat. 'Is name be George Wickham, the son of the *steward* of Pemberley, not the *master!*" Biggs informed the now angry group of men.

Before the crowd turned too ugly, Biggs and Johns each took an arm of the petrified liar, lifted him as if he were nothing, and walked out of the inn with George Wickham dangling between them. When they reached a dark alley behind the establishment, the one-time warning was delivered, leaving Wickham with a broken nose and a missing tooth. Before they left, Biggs turned to the snivelling coward.

"Mr. Darcy wants you t' know," Biggs stated menacingly, "if ya' ever use 'is name agin, there will be no mercy. 'E 'as bought your debts 'ere and you will go to gaol—if you are still alive—there will be no second chance."

In the moon's light, it was then George recognised them as two of the men who he had seen protecting the blonde after whom he still lusted. Up close they were much scarier than from a distance. He admitted then and there he could never use the Darcy name, or the names of any of their friends, ever again.

From Staffordshire he made his way to London, where he begged, borrowed, and stole whatever it was he needed to live, which is how he found himself in a tiny, rat-infested room in the worst part of Town. The next day, he was in a neighbourhood that was somewhat better than where he lived—any neighbourhood in London was better—walking down Edward Street. He saw a boarding house with a sign over the door that identified it as 'Younge's Boarding House.'"

There was a notice next to the door: "*Seeking a man of all work.*" Taking a chance it might get him out of the squalor he was living in, George Wickham knocked on the door, and told the woman who opened it he wanted to apply for the position.

~~~~~~~/~~~~~~~

Robert Darcy kept his word to his beloved wife. In July, a year after her passing, the master of Pemberley ended his year

162

of mourning. He was thankful beyond words for the support and friendship of his extended family, for they had never allowed him to sink into the depths of despair he would have otherwise allowed himself to drown in.

At the end of the three months of his children's deep mourning period, he had accompanied William to Cambridge to take up his studies, and then his daughter to Netherfield Park to be with the Bennets. His wife's wisdom was proved once again as Gigi had thrived with the Bennets. She had been surrounded by love and sisterhood, and a slightly younger adopted brother. When Darcy had joined William for Christmas at Netherfield the year Anne died, neither he nor his son recognised the self-confident girl who threw her arms around them in welcome. After her mother passed, Gigi had begun to withdraw into herself and exhibited a level of shyness not seen before regardless of her friends' attempts to draw her out. After a few months with the Bennets, the renewed shyness had all but evaporated.

Georgiana Darcy still missed her mother each and every day, but the love extended to her by the Bennets had done much to ameliorate her sorrow. She looked upon Aunt Fanny and Uncle Thomas almost as surrogate parents rather than merely adopted aunt and uncle. In addition, she had become very close with Mariah Lucas and the Long sisters. It also helped that Cassie—even though she was five years older—spent a few months at a time at Netherfield Park as well.

Her mother was always with her, Georgiana could feel her presence in her heart and when ever she was in doubt, she believed she could hear her late mother in her head giving her the advice she needed.

William was enjoying Cambridge. Yes, he was sad much of the time when he was not busy, and his mother's death had left a hole in his heart, but he loved the intellectual stimulation. In addition to cricket, the Darcy heir excelled at fencing and was a force on the chess and debating teams.

The latter he joined to sharpen his skills for the epic

debates he and Elizabeth tended to have when in company together, the former because he had been thought by his father
to be one of the best chess players in their extended family. He
needed every edge he could attain, and the debate team would
help with bolstering his defences against a certain highly
intelligent and strikingly beautiful young lady.

Georgiana had remained with the Bennets until her
father's year of mourning was complete. As his late wife and
friends suggested, Robert Darcy visited his daughter almost
every month she was at Netherfield, so she never felt abandoned.

Beyond the year of mourning, with the Bennets' ready
agreement, Gigi had spent a good deal of time in Hertfordshire
so she could keep studying with the masters the Bennets had
on staff, especially Mr. Mercury for voice and *Signore* da Funti
for her playing of the pianoforte, which was now on par with
the three eldest Bennet sisters.

Kitty had displayed an innate skill for drawing during
the last two years, so a new drawing and art master had been
hired, young Mr. Adam Lambert from London, of no relation
to Aunt Maddie Gardiner's family. Mr. Lambert was an added
incentive for Gigi to want to be at Netherfield Park as she, like
Kitty and her cousin Anne, loved drawing and sketching. He
would often sing with the group of masters when they had
their impromptu music sessions, as it seemed he had a voice to
rival Mr. Mercury's.

In the last few months, William had started to notice
Elizabeth, who was sixteen, as far more than a family friend.
He was attracted to her, not just to her looks—though there
was no arguing her striking beauty. It was her intelligence that
was the main attraction for him.

Some may have been intimidated by a woman as intelligent, if not more so, than themselves, but William considered
it a huge plus in her favour. She was also teasing, playful, and
could be impertinent if she so desired. The more time William
spent around her, the more he came to realise he was falling in

love with Elizabeth Bennet.

One evening, when William had arrived home at Pemberley for his Easter term break from Cambridge, he told his father he felt he was falling in love with Elizabeth. Robert Darcy threw back his head and laughed. Even though his stomach sank at such a reaction, William held his peace because it was the first time he had heard his father laugh since before his mother had received her diagnosis.

"I am sorry, William; I was not laughing at you," Robert told his son as he regulated his mirth, not missing the hurt in Williams eyes. "I am laughing at your mother's perceptivity. She told me she believed you would fall in love with Lizzy one day, and I thought she was out of her senses, as it was during the time you and she were standoffish to one another."

"Thank you, Father," William stated with relief. The fact his late mother had predicted his falling in love with Elizabeth made her all the more desirable, knowing he had his late mother's blessing.

"You know you will need to wait two years for her come out before you declare yourself," Robert reminded his son. "In addition, before you approach her you will need permission from her father." His son had no idea who the father was that was referred to. "Once York approves you will need the King's permission."

"It will be hard to wait, but I will use the time to deepen my friendship with Elizabeth so she will hopefully start to develop tender feelings for me," William voiced his hopes.

"What about the young men you assisted at Cambridge?" Darcy remembered his son telling him something close to the beginning of the current academic year at Cambridge. "Did you become friends?"

"You mean Bingley and Jamison," William reminded his father. "Some lordlings were attacking them for no other reason but that the former's father was in trade while the latter's father is considered an insignificant country squire with a small estate. We are acquaintances, nothing more, and this at Bingley's insistence," William shared.

"Why would this Bingley eschew a connection to you?" Darcy asked his son in confusion.

"As he tells it, his mother and younger sister are incorrigible social climbers, and he did not want to subject me—us—to their machinations," William shared. "Based on his description of the two, I think he did us a great service."

A few hours later, father and son had departed south to visit the Bennets and Gigi.

~~~~~~~/~~~~~~~

Louisa and Harold Hurst had been happy since their wedding in August of 1803. The only darkness in their otherwise felicitous life was when Mrs. Martha Bingley and Caroline, now seventeen, were in company with them.

The Hursts had a smallish town home on Curzon street in London, to which, when they were in residence, they felt obligated to invite Caroline. Caroline was attending Mrs. Hawthorn-Jones's Seminary for Young Ladies and when they were at the house, residing with the Hursts on weekends and holidays.

It had not taken Caroline long to feel the disdain of both titled and untitled daughters of the *Ton*, who considered her to be what she in fact was, the pretentious daughter of a tradesman. Rather than realise the way she was treated was wrong, Miss Bingley believed if she was to climb to the levels of society she craved, she would need to emulate the behaviour of the girls who belittled, bullied, and denigrated her.

She could not blame them for disdaining her father's roots in trade, as she felt the same. She had initially believed her dowry of ten thousand pounds would buy access to the upper echelons of girls at the school, only to discover that ten thousand was insignificant compared to the twenty thousand, or more, most others had.

She enlisted her mother to join her in working on her father to increase her dowry to twenty thousand, or higher if it were possible. No matter how much they cajoled, tried to manipulate, or simply begged, Mr. Bingley senior remained unmoved.

As her dissatisfaction built, Caroline Bingley was considered more and more of a chore to be around by all in her family other than her mother, who continued to indulge her spoilt shrewish daughter's whims.

Unbeknownst to his family, Arthur Bingley was saving for an estate to raise his family to the minor gentry. His desire to own an estate had nothing to do with the pretentions of his wife or youngest daughter; he was merely looking forward to retirement and had decided he would one day like to relax and enjoy the fruits of his labours.

All his plans changed in early September of 1806, when, in a twist of cruel irony for a carriage maker, a wheel broke as the conveyance he and his wife were travelling in was negotiating a sharp bend at speed. The vehicle turned over, breaking free of the horses, and then slid down a steep embankment and smashed to pieces on the rocks below. The coachman, a footman, and Mr. and Mrs. Bingley were killed instantly.

~~~~~~~/~~~~~~~

Fanny was expecting her two best friends to return from London after Jane's curtsy before the queen. In the end, to cater to Bennet's *aversion* to Town, Jane had gone with Ladies Edith and Elaine, with the former sponsoring her presentation as her godmother.

It was no secret among the families that Andrew Fitzwilliam, Viscount Hilldale, was in love with Jane and she returned his love in full measure. Both understood he could not declare himself until after she came out, but now Andrew was able to ask for, and be granted, the second, supper, and final sets with her at the ball to be held at Holder Heights.

While the two had always been friendly, in the last six months things had changed and both had developed tender feelings, one for the other. At six and twenty, Andrew felt he was ready to take the next step in his life, and he could imagine no one other than Jane Bennet making life's journey at his side.

Fanny would never forget the conversation she and her husband had with Jane when she insisted she wanted all of the family with her when she was presented. With Lizzy being sixteen, Mary fourteen, Kitty thirteen, Lydia twelve, soon to be thirteen, and Tommy almost ten, Jane could not understand why her father could not bring all of her sisters to London to witness her curtsy. She also asked why her, Anne, and Cassie's ball would be held at Holder Heights rather than in London.

"Jane, sit," Fanny had instructed after Jane joined her parents. "We must have your promise you will not repeat a word of what we are about to tell you to anyone, not until after Lizzy's eighteenth birthday or we feel she is ready to know what we are about to disclose to you," Bennet insisted.

Jane had looked at her parents questioningly. "What has this to do with Lizzy?"

"Will you promise us, Jane, to solemnly swear you will not repeat a word of what we are about to tell you to another soul until it becomes more widely known?" Fanny asked.

"I give you my vow; I will not repeat anything," Jane agreed.

"How much do you remember of Aunt Priscilla, Janie?" Fanny asked.

"Nothing beyond what you, Uncle Freddy, and others have told me, Mama" Jane admitted.

"Here is a painting of Aunt Priscilla. You will soon understand why I do not allow it to be hung with the other portraits in the gallery." Fanny handed the small portrait of Priscilla, which was painted soon after her marriage to Frederick, to Jane. There was no missing the gasp from Jane as soon as she saw the likeness.

"Mama, Papa, I am confused. Are you saying this painting of Lizzy is Aunt Priscilla?" Jane asked non-plussed.

"Jane, dearest, although Lizzy is our daughter and your sister in every way that counts, she is not related to us by blood," Bennet explained.

"But Aunt Priscilla's son... was it my brother who is buried with her?" Both her parents nodded. "So Lizzy was brought up as one of us, but she is a Royal Princess. Is Uncle Freddy her father?"

Jane asked carefully as the reality of what her parents were telling her sunk in.

Jane asked carefully as the reality of what her parents were telling her sunk in.

Fanny and Bennet explained all to Jane. "Do you understand why the Prince left her with us and did not consign her to be raised the same way he had to endure?" Fanny asked.

"I do, Mama. And I now understand why we are not able to go to Town as a family. I love Lizzy, and of course nothing you have revealed to me changes that; she is, and always will remain, my sister." Jane clarified for both should they have any question. "Am I to deduce from what you said about Lizzy's eighteenth birthday that it is when the truth will be revealed to her?"

"Which is as Aunt Priscilla requested, unless there is reason to do so sooner. We are aware she perhaps will not be happy initially at not being told the truth of her antecedents, but we hope when she regains her equanimity, she will see the reasoning behind our not telling her," Bennet stated.

"It will be up to her if she wants to be known to either or both sets of grandparents. As far as the King and Queen go, it will depend on them more so than Lizzy after she makes her decision. It is up to them whether they recognise her as a princess or not," Fanny explained.

"I hope Lizzy does not want to know Aunt Priscilla's family. They do not deserve to be acquainted with her after they cut their daughter in such a way," Jane had stated flatly, the steel in her voice making both of her parents smile.

After the discussion with her parents, Jane clearly saw the reasoning behind her ball being in Staffordshire rather than London and had accepted the necessity of the protections her parents and their Aunts and Uncles, Uncle Freddy in particular, had put in place to try and make sure Lizzy would not be seen by anyone who knew the late Lady Priscilla.

CHAPTER 17

Elizabeth had been disappointed in her hope she would accompany Jane to London for her presentation. She accepted the reasoning her parents and aunts gave her, that she was not yet out and the presentation was the smallest part of Jane's coming out.

Excitement was building for the ball to be held at Holder Heights as Elizabeth and Mary would be allowed to attend the ball until supper, at which time they would retire. They would be allowed to dance, but only with pre-approved friends and family. Elizabeth secretly hoped William would request a set with her.

Anne and Cassie were sharing the coming out ball with Jane, who would turn nineteen a month after Cassie turned eighteen; Anne had turned nineteen a few months earlier. The three made their curtsies on the same day. Even though Lady Edith was sponsoring Jane as her godmother, Lady Elaine had presented her together with Anne because the aforementioned lady had presented her own daughter.

None of the ladies saw the man leering at Jane as she returned to the carriage after her presentation. George Wickham took the position at the boarding house—which was in fact a brothel masquerading as a boarding house—on Edward Street, which, thankfully, included a room in the attic. It was far less that he thought he deserved but was worlds better than the hovel he had inhabited in Seven Dials.

George was on an errand for the owner of the house, Mrs. Agnes Younge. He thought about approaching the carriage to get a closer look at the blond beauty—that is until he spied one of the two huge footmen who had taken him to task in

Staffordshire. His bent nose and missing tooth convinced him to turn tail and make all haste in the opposite direction as fast as his legs would carry him.

Johns recognised the coward he and Biggs had paid a visit to in order to warn him off. He would thrash the man again if needs be. He marked the instant the man recognised him, and the fear he displayed. Before Johns could take a step towards the blackguard, he turned and ran.

Once all the ladies were seated, the coachman urged his team forward. Lady Edith would travel with the Bennets and Fitzwilliams from Netherfield to Holder Heights, where the Darcys would be waiting for them.

~~~~~~~/~~~~~~~

Mrs. Catherine de Bourgh had learned a lesson in abject humility during the last three years, relegated to a small cottage in Hunsford with one maid of all work.

Her brother had reduced her allowance to ten pounds per month, and all of her jewellery had been locked in a safe at Rosings Park. Once or twice during the first month of her changed circumstances she had attempted to enter Rosings Park. In both instances, she was unable to get close to the manor house before being apprehended by the guards her brother had patrolling the park.

She gave up after her second attempt, as she had been told in no uncertain terms that were a third such attempt made, she would be turned over to the local magistrate, Lord Metcalf, and be charged with trespassing.

Lady Metcalf was one of the only ladies in the neighbourhood who had received her prior to her courtesy title being stripped by the King. The royal decree the Prince had told her would appear had been in the papers had been published a few days after she was ensconced in her new abode. Her nightmare had become reality; that she was merely Mrs. de Bourgh was known far and wide.

She thought Lady Metcalf would offer her succour, but she had a rude awakening when she tried to visit her *friend.*

The butler had her wait outside, not even in the entry hall, as he went to notify his mistress she had a caller. He returned ten minutes later and told the humiliated woman his mistress was not at home to her, and never would be again.

It did not take long for Catherine de Bourgh to learn how much the people of Hunsford, her former tenants, and those from the Westerham area disdained her. None of them would forget the imperious lady who interfered in their affairs while offering them useless advice and subsequently haranguing them for not implementing her unsolicited and nonsensical guidance.

After railing at everyone except herself for the first six months, Catherine began to examine her actions and inter-actions with those around her. For the first time in her life, she admitted she was wrong. She had lost her family through no one's fault but her own.

In her desire for power and wealth, she had alienated each and every single member of her family. In her memory, she recalled the sneering look of disdain on her daughter's face the last time she saw her in the music room at Pemberley. As hard as it was to hold a mirror up to herself and her actions, she acknowledged her avaricious behaviour, especially towards Anne. She deserved nothing less than the scorn her daughter had looked upon her with.

Catherine reviewed her behaviour as far back as when she was a little girl and started to feel abject shame. She realised it all started when she became envious of Reggie. He was the Matlock heir and would receive, in comparison, both in wealth and attention, so much more than her pittance of a dowry. It was from that point she became more concerned with what she did not have in comparison to what others had. She elevated the desire for what she did not have over all of the blessings she had actually had in her life.

She knew she needed to apologise for her many wrongs but was intelligent enough to know she could not pay mere lip service. She needed to act, not talk. At first, when she started to help wherever she could in the little community of Hunsford, she was rejected by those who remembered the way she was.

She persevered, and slowly but surely those who lived around her started to accept that something had changed in the formerly arrogant woman. After her maid was paid and she had purchased food for the month, Catherine would donate whatever money she had left.

What she did not know was she was always under surveillance, both for her own protection and to make sure she did not cause trouble. When the initial reports reached her brother regarding the changes in his sister, he thought it was an act to try to regain what she had lost. It soon became evident the change was real.

Lord Matlock increased her allowance to twenty pounds. He was amazed when the reports told him rather than hire another servant or spend on herself, she merely increased the amount she was able to use to help others in the area.

By the end of the second year, her allowance was at fifty pounds a month. Her brother had conditioned the increase on her hiring a man to assist around the cottage and to buy better food for herself and her household. Even after complying, there was still close to forty pounds per month Catherine was able to use to help others in her small community.

If a lady was sick, or heavy with child, Catherine would volunteer to help, or if needs be pay for a maid to help. She would look after their children when needed, teaching them their letters and sums. As she approached her third year living among the people of Hunsford, Mrs. Catherine de Bourgh had gone from one of the most hated to one of the most loved people in the town.

There was no question as to her sincerity. Lord Matlock felt true pride in his sister Catherine for the first time since she was a young girl.

~~~~~~~/~~~~~~~

When her father's final will and testament was read, Miss Bingley was most displeased. Her dowry was unchanged, and she had inherited nothing beyond it. Everything had been left to her brother, the one who was happy to be in trade. What was even worse was that their Uncle Paul was executor and had become her guardian. Another tradesman!

If she did not marry, her dowry would be released to her when she was five and twenty. How was she ever going to find a husband from the first circles living in the house of a tradesman in Scarborough?

She did not notice—or care to see—the looks directed at her from her brother, uncle, aunt, and her married sister. Louisa had a difficult time believing they were born of the same parents. She did not want to think ill of the dead, but she held her mother responsible for planting the social climbing desire in her younger sister.

~~~~~~~~/~~~~~~~~

Louisa would return to her husband soon. She suspected she was at long last with child but did not want to get the hopes of Harold and her in-laws up until she felt the quickening. She prayed her uncle would not ask her to take her sister; she would have to refuse him. Her husband and his parents would not have Caroline in their houses again. There was only so much one could bear of the youngest Bingley.

At one and twenty, Charles Bingley graduated from Cambridge. When he reached the age of five and twenty, all of his father's fortune of more than one hundred thousand pounds would be his. After a disappointed Caroline stomped off, Paul Bingley asked his nephew to join him in his office.

"Uncle Paul, what are we to do about Caroline?" Charles asked, disgusted with his sister's attitude. "It seems she does not care about our parents' deaths; all she was concerned with was if she gained from the tragedy."

"My brother knew his daughter, which is why he refused to increase her dowry. He was worried it would make her even more insufferable than she is now," Paul Bingley told his nephew. "Your father recognised Caroline for exactly who she is and used to tell me often that she was far too high in the instep."

"Father often told me the same," Charles agreed. "With her attitude, who would want her as a wife? She thinks she will be wife to a member of the *Ton*, but if she truly believes that then she is more delusional than even I believe her to be." Charles paused. "Did Father tell you I turned down some offers of friendship as I would not subject potential highborn friends to Mother, may she rest in peace, or Caroline?"

"My brother told me," Paul Bingley nodded, frowning at the consideration. "I remember he told me about the Darcy fellow who helped you and young Jamison at Cambridge."

"All I could see was Caroline attaching herself to him and declaring herself the next mistress of Pemberley—that is his father's estate—as soon as she found out about his connections and wealth. If we had been friends, I am sure she would have resorted to engineering a compromise if she felt she had to in order to gain the position she craves."

"The reason I asked you to come see me in the office and not where Caroline could hear is because your father was seriously considering the purchase of an estate where he wished to retire. He wanted to relax and partake of the fruits of his labours—it had nothing to do with his wanting to rise in society. Unfortunately, that will never be," Paul Bingley stated sadly. He missed his big brother. "As you heard in the will, he and I owned the carriage works jointly. Now you own an equal share. Your share of the profits should be more than two thousand five hundred pounds per annum. If you add that amount to the interest from the money your father saved, you should have around six thousand pounds per annum.

"Arthur planned to lease an estate in 1808, in Hertfordshire. He prepaid for two years on an estate named Longbourn. The landlord lives three miles away on a second estate. My brother heard about the estate from his friend Edward Gardiner in London; his sister is mistress of both estates. The current lessee is leaving in early 1808. You will be able to take up the lease as soon as the agent, Mr. Phillips, notifies you."

SHANA GRANDERSON A LADY

"I thought Father was not interested in owning an estate, that he was happy in the business you two built," a confused Charles stated.

"His reasons were not the same as those of your late mother," Paul Bingley averred. "As I mentioned previously, it had nothing to do with social pretension. He told me that if anything were to happen to him before he took up the lease, he wanted you to do so. He is not dictating what you do in the future, hence there was no mention of it in the will. If you enjoy life as a landed gentleman, then you have the means to purchase an estate. If not, the business will be here. You will need to attend quarterly meetings with the investors, and the rest we will cover by post."

"I will honour my father's wishes," Charles informed his uncle. "Now, what about Caroline?"

"She is my ward, and therefore my problem. We will discuss her later." Paul Bingley stood and slapped his nephew on the back as the two made to re-join the family in the sitting room—except for Miss Bingley who was having a snit in her bedchamber.

~~~~~~~/~~~~~~~

"Sarah, could it be that my decision to break with Priscilla may not have been for the best?" Lord Jersey asked his wife.

Rather than be lauded for his decision as he had thought they would have been, the opposite had happened. Invitations had all but dried up, especially since their former son-in-law had turned his life around suddenly in 1795.

There had been no royal invitations, and now there was a coming out ball at Holder Heights from which they had been excluded. "We could not have expected to be invited to this particular event, Cyril. Lady Holder is a friend of Priscilla's, as is Lady Matlock. On your instruction we cut them when Priscilla was cut, so why would her friends want us present? The Bennet girl who is sharing the ball is daughter to Priscilla's friend in Hertfordshire. It is not surprising we were not invited," Lady Jersey stated bitterly. She had done her duty and obeyed her husband's edict but it never sat well with her. Her husband had forced her to cut her firstborn.

She had tried to write to Priscilla once or twice, but each time her husband intercepted the post and had been vociferous in his condemnation of her disobedience, so the Countess had given up, much to her sorrow.

"I suppose you are correct, Sarah. Even though we and Wes were not invited, at least there will be one representative of the family present, even if she is only included because she is a Rhys-Davies now," Lord Jersey opined.

~~~~~~~/~~~~~~~

The ball at Holder Heights was well attended. There had been not a single refusal as the invited members of the *Ton* invited simply delayed their return to London. The three ladies organising the ball had made sure they scrutinized invitations carefully to make sure no intimates of the De Melvilles would be included.

The Bennet parents stood in the receiving line with the Carringtons and the Fitzwilliams. One of the couples to enter were the Marquess and Marchioness of Birchington, Lord and Lady Rhys-Davies. He was the heir to the dukedom of Bedford.

Lord Sedgwick Rhys-Davies, Junior, known as Sed by all, had married the lady he chose to be a future Duchess, Lady Marie De Melville as was. Lady Marie was not close to her late sister in looks, but there were definite similarities.

Lady Marie had never felt reconciled to her father's decision to break with her older sister over the divorce the King forced on Priscilla and her husband. She was still remonstrating with herself for not being willing to go against her father even now and write a letter to her sister.

Lady Marie was well aware her parents were not held in high regard by many at the ball, especially the joint hostesses. She saw Lady Matlock, another of Priscilla's close friends, in the receiving line as she made her way down the line. She prayed her sister was present, for if she was, there was nothing she would like more than to hug her elder sister.

When the Marchioness greeted Fanny, she had been distracted until she looked up, and without hearing the name again, she knew exactly at whom she was looking—Priscilla's sister, about ten years her junior.

Ladies Edith & Elaine recognised the lady at the same time and understood Fanny's look of shock. If Lady Marie saw Lizzy, she would think she was seeing her sister, as the likeness was so close.

There was nothing to be done immediately, as the receiving line duty was not complete. After Lady Marie and her husband moved past the line towards the ballroom, both Fanny and Lady Edith pointed out Lady Marie to the Prince by inclining their heads.

Lady Matlock called Richard to her side and told him to delay the Marquess and Marchioness until the Prince could act. She then left the receiving line to seek out Lizzy and remove her from the ball room. It took a little longer than she would have liked, but she found Elizabeth and Mary with Jane, Cassie, her sons, Darcy, and Jamey.

"Elizabeth and Mary, my dears, we will have to ask you to retire now," Lady Matlock stated, giving a nervous look towards the doors leading to the hall outside. The Prince had engaged the Marquess and Marchioness in conversation to delay their entry into the ball room, so Richard joined them.

"But Aunt Elaine, Mama and Papa gave their permission," Elizabeth stated plaintively.

"Something has occurred that we believe may affect either your or Mary's safety, so as much as it pains your parents, they ask that you and Mary retire this instant," Lady Matlock insisted. After his mission to delay the Birchingtons, Richard joined his mother. Captain Richard Fitzwilliam was well aware that the Marchioness was someone who could identify Elizabeth as connected to Lady Priscilla.

"I will escort the fair maidens to safety, Mother," Richard gave a mock gallant bow.

"As will I," Darcy repeated Richard's bow.

Without further complaint, although neither was happy, Mary took Richard's arm and Elizabeth William's.

As Lady Marie Rhys-Davies entered the ballroom with her husband, she scanned the room, hoping to glimpse her sister. She was about to give up when she saw the back of a lady who was being escorted out of the ball room.

From what she could see from behind the lady, she swore it was her sister, Priscilla!

CHAPTER 18

"**S**ed, SED!" Lady Marie demanded her husband's attention.

"What is it, Marie?" the Marquess asked.

"I swear I just saw Priscilla being escorted out of the ballroom by the Darcy heir," Lady Marie insisted. "Why would she run as soon as I entered?"

"If it were my ex-wife you saw, it may have something to do with the disgraceful way your family treated her when the King forced the divorce on us," the Prince stated, none too quietly. The couple had forgotten he was nearby.

"Your Royal Highness," Lord Sed gave a deep bow while his wife gave the deepest of curtsies.

"I was but twelve when my father did what he felt he had to," Lady Marie managed. She was not able to explain how her father had forced the decision on them as the Prince spoke again.

"Do you try to defend their despicable actions toward their own daughter in my presence?" the Prince bristled. In his anger he missed that the younger lady had said it was her father's decision alone. "I understand you were a young girl at the time, but how many letters have you written since you came of age, since you married?"

"If you will excuse us, your Royal Highness, I think my wife is overwrought and we need to depart," the Marquess stated and then gently guided his wife out of the ball room to collect their outerwear and call for their carriage.

"Is the Marchioness not well, Lord Sed?" Lady Edith asked when she saw the distressed look Lady Marie was displaying.

"It seems that is the case. Lady Holder, Mrs. Bennet, Lord

Matlock, please accept our good wishes on your daughters' entry into society and our apologies for not being able to remain for the ball." The Marquess led his wife out to call for their carriage.

"Sed, I promised your parents that the royals did not hold the actions my parents took against us, as my father stated what he did was done in support of the crown," Lady Marie cried as their coach pulled away down the drive towards the exit from Holder Heights.

"It seems your father may have been incorrect in his calculation, Marie," her husband said blandly. "Are you sure you saw your sister?"

"My eyes did not lie to me, Sed," Lady Marie insisted. "Unless there is another who looks just like her, that was my sister."

"You need to write to your father and inform him the opposite of what he thought has happened as far as the royals are concerned," Lord Sed suggested. "My parents are not going to be happy, especially with my mother being a distant cousin of the Queen."

~~~~~~~/~~~~~~~

Elizabeth and Mary were escorted back to the ballroom. To assuage their confusion, they were told that the perceived threat was not an issue any longer. The two soon forgot about the oddity as the former was engaged for the first set by William and the latter by Richard.

Richard had Cassie's supper and final sets. The two had become close over the last few times Richard had liberty from his unit and both realised that they were forming tender feelings, one for the other. The feelings were creating a quandary for Richard.

He was not the typical poor second son; he owned an estate within five miles of Pemberley's western boundary called Brookfield. Richard had not joined the army out of necessity, but rather out of a sense of duty. If he were to ask for and be granted a courtship with Lady Cassandra Carrington, his honour would dictate he must resign from the army because unless he took a commission in the militia, he would not be able to ensure he would not die on a battlefield soon after engaging Cassie's affections.

As he saw it, his only honourable option would be to remain silent until after the upcoming deployment, and then, if he survived, he would be ready to resign. The danger in such a course of action, however, was he risked losing the lady to another if his deployment was long. It was a conundrum he needed some advice to help him sort through.

While Lord Holder was dancing the first set with Cassie, Lord Matlock and Bennet were doing the same with Anne and Jane. The three debutantes shined like the jewels of the first order they were. While they danced, Ladies Elaine and Edith, along with Fanny and Frederick, met in a corner out of earshot of anyone. "When the Duke and Duchess of Bedford declined and sent the Marquess and his wife in their stead, I did not consider who he had married," Edith apologised.

"Edith, we all went over the guest list carefully and we all missed that fact," Fanny reassured her friend. "I am sorry she was upset, but even had she remained, Lizzy was out of the ballroom, and, at best, Lady Marie saw Lizzy from the back as William escorted her upstairs."

"What I said to Marie was not just to take her attention off Lizzy," the Prince stressed. "I am still angry at the way the De Melvilles treated my beloved, and I honestly believe that the treatment at the hands of her family was a contributing factor to taking away her will to live."

"If the De Melvilles write to Priscilla now after this confrontation, what should we do?" Elaine asked.

"We do nothing, they will receive the letter after Lizzy turns eighteen," Fanny stated firmly. "Any contact now will be disingenuous, a reaction to a public berating by Frederick in front of many prominent members of the *Ton*. They proved what their priorities were when they cut Priscilla; if they suddenly deign to write, there will be no answer." Fanny paused to rein in the ire she felt towards the De Melvilles. "They had almost sixteen years to initiate contact, to make any sort of inquiry about Priscilla, and they did nothing. It will be Lizzy's decision if she desires a connection with them after her eighteenth birthday, not theirs."

"I agree with Fanny," Frederick stated simply. The Prince knew it was unfair to unleash his anger against his Priscilla's younger sister. He hoped the Marchioness would relay his displeasure to her parents. Frederick was sure the Marquess would not hide the confrontation from his parents, the Duke and Duchess of Bedford.

With the decision taken, the small group drifted back to where their family members were.

~~~~~~~/~~~~~~~

Jane, Anne, and Cassie were enjoying their ball immensely. All three received more requests to dance than spaces on their dance cards. Jane had the pleasure of dancing the second with Andrew, while Cassie danced with her brother. Anne danced the third with Jamey with much pleasure. Other than the small disturbance near the start of the ball—the reason for which none of the debutantes was aware—the ball was meeting and exceeding all of their expectations.

For Elizabeth and Mary, their first ball and dancing experience could not have been more pleasurable. After dancing the first with William, Elizabeth had the pleasure of his father's company for the second set. The three sets before dinner were taken by Andrew, Richard, and Jamey, respectively. The supper set was Lord Matlock's.

Mary enjoyed dancing with the dashing Captain Fitzwilliam in his regimentals. Even though she was young, she was not blind and rather perceptive. She had not missed the looks which passed between Cassie and Richard, and unless she was misreading the situation, they were a couple in the making. She danced the second with William, then Uncle Robert, Jamey —on whom she had a secret crush, notwithstanding the closeness between him and Anne—followed by Andrew, and then for the supper set she had the pleasure of her father for her partner.

Cassie and Jane each danced with their selected Fitzwilliam brother for the supper set, while Anne had the pleasure of Jamey as a partner for that set, so they had the pleasure of their partners' company for supper. When Jane and Andrew took the last two seats at the table with Lizzy and Lord Matlock, Mary and Bennet, Anne and Jamey, and Fanny and the Prince. Seeing there was no room for Cassie and Richard, Jane and Andrew volunteered to move, but were waved off by Cassie.

Cassie and Richard found a table close with another two couples, but neither of them had anyone sitting next to them. When Richard returned with their food, he noticed Cassie looked a little sad. "Cassie are you not enjoying your ball?" Richard asked softly.

"The ball is wonderful, Richard," Cassie replied. "I am just a little sad as I may have misread a situation."

"What is it?" Richard asked. "Is there aught I may do to alleviate the situation for you?"

"I had hoped so, but it does not seem so," Cassie averred.

"Please speak plainly, Cassie," Richard requested. "In the army an order is an order, there is no need to interpret it, unlike how people speak in society."

"Are you sure you want me to speak plainly?" Cassie verified.

"Yes, please. Mayhap if I understand what the issue is, I will be able to assist," Richard confirmed.

"Is there something wrong with me, Richard?" Cassie asked. The question was not one Richard was expecting, and he had to collect his thoughts.

"Why would you ask that?" Richard replied. "You are all that is good and proper, and any man who is lucky enough to win your hand will be most fortunate."

"Just not you, it seems," Cassie stated as a single tear rolled down her cheek.

"What has given you such an idea?" Richard asked with

alarm.

"You, Richard; you have given me that idea," Cassie answered quietly, her mouth close enough to his ear he could feel her warm breath. Seeing the quizzical look, Cassie expounded. "You used to be so warm and open with me, yet tonight I find you withdrawn. You did not ask me for a third set. I had started to believe you might return…" Cassie stopped herself just before she made a declaration.

"I have been such an idiot," Richard lamented. "In my inept attempt to protect your heart, all I have done is hurt you when it is the last thing in the world I want to do. Though I confess that until now I had forgotten the lesson from Aunt Anne's life and death."

"What do you mean, Richard?" Cassie asked, confused.

"Life is short; we should not defer to tomorrow that which we can do today," Richard explained. The other two couples stood and left the table after a perfunctory greeting, but Richard and Cassie made no move to stand. "I thought I had to first serve in the Dragoons and then, if you were still unattached, I would ask to court you."

Cassie lit up at his declaration. "Waiting for you would be no hardship, but what if you do not return from the continent?" Cassie asked the critical question.

"That is just it. As much as I like serving in the army, I love you far more, and it would be folly for me to risk my future with you," Richard stated. "It was as if I could hear Aunt Anne in my head telling me I was a fool for risking the chance of a future with you."

"You love me?" Cassie asked excitedly.

"Very much so, yes, I do," Richard confirmed.

"And I love you, Richard," Cassie declared.

"Lady Cassandra Carrington, will you accept a formal courtship with me?" Richard asked expectantly.

"Yes, Richard, a thousand times yes." Cassie felt like her heart was bursting with joy as it sped up to a rate she had never experienced before.

"Is there something you would like to ask me, Richard?" Lord Holder cut into the conversation as he approached the couple, who had just stood up.

"Mayhap at the ball is not best, Uncle Paul. May I meet with you in the morning?" Richard asked.

"I will see you in my study at nine," Lord Holder shook the hand of the man he had long suspected would be his son one day.

Lord and Lady Matlock had been watching their second son with bated breath. Even though he had Brookfield and its six thousand pounds clear per annum, Richard had insisted on joining the army. The Fitzwilliam parents were worried about their son's life once his regiment was moved to the Peninsula.

They knew from reports and speaking to the Prince how junior officers usually led the charge and just as often were cut down but had promised Richard not to interfere in his career in the army to make sure he never saw combat. As tempted as the Earl was, he had given Richard his word, so he did nothing once Richard's tentative orders to the continent were received.

"If I am reading this correctly, I think our son has just decided that life with a woman he loves is not worth risking by remaining in the army," Lady Elaine surmised.

"I think you have the right of it, my love," Lord Matlock replied. "As hard as it has been not to use my influence to keep him safe, I am glad I will never be tempted again. It seems both our sons have selected the women they wish to spend the rest of their lives with."

"Jane and Andrew may take longer to commence a courtship. I believe Thomas wants her to have a month or two of the little season after coming out before Andrew declares himself," Lady Elaine agreed. "I could not imagine two better daughters than Cassie and Jane. Reggie, have you noticed that Anne and Jamey were together for dinner? I believe he will dance the final set with our ward."

"Now that Catherine has finally changed for the better and does not obsess about rank and status any longer, how ironic that Anne seems to be considering becoming the next Viscountess Amberleigh," Lord Matlock opined. "When we return to Town, we need to talk to Anne and Frederick so we can decide what to do about Catherine."

"It seems removing her courtesy title may have been one of the best things for her," Lady Elaine agreed.

The rest of the ball went as smoothly; the only noticeable difference was that Cassie seemed to be floating among the clouds.

~~~~~~~/~~~~~~~

Lord Paul Carrington heard a knock on his study door. A glance at the clock on the mantle showed it was one minute before the hour. He smiled to himself, as it proved how keen Richard was to speak to him.

After the ball, he and his Edith had spoken to Cassie, who had let them know, in no uncertain terms, she was in love with Richard and did not need a season in London to know her heart. She shared the gist of their conversation, and that Richard had decided to resign his commission and take up his inheritance.

"Come," Lord Holder called out.

Richard—in full regimentals—marched into the study. Lord Holder found amusement in watching the nervous man who was normally so self-assured. "Good morning my Lord— Uncle Paul," Richard greeted.

"As tempting as it is, I will not sport with you, Richard," Lord Holder allowed. "My wife and I spoke to Cassie last night, so I have a few questions based on that discussion."

"Please ask anything you choose to," Richard averred as he sat in front of the oversized oak desk.

"You are resolved to leave the army?"

"Yes, I am."

"And you will not resent my daughter for giving up your military career for her?"

"No, as I did not give it up for her, but rather for myself," Richard stated evenly. "Cassie never once asked me to curtail my career for her. Last night, I was reminded of the lesson Aunt Anne taught all of us in her last month of life about the brevity of our time in the mortal world. I am not willing to trade the love of a good woman for glory on the field of battle."

"If that be the case, then I grant your request for a courtship. My condition is a minimum of two months. She will be eighteen in a fortnight, so her age is not an issue. If and when she grants you her hand, I ask for the same minimum length for the betrothal." Lord Holder stood and offered Richard his hand, which Richard shook vigorously.

When Richard and Lord Paul entered the breakfast parlour, Richard nodded his head to Cassie whose face was transformed by a gleeful smile. No one was surprised at the announcement; however, there had been no inkling of the one Lord Matlock made: "It is my great pleasure to tell you that Jamey has requested a courtship with Anne, and I have granted it with pleasure."

Everyone then looked to Bennet, who shook his head as he chuckled ruefully. "I have no announcement—yet."

Mary realised her crush on Jamey needed to be put out of her mind and wished both couples happy, sincerely, along with everyone else.

CHAPTER 19

"**S**arah, this is an unmitigated disaster!" Lord Jersey complained. "The Rhys-Davies are considering a divorce, claiming we misled them regarding the royals' support for us cutting our daughter."

"It seems your supposition was incorrect," Lady Jersey stated the obvious. "The other patronesses have requested I withdraw as a patroness of Almack's. How has it come to this?"

"We made a critical error; we cut Priscilla before asking for or receiving direction from the Crown," Lord Jersey said resignedly. "That miscalculation has turned us into social pariahs. The Prince's displeasure was not just simply directed toward us, it was publicly displayed!"

Lady Sarah was well aware it was her husband's decision and directive to cut her daughter, something she did not want to do. There was not much use arguing the point with him as he would dismiss what he found to be inconvenient. "If only Marie had not thought she had glimpsed Priscilla and made those remarks in his Royal Highness's hearing." Lady Jersey was sure her husband was upset at their behaviour being discovered rather than the pain his decision caused to their oldest daughter.

"Look at all it has cost us! A possible divorce for Marie, and Wes was refused when he requested a courtship with Huntington's daughter. Before this, Lord Huntington would have salivated at a connection to our family," Lord Jersey lamented.

"The only solution is to reach out to Priscilla." Lady Sarah knew her husband would read what she wrote so she would not be able to tell Priscilla she was sorry and never wanted to cut her. "We will have to appear to show deep contrition if there is to be any hope she will help smooth our way back into the good graces of the Royals and society at large," Lady Jersey stated in the vain hope her husband would allow her to write what she actually wanted to.

"Yes, Sarah; post her a letter. I must read it before you do so. I am sure she will be gratified for our condescension," Lord Jersey calculated.

Lady Sarah De Melville hated having to give her husband the letter before it was posted, but the situation they now found themselves in required it. He was too controlling to allow her to send a letter he did not approve of, so she sat down at her desk in the mistress's study and wrote her daughter a letter in a manner to ensure his approval.

The sad fact was Lord Jersey was only interested in what would look good to society, forgetting how he had cast out their daughter like yesterday's broadsheets. There were few nights Lady Sarah did not lament her separation from Priscilla. At least she did not cry every night anymore.

~~~~~~~/~~~~~~~

"You desired to talk to us, Jane?" Fanny asked as her eldest sat down in her father's study at Netherfield Park.

After her coming out, Jane had accompanied the Carringtons and Fitzwilliams to London for part of the little season. Unlike the coming out ball, none of her siblings—who were not yet out—had any expectation of accompanying her to Town.

During her two months in London, Jane and Andrew became very close. The attraction on both sides had grown to the point that both were sure the other's feelings were engaged as much as their own.

Before Jane left London, Andrew requested a courtship. Jane agreed—conditionally—she knew she could not tell him what the condition was, but she asked him to give her a few days at home before he presented himself.

As planned, Jane returned home in mid-November. Once she answered her siblings' questions about her time in Town— her sisters, as Tommy had no interest in who she danced with and at what ball—Jane asked for a private meeting with her parents.

"Andrew requested a courtship, and I want to give him an unconditional yes, but I am not sure I will be able to," Jane told her parents.

"Andrew is one of the best young men we know; why would you hesitate if your inclination is to accept his suit?" Bennet asked.

"I do not want to begin our courtship with a lie, even if it is one of omission," Jane revealed sadly. "I swore to keep the secret about Lizzy, and so I will, but that places me in a quandary."

"Jane, my darling sweet and thoughtful Jane." Fanny enfolded her daughter in a hug. "Richard was able to piece the facts together based on a small error by Uncle Freddy, so he told him the truth. He has not mentioned a word in three years, not even to his parents who know the truth. In fact, he requested that Richard join us in her protection and he has not yet wavered, and likely never will even after the world at large knows. I trust Andrew no less."

"Why was Andrew not informed when Richard was?" Jane asked pensively.

"Until now, there was no need. If Uncle Freddy had not had the slip of his tongue and Richard had not divined the truth, he would not have been told," Bennet informed Jane. "Now that Andrew is about to become your official suitor, he needs to know. Neither your mother nor I would expect you to be other than completely truthful with Andrew."

"Then when he arrives on the morrow, I am allowed to tell him the whole truth?" Jane verified.

"Yes, Janie. The whole truth," Fanny assured her in confirmation.

"Thank you, Mama and Papa." Jane was finally able to relax. Receiving her parents' permission to share everything with Andrew had been a boon and she felt extreme excitement at the idea of his impending arrival.

~~~~~~~/~~~~~~~

"Come in, Anne dear," her uncle Reggie welcomed her to his study.

"Is there a problem, Uncle Reggie?" Anne asked nervously. After her aunt's death, she was wary of being summoned for serious meetings.

"Nothing bad, Anne, we promise you," Aunt Elaine assured her niece who visibly relaxed.

"Anne, the reason we requested that you join us is because we would like to discuss your mother with you," Uncle Reggie informed her.

"What has Mrs. de Bourgh done now?" Anne asked testily. Since that day at Pemberley, Anne had put the woman who bore her out of her mind. Given all she was forced to suffer under her mother's control, nobody mentioned the woman in Anne's hearing.

"That is just it, she had undergone a complete transformation..." Anne's aunt and uncle shared all with her. If it had been weeks or months, Anne would have been sceptical, but it was going on three years, and Catherine de Bourgh was—if anything—more conscientious in her good deeds.

"She is unaware you are having her watched?" Anne asked, unwilling to credit her mother with anything that did not benefit her.

"Correct. In the last six months I increased her allowance to two hundred pounds a month. That is more than enough for her to move to a reasonably comfortable house with at least four or five servants, including a cook. The condition was she had to spend at least forty pounds a month on herself and her household. Every penny of the balance, she uses to better the lives of the people of Hunsford, Rosings Park's tenants, and citizens in the Westerham area," Uncle Reggie laid out. "There is no question she is sincere. She gives fifty pounds to the rector at the Hunsford church each month, to distribute as he sees fit to the needy."

"If only she had been like this when I had lived with

her," Anne stated wistfully as a few tears ran down her cheeks. What caused the sea change in her mother was not important. The only thing that mattered was she had changed, and this was the mother Anne de Bourgh desperately wanted to meet.

"From all the reports we have, she is nothing like she was. She has begun to educate herself and, believe it or not, she is using part of the extra money she had to spend on herself to hire masters, including a music master, who is teaching her the pianoforte," Aunt Elaine reported. "She has written to us requesting a chance to meet with the family to apologise in person."

"Why now and not two years ago?" Anne asked.

"She did not feel worthy, Anne," Uncle Reggie averred. "She felt crushing shame for the way she used to behave and did not know how to face us. After counselling from the clergyman at Hunsford, she has taken his advice and believes she has become the type of person worthy of begging our pardon."

"The same parson she used to command as if he were her personal servant is counselling her now?" Anne was flabbergasted.

"Yes, Anne, the very same one. I am waiting for Frederick's response before we go to Kent to see her, that is if you decide you want to come with us," Uncle Reggie's offer clarified that it was up to her alone.

"Before you jump to conclusions, she does not want her courtesy title back," Aunt Elaine stated. "Your mother has at last realised the value of character and not a title. The days of her lectures on the maintenance of the distinction of rank are forever gone."

"When do we depart for Kent?" Anne asked. She was starting to feel excited about seeing her mother—and thinking of her as a mother again.

"We will depart two days hence," Uncle Reggie informed his niece.

~~~~~~~/~~~~~~~

"Welcome, Andrew," Jane stated excitedly. She had missed Andrew greatly, even though it was but three days since they had seen one another in Town. As it was wont to do, her heartbeat sped up when Andrew was near.

"Thank you, Jane," Andrew bowed to the Bennets. "Uncle Thomas, Aunt Fanny, it is good to see you again."

"If I were a wagering man, I would say it is not us you are here to see—at least not yet." Bennet's quip caused Andrew's colour to darken.

"Papa, behave yourself," Jane gave her father a playful tap on the shoulder. "May we use your study?"

"You may, as long as the door remains partially open and a maid or footman is sitting in the hall nearby—out of earshot," Bennet granted.

Jane arranged the chairs so they were facing one another and indicated one for Andrew to sit in while she took the one opposite him. "This must be serious, Jane," Andrew tried to lighten the mood. He had been troubled when Jane was not willing to answer hm other than conditionally; he was worried he had overestimated her feelings for him.

"Andrew, I did not want us to start our courtship with any secrets between us." Jane handed Andrew the portrait her mother had shown her when she was told about Lizzy's true parentage.

"Why have you handed me a painting of Lizzy?" Andrew asked in confusion.

"That is just it. The painting is of the late Lady Priscilla, Uncle Freddy's late ex-wife." Jane stated evenly.

"Jane?" Andrew went still. The conclusion he jumped to seemed too remarkable to be true, but his Jane had been guarded, and their Lizzy looked exactly like the woman whose picture he held in his hand.

Jane told Andrew the story of the birth of the two babies in 1790 and what had occurred since. When she was done, Andrew was slack jawed. "I swore to my parents I would not share the story with anyone; I needed their permission to tell you. I want nothing more than to be courted by you, Andrew, but I refused to enter into a courtship with any secrets between us."

"My parents and Richard know?" he asked carefully. Jane nodded. "You say Richard picked up...I remember! It was not long after Aunt Anne passed away, Uncle Freddy stopped himself from saying something. William, Jamey, and I left with Uncle Paul and Uncle Robert, but Richard remained with Uncle Freddy, Uncle Thomas, and my father." Andrew puzzled out.

"Yes, that was when Richard discovered the truth," Jane confirmed. "It is less than two years until Lizzy will be told. I am not sure how she will react to being kept in the dark for eighteen years."

"William does not know, does he?" Andrew verified.

"No, he does not. In his case, it is a good thing," Jane opined.

"How so?" Andrew asked.

"Because his feelings for Lizzy developed before he knew she is a princess and one of the wealthiest women in the realm," Jane explained.

"I suppose...wait, did you say you want to accept a courtship with me?" The realisation hit Andrew like the kick from a horse.

"Yes, Andrew, I most certainly do accept your offer for a courtship for I love you already. If you need a courtship, then so be it but..." Jane never finished what she was going to say as Andrew pulled her into an embrace. He was about to kiss her when he remembered he had missed a critical step and dropped to one knee.

"Jane, I am in love with you too, and have been for some time now. Rather than a long flowery speech, will you accept my hand in marriage as you are my one and only love?" Andrew asked hopefully as he held Jane's hands.

"Yes, Andrew, Yes, yes, yes, YES!" Jane responded effusively.

Andrew stood and drew Jane into his arms again. She looked up at him, the marked difference between this time and the ones before when her heart would speed up was shocking, now it was racing as he closed the distance between them until Jane felt his lips on her own, which felt right, so very right.

The first kiss was nice, but then Andrew deepened his kisses, and Jane was thankful her arms had snaked around his neck as she went weak at the knees from the pleasure.

Neither one of the newly betrothed couple wanted to stop the moment they were sharing, but they knew they must. After one last lingering kiss, by silent mutual agreement they both took a step back.

"Does this mean the revelation about Lizzy does not change anything between us?" Jane teased her love.

"Not in the least, just like it changed nothing for you with the way you see her as a sister," Andrew stated firmly. "She is not the one to whom I am betrothed." Andrew waggled his eyebrows. "I think I need to talk to your father."

"Wait here; I will ask Papa to join you." Jane kissed her betrothed's cheek and was gone.

Not many minutes later, Bennet joined him in the study and took a seat behind his desk. "I presume you have a question for me, Andrew?"

"I do, Mr. Bennet, Uncle Thomas," Andrew began. "Jane did me the greatest honour in accepting my hand in marriage, so I now request your consent and blessing to marry her."

"I thought you were requesting a courtship," Bennet asked with raised eyebrows.

"So did I, until she informed me that a courtship was superfluous," Andrew informed Bennet.

"Rather than run afoul of my eldest, you have both, Son. Welcome to the family." Bennet rose and offered his soon-to-be son his hand and the two shook hands heartily.

~~~~~~~/~~~~~~~

William Collins had graduated the seminary and taken orders. He could not understand why no one at any of the livings he applied for would offer him more than a trial curacy, for he felt he was better than a curate.

His dearly departed father, who had passed away two years previously, had always told him this, which bolstered his belief that it was true. He intended to try one more parish, as he had read a notice that Longbourn church was interviewing clergymen to fill a vacancy upcoming after the incumbent who held the living retired.

He debated for some time, as the living was in the parish attached to the estate that his father told him had been stolen by the Bennets when they had a son. In the end, two things drove his decision to apply for the position. First was his need for a position and second, since his father's death he had started to realise that many of the elder Collins's pronouncements were less than factual. With the resolve taken, Collins started the journey from Loughborough, where he failed to win a position. He finally realised he would have to start with a curacy; he could not expect to be awarded a living until he proved himself.

~~~~~~~/~~~~~~~

Jane looked at her beloved Andrew when he and her father entered the drawing room. Andrew was grinning from ear to ear, which told Jane his petition had been granted. Bennet allowed them a moment to communicate silently while he looked at his wife and conveyed the situation the same manner. He asked Jane to join him and announced, "It is my pleasure to tell you Andrew has requested Jane's hand in marriage, and she replied in the affirmative. We congratulate both of you as we know you will be happy together."

"I know you could not be such a wonderful person for nothing, Jane," Fanny told her as she enfolded her daughter in arms and kissed her on each of her cheeks.

"At last, I will not be the only brother," Tommy exclaimed.

"You could not have chosen a better woman for your betrothed," Elizabeth told Andrew as she hugged him. He was mobbed by Mary, Kitty, and Lydia as soon as Elizabeth moved aside.

"Jane, you are gifting us with such a good and honourable new brother," Elizabeth told Jane as the sisters hugged one another tightly.

"Have you two decided on a date for your wedding yet?" Fanny asked.

"That is not a discussion we have had yet," Jane acknowledged.

"On the morrow, when I return to Town, I will inform my parents of our happy news," Andrew stated. "We are all headed into Kent soon thereafter. When we return to London, if you are ready for some guests, Aunt Fanny, we will join you here the day after we return to Town."

"You should know by now you and your family are welcome any time we are in residence, and I think from now on you need to call me Mother Fanny," Fanny told her daughter's betrothed.

"Bennet is good for me," Bennet clarified before anyone suggested a different appellation for Andrew to use for him.

"Thomas," Fanny got her husband's attention softly, "will you join me in the study, please?" Bennet noticed the letter in his wife's hand.

"Who is it from, Fanny?" Bennet asked after he closed the door to the study, presuming the recent scene and the expected fallout had finally come to pass.

"It is from Priscilla's parents, her mother to be exact," Fanny revealed.

"We guessed that they would try to contact her after their names were dragged through the mud after Holder Heights," Bennet stated.

"You are correct, Husband," Fanny averred, "and we all agreed how to treat the self-serving letter when it came."

"You will do as we all agreed and send it back?" Bennet verified.

"Absolutely yes," Fanny replied emphatically. Fanny called for the butler and instructed him to have the offending missive returned to whence it came.

~~~~~~~/~~~~~~~

The butler at Jersey House delivered the post and placed it on the master's desk, as he did every day. When Lord Jersey sat down, the first letter he spied was the one his wife wrote to their daughter, returned unopened.

Getting out of this trouble was not going to be as simple as a letter to their eldest daughter after no contact in sixteen years. The Earl went to find his wife so they could decide on a solution to their problem, as the Duke of Bedford was due to call on the morrow. Lord Jersey had hoped to receive a warm and welcoming reply from Priscilla before then. It seemed he had miscalculated again.

CHAPTER 20

"Thomas, there is a possibility for which we must be prepared," Fanny stated as she entered the study.

"What might that be, Fanny?" Bennet asked as he replaced his quill in the holder.

"Priscilla's parents have been ostracised, and their oldest living daughter is facing a possible divorce because they told the husband's family the royals supported them without ascertaining the truth of the matter first," Fanny said thoughtfully. "I think we need to be ready for them to arrive at Netherfield Park uninvited."

"I think you are correct, Fanny," Bennet responded. "From today onward, there will be two of our footmen guards posted at the entrance to the drive. If the De Melvilles dare show their faces here, they will be turned away before being allowed onto the estate."

"If only they had acted as Priscilla's parents and not been so worried about what society would think, they could have been part of Lizzy's life these many years," Fanny lamented. "They will find out about Lizzy in less than two years now."

"There is little to be done when what people may or may not think is more important than the love of your own flesh and blood," Bennet stated sadly.

As soon as his wife departed, Bennet summoned Biggs and instructed that the gate be manned by two men at all times. He was very clear in telling his man that no matter how much they blustered and demanded, the De Melvilles—if they arrived—were not to be allowed on the estate under any circumstances.

~~~~~~~/~~~~~~~

'How is it I have begun to have tender feelings for William?' Elizabeth asked herself. Only a few months away from turning seventeen, Elizabeth was trying to puzzle out the conundrum. In the last few months, especially since opening Jane's coming out ball with him, feelings she never expected to have for William had developed.

Elizabeth, who knew she could talk to her mother or Jane about anything, decided to keep the revelation to herself—for now. Jane was busy preparing for her wedding—or at least choosing a date for the wedding, and her mother was preparing for friends and family who would arrive in early December —William among them.

Elizabeth had little more than a year before her own coming out, and William was looking forward to spending time with the Bennets for Easter next year, soon after her seventeenth birthday. The big question to which she needed to find an answer—and she did not know how to go about finding that answer—was did he see her as more than an adopted cousin?

She could not understand her mixed feelings about William coming to Netherfield. On the one hand, she could not wait to see him; on the other hand, she was very nervous at the idea he would soon be there.

The fact that he never talked down to her, respected her opinions, and debated with her as an equal were incredibly attractive traits which drew Elizabeth to William. That he was one of the most handsome men of her acquaintance did not hurt at all. Of late, there were times when Elizabeth had found her breath speeding up and becoming tongue tied in his presence—something which was most disconcerting to her—and she did not know how to resolve all of the feelings she was experiencing.

She resolved to talk to Jane she and Andrew had selected a date for their wedding. Elizabeth knew she needed to talk to her mother at some point, but on this subject she preferred to talk to Jane first.

~~~~~~~/~~~~~~~

When Andrew arrived at Matlock House, his father was at White's. Andrew found his mother in the master suite sitting room and kept his facial expression neutral. "I assume that Thomas consented to your courting Jane?" she asked, her smile growing wider as she saw him attempt to school his features.

"When I arrived, Jane asked to talk to me. Uncle Thomas allowed us to use his study, and after telling me she did not want any secrets between us, she told me what my little brother has known and had to keep secret this last three years," Andrew informed his mother.

"So, you know about Lizzy," Lady Elaine stated. "Unlike the vow required of Richard when he unravelled the truth, the time for you to guard the secret is much shorter."

"Once I told Jane it made no difference in how I felt about her, I requested a courtship," Andrew related, and then he paused as his mother looked at him questioningly. "But Jane stated she did not want a courtship." Andrew affected a saddened look.

"Oh Andrew, I am so sorry," Lady Elaine said sympathetically. "We all believed she was in love with you."

"That she is, Mother," Andrew relayed joyously. "If you had allowed me to finish, I would have told you she said because she loves me, a courtship was not needed. I am officially betrothed to Jane."

"Andrew!" Lady Elaine swatted her eldest playfully. "How could you make it sound like she had rejected your suit. You are not too big for me to bend you over my knee, you know."

"What has our eldest done now, Elaine?" Lord Matlock asked as he entered the sitting room.

"He was making sport of his mother," Lady Elaine reported. "All is well; Jane accepted a proposal of marriage; your son is betrothed, Reggie."

"Congratulations, my boy, you could not have chosen better," the Earl stated happily, then gave his son a bear hug.

"Hello Andrew," Anne greeted her cousin as she joined them in the sitting room. "You look rather pleased with yourself. Jane is well?"

"She is well, and as I am betrothed to your good friend; I have many reasons to be pleased," Andrew informed Anne.

"I wish you and Jane happy, Andrew," Anne gushed joyfully, "I do not know if you are good enough for my Jane; you will just have to try to be." Anne smiled as she teased her cousin. "Will you join us when we travel into Kent on the morrow, or do you have a ring to deliver to Netherfield Park?"

"The Bennets know I am joining you, so they are not expecting me to return until we return from Kent," Andrew relayed to his family. "When do Uncle Robert, William, and Gigi arrive?"

"Robert and Gigi plan to collect William from his friend's estate and then journey to London," Lady Elaine stated. "They should be here well before we are to make for Netherfield Park for the holiday."

"It will be good to see the Darcys. How does Richard's courtship of Cassie progress?" Andrew asked.

"He is at Holder House as we speak," Anne reported. "From what I have observed, the courtship seems to be proceeding anon."

"And your courtship with Jamey, Anne?" Andrew asked. Anne blushed deeply as her cousin asked about the man she loved. "You deserve to be happy, and I have reservations on his being good enough." He winked at her.

"Things are progressing." Anne allowed. The truth was their courtship was nearing its natural conclusion, but until Jamey spoke, Anne would not be willing to state more than she had.

~~~~~~~/~~~~~~~

George Wickham was sitting in his small attic room of the boarding house on Edward Street. After three years on his own, he finally understood the rectitude of his father's words about having to earn one's way and nothing being given to one because they thought it was their due.

He considered his animosity towards the Darcys and was able to admit they had never done anything to him. In fact, as painful as it was to accept, everything bad in his life was self-inflicted.

It was his behaviour alone which caused him to be sent away from Pemberley. He felt shame as he remembered the way he used to leer at the blond while promising himself she would be his, never once considering her preferences or that she might not have desired a connection with him. He owned that the chances of her wanting the connection were less than naught. One of many reasons why she might reject him was he had never behaved in an honourable fashion.

If he had not gotten in his own way, he would have received an education and might have gone into the church or the law. Was it too late for him to change the direction of his life? What had his father said about consequences? George remembered the words: *There are always consequences, good or bad.* His father had given him the key to his future, and George realised he had rebuffed it without consideration.

After his epiphany, he decided realisation was not enough; he needed to back up his thoughts and words with actions. He intended to do something to prove to his father he had finally learnt his lesson, that he was more than his past mistakes. George knew he would have to apologise to Mr. Darcy for trying to use his name, and regardless of how long it took him to do so, he needed to repay every farthing of the debts he had accumulated in that gentleman's name.

The first step he decided to take was to save his wages rather than follow his late mother's folly and throw his money away on games of chance that he invariably lost. He also needed to find a job—a good job—better than the one he had at the boarding house, which was little more than a brothel.

The next day, George was sent to Gracechurch Street by Mrs. Younge to acquire a bolt of fabric needed to make new dresses for some of the girls who plied their profession at the house.

When George arrived at Gardiner and Associates, he saw a sign proclaiming the business was looking for a new clerk. "Who do I see to apply for the position?" He asked one of the men in the warehouse. The man pointed him to the offices raised above the sales floor.

"Please wait here," a man requested. After a few minutes, the man returned. "Mr. Gardiner will see you now."

"Mr. Wickham, how is it you have no characters?" Gardiner asked pointedly after the applicant sat in the chair indicated.

"Until this point, Sir," George stated evenly, "I did not deserve any…" With brutal honesty, George Wickham told Mr. Gardiner all. He did not gloss over his theft from the carpenter in York, or the use of the Darcy's name in Staffordshire. He admitted very last detail, as if he were in a confessional, though he was taking a huge chance and half suspected that Mr. Gardiner would have him thrown out the door. When his recitation was completed, George sat in silence waiting for Mr. Gardiner to pronounce his fate. "It could not have been easy for you to admit to so many *past* failings, Mr. Wickham," Gardiner stated.

"No, Sir, it was not," George owned. "However, I am determined to walk an honourable path; if by some small miracle you employ me, I could not have you know anything less than the unvarnished and complete truth about me."

"You say you did not receive a formal education, but you have always had an aptitude for numbers?" Gardiner verified. George allowed it was so. "As Christians, it is our duty to forgive and to allow a man to prove he can change. As a businessman, if you apply those principles blindly, you do so at your own peril."

George was sure he was about to be shown the door, but at least Mr. Gardiner was being gracious about it and not having him thrown out—yet. "I understand, Sir. I would not employ me either had I heard what I revealed to you. I do thank you for your time," George made to stand.

"If you will allow me to finish what I was about to say, Mr. Wickham." Gardiner looked at the chair and George sat again. "I am willing to take a chance on you. You will begin in a training position where you will have no direct contact with any money. Forgiveness is between you, God, your father, and it seems Mr. Darcy. I cannot grant you absolution and based on your past, trust must be earned."

"Anything you require of me, I will do." George could not believe the man was willing to give him an opportunity to prove himself worthy.

"In the spirit of honesty, I must tell you I am well acquainted with Mr. Robert Darcy," Gardiner revealed. "Both in business and as a very close friend of my sister's and brother-in-law's family. I will see him when my family and I spend Christmastide with our relatives in Hertfordshire. At this point, I will not mention you to him unless you break my trust, then I will be sure to talk to him. Conversely, if you prove yourself over time, I will be very happy to inform him, and by extension, your father will also be aware of the fact," Gardiner shared with young Wickham.

"I thank you from the bottom of my heart, Mr. Gardiner." George knew this was his one and only chance and he would do nothing to spoil it.

"I own a house across from the warehouse where our single male employees can live if they choose to. You will be paid the minimum of five pounds a month. If you choose to avail yourself of room and board, one pound per month will be deducted to cover your rent and meals," Gardiner explained.

George Wickham accepted a room at the employee house. It was not in the attic like the one at Edward Street and the bedchamber was much larger than he had lived in since he left his father's house. It was with glee he returned to Edward street for the last time, dropped off the bolt of sprigged muslin, and collected his meagre belongings. Mrs. Younge paid him the few shillings of outstanding wages she said he was owed. He knew she shorted him, but he was so happy to depart, he did so without complaint.

He was determined his father would finally have a son worthy of the Wickham name.

~~~~~~~/~~~~~~~

After meeting with Rosings Park's steward, Lord Matlock sent his sons to invite their aunt to meet with the family. The man at her cottage told Andrew and Richard that Mrs. de Bourgh was not home and were directed to the school his mistress had established, used some of her monthly funds.

The school was a large cottage which had been converted for teaching. In one room they found children being taught sums, and in the other their aunt was teaching children their letters.

She was dressed in the same style of dress as the other ladies the brothers had seen in Hunsford. If they did not know their aunt's profile so well, they would have thought they were hallucinating. The thing that struck them more than anything else was the pure contentment that seemed to radiate from their aunt.

Rather than disturb the class, Andrew and Richard stood in the doorway until the lesson was complete and were surprised anew when most of the children hugged their teacher —the hugs were received and returned with genuine warmth —before leaving the classroom. It was then then Catherine noticed her nephews.

"Andrew, Richard!" she exclaimed with joy. "I had no idea you would be in Hunsford today. How are my family, and how is Anne?"

"We are here to invite you to a meeting at Rosings Park, Aunt Catherine," Andrew informed his aunt.

"As long as you are sure I will be welcome, I will accompany you there," Catherine accepted. Her nephews assured their aunt she would be welcomed with open arms.

A little under an hour later, the carriage halted under the portico at the manor house. Mrs. de Bourgh wore the same

SHANA GRANDERSON A LADY

dress she had worn while teaching. She had a shawl around her shoulders, and other than a little cross her late grandmother had given her on her fifth birthday, she wore no jewellery even though her personal jewellery had been restored to her almost a year past.

The brothers noticed she was hesitant as she was shown into the drawing room—the one she used to rule over from her raised throne-like chair. It did not escape her notice that the house had been redecorated and the décor looked similar to that in the Fitzwilliam and Darcy houses—understated elegance with no gaudy or ostentatious displays.

"Welcome, Mother," Anne said warmly.

"Anne?" Catherine froze as she saw the pretty woman who stood before her. Anne was the picture of health and looked much like Catherine had around the same age, except Anne was happy rather than looking to find fault as her mother had been prone to do.

"Hello, Catherine," her brother welcomed her.

"Reggie and Elaine," Catherine acknowledged her brother and sister, but her eyes were locked on the commanding presence of her daughter. She thought after that day and her disgusting behaviour at Pemberley she would never see Anne again. Catherine's overwhelming gratitude caused tears to flow freely down her cheeks. "Anne, you look wonderful; I never dared to hope you would allow me in your company again."

"As you used to be, Mother," Anne stated as she approached her weeping mother, "no, I would not have wanted to know you. However, the lady you have become, the one that sees to the needs of others to the exclusion of her own needs, the lady who is happy among the people of Hunsford and Westerham and does not try and exert her authority over them, that mother is the one who I would very much like to come to know."

"You will forgive me?" Catherine asked between sobs.

"How could I not?" Anne enfolded her mother in a hug.

"Many would have become bitter and resentful, refused to see the error of their ways. You have made many more changes than most are forced to make, and I—no, the whole family—want to get know Mrs. Catherine de Bourgh."

"My brother Darcy would welcome me back into his company, William and Georgiana too?" Catherine asked in wonder.

"You are not the only one who is able to change, Cathy," her brother informed his sister. She felt warmth and gratitude when Reggie used the name he used to call her as a little girl for the first time in almost forty years.

"Cathy, would you like me to ask the Prince to restore your courtesy title?" Lord Reggie asked.

"No, Brother," Catherine replied emphatically. "That title used to encompass my identity and led to my wrongheaded ideas about the distinction of rank. In the last three years without it—without all the finery I used to have—I have been happier than I have since I was a little girl, before I allowed jealousy to rule me. Now I choose to see my self-worth as being tied to how I behave and the good deeds I try to do rather than title or rank. I never want to go back to how I was."

"From what we saw at the school, Aunt Catherine," Andrew interjected, "there is no possibility of your returning to who you used to be, with or without the honorific. The pleasure of what you were doing was radiating from your whole expression as you taught the children."

"Mother, we want you to be part of our lives again," Anne told Catherine as she held her hands, "and I have news. I am being courted by Jamey Carrington, and Richard will be my brother as he is courting Cassie."

"Do not forget me," Andrew added, "I am betrothed to a wonderful woman, Miss Jane Bennet."

"Anne, if you are happy with him, then I am happy for you." No one missed that there were no effusions about Anne becoming a future countess or talk of the Carrington wealth.

"Thank you, Mother," Anne gushed, "we love one another."

"As much as I want to be with all of you, I cannot just leave all of my responsibilities in the area," Catherine informed her relatives, in yet another confirmation of the changes which she had undergone.

"We have a solution, Catherine," Lady Elaine informed her sister. "You remember Mrs. Jenkinson?" Lady Elaine motioned for the aforementioned lady to come forward as Catherine nodded. "As Anne will have you with her until she marries, Mrs. Jenkinson will take over here. She will have funds at her disposal to continue all of your good works here and will teach the classes you would normally teach."

"Are you saying I am to return to the bosom of my family?" Catherine asked with trepidation. She received nods from all five family members looking at her. "Even after all of my atrocious behaviour?"

"Cathy," Lord Reggie took his sisters hands from his niece, "none of us can change what we did in the past. We can, as you have done over the last three years, change the present and the future. I leave it to you to make your amends to others, but we *all* know that the steps you have taken have changed your life—and the lives of those around you—for the positive."

Mrs. Catherine de Bourgh was finally able to accept that her family wanted her as a part of it again, and more importantly, that her daughter wanted her as a mother.

CHAPTER 21

Andrew arrived at Netherfield Park before the midday meal, and after greeting the family and Uncle Freddy, he answered Tommy's many questions—those expected from a boy of ten years—about his ride and how his horse fared. Andrew then requested a little time with Jane.

"It was not the same without you, Jane," Andrew told her as they sat in the east parlour with Elizabeth and Mary as chaperones. "You will want to get married from Netherfield Park, will you not?"

"The wedding breakfast will be here, but as we still attend the church at Longbourn, it is my choice to marry from there and not from St. Alfred's in Meryton," Jane related to her betrothed.

"That is completely understandable," Andrew acknowledged. "Please tell me you do not require a lengthy betrothal."

"While you were away, I spoke to my mother," Jane informed him. "She has left it up to us, as long as for propriety's sake the date is one month or more from the date of our betrothal." Jane paused. "Mary dear, will you retrieve the calendar on Papa's desk for us?"

Mary returned and handed the calendar to Jane. "The fifteenth day of December would be good, would it not?" Andrew suggested after the two examined the month of December. "It is a Monday."

"Yes, the fifteenth will suit, and it is just past a month, so Mama will have no complaint," Jane enthused. It made her betrothal that much more real now they had selected a date. "Let us inform my parents and the rest of the family. Elizabeth and

Mary followed their sister and soon-to-be brother to the drawing room.

~~~~~~~/~~~~~~~

"This is my daughter's estate! Do you know who I am?" Lord Jersey spat out in frustration.

Things had grown so bad socially for the De Melvilles that the Earl decided the only way out of their problem was to humble themselves before their eldest daughter and beg her assistance in alleviating the situation they now found themselves in.

His wife secretly prayed they would be allowed to see Priscilla. She would tell her daughter the truth, that she never wanted what her husband had forced on her. She knew it would engender her husband's wrath, but she was willing to take that chance if she were able to see her daughter.

Their coach was halted at the gates of Priscilla's estate, and no matter how much he blustered, the men guarding the gates would not allow them to pass. The Earl did not notice a groom riding swiftly down the drive from the gates towards the house.

Andrew and the three eldest Bennet sisters had just entered the drawing room when Mr. Nichols entered and handed his master a note, which Bennet handed to the Prince. "I think I need to see these people," Frederick stated as he gave the note to Fanny. Both Bennet parents nodded their agreement, and Frederick followed Mr. Nichols out of the drawing room.

"Is there a problem, Mama and Papa?" Elizabeth asked. "Uncle Freddy did not look happy."

"There are some people who are connected with Uncle Freddy demanding entrance to the estate," Bennet stated, not one word of which was false. "Your uncle is going to inform them they are not welcome and why."

Elizabeth would have preferred to know who the people were and why they were not welcome, but she decided if her father and mother desired to share more information, they would in their own time. Her mind returned to more pleasant thoughts as William would arrive in a fortnight, and there was now a wedding to look forward to before Christmas.

~~~~~~~/~~~~~~~

Lord and Lady Jersey saw a coach approaching and the last man the Earl wanted to see at that moment stepped out of it. "Your Royal Highness," Lord Jersey intoned as both he and his wife inclined their heads to the Prince.

"Lord and Lady Jersey," the Prince drawled. "What an unpleasant surprise to see you here at Netherfield Park. After the way you have treated your daughter, what possible excuse could you have made which caused you to believe you could gain admittance here?" The Prince did not notice the look of sorrow on the Countess's face as he was looking at the Earl.

"We did what we did in support of the Crown," Lord Jersey insisted.

"What stuff and nonsense," the Prince bit back, and both De Melvilles were taken back at the vehemence in his response. "You did what you *thought* would gain you notice from my family, without asking what we desired." There was no mistaking his disdain.

"How could we not support you when his Royal Majesty found Priscilla too low to be your wife," Lord Jersey tried.

"Are you senseless, Jersey?" the Prince shot back. "My father found my ex-wife wholly appropriate to be my wife. The *only* reason he did what he did was for an alliance with Prussia, and now that we are at war that alliance has become invaluable. The King was *never* happy with what he had to do. All of Priscilla's true friends have asked the same question: How could a parent who loved their child in the smallest measure cut ties with said child so wholly and without remorse?" The Prince was looking directly at the Earl and missed the look of great sorrow on the Countess's face. She shrunk back into the corner of the coach and released the tears which had been threatening to fall since they arrived at Netherfield Park.

"We are here now to reconcile with Priscilla," Lord Jersey understated the truth. Neither the Earl nor the Prince saw Lady

Jersey pressed into the corner of the coach, crying quietly. She would not see her daughter and the Prince was too incensed to listen to her.

"If I were you, I would be wary of lying to the person second in line to the throne. You are here because you are reaping the rewards of what you have sown. You would not have come had you not been rejected by society." The Earl blanched at the Prince's accurate portrayal of his reason for coming. The Countess hung her head in sadness. "This I can guarantee you; Priscilla will *never* be in your company again. Now turn your carriage around and be gone. If you ever attempt to come here without explicit invitation, I will strenuously recommend to the King that he strip you of your title and return any land awarded to the earldom back to the Crown." Frederick excoriated the Earl and Countess happily, as he had wanted to do since he had heard of them cutting all connection with his beloved. The Earl had no doubt the King would act on the Prince's recommendation.

"I would write to my daughter again, but the last letter was returned unopened," Lady Jersey stated softly. The Prince did not look at her right away so he missed the look of pure anguish on the lady's face.

"You mean the first letter you have posted her in sixteen years? If you had reached out to your daughter before it was for selfish reasons, your reception here would have been vastly different," the Prince informed the couple.

'*On more than one occasion I tried, but my husband consigned my letters to the fire. He has me watched so I am not able to contact my daughter,*' Lady Sarah told herself. How she wished the Prince were in a mood to listen to her.

Knowing that any further attempts to contact his daughter would cost them their titles—and by extension their children's—the Earl departed with his tail between his legs. His wife sat in silence, refusing to look at her husband and her heart breaking all over again. She had been so close to her beloved daughter, and yet so far.

~~~~~~~/~~~~~~~

The Prince returned to the drawing room an hour later, and when Bennet and Fanny looked at him in question, he gave a curt nod of his head and informed them the unwanted guests had been sent on their way.

"While you were away, Jane and Andrew informed us they will marry on the fifteenth day of December." Fanny related.

"Please say you will attend, Uncle Freddy," Jane beseeched.

"If I have any conflicts, I will move them, so yes, Janie, I will not miss your wedding unless my father issues a royal decree in opposition to my intent," the Prince teased his adopted niece.

"Will we ever see any of the palaces?" Tommy asked enthusiastically.

"I have a feeling that will happen in the next year or two," Frederick responded to his godson.

"Would it not be grand to see a palace and meet the royal family?" Elizabeth enthused.

"I suppose it would," Jane said as her parents, Uncle Freddy, and Andrew looked anywhere except at Elizabeth.

"Aunt Catherine will be with us for Christmastide," Andrew reported to change the subject. He informed them of the meeting in Kent and the pleasure his aunt took from the simple things in life now.

"It will be good to see how she has changed, as I only remember the imperious lady we met soon after Aunt Anne passed away," Elizabeth stated.

"As she is your aunt, she will be more than welcome here," Fanny stated generously.

When there was a lull in the conversation, Elizabeth approached Jane. "Jane, may I talk you in private?" Elizabeth asked.

Worried Lizzy suspected something of her true parentage, Jane looked to her betrothed. "Will you join us?" Then Jane turned back to Elizabeth, "Do you object to Andrew being with me?

"No, I suppose not," Elizabeth averred.

The three returned to the same parlour they had been in earlier. "Lizzy, if I judge I must speak to Mama and, or Papa, regarding what we speak about here, you know I must, do you not?" Jane asked forthrightly. Elizabeth nodded, because she knew it was only true concern which would cause Jane to break the request of a confidence.

Elizabeth sat for a minute trying to marshal her thoughts. "How do you know if your affections are returned?" Elizabeth opened.

"Who do you hold in high regard, Lizzy?" Jane asked, though she suspected who it was.

Elizabeth blushed as she looked at Andrew. He was William's cousin and she wanted to make sure he would not relate anything she said to William. Andrew made a move to leave the ladies alone, but Elizabeth shook her head. "Will you both swear, unless I say something which you feel Mama and Papa need to know, that you will not mention a word of this to anyone else?"

"You have my word, Lizzy," Jane vowed.

"And mine, besides; I would not tell William anything as it would just puff up his ego," Andrew replied.

"How did you know it is William?" Elizabeth asked in alarm.

"Until this instant, I only suspected; you just confirmed my suspicions, little sister-to-be," Andrew revealed.

"Do you have tender feelings for William?" Jane asked.

Elizabeth blushed a deep red and nodded her head. "I believe I am falling in love with him. How will I know if he sees me as more than a friend and cousin? How did you and Andrew know each loved the other?"

"Lizzy, let me answer your question with a question," Jane responded. "When the two of you are in company at the same time, who do each of you spend the most time with?"

"Each other I suppose," Elizabeth stated as she thought back over the last number of years. "But that is just because we both like books and debating."

"And you are the only one available?" Andrew prompted.

Yes—no—I suppose I am not," Elizabeth realised. "Are you saying William chooses to spend time with me because he may have tender feelings for me?"

"There is no way to know for sure, until and unless he declares himself, which he will not do until after you come out," Jane opined. "Until then, as long as you both enjoy one another's company, keep doing what you have been doing. A deep friendship is a good basis for a future romantic relationship."

"Jane has the right of it, Lizzy," Andrew agreed. "William can be very hard to read sometimes, but there is no mistaking the pleasure he takes in spending time with you."

"Thank you both; I find your advice both useful and comforting," Elizabeth stated appreciatively.

"If Mama asks why you wanted to talk to me privately, may I inform her?" Jane asked.

"Yes, you may, as I will not ask you to tell Mama an untruth on my behalf," Elizabeth averred.

~~~~~~~/~~~~~~~

In London, Cassie accepted Richard's proposal of marriage. He was not sure if he could share the secret he had known for the last three years with her. When he asked his parents, they advised him to talk to Uncle Freddy and the Bennet parents when he went to Netherfield Park.

Lord and Lady Matlock felt they needed to have a serious talk with the three. They realised that the wider the circle of those who knew the truth of Lizzy's parentage became, the more likely that Elizabeth could discover her true heritage by chance. It would be up to Elizabeth's parents—adopted and birthfather—to make the final decision, but in their opinion, it was time to tell Elizabeth the truth.

Anne was visiting Holder House with her mother . Anne missed Mrs. Jenkinson remained in Kent to take over the work

Mrs. de Bourgh had been doing, but she knew from their correspondence the lady felt very fulfilled after taking over for Catherine.

Each day Anne spent with her mother, the closer the two became as more of her mother's new character was revealed. The first visit with the Carringtons after their return from Kent with Mrs. de Bourgh left the Carringtons amazed. They had heard about the changes to Anne's mother, but to see them in person was a wonder to behold.

The party that travelled to Holder House returned and Jamey was with them. Out of respect for her mother, Jamey asked if she could be included in the meeting in the Earl's study. He then explained he had requested Anne's hand in marriage, and that she had granted him his dearest wish.

It was a matter of minutes to receive Anne's uncle's hearty permission and blessing, wholeheartedly echoed by Mrs. de Bourgh who, after hugging her future son, wished him happy and admonished him to make her daughter happy all the days of his life.

Lord Reginald Fitzwilliam had the pleasure of announcing his niece's betrothal to his wife and younger son. Thoughts of the upcoming conversation at Netherfield Park were deferred as the Earl and Countess of Matlock revelled in both of their sons and niece finding estimable people to marry that each loved deeply.

CHAPTER 22

A few days before the family was to arrive, Bennet met with the man who was applying to replace the parson at Longbourn—his distant cousin, William Collins. Luckily for Collins, his rejection for every position he applied for had taught him some genuine humility.

"Mr. Collins, there is a reason no one will offer you a living fresh out of seminary and taking your orders," Bennet explained gently. "You are unproven. Unfortunately, only one with little sense would award a green clergyman a living. Before we proceed on that topic, I need to clear something up."

"After much reflection, I had arrived at that very conclusion, Cousin. What do you need to clear up?" Collins asked.

"After my son was born, your late father was rather abusive and made veiled threats against my boy. If your aim is to come here to try to remove the impediment to your becoming the heir presumptive of Longbourn, I will find out soon enough and it will not go well for you," Bennet stated.

"My father was disappointed as his hopes of becoming a landed gentleman—for himself or myself—were dashed the day the notice of your son's birth was received and read to him. Yes, he blustered, but I convinced him that it must be the will of God that a Bennet was to remain at the helm of Longbourn," Collins related. "I read over all of the entail paperwork, and unlike him, I understood even if one of the Collins line were to inherit, he would have only the land listed in the entail and future earnings from the date of inheriting, and that nothing from before is included in the entail. The gain of the additional wealth was my father's dream, and it died the day I explained the restrictions of the entail to him."

"You are happy to be a clergyman and know that unless God takes our Tommy from us, you will never be master of Longbourn?" Bennet pressed.

"Yes, Cousin. I am here to apply for a clerical position, not master of any of your estates," Collins vowed.

"In that case, I will accept you as a curate, with an eye to receiving the living when Mr. Dudley retires in less than a year. You will have the use of a cottage with all meals included and receive five pounds a month on top of that. If you accept, you will learn from Mr. Dudley, who has had close to forty years in the pulpit," Bennet offered. "Do you accept my terms?"

Collins acknowledged to himself what his cousin was offering him was two to three times as generous as he had been proffered anywhere else he had applied, so he accepted happily.

He met all of his cousins the first Sunday when he was invited to dine and was taken by the beauty he saw arrayed among the Bennet sisters. He was aware only the oldest, who was betrothed, was out. As much as the second daughter captivated him with her green eyes, she was not out. It was also true as the daughter of a gentleman of means, she was far out of his reach, and he had no intention to test his cousin's boundaries.

It was that Sunday when he first met Miss Charlotte Lucas, who was about a year older than he.

~~~~~~~/~~~~~~~

Once the date for Jane and Andrew's wedding had been decided, notice was sent to Pemberley, and Robert Darcy departed with his daughter to collect William from a friend's estate a week earlier than originally planned. He wanted to arrive at Netherfield Park well ahead of the festivities, which would include a betrothal ball, arriving on the first Wednesday in December.

The coach had barely stopped, and the footman had just managed to open the door when Georgiana was out of the interior as if shot out a cannon. It had been some months since she had been at Netherfield, and she missed all of the Bennet offspring.

As much as she wanted to spend time with her best friends, Georgiana was also looking forward to taking up her lessons with the masters again and would remain with the Bennets while her father was in London for part of the season after Twelfth Night.

"I have missed all of you so much," Georgiana stated as she hugged each Bennet child in order, even—to his dismay— Tommy, who was at the stage when he found girls strange and foreign creatures.

"It is good to see you again, Gigi," Jane stated for herself and her siblings.

"In less than a fortnight you will make us all cousins when you marry Andrew," Georgiana gushed.

Robert and William Darcy stood back as the whirlwind that was Gigi made her way greeting everyone. After Andrew, she moved to the Bennet and Fitzwilliam parents and ended with Uncle Freddy, having missed her Aunt Catherine who was standing a little away from the main group.

"Welcome, Robert and William," Fanny stated once Georgiana had moved off with Kitty and Lydia.

"You would swear Gigi had not been here in a few years, rather than just a few months," Darcy observed.

"You look so much like my late sister, Georgiana," Catherine stated softly.

"Aunt Catherine, I did not see you," Georgiana stated. She was not sure how to greet her aunt when Catherine opened her arms and enfolded her niece in a warm hug.

Robert and William Darcy had to rub their eyes. They had heard the reports of Catherine's reformation, but to see the demure woman who only spoke when spoken to and did not offer any unwanted useless advice was beyond anything either had expected.

William greeted each one in turn, wishing Jane and Andrew happy on their betrothal as it was the first time he had seen them since that joyous day. "How are you, Lizzy?" William asked, not missing the blush on her beautiful face as he took her hands in his and bestowed a gentle kiss on the back of one of her hands.

"Ahem, I am well, thank you, William," the discomposed young lady responded. It was at that moment William first understood that Elizabeth might have tender feelings for him just as he did for her.

"After I wash and change, will you be in the library? There are some new works by Byron I would like to see if you have read," William asked.

"Yes, I believe I will be there with Jane and Andrew," Elizabeth replied, her eyes not quite meeting William's.

William next wished Richard and Anne happy on their betrothals. Both thanked him. It was then he remembered his Aunt Catherine standing off the side. "Aunt Catherine, I want you to know that my mother would be so very happy at the changes you have made in your life. She would be proud of you." William hugged his aunt and was genuinely happy to see her for the first time in many years.

It had taken the Bennet parents and the Prince a little while to accept that the Catherine who had arrived with the Fitzwilliams was the same woman who had barged into Pemberley making demands, tried to lie, and insulted everyone. Like the Darcys, they had heard the reports of her change, but until they saw it for themselves, and heard the absolute contrition in her apologies, they had been somewhat sceptical.

The six adults standing together were watching the interaction between Elizabeth and William shook their heads, all remembering the perspicacity of the late Anne Darcy. "My Anne knew what she was about," Darcy said softly so only those right next to him would hear. "I should have known better than to think she was incorrect about those two."

"We need to talk privately as soon as we can now that Robert is here," Bennet told the others in their group. It was agreed they would meet in the master suite's sitting room in an hour.

Before everyone dispersed, Darcy hugged his sister-in-law and echoed the words his son had spoken about how proud his late wife would have been of Catherine.

~~~~~~~/~~~~~~~

Edward Gardiner was impressed. Seldom has he been so impressed with a new man, but in the short time George Wickham had been an employee there was no task too menial for him to do, no hours too long for him to toil, and the man was intelligent.

He caught onto what was needed in his position of a clerk in a fraction of the time others trained for the same position had taken. Not only that, but the man was good at solving issues which would otherwise have taken Gardiner's own time to solve.

Gardiner was not proud of it, but he had placed temptation in young Wickham's way. His purse had *dropped* out of his pocket onto the floor. There was more than twenty pounds in notes, two guineas, and some coin in the purse. Wickham discovered it when he was alone in that section of the office. He picked it up, promptly found Mr. Gardiner, and returned it without opening it to see how much was within.

His employer thanked him and rewarded his honestly with a single guinea. Gardiner knew he would need to watch the man over a longer term to see if he was genuine or if he was acting a part to gain access to larger amounts to steal, but his gut told him it was the former, not the latter, the same instinct that had helped him create his more than moderately successful business.

Before Gardiner, his wife, and four children departed for Netherfield Park, he put Wickham in charge of two other clerks. He spoke to his manager and told him to keep a weather eye, as he wanted to know how the young man did when not under the owner's constant supervision.

By ten that morning, the Gardiner carriages were on their way to Netherfield Park, taking the family to the ball, wedding, and Christmastide celebrations. Gardiner had a report on both the Bennets' and Lizzy's investment portfolios. After sixteen years of wise investments, the more than three hundred thousand pounds Lizzy had inherited was approaching a million pounds as of the drafting of the report.

~~~~~~~/~~~~~~~

"Elaine and Reggie, you asked us to meet. Is there a specific worry we need to address?" Fanny asked.

"We think it is time," Matlock stated without preamble. "In barely three months Lizzy will be seventeen. She should be told the truth. You all know how intelligent she is, and especially now as there seems to be a mutual attraction between her and William, we—Elaine and I—do not think you are protecting Lizzy any longer but may be hurting her by not telling her the truth."

"Why now, Matlock?" the Prince asked.

"Richard has been aware of the truth these past three years, then Jane was told, and now Andrew is aware. Richard does not want secrets between him and Cassie, just like Jane did not want before she and Andrew began their betrothal," Lady Elaine explained.

"You think the more people know the more the likelihood of it will coming out, and then Lizzy will be angry at us because we hid it from her for so long," Fanny surmised. When Lizzy is told, so must William be.

"What about you, Freddy? Will your parents try to force their will on Lizzy at this stage?" Darcy asked. "I agree it is time as well. She is an extremely intelligent young lady and I believe she will understand, especially as you have a letter from Priscilla for her."

"At this stage," the Prince stated thoughtfully, "if Elizabeth wants to be known to them, they will defer to my judgement. My father still feels much guilt after forcing the divorce on Priscilla and me; that more than anything else will stay his hand. When she is ready, they will welcome her as a granddaughter, but I told you what Father will do regarding the line of succession."

"Not to mention that William will have to come to terms with her true rank and wealth," Fanny stated. "Today they are equal; mayhap William believes his position is slightly better. However, after her true parentage and rank are revealed, he may not think himself worthy of one so high."

"What of the younger children, Fanny?" Bennet asked.

"If we decide now is the time, then we will need to talk to them after Lizzy has been told; the delay will depend on what her reaction is," Fanny responded.

"Do we need to wait for Edith and Paul—who also agree it is time—or are we all in agreement?" Elaine asked.

"It is time," the Prince stated simply.

"When should we talk to her?" Bennet asked.

"I agree William be with us when she finds out; he needs to know and she will draw strength from him being present because he did not know," Fanny opined. "If they are to have a chance at a mutual future, she needs to have it proven that he knew nothing and is not interested in her for any reason but love and respect."

"The Carringtons will be here on Friday; I see no harm in waiting until they are present," Bennet recommended. "We will, of course, include Catherine."

"Yes," Matlock agreed, "we want her to know she is not excluded from the bosom of the family now that I finally have the sister I have missed for over forty years back."

"Are you sure your sister does not want me to have my father reinstate her title?" the Prince asked.

"No Frederick, she was adamant," Lady Elaine stated. "She loves her life as it is now without any courtesy title." Then the Countess got a malevolent look on her mien. "Let us hope the De Melvilles do something to cause you to strip their titles. We are not sending their letter yet, are we?"

"Only if the news of Lizzy's existence becomes public knowledge. Otherwise, they will wait until she is eighteen," Bennet stated with purpose.

"I agree with Thomas," Fanny stated. "We have all been

through this together so there is no pressing reason not to wait, and it will relieve Richard of the need to keep this secret from Cassie for one more day." Then Fanny had a thought. "Most of you do not know this, but Mrs. Nichols was witness to everything that day, I think she should be included to answer any questions Lizzy might have." There were nods from the others in the sitting room.

So, it was agreed. There would be a meeting two days hence after dinner.

~~~~~~~/~~~~~~~

Andrew, Richard, and Jane were summoned to the master suite, thinking it had something to do with their recent betrothals—which, in a roundabout way, it did. They found the Bennet and Fitzwilliam parents waiting for them; Richard closed the door and the three took seats.

"We will be revealing Elizabeth's true parentage to her, and William too, on Friday after dinner," Bennet informed the three who were party to the secret without any preamble.

"Why now, Papa?" Jane asked, "It is only a little more than a year before Lizzy is eighteen."

"The circle of those who know is ever widening..." All four parents told the three about the meeting and the decisions taken.

"It makes sense," Andrew postulated as he unconsciously held Jane's hand. "Lizzy has more than enough maturity to assimilate the information."

"Poor William," Richard pointed out. "He is going to be flummoxed. I wager he will apologise all over again for his comments at Pemberley more than eleven years past."

"You could be correct, Richard," Fanny smiled. "Another advantage is that they will both be able to become comfortable, one with the other, if this creates any distance with more than a year before Lizzy is launched into society."

"She will not be sanguine about the way the truth has been bent. She knows Papa has an aversion to Town but will quickly see it is not as it was made to be and it was not the main reason for her never going to London," Jane pointed out.

"I pity her De Melville Grandparents if they meet her once she understands what they did to her mother," Fanny stated. "If Lizzy unleashes her anger on them once she knows she is a Princess of the United Kingdom of Great Britain and Ireland, they will pray for her birthfather to take them to task in comparison."

"The Christian thing to do would be to forgive them," Jane highlighted.

"If they had shown any contrition for what they did rather than to have it forced by motivation to keep their position and the good opinion of society, I would agree, Jane," Andrew stated. "They had sixteen years to offer amends, but they did not until they paid a social cost."

"Thank you for not making me think about keeping a secret from Cassie." Richard felt a sense of relief; he hated keeping secrets from the woman he loved beyond all others.

~~~~~~~/~~~~~~~

"Charles," Caroline Bingley whined, "when will you take me to Town? How will I meet men of the first circles when we only associate with tradesmen?"

"Do I need to point out to you again, Sister, that I am a tradesman? So is Uncle, who is your guardian," Bingley countered. He had lost count of how many times they had this conversation, or a variation of it, with his pretentious harpy of a younger sister.

"How could our father make another man stinking of active trade my guardian?" Miss Bingley complained. "Mother would have never..."

"As it was not her choice, but rather father's, what you were about to say is as irrelevant as it has been each time we have had this self-same conversation," Bingley sighed with frustration. "If you continue in this vein, I will not ask Uncle if I may take you with me when I take up a lease at the estate in another year or so. Before you tell me I will need a hostess, I will simply request that Louisa and Hurst join me, and she will be my hostess if Uncle refuses his permission."

As she always did, as soon as her brother mentioned the need for her guardian's permission, Miss Bingley subsided. Her brother refused to introduce her to anyone other than the nobody Jamison friend of his. She would do her late mother proud and find a husband of the first circles, even if she needed to engineer a compromise.

CHAPTER 23

Once the Carringtons arrived, Mrs. de Bourgh asked if she could meet with all of the adults and the younger set from Miss Mary upward. As soon as everyone was seated, Catherine made her sincere, heartfelt apologies to everyone in the room she had wronged.

The longest was the public one she made to Anne. She had apologised to Anne in Kent but felt that she owed her daughter an apology with all of the family present as well. She fully acknowledged who she used to be and told them all how happy she was to be who she was now. When Catherine was complete, Anne was the first to tearfully hug her mother, and then each person present fully forgave Mrs. de Bourgh for any transgressions against them.

The last person to hug her and tell her proud he was of the way she had changed her life was Robert Darcy. He reiterated that his late Anne would have been proud of her, as were he and his children were.

After her apologies and her family's acceptance, Catherine de Bourgh felt the last vestige of the weight of her former misdeeds lift from her shoulders.

~~~~~~~/~~~~~~~

Before entering the meeting where Catherine made her apologies, the Carringtons were waylaid by the other parents and the Prince. After a short conversation with the Prince, Darcy, and the other two sets of parents, the Carringtons agreed that it was time to tell Elizabeth the truth. It was decided that while Elizabeth and William were meeting with the parents and the Prince, Andrew, Richard, and Jane would sit with Jamey, Anne, Cassie, and Mary in a separate sitting room.

The four youngest children would be informed by a group of their parents on Saturday morning.

Elizabeth could tell there was a certain tension in the atmosphere on Friday, but she had no clue what the source was and from what she could tell, William was as clueless as she. Assuming it was due to having Mrs. de Bourgh with them, she assessed the woman carefully, but it did not take her long to warm to Aunt Catherine. Elizabeth had met the lady only once, at Pemberley just after Aunt Anne passed away, but she was able to tell that Aunt Catherine had won approbation from all those she trusted when before she had garnered naught but disdain.

From Catherine's perspective, she was drawn to the smart as a whip, sometimes impertinent, young lady with a rapier wit. She could not image hearing better musical talents than those of the Bennets and her niece Gigi. When she asked who taught them, she was told that *Signore* da Funti would return with the voice master after Twelfth Night, and that if Aunt Catherine was in residence, she would be welcome to take lessons with the *Signore too.*

~~~~~~~/~~~~~~~

Once dinner was over, Bennet told everyone there would be no separation of the sexes and requested Mrs. de Bourgh, Elizabeth, and William to join them for a meeting. Having no clue as to what they were being called to discuss, William and Elizabeth followed the group of parents, the Prince, and Catherine to the family sitting room. Biggs was stationed outside the door in the hallway. It made Catherine feel warm all over that she was to be included in an intimate family discussion.

Elizabeth was asked to sit on a settee between her father and Uncle Freddy, while William and Aunt Catherine sat on another with Robert Darcy. The Fitzwilliam and Carrington parents found seats close to Lizzy. There was a short silence, followed by a knock on the door, and Mrs. Nichols entered the room.

"Lizzy, no matter what you hear or read here, you must

know that you have been, and always will be, a most beloved daughter to your father and myself. I want you to hear this clearly, that no matter what, you will be loved as much tomorrow as you are today," Fanny began, her voice tremulous.

"Mama, what are you saying? I am starting to worry," Elizabeth asked nervously as she felt her father take one hand and Uncle Freddy the other as each gave her a reassuring squeeze.

"I need to tell you the tale of the day you were born, Lizzy," Fanny stated. "Mrs. Nichols is with us now because she is one of the few others that attended your birth. I have told you—all of my children—many times of my sister of the heart, Lady Priscilla, have I not?"

"Yes, Mama, she is the lady who gave us Netherfield," Elizabeth verified.

"Correct, and we will return to the topic of Netherfield later in our discussion," Fanny confirmed. "You know Uncle Freddy was married to Priscilla and his father the King forced them to divorce for a political alliance with Prussia." Elizabeth and William both nodded.

"What has that to do with why we are here, Mama?" Elizabeth asked cautiously.

"It has everything to do with it, *Princess*," Fanny used the now rarely used term of endearment. "My friend was weak; she had a broken heart. She knew Uncle Freddy had no choice in the matter of their divorce and he had to do as the King commanded. Priscilla's family name before marrying was De Melville. She was the eldest daughter of the Earl and Countess of Jersey. Even though the divorce was through no fault of her own, they disowned Priscilla and cut all ties with her. I believe it was their callous action that completely destroyed Priscilla's will to live."

"How can anyone do that to their own child?" William asked indignantly.

"That is a question we have all asked many times over, William," his father agreed.

"Your father was visiting Uncle Paul and Aunt Edith when both Priscilla and I entered our final confinements. As I have told you, she died from complications of the birth; all of that is true. What was not true was what we told everyone the sex of the baby we each bore was," Fanny said the last slowly.

William was quick to apprehend what Aunt Fanny had just said. His father placed his hand on his arm to stay any words from his son. "Mama, what are you telling me?" Elizabeth asked. The shock was sketched clearly on her face. She understood what was being said but she wated to hear her mother say the words. She felt anger bubble under the surface for a reason she could not yet comprehend.

"You are too intelligent not to understand what I am telling you, my Lizzy," Fanny told her second daughter. "Here is a portrait of your birthmother." Fanny handed the portrait of Priscilla to her daughter.

Elizabeth was about to protest it was a portrait of herself, one she did not remember sitting for and where she looked older, until she noticed the date: 1798.

"I had an artist paint that of my beloved wife shortly after we married," the Prince stated softly.

"If Uncle Freddy is my father, why did I live with you and not him? Did he not want me?" Elizabeth asked in alarm. She was doing all she could to regulate the anger that wanted to burst forth.

"That could not be further from the truth, Lizzy," the Prince told her firmly.

"Lizzy, your birthmother wrote a letter to you, one I swore to her on her deathbed I would give you when you were ready. She suggested eighteen, but we all feel you are ready now," Fanny told her daughter.

"Who else knew about my true parents?" Elizabeth asked with some asperity showing.

"Do you remember in 1795 when we went to Holder Heights after Uncle Edward's wedding, and you asked why Aunt Anne was staring at you?" Fanny reminded her and Elizabeth nodded. "Until then, beside Mrs. Nichols who was at your birth, I was the only one who knew the truth. Your birthmother's letter will explain her reasoning for asking what she did.

"When Aunt Elaine saw you she, like Aunt Anne, recognised your birthmother in you. The Darcys and Fitzwilliams were unmoved in their belief that I needed to tell your father, and I did when we returned to Netherfield Park. It was only then your birthfather was informed he had a daughter, and after reading the letter from his Cilla, he agreed to allow us to continue to raise you, but he wanted to be part of your life, and he is, though as your Uncle Freddy."

"Here is the letter from your mother; we will all sit here while you read it. We will answer any questions you have when you are finished." Fanny handed her daughter the letter from Priscilla.

"Before I read, I saw William's face, he was as shocked as I was. He did not know, did he?" Elizabeth wanted to know.

"No Lizzy, I knew nothing," William confirmed.

27 February 1790

To my dear son or daughter,

If you are reading this, then you have been raised by Fanny and Thomas Bennet as the worst has come to pass; I have been called home by God. I implore you not to be angry with your adoptive parents. If Fanny has shared the truth of your birth with Thomas—as I suspect she has—before you are eighteen or whatever age my sister Fanny decides to disclose all to you, remember that you are loved.

If you are a daughter, I will name you Elizabeth Sarah. Elizabeth is for my late maternal grandmother Beth, and Sarah for my mother. Before you say it, yes, their breaking with me has cut me to the quick, but she is still my mother. If you are a son, then you are named for your father—who I love more than there are words to describe—and your grandfather, my father for the same reasons as I would use your grandmother's name if you were a girl. If you are a boy your name will be Frederick Cyril.

"I will not bear the name of the woman who rejected my mother," Elizabeth told no one in particular. "I want my middle names to be Priscilla Francine and *not* Sarah!" The anger she had been feeling was now directed at the grandparents who had hurt her birthmother so badly.

"Then it will be so, Lizzy," Fanny said softly, almost overcome with her being so included as she had long feared her daughter's reaction and if she would be forgiven.

Elizabeth continued to read.

So, you understand my reasons that I will swear Fanny to years of secrecy—yes even from you my child—they are as follows...

Priscilla told her child how her father and his siblings had been raised in a royal household, and how she would never want the same for her child. She made sure that Elizabeth knew her father had not rejected her, but for the reasons she enumerated as well as not wanting to pain him more than he had been by being forced to divorce her, he was not aware of her existence.

I hope you understand that what has been done has been done to protect you, my child. It is my firm belief that more than blood, what defines family—a parent—is love. Before you become angry with your mother and father, ask yourself this: Have they loved you as well as the rest of their children? It was a pleasure for me to have met your sister Jane and I am sure Fanny will provide you with more siblings, so again I ask you—have your adoptive parents ever treated you less than their other child or children?

"No, no they have never treated me as anything but one of their children they love," Elizabeth told her long dead birthmother as her tears flowed down her cheeks. "You could not have left me in the care of better or more loving parents, sisters, brother, and extended family." As Elizabeth spoke, the anger she had been feeling dissipated.

On hearing such a declaration, Fanny cried tears of relief

as she heard Elizabeth's pronouncement. Her daughter would not reject her and her family. She lifted her head to the heavens and said a prayer of thanks for the words her dearest friend had written in her letter to placate Elizabeth's anger at not being told before this day.

Elizabeth continued to read.

As much as I miss your father each and every day, I do not hold any animus against your grandfather, King George III. He has the weight of the Crown on his head and must consider much more than personal desires when making decisions. Your birthfather will confirm for you his love of his father and that of his father for him.

When my Frederick returned with the news that we must divorce, he was devastated and told me how it hurt his father to inflict pain on his beloved son. The most important thing for you to know, my son or daughter, is you were created out of the deepest of love, and we were legally married when I became with child. That, my child, makes you a legitimate Prince or Princess of England—of the United Kingdom of Great Britain and Ireland.

I know it is much to take in, but remember this; no matter your title, you are still the boy or girl who has been raised by two of the best parents I know. When one day you choose a mate, make sure that you love him or her with all of your heart. My Frederick will make sure you are not used to further some treaty as he was. I believe the fact you were born after the divorce will protect you to a large extent.

Beware of false friends and fortune hunters, my child, as Netherfield and all of my wealth not bequeathed to others is yours. It is a vast fortune and will bring many such vile avaricious men slithering out of the woodwork if the extent of your fortune becomes known before you choose your life partner.

Besides your mother, my good friends who did not drop my connection are Anne Darcy and Elaine Fitzwilliam. If you ever need help, they will provide it to you as will their husbands, who are the best of men. Although not as close a friend—but still a very good one—as the former two I mentioned, Edith Carrington too tried to keep our acquaintanceship alive after the divorce.

I withdrew into myself after my parents cut me and was not ready to contact anyone and only wanted to be with your mother—our Fanny—so as you are reading this, I did not get to contact them while I was alive. Your mother has other letters, other than the one you are reading, and I trust she had passed them onto each of those I addressed them to—and is holding some I asked her to hold.

Let me close by reiterating that everything *that has been done has been done out of love and to protect you.*

I love you, and hope to meet you in heaven many decades from now,

Your Loving Mother, Priscilla

Elizabeth read the letter twice more before she silently handed it to her mother. Her birthfather drew her into his arms, and he rocked her back and forth as she assimilated the information her birthmother had shared with her.

"Mama, have all of the letters been delivered?" Elizabeth asked after she dried her eyes.

"All except one. There is one for Priscilla's parents to be posted on your eighteenth birthday or when your existence becomes public," Fanny averred. "Whether you decide to have contact with either set of your grandparents is up to you, but as Uncle Freddy—your birthfather—will explain, you will have to be presented to their Majesties before you come out into society.

"I never want to meet the people who were so cruel to their own daughter; they do not deserve to be my grandparents," Elizabeth stated vehemently. "When they rejected my birthmother, they rejected me too."

No one said a word in opposition to Elizabeth's statement. "Lizzy, besides those in this room, Jane, Andrew, and Richard are aware of your true birth and heritage..." Fanny explained how each one found out or was told and why.

"Jane has known since before her coming out and has never treated me differently," Elizabeth observed. "Why could others be told and not me?"

"It was partly your birthmother's instruction as well as our," Bennet indicated all the adults in the sitting room, "desire to protect you. I suppose we could have told you sooner, but we wanted you to live a carefree life without the weight of being a royal on your shoulders."

"Jane's sisterly love for you did not change, nor will it ever," Fanny reassured her daughter. "As Priscilla pointed out in her letter and you have seen for many years, family ties are so much more than just blood.

"I cannot be upset they knew before me as there was sound reasoning behind each disclosure," Elizabeth decided.

"At Pemberley, after insulting the Prince, I then proceeded to screech in front of his daughter, a Princess?" Catherine shook her head at the depths of her former bad behaviour.

"You did not call a Princess riffraff, Aunt Catherine. I believe as far as insulters of royalty go, I am far ahead of you," William stated as the shock of the revelations started to wear off.

"William, neither you nor I knew who I was then," Elizabeth stated with arched eyebrow, "and besides, I believe I pardoned your offence almost twelve years ago—after delivering a kick to your shin."

"There is a story here I need to hear—later of course," Catherine said with amusement.

"Lizzy, at the same time we have been meeting here, Jane, Andrew, and Richard have been sitting with Jamey, Anne, Cassie, and Mary and telling them of your true parentage," Bennet revealed. "We felt that when we inform the younger children on the morrow, you should be with us."

"How hard is it to have my middle names changed?" Elizabeth asked pointedly. "The sooner I do not carry the name of the woman who treated my birthmother in so callous a fashion, the better." Elizabeth, like the rest present, never considered that Lady Sarah may have been acting under duress.

"On the morrow. I will request Uncle Phillips to make

the change and it will be done," Bennet responded. "Both he and Uncle Gardiner know the truth. Uncle Phillips drew up your late birthmother's final will and testament, and Uncle Gardiner manages your fortune."

"The letter said I own Netherfield, is that correct Papa?" Elizabeth enquired.

"Yes Lizzy, when you reach one and twenty or marry, it and your fortune become yours. At that point, we will move back to Longbourn," Bennet clarified.

"No, Papa, I will never ask you, Mama, or my siblings to leave this house, unless," Elizabeth looked at William, "I marry a man without his own estate." Both blushed and no one commented. "You mentioned a fortune, Papa?"

"Yes Lizzy, it has grown to close to a million pounds, thanks to Uncle Edward's management of your wealth," Bennet revealed.

There was silence in the room. Other than Fanny and Frederick, no one had ever heard the exact amount of Elizabeth's wealth before. William realised she was wealthier than the Darcys and their combined holdings.

"I think we all need to rest and allow Lizzy—and William —to come to grips with all these revelations," Fanny suggested.

It was agreed they would talk more on the morrow, and at that time Elizabeth would meet with her birthfather to discuss when and how to make the revelation to the King, Queen, and the rest of the royal family.

CHAPTER 24

"Mother and Father, Prince Frederick has informed his cousin Lady Rose and her husband that it is not his desire they push for a divorce," Marie Rhys-Davies née De Melville, Marchioness of Birchington, informed her parents. Lady Marie was meeting—two days before the revelations at Netherfield Park would be made—with her parents and her brother Wes—Wesley De Melville, Viscount Westmore— at the family estate, Broadhurst in Essex, in their parents' private sitting room to be sure no one in the household could overhear them.

"We are saved," Lord Jersey exclaimed gleefully. It was the first good news in the sea of bad news that had befallen the De Melvilles since the displeasure of the royals—not only restricted to Prince Frederick—had become known to the *Ton* which had necessitated the flight back to their country estate.

"No Father, that is *not* what this means," their daughter informed her parents firmly. "I am afraid the condition for no divorce is that I am to cut ties with you."

"How can anyone be so cruel?" Lord Cyril asked indignantly. He knew full well as soon as word of the split with the Rhys-Davies became common knowledge—and it would as surely as the sun would rise in the east on the morrow—the De Melvilles' fall from grace would be complete.

"Father," Wes interjected. "how can you be so hypocritical? Did you not cruelly reject your daughter—our sister—in exactly the same manner and ordered our mother to do the same? It seems to me you are reaping what you have sown."

"How dare you disrespect your parents thusly?" Lord Jersey blustered angrily.

"Over sixteen years ago, at a time she needed her family more than ever, you cut ties with Priscilla, denying her the succour of family, of her mother and father," Wes shot back. "If I were not a boy of six or seven years I would have objected then." Wes paused allowing his words to sink in. "At least Marie has come to deliver the news in person, and not like you did in a short, impersonal letter you ordered my mother to write. I know we are supposed to respect our parents, but enough is enough! Your only worry was what society might think— which as we all know you were wrong about—when your only concern should have been for your daughter."

Lady Jersey was about to tell her children how sorry she was for not standing up to the Earl when her husband placed a hand on her arm and gave her a warning look. "Our son and daughter are tired. We need to give them time to come to their senses," Lord Jersey deluded himself.

"No, Father, we do not need time," Wes stated, and Marie nodded. "All we can do is beg our sister's forgiveness and her pardon for following your dictates since we have been old enough to know them to be wrong. Come, Marie, I will away with you."

Marie turned without another word and walked out with her brother. It did not take long before the father whose pride would not allow him to admit he had been wrong, was left alone with his devastated wife at Broadhurst in Essex.

The Earl and Countess did not know it, but the two children they had just lost were on their way to Hertfordshire to throw themselves on Priscilla's mercy and beg her forgiveness. If Lady Sarah had been aware of that fact, she would have begged to accompany them regardless of her husband's edicts.

~~~~~~~/~~~~~~~

"It is done, Lizzy. Your name is now officially Elizabeth Priscilla Francine," Phillips informed Elizabeth as she sat in her father's study with him, her birthfather, and her father.

"Thank you, Uncle Frank," Elizabeth replied. "I appreciate not having to have my late birthmother's mother's name as my middle name another day longer." Elizabeth thought for a moment as she turned to the Prince. "What am I to call you now? It does not seem right to call you Uncle Freddy any longer now that I know who you truly are."

"Bennet, would you have an objection if Lizzy calls me Father and you Papa?" The Prince asked.

"Not at all, York," Bennet averred. "I think, though, that if Lizzy is to address you thusly, should you not inform the King and Queen before they hear the news from another quarter?"

"Before you discuss anything further," Phillips interjected, "am I needed here?"

Bennet looked at the Prince, who shook his head. "Thank you, Brother, but we need nothing further at this moment." Phillips took his leave with a bow to the Prince and closed the study door on his way out.

"The disclosure to my parents cannot be delayed now that Lizzy is aware of the truth," the Prince acknowledged. "I am expected at court the day after Jane and Andrew's wedding. While there, I will request a private audience with my parents and older brother."

"Father, the King and Queen will not order me to leave my mama, papa, sisters, and brother, will they?" a concerned Elizabeth asked.

"How long have I dreamed of hearing you address me so," the Prince exclaimed. "I will not lie to you, Lizzy, there is a very small chance they may demand that of me; however, it is my solemn belief that is not what they will do."

"Why do you think that?" Elizabeth followed up.

The Prince explained his reasons, which were largely centred on the guilt his father felt for tearing a loving couple asunder for political reasons. Although she knew there was always a chance, Elizabeth felt somewhat more confident she would not be taken away from the family she loved.

"May I solicit the first set from you at the ball on the morrow, Lizzy?" her birthfather requested. The betrothal ball for Jane and Andrew had the same rules for Elizabeth and Mary as

Jane's coming out ball. The difference was that they would be allowed to remain for the whole of the ball.

"Yes, Father, those dances are yours," Elizabeth granted happily.

"In that case, I will take your second set of dances," Bennet stated.

"Of course, Papa," Elizabeth allowed just as happily.

"York, I assume you do not want word of Lizzy's rank to be disseminated in the neighbourhood until the King and Queen decide whether or not they will acknowledge her?" Bennet asked.

"That is correct, Bennet," the Prince averred. "We will be telling the younger children later today, will we not?" Bennet nodded.

"We will need to impress on them the need to be silent on the subject until there is an official response from the palace," Bennet pointed out.

"Even though Tommy is the youngest, Papa," Elizabeth noted, "he will understand the need for discretion, as will the other three girls."

~~~~~~~/~~~~~~~

The younger group of children had just been informed of the truth of Elizabeth's parentage and rank when they were summoned to the family sitting room, where all of Netherfield's residents and the Prince were present. "Does this mean I need to bow to you and address you as *Your Royal Highness* each time I see you, *Princess* Elizabeth?" Tommy, who had just turned ten some days previously, asked cheekily.

"If you are not careful, *Master* Thomas Bennet Junior," Elizabeth replied with mock affront, "you will have to address me thusly and stand whenever in my presence."

"I have heard the story of your insult on the Bennets' first visit to Pemberley many times, William," Georgiana reminded her brother whose pallor darkened as he looked anywhere except at Elizabeth.

"Gigi, and everyone else," Elizabeth responded, "It has

been well over ten years since that occurrence. William was granted our pardon many years, ago and I know it is amusing to embarrass him over his intemperate words then, please let us leave it in the past where it belongs."

William gave Elizabeth a thankful look. He did not need anyone to remind him, as he would never forget the day or his ill-advised words. Thankfully for William, it was the last time he was reminded of the incident by any in the extended family.

"You four do understand why you may not discuss this with anyone outside of this room, do you not?" Fanny asked. "And, if you do want to talk about it with one of us, you must make sure we are alone and have complete privacy. Once the King and Queen accept Lizzy as their granddaughter and make a formal announcement, then you will be free to talk about Lizzy's rank openly if you need to."

"We understand," the three girls and one boy chorused.

"The Gardiners and Phillipses will be arriving for the betrothal ball in the morning on the morrow," Bennet informed the family. "Both sets of adults are aware of Lizzy's true parentage, but your Gardiner cousins are not. The restriction regarding discussing what you have been told here includes them." The four nodded their understanding and agreement.

"You are still our Uncle Freddy, are you not?" Lydia asked.

"Of course, my dear, yes," the Prince confirmed. "The only change is that Lizzy now knows I am her birthfather, as do you all."

"It is so exciting that I will be attending my first ball tonight," Kitty gushed.

"We have set thirteen as the minimum age for attendance; however," Fanny stated, "unlike Lizzy and Mary, you will retire after supper."

"Yes Mama," Kitty acknowledged.

"We still have some last-minute things to see to for the ball, Fanny," Lady Elaine pointed out, "Are we finished here?"

There was general agreement there was nothing else to discuss. The family dispersed to their own pursuits, not before Kitty, Lydia, and Gigi gave Elizabeth a deep curtsy, each of which elicited a tinkling laugh from the object of their deference.

William felt forlorn when he heard the laughter he loved to hear. *'I love her, but she is so far above me! I am a mere gentleman, and she is a princess. I will always love her, but I will have to reconcile myself to the fact the King and Queen will never sanction a match to one as low as me for their granddaughter especially with the new law.'* William told himself as he felt melancholy set in as he thought about the future he thought he would never have with Elizabeth.

~~~~~~~/~~~~~~~

When the De Melville siblings arrived at Netherfield Park, they were able to drive up to the manor house as the man stationed at the gate had not been instructed to halt carriages and verify they were not the De Melvilles, since the Prince had dispatched the Earl and Countess of Jersey with a major sized flea in their ear.

The Prince and Bennet were playing chess to see who would play against Darcy; Matlock and Holder were playing billiards. The men were in the game room to keep out of the way while the last of the preparations for the betrothal ball were put in place by the ladies of the house.

Nichols cleared his throat to announce his presence. "Master, we have unexpected guests," the Butler reported.

"Who is it Nichols?" Bennet asked.

"The Marchioness of Birchington and Viscount Westmore," Nichols reported. The two names caused all of the men present to stop what they were doing. "They desire an audience with Lady Priscilla to beg for her forgiveness."

"What do you recommend, York?" Bennet asked.

"Let us hear them," the Prince suggested. "If they are truly here in contrition, then we will do as my Priscilla would have and grant them forgiveness. If they are here to try and save their parents' place in society or some other selfish reason, I will know how to act."

"Everyone who will be at the ball is resting so they won't be able to see Lizzy," Bennet articulated his thoughts. "Show them into the study in a few minutes, Nichols." The butler bowed and departed to fulfil his orders.

~~~~~~~/~~~~~~~

When Marie and Wes were shown into the study, they were not sure what to expect, though it was certainly not the group of men waiting for them. Wes immediately recognised his Highness, the Earls of Matlock and Holder, and Mr. Robert Darcy. He did not know the man seated behind his sister's desk, though because he was in the seat of the master of the estate he assumed Priscilla had remarried.

"As I can see you recognise everyone else, I am Mr. Thomas Bennet, the custodial master of Netherfield Park," Bennet informed the two who looked rather confused.

"Lady Marie, Viscount, what brings you to Netherfield uninvited?" the Prince asked.

"If it is all the same to you, Your Royal Highness," Wes bowed as he addressed the Prince, "our business is with our sister."

"We," the Prince indicated the men with him with a sweep of his arm, "are all protectors of your sister's interests. You can tell us why you are here, or you may leave now and never return."

"When you confronted me during the ball at Holder Heights, you asked me a very pertinent question, Your Royal Highness," Lady Marie stated. "The truth is, I have been ashamed that I did not ignore the edicts of my father and reach out to Priscilla as soon as I came of age. It was unconscionable, and I—we both are—here to beg my sister's forgiveness and to make amends in any form she sees fit. We will, however, truly understand if she chooses not to see us since we obeyed our father for so long."

"How is it to be known that you are not here to try and repair your and your parents' positions in society and not for the reasons you have stated?" Darcy asked.

"As of two days ago, Your Royal Highness, your Lordships, and gentlemen," Wes replied, "My sister Marie and I broke with our parents. After all of these years, they—my father—could only see the problems they are living with and not that the cruelty towards Priscilla is the root of all of their problems." The men listening did not notice that Lord Kersey was identified as the one who demanded the break, not Lady Jersey.

"We do not expect any public acknowledgement of our seeking her forgiveness, whether she grants it or not; we are only trying in some small measure to correct a wrong perpetrated on our sister many years ago," Lady Marie added.

The four men looked to the Prince and each nodded. The Prince in turn inclined his head to Bennet. "Please be seated." Bennet indicated the chairs in front of his desk. "Priscilla *would have* liked nothing more than to grant you forgiveness, as all she ever desired was the love of family. Unfortunately, she passed away after giving birth almost seventeen years ago," Bennet revealed.

Brother and sister reached for one another and held the other's hand as Lady Marie started to cry quietly. Wes fought and failed to stop some tears running down his cheeks. "But I saw Priscilla at the ball; I am sure of it," Lady Marie managed once she dried her eyes.

"No, you saw my daughter, your niece," the Prince elucidated. "Her name is Elizabeth, named after your late grandmother Beth, and she will be seventeen in March."

"How did we know none of this?" Wes asked.

"Priscilla did not want any of you contacted unless there was a genuine attempt—such as the two of you have made this day—to contact her to repair the rift," Lord Matlock stated.

"Would we have gone the whole of our lives without knowing our sister was in heaven and we had a niece?" Lady Marie inquired.

"This is what we were instructed to do by your sister..." Bennet and the rest of the men explained what Priscilla had instructed and why. When the recitation was complete, brother and sister understood why Bennet called himself the *custodial master* of the estate.

"You say you will inform the King and Queen of their granddaughter, a Princess of the United Kingdom of Great Britain and Ireland, next week?" Wes verified.

"Yes, after the wedding," the Prince confirmed.

Seeing the quizzical looks from the siblings, they were informed that eldest Bennet daughter would be marrying Viscount Hilldale on Monday coming. "If you will show our guests to the family sitting room, I will see if my wife and Lizzy would like to meet them," Bennet asked his friends. "As you can imagine, she was not happy with your parents for the actions they took against her mother." Brother and sister were so excited they may meet their late sister's daughter, they did not correct Mr. Bennet's statement about the culpability for the break.

~~~~~~~/~~~~~~~

Bennet found his wife and gave her a synopsis of what had occurred in the study. She agreed with the decision to tell the brother and sister the truth about Priscilla and Lizzy. Together, they knocked on Lizzy's bedchamber door, and when summoned to enter they found her in the window seat, her legs curled up under her while she read.

Elizabeth's immediate reaction was to refuse to meet her aunt and uncle. After some conversation, she understood the two were nothing like their parents and agreed to accompany her adoptive parents to the sitting room.

When the door opened both Lady Marie and Wes stood; they saw Bennet enter with a woman who still held her looks, who they correctly assumed was his wife. As soon as they beheld their niece, both gasped audibly. Elizabeth was an almost exact copy of her late mother.

"Lady Marie, Viscount Westmore, my wife Mrs. Francine —Fanny—Bennet, and my daughter, Her Royal Highness Elizabeth Priscilla Francine *Bennet*." Bennet made the introductions.

After her experience—even though at the time she did not understand why—of the way Aunts Anne and Elaine had at stared at her the first time they met her, Elizabeth was prepared for her newly-met aunt and uncle to stare at her given how much she looked like her birthmother. So prepared, Elizabeth stood and bore the scrutiny with aplomb.

"No wonder I thought I saw my late sister," Lady Marie stated as the tears began to flow again. "May I hug you, Your Royal Highness?" Elizabeth gave a nod and Marie approached her tentatively until she enfolded Elizabeth in her arms, and the tears flowed in earnest.

When Lady Marie stepped back, she was replaced by her brother who opened his arms for his niece and Elizabeth stepped into his hug. "On behalf of myself and my birthmother, I forgive both of you," Elizabeth granted, "but never ask me to forgive your parents." Elizabeth returned to sit with her parents and birthfather after Wes released her.

"We understand why you do not feel like you can grant my parents forgiveness, and we will never ask you to do that which you do not desire to do," Wes assured Elizabeth.

"I second my brother's statement," Lady Marie said with purpose as she dried her eyes.

"Once there is a Royal decree about Princess Elizabeth..." Wes started to say when he was interrupted.

"Elizabeth or Lizzy, please," Elizabeth interjected as she looked from brother to sister.

"In that case, about *Lizzy*, I would suggest posting the letter to my parents then," Wes completed his suggestion.

"I think that is a good suggestion," Lady Edith opined, and those present allowed it was so by general agreement.

"As you are Lizzy's aunt and uncle, you are invited to the ball this night and the wedding on Monday," Fanny insisted after a nod from her husband.

"It would give me great pleasure to remain for the festivities. Thank you, Mrs. Bennet," Wes replied.

"I must return to my husband and parents-in-law in Town," Marie explained. "As much as I would love to be here, there will not be enough time to return from London today. As Long as the Duke and Duchess agree, we will depart London at sunup and will join you on Monday."

Not long after, Lady Marie started her journey back to Birchington House on Russel Square to inform her husband and the Duke and the Duchess of the outcome of her trip into Hertfordshire, and to share the invitation to the wedding with them.

CHAPTER 25

Wes was introduced to the rest of the family. He had met Andrew, Richard, and Jamey previously. Although he had not met William before, he did know him by sight.

His father's—he knew his mother had been forced to follow her husband's directions—actions had cost him a courtship, but in hindsight he owned the truth. He had not loved the lady—he was not sure he liked her much; it was an alliance his father wanted to bolster their position in society and to gain another ally in the House of Lords, so Wes could not repine the family's defection.

When he looked at the three betrothed couples present, Wes saw the obvious love between them and decided then and there he would not be induced to court a woman again unless he too found what they so obviously shared.

Marie had been pushed toward Sed Rhys-Davies by his father, using his daughter to bolster his position in society. He would always love his parents, but he could not repine the price his father was paying for the cruelty he had visited on his late sister. It was sad that they would never know their granddaughter—he felt badly for his mother, but as long as his father's pride was an obstacle, she would be stuck where she was—but he knew the situation they found themselves in now —ostracised from society—was entirely of his father's own making.

"What do we call you?" Tommy asked. "Uncle? Cousin?"

"Just Wes, Tommy," Wes responded. "Just like you address the rest of the younger men without a prefix before their names."

"You are like me, the youngest in your family, are you not?" Tommy verified.

"Yes, you are correct," Wes confirmed.

"How old are you? I am ten," Tommy enquired.

"I am two and twenty," Wes averred.

"You and William are the same age. Did you know him at University?" Georgiana interjected.

"We were not at the same schools, Gigi," William informed his younger sister. "I, like Andrew, Jamey, and Richard, went to a *good* school—Cambridge—while Wes went to Oxford."

"As those who go to the *inferior* and *newer* Cambridge know, Oxford is more than one hundred years older," Wes countered in the good-natured banter of rivals.

"Older does not mean better," Andrew joined the fray.

"Peace, young men," Bennet interjected. "Do not pick on Lizzy's uncle because he had the misfortune of not studying at Cambridge."

"I know when I am outnumbered," Wes capitulated playfully. "Do any of you Cambridge men know how to play chess?"

"We all do," the Prince informed his former brother-in-law.

"Mayhap after church on the morrow we can have an Oxford versus Cambridge competition?" Wes suggested.

The challenge was happily accepted by the Cambridge men who knew they had both Darcys as their secret weapons.

~~~~~~~/~~~~~~~

Gardiner requested to meet with Darcy after he washed and changed out of his travel attire. "Is there news about my investments?" Robert Darcy asked.

"No, it is not about your funds, rather about a new employee of mine," Gardiner responded. "For some months now, a new trainee clerk has been working in my employ—one George Wickham."

"What manner of lie did young Wickham tell you to gain a position of trust in your business?" Darcy asked.

"Actually, he told me the whole, unvarnished truth from his theft in York to his fraud in Staffordshire and everything in between," Gardiner related. "He had a genuine desire to change, to make a better life."

"Just do not turn your back on the young man," Darcy warned.

Gardiner proceeded to tell Darcy all, including the test he had engineered and all about the honest work ethic George Wickham had. Darcy was disbelieving at first, but he knew Gardiner would neither prevaricate nor exaggerate.

"I am amazed, as this news is the last I would have expected to hear about George Wickham," Darcy owned. "Do not misunderstand me; both his father and I would like nothing more than to see him succeed in an honest life. I will write to my steward and inform him of what you have told me. I will reserve judgement until more time has passed."

"You will hear no argument from me, Darcy," Gardiner stated. "Given his past, I understand why you are not ready to embrace his changes as permanent. Although I am sceptical as well, I will give him every chance to succeed. I will also give him enough rope to hang himself if he is not genuine. That being said, I believe he is sincere in his desire to make meaningful changes to his life."

~~~~~~~/~~~~~~~

Paul Bingley was exasperated. His niece—his ward—was incapable of change or of learning the error of her ways. As much as he preferred not to speak ill of the dead, he was not happy with his late sister-in-law, who had planted the nonsense about rising in society in Caroline's head.

He found one effective way to bring her to heel—withholding her allowance. Money had become the biggest stumbling block between them. When he refused to give her money for unnecessary clothing, she unleashed a tantrum of epic proportions and then took herself to a dressmaker and ordered a large number of dresses, telling them to send the invoice to her uncle.

By providence, Paul's wife, Henrietta, picked up a dress at the same store a day after Caroline's extravagant order. When the proprietor thanked her for the massive order, Mrs. Bingley told the lady, in no uncertain terms, that her husband had not authorised their niece to charge on their account. She berated the woman for accepting an order from a young lady without first checking with her guardians.

The order was cancelled forthwith, and the small cost incurred was deducted from Caroline's allowance. The dressmaker was told that unless Miss Bingley was accompanied by Mr. or Mrs. Bingley and they authorised the charge to their account, they would not pay any of those bills in the future.

Word spread quickly among the merchants of Scarborough that if they granted Miss Bingley credit, it would not be covered by her guardians. This cut off any avenue for Caroline Bingley to place orders for unneeded and excessively ostentatious gowns in her preferred colour—burnt orange.

The Bingleys did not mention anything to Caroline, hoping she would learn a lesson from her coming embarrassment. A week later, Miss Bingley, nose in the air, flounced into the dressmaker's shop for her fittings as if she were the Queen. She came very close to an apoplexy when she was told her order had been cancelled and she was not allowed to charge anything to the Bingleys' account.

For someone who dreamed of rising in society, Miss Bingley's behaviour was that of a shrew; her language that of a sailor. She was evicted from the shop, and after being refused at four other stores, she stomped off—the poor maid having to run to keep up with her—to return to her uncle's house in high dudgeon.

Before she could scream as she desired, her aunt and uncle sat her down and explained the way forward. She would behave like a lady in their house with decorum and respect, or she would forfeit her allowance—one week's worth at a time—until such time she changed her behaviour.

After four infractions which cost her a month's allowance, Caroline understood her guardians were serious. She would have to work on Charles to remove her from their custody. Unfortunately for her, her brother had neither the inclination nor the authority to do so.

~~~~~~~/~~~~~~~

"Father, may I have some of your time?" William asked after being admitted to his father's suite by the valet, Snell.

"You know I am always available to you, William," Darcy returned warmly.

"I have fallen in love with Lizzy, and now that I know her true rank—a Princess of the United Kingdom of Great Britain and Ireland, she is too far out of my reach—especially with the stipulation the King has made to marry a Prince or Princess—and it is breaking my heart," William lamented.

"William, I love you dearly, but sometimes you can be a dullard," Darcy retorted jocularly.

"Do you jest at my sorrow?" William asked.

"No son, not at your *self-inflicted* pain, at your wilful blindness," Darcy averred seriously.

"To what do you refer?" William attempted to understand.

"Let me ask you a question. Since Lizzy was informed of her true parentage and heritage, has she behaved any differently toward you or any of us?" Darcy asked.

"No," William owned.

"So, this is all in your head," Darcy pointed out. "You are assuming she will think you below her because you used to—albeit many years ago—think her below you. Is your love for her so weak you are willing to give her up without a fight?"

William sat in silence for a minute or two as he assimilated his father's words. "No, I love her with all of my heart and soul," William admitted.

"Then why are you already adopting a defeatist attitude and giving up a year before she comes out?" Robert Darcy asked his son pointedly.

"The King will have to approve of her suitor," William

stated, changing direction slightly. "And what of the new law that one must be a certain rank to marry a prince or princess?"

"Yes, and what of it?" his father asked.

"You are not a duke and I am not a marquess; how will the King consent to a mere gentleman as a suitor for his grand-daughter—a royal princess? He will not make an exception to his new rule," William tried to explain his rationale to his father.

"Do you think your Uncle Freddy—who has seen the attraction between the two of you as plain as day for some time now—disapproves of you, William?" Darcy answered with a question of his own.

"No, I suppose not, but..." William started to respond when his father held up his hand.

"How many times have you heard the Prince tell us how his father will not interfere as far as Lizzy is concerned due to the guilt the King feels after forcing the divorce and the marriage to Princess Frederica on him?" Darcy pushed.

"Many times," William acknowledged.

"If Lizzy is amenable to your suit—and I believe she will be—from whom do you think you need to request consent? The Prince or the King?" Darcy sat back and waited while William cogitated. "Also," he added cryptically, "rank will not be an issue."

It was one of the characteristics—one of many—Robert Darcy admired in his son. He was not impulsive and always took his time to think when considering weighty issues. Darcy saw the moment his son reached the correct conclusion, as his whole mien brightened.

"I understand why you told me my pain was self-inflicted," William admitted. "It seems I was trying to protect my heart prematurely. If I did not venture anything, I could not get hurt. It seems I need to look at what is rather than operate on assumptions. I do not understand why you say rank will not be a factor, but I trust you, Father."

"Your mother and I always said you could not be so intel-

ligent for no reason." Darcy gave his son a pat on the back as
William departed to go complete his ablutions prior to the ball.

~~~~~~~/~~~~~~~

"I know your birthfather has the first and your papa the
second," William bowed over Elizabeth's hand, entranced by
the vision she made as she descended the stairs before the first
guests were expected. "I would like to ask for your supper and
final sets, if you will grant those to me."

"You have been distant since we were told of my birthparents, William," Elizabeth pointed out archly. "I was not sure
you wanted to dance with me at the ball."

"Lizzy, I am sorry," William replied contritely. "After the
revelation of you true rank, I was afraid I was too far below
you. I should have relied on our bonds of friendship and not allowed my self-doubt to rule me."

"You are forgiven. I will grant you the two sets you have
requested," Elizabeth allowed. "Please remember this, William.
It is critical to me that my friends and extended family treat
me as they always have. I may be a Princess, but that is a rank,
not who I am. For me *nothing* has changed among those I esteem and count as my closest friends and family."

William's heart soared as he understood her message
clearly. He would never allow his head to overrule his heart
again.

"Do you have a set open for your *very old* uncle, niece?"
Wes asked with a grin.

"As William here is a few months older than you, that
must make him ancient," Elizabeth volleyed playfully. "Yes, my
third set is open, and if you desire those dances, they are yours,
Uncle Wes."

"Thank you, my impertinent niece." Wes looked around
and saw the warm camaraderie among those assembled for
an aperitif before the receiving line formed. These people
were genuine, warm, and loving. Nothing they did—unlike
his father—was to impress society or anyone else. If not for
his father's wrongheaded decisions, both of his parents would

have been part of this family for many years. He felt sympathy for his father, who was driven not by love but by what he thought society expected from him.

Wes solicited, and was granted, a set each from Jane, Anne, Cassie, Mary, and Kitty. He had to admit he was intrigued by the third Bennet daughter. She was almost as pretty as her eldest sister and had a wit and intelligence that matched his niece Elizabeth's. Earlier, Wes met the resident masters the Bennets employed, which helped him understand why all six Bennet children were so well educated and accomplished.

He smiled to himself as he thought of the drubbing he had suffered at the hands of both Darcys across the chessboard. He could not remember clashing with players of that calibre before.

Before the receiving line formed, Elizabeth, Mary, and Kitty had filled their dance cards. Kitty would have much to tell Gigi and Lydia when she departed the ball after supper to join the other two above-stairs. When Wes requested her final set, Mary had blushed with pleasure. She was days away from turning fifteen, so she had three more years before coming out, but it did not stop her glowing with pleasure with the attention from Lizzy's handsome uncle.

~~~~~~~/~~~~~~~

Jane and Andrew were at the head of the line, followed by Jamey and Anne and Richard and Cassie. Although Jane and Andrew were to wed in two days, the ball had become an impromptu ball for all three betrothed couples, which necessitated the addition of the Carringtons and Mrs. de Bourgh to the receiving line. If anyone from high society questioned the latter's presence in the line, none had the bad manners to comment on it within earshot of those in the receiving line.

Elizabeth enjoyed dancing the first with her birthfather. Again, if any of the guests questioned why the second Bennet daughter danced the first with the Prince and the second with her father, none voiced their questions aloud.

Most surprising was when Robert Darcy requested the

supper set from his late wife's older sister. Darcy would have loved for his Anne to have been present to witness how much her sister Catherine had changed. Darcy felt it was only right he recognise Catherine's efforts by dancing with her. The dance signalled to the *Ton* the complete reconciliation within the family.

"Come, William," Elizabeth said archly, "we cannot dance the whole half hour complete without some conversation; what will people say?" Lizzy teased lightly as they danced the first of their two scheduled sets—the supper set.

"Do you talk as a rule when you dance, Lizzy?" William returned. "Name the topic and we will discuss it. Would you like to discuss the new edition of Cowper's you are reading?"

"No, books are not a fit subject for discussion in a ballroom," Elizabeth replied with mock severity. "I could comment on the number of guests, and you could remark about the lovely decorations Mama and her helpers have made."

"I am at your disposal your Roy...madame." William stopped himself before he completed his attempted jest knowing how close he came to making an unintended revelation in a crowded ball room.

The guests were split between those representing the four and twenty families of gentlefolk in the area and those from London. He might have been able to explain his slip as a jest, but he would rather not take such a chance.

"That is enough conversation for now," Elizabeth granted, and they enjoyed the rest of the set in companionable silence. At its completion, William led Elizabeth to sit at a table with her three sisters and their partners.

William Collins, as a family member—albeit distant— had been invited to the ball. He was awestruck at the number of highly ranked personages, from a Prince on down. Luckily, he schooled his features and did not fawn over anyone. It was not the first time in his five-and-twenty years Collins had been thankful he had not taken his father—who used to fawn over the high-born—as an exemplar of how to behave towards others.

Collins passed supper most pleasantly with his partner for the supper set—Miss Charlotte Lucas. Before the meal was complete, Collins solicited the final set from his partner, who gladly granted those dances.

After supper, Kitty departed without complaint, and it was not long before she was regaling Gigi and Lydia with her experiences at her first private ball.

The rest of the ball passed as balls do, without any remarkable occurrences.

CHAPTER 26

On Sunday evening, Fanny gave Jane the pre-wedding night talk. Jane had the example of her parent's felicitous marriage, and even before her mother stressed the marital bed was not a duty but rather could and should be a pleasure, Jane had realised such based on not only her parents' marriage but based on the example of their closest friends as well.

Deeply in love with Andrew, she was confident he would be solicitous of her needs before listening to her mother's talk, but the last vestiges of nervousness Jane had felt were banished by her mother's assurances.

Andrew and Jane had managed some stolen kisses. From the way her body had reacted to him, Jane was anticipating more eagerly—both his kisses and what was to follow. Every time they allowed themselves such a moment—when they managed to gain some much wanted privacy—and forced themselves to stop well before either of them wanted to, the more she anticipated discovering the passions hovering just below the surface she knew were waiting to be freed for their wedding night. Considering that, she had to smile. It was both well considered and sweet that he was helping her overcome her concerns by allowing her to feel such powerful desires as he inspired.

After her mother departed, Lizzy—who would stand up with her—joined Jane in her bedchamber. "I will miss you, Janie, but I could not ask for a better older brother than Andrew. You two fit together like a hand in a glove," Elizabeth enthused as the two laid on the bed next to one another.

"I will miss you, my sisters, and my brother," Jane responded wistfully. "But it is the way of things, is it not? As women, if and when we marry, we cleave unto our husbands and go whither he goes. The truth is, Lizzy, that even though I will miss all of you and Mama and Papa, I am excited to begin my life with Andrew."

"How did you know you were in love with him?" Elizabeth asked shyly.

"Is your question related to your feelings for a certain tall and studious cousin of Andrew's?" Jane prodded.

"Possibly." Elizabeth blushed deeply.

"Elizabeth Pricilla Francine Bennet! Do not try to be evasive with me. Neither I nor any of the rest of us are blind. We have long seen the way the two of you look at one another." Jane replied gently.

"It is him I am drawn to above anyone," Elizabeth admitted softly without lifting her eyes to look at her sister.

"In my case, there was not one thing that proved to me I loved Andrew, but two," Jane revealed. "Whenever Andrew was not with me, I would be thinking of him, willing him to come back to me. The second—which to me was even more indicative of love—was there was no version of my future I could envisage of which Andrew was not a part."

"If that is the case, then I am in love with William," Elizabeth admitted both to herself and Jane. "I was worried he thought me too high for him as he seemed to pull back after I learned of my parentage. There was a time I thought he would not ask me to dance at the ball, but whatever was holding him back no longer seems to be an issue."

"Andrew told me that William is not one to act impulsively. Surely you have seen in your debates with him how deliberative he is?" Jane asked.

"It is true, he does like to cogitate fully before giving his opinion. I cannot wait until we are able to move forward together as more than just friends. I would give up my title and my wealth if they were impediments to my one day being with William," Elizabeth told her older sister.

"That will not be necessary, Lizzy, but your statement only proves the depth of your feelings and love for William. He is a very lucky man to have won your heart, sister dearest." Jane squeezed Elizabeth's hand.

"Are you nervous for—well you know—the wedding night?" Elizabeth asked despite her embarrassment.

"That is not the question I would expect from a younger sister not yet out," Jane teased.

"We do live on a working farm, and you know I love to read," Elizabeth countered.

"No Lizzy, I am not nervous. If anything, I am in anticipation," Jane shared.

"First you, then in March—the day after my birthday—a double wedding for Cassie and Richard and Anne and Jamey. The number of us who remain unattached is dwindling," Elizabeth stated.

"And you, Lizzy, will have a year to prepare for your coming out. The *Ton* will be in a frenzy. It is not every day that a previously unknown Princess of the United Kingdom of Great Britain and Ireland is launched into society," Jane opined.

"That is what I am dreading most, Jane. At least with everyone who knew and liked me before my position and fortune was known, I know they liked me for myself. In society, I will be like a sardine swimming in shark infested waters; many will only be interested in a connection to my royal grandparents and my wealth," Elizabeth expressed her worry.

"Never forget, Lizzy, if you and William become more than friends, you have known one another for years before your true status was revealed," Jane reminded her sister.

Deep down, Elizabeth would have preferred to simply be Elizabeth Bennet, daughter of a country squire. But she would not shirk her duty, and as Jane had reminded her, if she and William became more, he knew her as Lizzy and as not as 'Princess Elizabeth, incredibly wealthy heiress.'

~~~~~~~/~~~~~~~

On Monday morning, Andrew—who had moved to the

Red Rooster Inn for the night before his wedding so he would not see his bride beforehand—was joined by the men to break his fast before they made the one-mile trip to the church at Longbourn.

Despite a lack of sleep due to both anticipation and restlessness, at least he had not been alone at the inn. Richard, who was standing up for him, William, and Jamey had joined him in his removal from the rest of the family.

The day was cold, a typical winter day in Hertfordshire. Thankfully, it was mostly clear and there was no snow on the ground. After the wedding breakfast, which would be held at Netherfield Park, the newlyweds would make their way to Hilldale House, on London's Portman Square, where they would overnight. Then they would depart to Uncle Robert's Seaview Cottage near Brighton, where they would remain for a month complete.

It would be the first Christmas that Jane would be away from her family, and the only other for Andrew since he missed one while on his grand tour. They had long spent the holidays together with family, but neither could regret missing this year for the reason of being on their wedding trip. It would be the first one they would share as the family that would be created as soon as the rector announced them man and wife.

~~~~~~~/~~~~~~~

At Netherfield Park, Jane was in the private sitting room attached to her suite breaking her fast with her sisters, brother, Cassie, Anne, and Georgiana. Excited, Jane could not manage more than tea and toast with strawberry jam, one of her favourites.

Once they were done eating, each of her siblings and friends stood to depart. Tommy came forward first to give her a hug and a kiss on the cheek. Mary then hugged her eldest sister for a long time before bestowing her kiss on Jane's cheek. Kitty, Lydia, Georgiana, Cassie, and lastly Anne, who gave her friend the longest hug, followed and departed, then it was she and Elizabeth alone.

"Lizzy, you should go dress so you can return and assist Jane," Fanny shooed her second daughter once she entered the sitting room. "You are standing up with Jane, so you need to be here to help her."

"Yes, Mama," Elizabeth gave her mother a kiss on her proffered cheek and then went into her own bedchamber, which was on the other side of the sitting room from Jane's. That was yet another change for her; since she had turned ten, Elizabeth had shared a suite with Jane, but the previous night had been the last one for them both. When Elizabeth entered her bedchamber, her maid since she turned twelve, Miss Jacqueline Arseneault—Jacqui— welcomed her with a warm smile.

Once Jane completed her bath, her maid dried her hair in front of the fire as she brushed her mistress's long, blond locks. Once de Chambé helped her into her stays and chemise, Jane asked her to call her mother and Lizzy, if she too was ready, to return to her chambers.

It was but a minute before Fanny and Elizabeth joined Jane to help her with her gown. It was relatively simple, but then again, with Jane's beauty, she did not need to detract the eye with elaborate gowns.

~~~~~~~/~~~~~~~

At the same time Jane was being helped into her gown, an enormous coach arrived at Netherfield Park carrying the Duke and Duchess of Bedford and the Marquess and Marchioness of Birchington. They were shown into the largest drawing room, where they were met by Bennet, the Prince, Lord Holder, Darcy, and Gardiner. Lord Matlock had left to join his son and younger men at the inn.

"Your Royal Highness," the Duke intoned as he and his son made deep bows and their wives deep curtsies.

"Come now, Bedford, there is no reason to stand on such ceremony; we are cousins after all. How are you Cousin Rose?" the Prince asked.

"I am well, thank you, Cousin Frederick," the Duchess returned.

"I believe you have met all of the gentlemen here except for Mr. Bennet, the master of this estate," the Prince said, and the Duke of Bedford confirmed it was so.

"This is Thomas Bennet, who I am sure by now you know from Marie is the adoptive father of my daughter, Princess Elizabeth. Bennet, Lord Sedgwick and Lady Rosamund Rhys-Davies, the Duke and Duchess of Bedford, and their son, Lord Sedgwick Junior, Marquess of Birchington. You met the Marchioness the other day." The Prince performed the needed introductions.

"Will we meet our cousin Elizabeth?" Lady Rose asked hopefully.

"You will, your Grace; however, she is assisting her sister into her wedding gown, I believe," Bennet stated.

"As your adoptive daughter is our cousin, please call me Bedford, my son Birchington, and I am sure my wife would want you to call her Lady Rose," the Duke allowed. "There is no need for 'your Grace.'"

"Now, Cousin, who is this *Uncle Freddy* Marie was telling us about?" Lady Rose asked with a smile.

"I will explain, but I want to apologise to Lady Marie for my anger-fuelled rebuke. It should have been reserved for her parents, not her. Believe me when I tell you, I understand better than most how one is forced to live with the dictates of parents," the Prince granted.

"Your anger is justified, your Highness," Lady Marie replied. "It also helped open our eyes to the cruelty my parents visited on our late sister. To keep peace with our parents, we tried to ignore their actions and carry on as normal for too long, but those days are past."

"It is a pity it came to this point, but my Cilla left clear instructions, and as her parents never attempted to reach out to her, there was nothing to be done," The Prince clarified.

"You mentioned Priscilla is resting eternally at St. Alfred's near Meryton?" Lady Marie asked. Bennet nodded once that this was true. "Wes and I intend to visit her grave before we depart for London after the wedding."

Just then Fanny entered the drawing room with Jane and Elizabeth. "That is a good idea," Fanny approved the idea without reservation.

The Duke and Duchess, who had known Priscilla before she married, instantly knew who her daughter was even before she approached Marie and hugged her aunt. Introductions were made, and Jane and the Bennets were congratulated on Jane's imminent nuptials. It was decided that there would be time at and after the wedding breakfast to talk to Elizabeth as the hour to depart for the church at Longbourn had arrived.

~~~~~~~/~~~~~~~

Charlotte Lucas was not devoid of intelligence and for a while now had suspected 'Uncle Freddy' was more than the late Lady Priscilla's ex-husband. Seeing the array of peers of the realm seated in the church was one thing, but then four people entered just before the start of the wedding rites and Charlotte did not miss the greetings. From what she heard, they were the Duke and Duchess of Bedford and the Marquess and Marchioness of Birchington.

Charlotte's parents used to be the only titled persons in the area before Lady Priscilla took up residence at Netherfield —even though her father was a lowly knight. Then sometime after the lady's death, the neighbourhood found out her former husband was none other than a Prince, second in line to the throne. About ten or eleven years ago the Bennets seemed to become close connections of a number of peers and an extremely wealthy and well-established family from Derbyshire.

Charlotte did not fail to recognise the protective cocoon around her friend Eliza either, although she had never verbalised her thoughts. Given what she was seeing at Jane's wedding, Charlotte decided it was time to have a conversation with her friend.

Before Charlotte could muse further on the subject, Mrs. Bennet and the members of her family who were not involved in the wedding party took their seats. Charlotte saw the handsome Viscount take his position to the right of the altar with Mr. Fitzwilliam behind him. Mr. Dudley and his curate, Mr. Collins, assumed their positions. Charlotte smiled shyly to herself; she felt as if there were butterflies in her stomach when she watched Mr. Collins on the dais.

Just then, the vestibule door opened and Elizabeth glided up the aisle to take her position opposite Richard. William Darcy was struck dumb at the sight of her, for he had never seen her look better. Her maid had done wonders with her sometimes unruly tresses, and her light-green velvet gown accentuated all of her bountiful womanly assets.

Once Elizabeth took her position, Mr. Dudley indicated the congregants should stand. Both vestibule doors opened, and Jane entered the church on her father's arm. She was glowing with happiness as her eyes sought and found her groom's; his awe and obvious approval were apparent in the smile which seemed to grow with every step that she took toward him.

Bennet stopped and lifted Jane's delicate, gossamer veil. "I could not have parted with you for one less worthy, my Jane; you will be a very happy woman," Bennet told his daughter quietly as he kissed her on the cheek.

"Thank you, Papa, I will be," Jane averred and kissed her father on his cheek before he lowered her veil again. Her attention shifted to Andrew who was standing ready as Bennet placed his eldest daughter's hand on her groom's arm. The two then turned as one and took their place in front of the parson.

Before they knew it, the two had recited their vows and the rector intoned the final benediction of the wedding ceremony. "God the Father, God the Son, God the Holy Ghost, bless, preserve, and keep you; the Lord mercifully with his favour look upon you; and so fill you with all spiritual benediction and grace, that ye may so live together in this life, that in the world to come ye may have life everlasting. *Amen.*"

Save signing the register in the vestry, it was done. The congregation stood as Mr. Collins led the couple and their two attendants to the vestry where the register was open to the relevant page. Jane signed 'Bennet' for the final time, was followed by her husband, and then the two witnesses. Once the register was signed, Elizabeth, Richard, and Mr. Collins withdrew and closed the door.

Andrew pulled his wife, who went most willingly, to him and captured her lips. This was not as chaste a kiss as most of their previous ones had been. It was a toe-curling kiss that held a heady promise of things to come, which caused Jane's heart to speed up beyond anything she had ever experienced.

After inducing him to bestow another that left both husband and wife gasping for breath, they forced themselves apart because their family was waiting for them just beyond the door, and it was the vestry at a church, after all. Neither of them realised Andrew's hands had dislodged some of the pins in Jane's hair until they were settled and one of Jane's tresses was teasing her neck. The pins were located on the floor and Andrew assisted his wife in replacing them. Once they had put themselves to rights, the couple exited the vestry to welcoming cheers and wishes for their happiness from the waiting extended family.

~~~~~~~/~~~~~~~

"Andrew and Jane Fitzwilliam, Viscount and Viscountess Hilldale," Nichols announced proudly as the newlywed Fitzwilliams entered the ballroom at Netherfield Park where a sumptuous wedding breakfast, planned by Fanny, Elaine, and Edith, was laid out on groaning tables.

For the next hour, the couple made their rounds of the room, greeting and thanking one and all for their attendance and good wishes. When they reached the tables where the family was seated, Jane was introduced to the three Rhys-Davies she had not yet met.

Elizabeth's newly met aunt and uncle looked on with happiness, appreciating anew their decision to go their own way, which had brought them into the bosom of a large and loving family.

"Eliza, will you join me on the balcony please?" Charlotte requested.

"Was there something particular you wanted to show me, Charlotte?" Elizabeth asked once they gained the chosen balcony. It was cold, but after being in the hot ballroom neither repined the fresh air.

"Eliza, long have I suspected there was a secret about you. Seeing the number of peers, the way you are guarded and protected, and the way the Prince looks at you with fatherly pride, my suspicions have risen to the point I must ask you what is the secret about you? If you choose not to tell me, I will understand, but you know me well enough to be assured of my discretion." Charlotte waited, watching a number of emotions play across her friend's face both as she asked her question and while she waited for a reply.

"You know I prefer not to keep this from you, my dearest," Elizabeth opened. "It started the day I was born..." Elizabeth told Charlotte an abbreviated version of events up until she was informed of her heritage some days before.

Now it was Charlotte's turn to be silent as she stared at her friend in wonder. "My goodness, Eliza you are a royal—a Princess!" The two looked around after Charlotte's exclamation and fortunately there were none close enough to them to hear.

"I am still Elizabeth—or in your case only, Eliza—so please do not treat me any differently. My birthfather will return to London on the morrow and speak to his parents. Once they decide how they want to proceed—whether they want to acknowledge me even—then I will know more about my way forward," Elizabeth explained.

"It goes without saying I will not mention what I now know to another living soul until your rank and parentage become public knowledge," Charlotte assured her friend.

"Your integrity and confidence were never in doubt," Elizabeth stated meaningfully. "Now, let us return to the ballroom." The two friends linked arms and made their way back to Elizabeth's family.

After Jane and Andrew enjoyed a small repast and some lemonade, they continued to mingle with the guests for another hour. Jane gave Elizabeth a nod, and the two made their way to Jane's former bedchamber.

"Jane, I have never seen you glow with happiness as you do now. Thank you for giving us such an honourable and fine brother," Elizabeth hugged her sister after she had changed into her travel attire.

"Oh Lizzy, why cannot everyone be so happy as I am?" Jane gushed.

"When each of us find a man—or in Tommy's case, a lady —so well matched to us, I am sure we will know the same joy you are experiencing today, Janie," Elizabeth opined.

"You mean like a certain tall, dark-haired, blue-eyed man of our acquaintance," Jane teased.

"Much can happen before I come out in more than a year. You know I hope it will be William, but we none of us know the future," Elizabeth stated evenly.

"It is time, Lizzy," Jane informed her sister as her maid took her wedding gown and remaining valise down to be loaded into the coach. After one last wistful look around the suite of her childhood, Jane and Elizabeth joined Andrew and the rest of the family under the portico in front of the manor house.

There were many hugs and kisses for Jane, and not a few backslaps for Andrew interspersed with a bear-hug or eight. Once all the farewells were received, the newlyweds boarded the comfortable Hilldale chaise and six.

Andrew knocked his cane on the ceiling, and the driver gave a flick of the reins, which put the team in motion. The family remained waving until the carriage reached a turn in the drive and it disappeared from view.

Later that evening when Elizabeth informed her parents and birthfather she had disclosed the truth to Charlotte, none were surprised to learn she had suspected part of the truth on her own, given the lady's intelligence.

CHAPTER 27

Once the celebration of Jane and Andrew's wedding was over and the guests departed, only the four Rhys-Davies remained at Netherfield Park with the extended family. "Not seeing Jane here with her sisters and brother will take some getting used to," Fanny reflected as she watched her family.

"That it will," Bennet agreed. He had no doubt Jane was with the man she was supposed to be with, but that did not stop him from feeling a small part of his heart was missing.

"Elizabeth, you remember you met the Duke, Duchess, and Marquis before we departed for the church, do you not?" Fanny reminded her daughter.

"Yes, Mama, I do," Elizabeth replied.

"Lady Rose is a cousin to your grandmother," Fanny did not miss that Elizabeth bristled, assuming the wrong grandmother, so she added quickly, "Your *paternal* grandmother, Queen Charlotte."

Elizabeth relaxed visibly. "It is good to make the acquaintance of more cousins, your Graces," Elizabeth allowed.

"The pleasure is ours, Your Royal Highness," Lady Rose returned. Elizabeth had tried not to think too much about her rank, but it was at that moment she assimilated the fact that in society at large she was ranked higher than a duke and duchess.

After hearing of the musical prowess of the family, Lady Rose requested the young ladies exhibit for her. The Rhys-Davies and Wes, listening to their performances, realised their abilities, if anything, had been understated. The singing, especially Elizabeth's, was sublime.

"Your mother will enjoy her granddaughter's accomplishments greatly, Cousin," Lady Rose remarked to the Prince.

"I cannot but agree, Cousin Rose," the Prince said. "All I can hope is that my parents are not too angry with me for hiding their granddaughter's existence from them for so long."

"I agree with your opinion. His Majesty will have parliament remove Elizabeth from the line of succession; therefore, it is my opinion that the King and Queen will not be too put out," Bedford surmised with a small smile for the princess.

"Will you bring your daughter with you when you travel to Buckingham House on the morrow?" Lady Rose asked.

"No. If my parents want to meet her—as I assume they will—I will send an express to Bennet and he and the whole family will travel to London," the Prince averred. "Once her existence becomes public knowledge, the royal guard around her will no longer have to be disguised as footmen and outriders."

"I have a suggestion," Darcy stated. "Why do we not all travel to London? The Bennets can stay with us at Darcy House or across the square at Matlock House, or Holder House is available for their use. This way their Majesties will not have to wait the length of a day to meet their granddaughter if they request it."

"Unless there is an objection," Bennet replied thankfully, "we will take you up on your invitation, Darcy."

"What about your aversion to Town, Papa?" Elizabeth challenged; her eyebrow perfectly arched to convey her expectation.

"I will survive, Lizzy. I know Darcy House's library is not Pemberley's, but if I know my friend here, it is impressively stocked and will provide me adequate reading material," Bennet told his daughter.

"As we are to travel, I have much to arrange," Fanny stood and was followed out by Ladies Elaine and Edith.

"We are for Town, but as soon as you know the schedule of events with the royals, let us know as we would enjoy having you all for dinner at Bedford House on Russell Square,"

Lady Rose invited.

Not long after, the Rhys-Davies departed for London, Wes De Melville with them.

~~~~~~~/~~~~~~~

"Sarah, I am sure our children will relent," Lord Jersey told his wife with confidence as they sat in their lonely house. It had been many months since they had received an invitation or even a response to one they had issued.

"How can you be sure they will?" Lady Jersey asked. "Why did you force us to break with Priscilla? Look where it has left us; you were so worried about society and now your cruel decision has made us pariahs."

"I was sure I was doing the right thing to protect our social position and look at where we are now. How can the *Ton* treat me, the Earl of Jersey, thusly!" Lord Jersey spat out.

"Wes was correct; we are now reaping what we sowed. I should have found a way to contact our daughter regardless of your wishes. I will never forgive you for separating me from my daughter," Lady Sarah stated in rare open defiance of her controlling husband.

Lady Sarah knew from the very beginning what her husband had done to their daughter when she needed their support the most was neither moral nor correct, but even if he now realised this, her husband would never allow himself to admit it to her, never mind anyone else.

If Lord Jersey were pressed to be honest, he would have admitted there was a determination in his younger two children. No matter what he told his wife, and regardless of the bravado it was proclaimed with, Lord Cyril De Melville had the feeling they had lost their two remaining children. His over developed pride would not allow him to admit how great an error he had made.

~~~~~~~/~~~~~~~

The carriages arrived at Darcy House just after midday on Tuesday. The Killions, Darcy House's butler and housekeeper, were waiting at the entrance to the house by the time the footmen placed the steps and opened the doors.

It was the first time the Bennets had visited Darcy House. They were impressed at the understated elegance of the décor and furnishings of the house, along the lines of what they had seen at Pemberley, which the master credited to his late wife's excellent eye for decoration. There was no doubt that everything was of the best quality, but like Pemberley it was designed for comfort, not for display.

"Uncle Robert, your house is wonderful," Elizabeth exclaimed when she returned from her bedchamber after washing and changing. By the time she arrived in her assigned chambers, Jacqui had almost completed unpacking. As he always was—and now Elizabeth understood why—Mr. Taylor was in a suite towards the end of the hall on the family floor.

"Thank you, Lizzy; it was your Aunt Anne's mission to make a comfortable home for all of us to live in, and she took much pleasure in so doing," Darcy shared wistfully as he thought about his beloved wife. "She would have loved to see everyone here, and your pleasure in it even more so."

"When will we hear from Father?" Elizabeth asked. She was full of frenetic energy and would not be able to relax until she knew one way or the other.

"He should have arrived at Buckingham House about the same time we arrived here," Fanny informed her daughter. "It will not be too long before we hear something."

~~~~~~~/~~~~~~~

"You requested to see us," the King intoned. The King, Queen, and the Prince of Wales were in a parlour with Frederick.

"Yes, Father, Mother, and George. I need to inform you of something. There is something I have kept from you on the strength of my late Priscilla's request. You remember some years ago I told you my beloved had passed after birthing a stillborn son?" Frederick reminded his parents and eldest brother.

"Yes, Son, we remember your telling us," the King replied

carefully, unable to fathom the turn of conversation. "Why do you bring this up now?"

"The account I gave you was not entirely factual," Frederick owned.

"You would never have lied about your ex-wife's death, so that means the son lived," the Queen reckoned.

"Not quite. Priscilla did not birth a stillborn son; she gave birth to a healthy and beautiful baby girl," Frederick revealed. "She has been raised as the daughter of my Priscilla's best friend—her sister of the heart—since she was born."

"Are you telling us that a royal Princess was kidnapped? That is treason!" the King pronounced.

"No, father, that is most certainly *not* what I am telling you. Priscilla made the Bennets our daughter's guardians, so they have done nothing except fulfil her and *my* express wishes," Frederick explained. "In fact, I issued the Bennets a royal indemnification certifying that my daughter was placed with them with my full agreement."

"Why did Priscilla not want her daughter—your daughter—to know her grandparents?" the Queen asked, having had a moment to digest the news. Her hurt was undeniable. She was a queen, but she was also a loving grandmother who ached for the child she had long been denied.

"That is a complicated question. She did not object to your knowing Elizabeth; she only wanted her to have a chance to grow up in a loving family and not in a country house with the coldness of governesses and tutors," Frederick explained. It was easy to see his parents understood the implied rebuke in his words, and both winced at the facts so boldly stated.

"Did you know from her birth?" the Prince of Wales asked, insightfully.

"No, I was not to be told until she was eighteen to make sure she was allowed to be raised as Priscilla desired, however..." Frederick told of the reasons for the disclosures more than eleven years ago.

"So now we understand why you spend so much of your

time in Hertfordshire," the Queen stated, more to herself than anyone. "Has your daughter ever been in London?"

"No, Mother. Today is her first day in town. She is the splitting image of her mother, which is what led the late Lady Anne and then Lady Elaine to know whose daughter she was. It is less than a sennight since my daughter was told of her parentage. She is extremely angry—almost as much as I am—at her maternal grandparents and has no desire to know them." Frederick paused to internalise his anger at the Earl and Countess of Jersey before it boiled up again.

"Brother are you telling me your former wife's parents do not know their daughter has been dead these sixteen years?" the Prince of Wales asked in utter disbelief.

"Yes, and until recently neither did the Marchioness of Birchington and Viscount Westmore. When they came to apologise to Priscilla and beg her pardon, they were informed and have met Elizabeth, as have the Duke and Duchess of Bedford and their heir," Frederick informed his family members.

"Technically, she is fourth in line for the throne, but given her birth was after the divorce I will not anger the church; I will see she is removed from the line of succession by Parliament," the King decreed.

"I expected that, Father. In fact, she has been promised it would be so, to her relief. When you meet her you will see titles, pomp, and ceremony are not things that interest her. She and her sisters are wonderful musicians. My daughter has the voice of an angel, and can speak many more languages than I," Frederick owned.

"Then her education has not been neglected?" the King asked.

"Not at all. She is as educated as any man I know. She debates rings around the Darcy heir, who studied at Cambridge. My daughter is beautiful inside and out, my natural bias notwithstanding," Frederick reported proudly.

The Queen looked at the King who nodded. "We will recognise Princess Elizabeth as our granddaughter with all rights and privileges of a Princess of the United Kingdom of Great Britain and Ireland, excepting her ineligibility to be part of the line of succession once Parliament acts. When may we meet her?" the Queen asked hopefully.

"Before you answer that, and given her feelings for the Jerseys, is she not also angry with us for forcing the divorce on you and your Priscilla, Frederick?" The King asked, not wanting to upset his granddaughter. He felt a renewed remorse for having forced that which had separated his second son from his beloved wife, and in turn his granddaughter from her birthparents. Hearing that the upbringing of his favourite son was amongst the reasons her late mother had wanted her raised as she had been, he longed to see the hitherto unknown princess and begin to make up for his actions, even if they had been right for the Kingdom and could not be corrected.

"She is not, and you have her birthmother to thank for that…" Frederick explained what Priscilla had written and her explanation of the King's duty to crown and country.

"We are very sorry she is no longer with us; she was an exceptional lady. What were Jersey and his wife thinking? Did they not know what we did, we did for England and did not want to hurt either of you? They presumed we would take pleasure in being so cruel?" the King mused. "We are tired, we will rest."

Once his father had left the parlour, Frederick turned to his mother to address her question. "May we bring her on the morrow, Mother?" Frederick requested. The Queen nodded her assent. "Would ten o'clock be agreeable to you?" The Queen nodded again, a small smile showing she was looking forward to it.

~~~~~~~/~~~~~~~

"The King raised the spectre of treason?" Bennet asked with no little trepidation. "I have long worried that he might."

"It took me less than a minute to point out the truth of the matter to my father, and he understands it was with my full permission and approval you and Fanny raised Lizzy. It all went very much as I predicted. Lizzy will not be in the line of succession; it needs an act of Parliament, but it will be quickly and quietly done. Other than that, she will be recognised as a legitimate Princess of the United Kingdom of Great Britain and Ireland." Frederick went on to tell Bennet, Fanny, and Darcy about his meeting and the King's sentiments regarding the Earl and Countess of Jersey.

"It is only right they should suffer now after the way they treated their own flesh and blood!" Fanny stated vehemently. "As she had stated she wants nothing to do with them, what will happen if they importune Lizzy?"

"Then I will execute my threat and my father will act on my recommendation. The King will have the Earl and Countess stripped of their titles, but rather than confiscate their lands, Wes will be elevated to Earl as soon as it happens—if they are so foolish as to attempt such a thing," the Prince stated emphatically.

"Who will be with us when we meet the King and Queen on the morrow?" Bennet asked.

"All of the Bennets, excepting the newlyweds. They know Jane is on her honeymoon in East Sussex," the Prince averred.

"Let us inform the children," Fanny suggested.

~~~~~~~/~~~~~~~

At a few minutes past ten, the Lord Chamberlain showed the Bennets into the receiving room in Buckingham House. The gold everywhere made it the most ornate room any of them had ever seen. On the opposite wall were two thrones; both had gold frames with red velvet upholstery. The King was seated on their right and the Queen on their left.

Prince Frederick stood next to his father, and to his right was a rotund man the Bennet parents assumed was the Prince of Wales. Elizabeth walked between her parents as they approached the thrones, with her sisters and brother walking behind them.

When the Lord Chamberlain indicated they should stop, all seven bowed low and curtsied deeply to the King and

Queen. "We welcome you to Buckingham House, Mr. and Mrs. Bennet," the King drawled. "And a special welcome to you, Princess Beth. We welcome the Misses Bennet and Master Bennet as well." The King turned to Frederick. "From what we remember of the late Lady Priscilla, you are correct, Frederick, our granddaughter is a true likeness of her mother."

"You mean her *birthmother*, Father. Mrs. Bennet is Princess Beth's mother." Frederick pointed out quietly. The King nodded, verbally agreeing it was so.

"Approach, Granddaughter," the Queen ordered. "We do not bite." Elizabeth approached the Queen's throne until she was a foot away. "You did not exaggerate, Son; your daughter is a true beauty." The Queen's focus turned back to Elizabeth. "We have a daughter Elizabeth, so when you visit us and she is present, there will be two Princesses Elizabeth at court."

"I am sure we can find a solution that will not cause confusion, your majesty," Elizabeth stated. Her decided lack of fear above all was impressive to the person she was addressing.

"What is your full name, child?" the Queen asked.

"Elizabeth Priscilla Francine Bennet," Elizabeth replied.

"It is good your name honours both your birthmother and your mother," the Queen opined. The Queen turned to her second son. "She is delightful, Frederick." Then her Majesty turned back to her granddaughter. "We will call you Beth so we do not confuse you with our daughter Elizabeth. Welcome to the family, Beth." The Queen stood and opened her arms for her granddaughter, bestowing a warm hug upon Elizabeth.

As the Queen sat, the King held out his hand and Elizabeth kissed it, then she backed away and re-joined her parents. "Our son had told us of the love and care you have shown our granddaughter," the King stated. "We will reward you."

"With all due respect, your Majesty, nothing we did was done with an eye to a reward. It was done out of love and to honour the dying wish of my best friend in the whole world," Fanny informed the monarch.

"We are well aware you did nothing expecting a reward,

but it is our prerogative to grant one," the King returned.

The Lord Chamberlain instructed Bennet to kneel in front of the King. "I name you Baron Longbourn." The King stood and tapped Bennet on the shoulder with his ceremonial sword. "Arise, Lord Thomas."

"Lady Francine, our son has told us our granddaughter is most accomplished, as are her adopted sisters. We invite you and your daughters to tea, two days hence at eleven. My lady in waiting, the Duchess of Wolverhampton, will send you the pertinent details." The Queen had issued an invitation, but Fanny—Lady Francine—was well aware it was a summons and not an invitation.

"It will be our pleasure, your Majesty. As you are a connoisseur of music, may I be so bold as to suggest Ladies Matlock and Holder, their daughters, and Miss Darcy be included?" Fanny replied.

"We will have our lady send invitations to them as well. We understand our Cousin Rose was at your eldest daughter's recent wedding." The Queen stated and Fanny nodded it was so. "We will invite our cousin and her daughter-in-law as well," the Queen decided.

After the Bennets backed out of the receiving room, they were joined by Frederick. "Did you know the King was going to make me a baron?" Bennet asked, a decided frown on his countenance, as he had loved their daughter from the day she was born and had needed no such reward.

"It was as much a surprise to me as it was to you," the Prince averred.

"Well then, Lady Francine, I think it is time to return to Darcy House to prepare for the dinner at Bedford House this evening," Lord Thomas, the Baron of Longbourn stated.

"Papa am I *Lord Tommy* now?" the youngest Bennet asked.

"No, Son. One day, when you inherit Longbourn, you will become Lord Tommy, now you are the Honourable Tommy Bennet," Bennet explained, mussing his son's hair as they stepped into the carriage.

With the Prince accompanying them, the Bennets departed Buckingham House for Darcy House.

CHAPTER 28

On Wednesday morning, the Fitzwilliams and Carringtons were visiting the Darcys and Bennets when the Prince stopped by after meeting with his parents and siblings at Buckingham House.

His other brothers and sisters who were in Town were informed they had a hitherto unknown niece and were keen to meet Princess Beth and introduce her to her cousins. The King and Queen told their son that a royal notice would appear in the evening editions of the papers announcing Princess Elizabeth Priscilla Francine Bennet, which would state that she was recognized as a legitimate grandchild.

"It seems that Lizzy's introduction to the King and Queen could not have gone better," Matlock stated just before the Prince informed the group of the impending notice.

"True, except I believe Bennet has omitted to share his news with you. Will you tell them or should I, *Lord Thomas*?" The Prince was distracted momentarily as Bennet rolled his eyes.

"Did the King elevate our friend?" Holder asked.

"How is it you never mentioned anything after your return from Buckingham House?" Darcy added.

"The King named Bennet Baron Longbourn in thanks for looking after his granddaughter all of these years," the Prince informed the group. "The announcement will be with the one about Lizzy and list the elevation of Lord and Lady Longbourn."

"Lady Francine," Lady Elaine stated, "how well that sounds."

"York, were you aware your father was going to bestow a

title on Bennet, here?" Holder asked.

"Not until the Lord Chamberlain had Bennet kneel. Even though Bennet and Fanny protested the need to honour them thusly, in my opinion they deserve this and more." The Prince met Bennet's stare, challenging his daughter's adopted father to gainsay him.

Bennet raised his hands in surrender. "It is not something I wanted, imagined, or needed, but one does not tell the King they are not willing to accept an award from him," Bennet stated stoically. "It was not a question of my preference, it was quite decided already so there was nothing to be done but accept grasciously."

"Poor Sir William and Lady Lucas. They thrived on the fact they were the only titled ones in the neighbourhood—that is until *Uncle Freddy* was revealed to be a Prince—then all of the titled visitors in the neighbourhood made them feel their own insignificance," Fanny told the group. "Before that, they were the only citizens of the area with titles, but now we are above them in rank, not to mention what they will say when they find out our Lizzy is royalty. We will include them in our social life as we always have so they can see we are as we have ever been. The new titles will not change us, save our address in formal situations."

"That reminds me," the Prince stated, "now that Lizzy is being recognised and the notice will mention her *late mother*, I believe it is time to post Priscilla's final letter."

"You have the right of it, York," Bennet agreed, then looked at his wife to gauge her opinion on the matter.

"There is no choice now," Fanny allowed. "I suspected it would need to be done so I have the letter with me. I will write the direction and place it with your outgoing post, Robert."

"If I may, I would like to write a note to be included with the letter to warn my daughter's other grandparents not to dare approach or importune her or my wrath will be great," the Prince stated firmly.

Darcy gave the Prince the use of his desk. It did not take

long to write a succinct missive, and its meaning could not be missed. If the Earl and Countess of Jersey ignored the warning contained in the letter, it would be at their peril.

~~~~~~~/~~~~~~~

The next day, the post arrived at Broadhurst, along with the previous evening's broadsheets from London. As usual, letters were placed on the master's desk by the butler, and the newspapers on the table in the breakfast parlour.

Lord Jersey was enjoying his repast, trying once more to ascertain a way to regain the society which they had once enjoyed, when he heard his wife dissolve into tears and wail in anguish. "Sarah, what is it?"

"Priscilla is dead, and she had a daughter!" Lady Jersey cried. "Your cruel actions have forever denied me seeing my daughter again!"

"What makes you utter such nonsense?" Lord Jersey demanded. Without another word, his crying wife passed him the paper opened to the page she was reading.

Lord Jersey's eyes nearly popped out of his head. There was a royal decree announcing the King and Queen's acceptance of their granddaughter, Princess Elizabeth Priscilla Francine *Bennet*. The notice mentioned the sad passing of her birth-mother, Princess Priscilla, in childbirth. There was not a word about her maternal grandparents, but in the same notice it mentioned the elevation of a new baron, Lord Thomas Bennet.

"The last thing my daughter knew of us in this world was that we rejected her," Lady Jersey lamented, the guilt over not finding a way to circumvent her husband crushing her. "There is no mention of us. First your actions denied me my daughter; now it seems we will not be allowed to be part of our granddaughter's life."

"Pish tosh," Lord Jersey returned dismissively. "The girl will be our way back into society."

After he broke his fast, as was his wont, the master of the estate repaired to his study, noticing Prince Frederick's seal on a thick letter waiting at the top of the pile. In his mind this was the redemption Lord Jersey was hoping for. When he opened it, he noted there was a single sheet he presumed was from the prince, but he focused on the second missive because the names—his and his wife's names—were in his late daughter's hand, though the direction was in a hand he did not know at all.

Lord Jersey had his wife summoned, and he handed her the letter from their daughter to read, wanting to know what she had written, then he would turn his attention to that which the prince had added. Lady Sarah read aloud.

27 February 1790

Lord and Lady Jersey,

I will not use the appellation of mother and father, as what you have done to me—broken with me when I needed your succour the most—are not the actions of those worthy of the name Mother and Father.

If you are reading this letter, then I did not survive the birth of my child, so this will serve as a final goodbye. No matter the sex of the child, if I am alive to do so, I will use your names as the child's middle name, Sarah if it is a girl and Cyril for a boy. No matter how you have treated me, you are my parents and gifted me with life.

"Let me read the notice again," Lady Sarah found the page. "There is no Sarah in her name; I have a feeling our granddaughter demanded her name be changed once she was informed of the way we treated her mother. She assumed I supported your cruel cutting of our daughter; I cannot blame her as she had no way of knowing." Her tears flowing anew, she returned to read the rest of the short message.

Whether or not you have my child in your lives is up to you. If you try to contact me because you are contrite for your treatment of me—your firstborn—then you will be welcomed with open arms.

If you are motivated by anything else, my sister Fanny knows my wishes and you will only receive this letter when my child's existence becomes public knowledge, or he/she reaches the age of eighteen, whichever occurs first.

Your heartbroken daughter,

Priscilla

Lord Jersey saw his dreams of redemption through his granddaughter crumble before his eyes. The only hope now was the letter from the Prince; mayhap there was still some salvation in that missive.

"I should have never acquiesced to your decree, Cyril. For shame, I did not have it in me to stand up to you even when I knew it was wrong. That guilt will be with me for the rest of my days. Now I will never see my firstborn until I am granted entrance to heaven—if I am granted such," Lady Sarah stated firmly.

Without comment, her husband read the note from the Prince, still telling himself their—his—vindication would be contained within.

18 December 1806

London

Do not for one moment think about importuning my daughter!

If—and only if—she indicates her desire to know you—which after the way you treated her birthmother is unlikely—then you may approach her. If you do so without expressed invitation, the penalty I enumerated that day at Netherfield Park will be executed immediately. I have the full support of my father—the King!

Frederick, Prince of the United Kingdom of Great Britain and Ireland, Duke of York and Albany, Earl of Ulster.

Lord Jersey's delusion of being saved evaporated as the unambiguous letter from the Prince dropped to his desk. He felt a burning pain in his left arm, followed by a massive and excruciating pain in his chest. He pitched forward, his head bouncing on his desk before he fell to the floor. His eyes were unseeing even before his head hit the floor of his study.

For some moments, Lady Jersey sat motionless. Her husband was not moving at all, and it took her a little while before she summoned the strength to call out. The footman on duty outside the study looked in. Seeing the master lying prostrate on the floor, he made haste to summon the butler and house-keeper. Before making for the study, the butler sent the footman to request the local physician come to Broadhurst with all speed.

Lady Sarah knew she should feel sadness at her husband's death, but she could not. She felt a wave of relief knowing he would never control her again. Her husband's cruelty had cost her so much—far too much.

~~~~~~~/~~~~~~~

There was insistent knocking at Darcy House later that afternoon. Mr. Killion showed Wes into the drawing room where the Bennets, Darcys, and the Prince were seated. No one missed the look of anguish on young De Melville's face.

"I must to Broadhurst; my father is no more," Wes reported.

"You have our deepest sympathy, Lord Jersey," the Prince spoke for them all.

"Marie, her husband, and I depart within the hour. I am sure you will not want to, but I have to ask, Lizzy. Would you like to be with the family?" Wes asked. "I should have made this plain to you before, my mother did not want to break with my late sister, my father ordered her to do so and had her watched to make sure her letters she tried to write to Priscilla were intercepted."

Elizabeth looked to her adoptive parents and her birth-father for guidance. "It is your choice, Lizzy," Fanny informed her.

"It seems I must go, if for no other reason to support my aunt and uncles. It seems I may have judged my maternal grandmother unfairly. I would feel better if we all made the journey together," Elizabeth stated contemplatively.

"Darcy, may we leave the rest of our children here so Fanny and I may be with Lizzy?" Bennet requested.

"That goes without saying, Bennet. I am sure Gigi will

be very happy with the arrangement," Darcy returned with no hesitation.

"Papa and Mama, may Mary come with me, please? I will feel easier if I have one of my sisters with me." Elizabeth asked.

"Of course Mary may join us," Fanny granted.

"I will join you as well," the Prince stated.

Within the hour, a caravan of coaches departed London for Broadhurst.

~~~~~~~/~~~~~~~

It was dark when the convoy passed the gateposts of Broadhurst, which had been draped with black cloth. The full moon enabled the drivers to press on safely—albeit slowly—which negated the necessity to overnight at an inn.

Marie and Wes were the first to enter the house. They found their mother sitting with their late father in the largest of the drawing rooms. He was in an open coffin for viewing purposes. Wes was about to warn his mother about how much Lizzy looked like her late daughter when the dowager countess heard voices in the hall and stood to welcome the guests to her home. Even in mourning, Lady Sarah's instincts as a hostess kicked in.

Luckily, Wes was close to his mother when she saw Elizabeth. Lady Sarah fainted at the spectre of her late daughter coming to haunt her for the cruelty she had not been able to mitigate and which her husband had visited on Priscilla all those years ago.

Wes caught his mother before she fell to the marble floor of the hallway. He carried her to an armchair in the drawing room opposite the room with the coffin, and the housekeeper revived her mistress with salts. It was all the housekeeper could do not to faint away herself when she saw the young lady who was the image of Lady Priscilla.

When their mother started to revive, Wes and Marie stayed close by so that they could introduce her to her granddaughter. "Priscilla is dead, and she has come to haunt me for my not standing up to your father." Lady Sarah's voice quivered.

"Mother, we had hoped to tell you before you saw her, but that is not your daughter's spectre, but your granddaughter, Princess Elizabeth. You needed to be prepared for the fact Lizzy is an almost exact image of my sister," Marie informed her mother gently.

"Why does everyone refer to Priscilla as her *birth*mother rather than as her mother? Her father used the same term in his short note of warning," Lady Sarah asked.

Wes and Marie informed their mother about the newly elevated Bennets, and the fact they had raised Elizabeth with the Prince's full approval, so they were acknowledged by all—from the King downward—as her parents.

Once Lady Sarah assimilated this information, she looked from son to daughter. "I thought I would never see you two again," she admitted, finally so relieved her tears, held at bay when they arrived, were allowed to flow unchecked at last. "You are the Earl now, my son, and will be a good steward of the earldom; of that I am sure."

"Mother, I was aware you had to follow father's edicts. I am loathe to speak ill of one who has just passed away, but I suspected for some time you had no choice but to obey him once he made the decision to cut Priscilla. I explained this to Lizzy on our way here, so she has agreed to meet you," Wes explained.

"Would you like to meet your granddaughter?" Marie asked. Lady Sarah simply nodded, not trusting herself to speak at that moment.

Not many minutes later, Elizabeth, her adoptive parents, Mary, and the Prince entered the drawing room. "Will you introduce us please, Wes," Elizabeth requested.

"Your Royal Highness, Lord Thomas and Lady Francine Bennet, the Honourable Miss Bennet, my mother, Lady Sarah De Melville, Dowager Countess of Jersey. Mother, your granddaughter Elizabeth, her parents Thomas and Fanny Bennet, and her younger sister Mary," Wes intoned.

"Your Royal Highness, you look just like my Priscilla," Lady Sarah marvelled at the vision before her as the young woman's intelligent green eyes watched her intently. "I wish I was able to apologise to Priscilla. Even though I knew my late husband's decision was cruel, I ceased objecting when he commanded it should be so. He intercepted my letters and had me watched. I should have..." Whatever Lady Sarah was about to say died on her lips as Elizabeth sat next to her on the settee and placed her hand on her grandmother's arm.

"I forgive you, *grandmother*, as I am sure my birthmother would have as well," Elizabeth granted. Her statement caused Lady Sarah to break into great wracking sobs as she understood how many years had been wasted by her not standing up to her husband. "I cannot imagine what it was like for you to be denied contact with your daughter."

"I am so very sorry," Lady Sarah managed as her sobs subsided.

The funeral service was held the following day, the day Elizabeth was supposed to have tea with her other grandmother, but the Prince had sent a note requesting it be rescheduled for the following week after they returned to London, and before the Bennets and the rest of their party were to return home to Netherfield Park for Christmastide.

The Prince felt badly about his uncharitable feelings toward his former mother-in-law, but he consoled himself with the knowledge he had no way of knowing. He did know his Cilla was smiling in heaven to know her mother never wanted to abandon her.

It was a small group of men who attended the service and interment. On Monday morning everyone began the journey back to London—including Lady Sarah.

~~~~~~~/~~~~~~~

It did not take long for word to be disseminated that Lady Sarah was accepted as a full member of society once again and that she had reconciled with her children and granddaughter. Any who had residual doubts were convinced when, two days after returning to London, word was spread abroad that Lady Sarah would have been one of the parties who attended the tea with the Queen at Buckingham House if not for being in deep mourning.

The tea was reported to have been a resounding success. It was soon known far and wide how impressed her Majesty had been with the musical talents of her granddaughter, her adoptive sisters, Lady Cassandra Carrington, Miss Anne de Bourgh, and Miss Georgiana Darcy. She was impressed with both their playing, and their singing, especially when they combined for a song and harmonised perfectly.

Lady Sarah was invited to reclaim her position of one of the patronesses of Almack's to begin after her year of mourning, but she demurred, claiming she would spend her time getting to know her granddaughter and her extended family.

By the time the convoy of carriages departed London that Thursday, the denizens of Meryton and the surrounding area were on tenterhooks waiting to call on their elevated friends and the Princess who had been hidden in their midst for so many years.

Sir William and Lady Lucas finally accepted that the honour Sir William had received from the King was the lowest on the rung of those available. They decided they should hope to be accepted for who they were rather than for a title they held. None at Lucas Lodge missed Charlotte's knowing smile as she waited to meet her friend again now the truth was known.

At Netherfield Park, the four Gardiner children could not wait to see their cousin, the Princess, again. Their parents pointed out that the same Lizzy they had known the whole of their lives would be arriving. That did not dim the excitement of the four young Gardiners, who were excited to see *Princess Lizzy*.

CHAPTER 29

February 1808

Rather than slip back into his former ways, George Wickham had gone from strength to strength working for Gardiner and Associates. During the year and a half George worked for Gardiner, he had been promoted three times; he was now an assistant manager of the warehouse.

When Mr. Lucas Wickham read the report from his employer, Mr. Darcy, in December of '06, he had been cautiously optimistic that his son had finally chosen to walk an honourable path. Darcy provided his steward with Gardiner's direction, and Wickham senior wrote to his son's employer, thanking him profusely for giving his son a chance after hearing the truth of George's past.

When the Darcys returned to Pemberley in May of '07, Mr. Wickham requested and had been granted a holiday. After he arrived at the Gardiners' house, Gardiner had accompanied Lucas Wickham to the warehouse, where the father watched his son diligently performing his duties for some time—George now supervised five clerks.

To say the reunion of father and son was a happy one would be an understatement. When he had parted from his son in York, Mr. Wickham believed it might be the final time he would see George. The gratitude and gratification he felt at having his son back was hard for the man to articulate.

As George's wages had increased, rather than spend more, he saved more. Before his first year of employment was completed, he had saved the fifty pounds and change he owed

Mr. Darcy. It gave him untold pleasure to burn the vowels Mr. Darcy had sent to him on receipt of the payment. What George did not know is Mr. Darcy turned the money received to pay the debt over to his steward to add to the amount he was saving for his son's legacy.

Given George's innate intelligence, Gardiner suggested he start taking classes at a local school. It was not Oxford or Cambridge, but if he graduated in a few years, he would be eligible to read the law, which had become George's dream.

Once George had been with Mr. Gardiner for a year, and the reports of George's work ethic and honesty remained as good—or better—as any others', Robert Darcy presented his steward with bank draft for two thousand five hundred pounds to be added to George's future legacy.

The irony was that although he was unaware of it, some of the projects he was in charge of for Mr. Gardiner were increasing his own legacy, as his father had invested his savings with Gardiner and Associates.

~~~~~~~/~~~~~~~

Miss Caroline Bingley had learnt to control the supercilious side of her character in order to save herself from going without any allowance. Based on her behaviour over the last year—which had been acceptable—her Uncle Paul agreed to allow Caroline to accompany Charles to Hertfordshire to act as mistress of his leased estate.

Caroline read the royal decree in December of '06 but did not pay attention to the details, nor to the names of the newly minted Baron and Baroness. Even though she had tamped her desire down for some time—in front of her family that is —Miss Bingley still believed she was destined to rise to the heights of society and was on the lookout for a man who would be able to help her achieve her aims.

After they arrived in the neighbourhood, Charles Bingley's level of frustration had risen significantly. His sister complained about everyone. The locals were savages, no class, no fashion, and on and on she went. When Bingley tried to explain to his younger sister that not only were all the landed gentry above her in rank, but that there were titled families and even royalty in the neighbourhood, Miss Bingley dismissed his words as nonsense.

She met Sir William when he called on Bingley soon after he took up the lease at Longbourn. Before the man left, Caroline denigrated him, proclaiming to all who could hear her that a knighthood was nothing. She was not present in the drawing room when Bingley's baron Longbourn, visited. Hearing her brother talk about the man after his visit she assumed it was another bumbling knight with delusions of grandeur, as he used the title of 'Lord'.

Louisa and Hurst joined Bingley at Longbourn a few weeks after he took up residence, and they agreed with Charles that it was pointless trying to tell their sister the truth as she heard naught that did not fit her preconceived notions. She would have to learn the hard way.

After Twelfth Night, the Darcys resided at Netherfield Park for a month before returning to London, and William made the mistake of calling on his acquaintance from Cambridge—at Longbourn.

Even though the Darcy heir paid her no attention and refused to answer any of her vulgar questions about Pemberley and his family's wealth, Caroline Bingley decided she had met her future husband. When her brother pointed out that from what he knew, Darcy was unofficially courting a lady—who was a royal and would be out in two months—his sister dismissed the information as meaningless, sure that once the Darcy heir became aware of her advantages, he would turn to her. She did have ten thousand pounds, after all.

~~~~~~~/~~~~~~~

Mrs. Charlotte Collins was a happy woman. William Collins asked for a courtship a few months after he became the curate at Longbourn's church; two months later he requested and had been granted Charlotte's hand.

Charlotte had always told the oldest two Bennet sisters

she was not a romantic, yet she had made a love match. They married in May of '07, and Charlotte had just felt the quickening of their first child. She and her husband were very comfortable in the Longbourn church's parsonage.

Mr. Dudley retired in June of that year, and after the good work Collins had done in the parish, coupled with the fact he was liked by the parishioners, and was given a glowing recommendation by the retiring clergyman, Bennet awarded the living to his distant cousin and never repined doing so.

At first, Collins had been wonderstruck by his titled cousins after their elevation in London. In addition to Bennet being named baron, and thanks to the recent weddings, he counted a number of peers, a viscount and viscountess, and a royal princess among his relations. Luckily, he did not have sycophantic tendencies, so as soon as he saw his family did not expect any special deference, Collins was able to relate to all in a way that never gave offence. Charlotte was happy to be related to the Bennets, cementing their friendship of many years, and continuing to enjoy her visits with Eliza.

<center>~~~~~~~/~~~~~~~</center>

The double wedding held at Snowhaven, the Fitzwilliam estate, had been an event everyone enjoyed. Richard and Cassie were given the use of Seaview cottage for their wedding trip, and Jamey and Anne travelled north to a small estate owned by the Carringtons, a little southeast of Dumfries in Scotland. The estate of Caerlaverock Heights boasted a triangular castle with a moat that had been built in the thirteenth century.

The former couple spent a month near Brighton, while the latter couple spent three weeks in Scotland. After their wedding trip, Richard and Cassie moved into Brookfield Meadows, where they had remained until joining the family in London for the little season of '07. Jamey and Anne took up residence at Rosings Park. Jamey's estate, Amberleigh, was smaller than his wife's; because they hoped to have visitors often, it was an easy choice to spend more of the year at Rosings Park than at Amberleigh.

Cassie believed she was with child, as she had just missed her third cycle of courses. Her new sister Anne had not missed any courses yet, which saddened her. Cassie had not mentioned anything to Richard—yet, but he—attuned to his wife's health—had a very good idea that she was with child. He respected her silence and the cause of it and would not mention it until Cassie spoke to him first. He understood she was waiting for the quickening. Thankfully, she had no significant illness in the mornings—so far.

~~~~~~~/~~~~~~~

Catherine de Bourgh would have been happy to return to her cottage in Hunsford after Anne's wedding, but Anne would not hear of it. She invited her mother to live with them. While Anne and Jamey had been enjoying their wedding trip, Catherine returned to her cottage and was most pleased with the way Mrs. Jenkinson had managed everything; she had even expanded the learning programmes begun by Catherine.

Once Catherine had gained access to all her funds, she had made plans to build a school in Hunsford to accommodate many more children—and offer subjects for adults in the evenings—as the converted cottage was too small to accommodate her long-term hopes.

Once other family members heard of her plan, more than enough money had been donated. The Prince adding ten thousand pounds of his own funds, so in addition to the school, a clinic was built, and money reserved to employ a doctor and an apothecary who would offer their services free to those in the area.

Once Lady Metcalf—who had cut Catherine over three years previously—realised her erstwhile friend was welcomed back into the bosom of her family and by royalty as well, she attempted to rekindle their friendship. Catherine had no time in her life for false friends, and rather than cutting the woman as had been done to her, she told her such politely to her face.

~~~~~~~/~~~~~~~

Elizabeth had cheerfully borne all of the 'Your Royal

Highness' greetings she had received when they returned to Meryton from London. Luckily, the novelty wore off quickly. Other than when Tommy, eleven, tried to annoy her or when she was addressed by those not acquainted with the family, she was Miss Elizabeth, Elizabeth, or Lizzy, to all who knew her. The exception was Charlotte Collins and the Lucas clan, who called her Eliza.

Since the public announcement concerning Princess Elizabeth, the friendship and feelings between her and William had deepened considerably. Only a fool who saw them together could not see that the two were irrevocably in love.

As she sat with her book in Netherfield's library, Elizabeth smiled as she recalled the conversation she had been a party to between her birthfather and Uncle Robert a month previously. William was not aware yet, as his father decided his son would be told the news when and if—as if it were a question—he requested a formal courtship with Elizabeth.

The family was at Pemberley to celebrate Christmastide. All of the extended family was present except for Jane and Andrew, as Jane had delivered a baby boy not eight weeks previously. Both Elizabeth's mother and Aunt Elaine were present for the birth of Andrew Thomas Fitzwilliam Junior in late October and remained with Jane for over a month.

Elizabeth had been playing chess with Uncle Robert. She was not quite at his level yet, but she did win—without him giving her quarter—occasionally. Her birthfather sat down with them, while the rest of the family was enjoying a sleigh ride. As Elizabeth had a slight cold, Mr. Taylor had recommended she keep warm and out of the snow.

"My parents are aware of William's ardent interest in their granddaughter," the Prince had stated.

"Will they approve of William, Father?" Elizabeth had asked worriedly.

"They will under one condition," the Prince stated as he gave Uncle Robert a conspiratorial look.

"I will not be able to refuse the King this time, will I?" Uncle

Robert stated with amused resignation.

"Of what do you two talk, if I may know?" Elizabeth asked inquisitively.

"In order to marry a royal prince or princess, one must be a marquess or, in a lady's case, a marchioness or higher," the Prince had explained to his daughter.

"In my father's time, the Darcys were offered the vacant dukedom of Derbyshire," Uncle Robert explained. "My late father respectfully refused the title, as did I—twice."

"Why did you refuse it, Uncle Robert?" Elizabeth followed up.

"We felt we did not need it, we—my father and I—were happy to be gentlemen farmers without being a member of the peerage and having to spend time in the House of Lords," Uncle Robert had clarified.

"But now, Darcy here will not refuse it again, so that if you and William decide it is what you want, he will be allowed to court you officially—and become betrothed, if the courtship reaches its natural conclusion," her birthfather stated with a smirk. Uncle Robert had said not a word to refute the statement.

Elizabeth smiled, not because of the way the Darcys would be forced to accept a dukedom they had previously refused—multiple times—but the demonstration of a father's love for his son that he would accept the title to ensure William's—and by extension her own—happiness.

On the way home from Pemberley, the family spent a few days at Hilldale, where all of little Andy's Bennet aunts, and lone uncle, had made his acquaintance. Mary, who would be sixteen in a matter of days, could not get enough of Andy. All of them loved their nephew, but for some unknown reason, Mary more so than the rest.

Elizabeth smiled as she thought about Mary and the close friendship that had grown between her and Elizabeth's Uncle Wes. He did not have much time with them as his sister had, because he assumed the role of the Earl of Jersey. However, when not busy in the House of Lords, Wes could be found not far from his niece's family, specifically not far from Mary.

The more Elizabeth came to know her Grandmother Sarah, the more she came to love the woman. Grandmama Sarah, as Elizabeth called her, had apologised many times for not being stronger in standing up to her late husband. Since Elizabeth shared her philosophy that one should remember the past only as the remembrance gives one pleasure, Lady Sarah chose to live in the present. Her year of mourning ended in December, six months after Wes and Marie's mourning period. Elizabeth had been willing to add her grandmother's name back as a middle name, but Lady Sarah demurred telling her the names were perfect as they were.

Elizabeth spent hours asking questions and hearing all about her birthmother, as a little girl as she grew up, whenever they were in company. She loved hearing how similar she was to the woman who had given her life.

As Lady Sarah came to know the Bennets, it was not long before she understood why Priscilla had chosen them to raise Elizabeth as a normal little girl rather than the childhood she would have had in a gilded royal cage. It was not many months before Ladies Sarah and Francine became quite close.

Fanny told her new friend how sorry she was that Priscilla went to her grave believing she had been rejected by both parents, which had led to Lizzy changing her middle names. Sarah relayed she had no ill feelings about the name change, as it was done with the information at hand and no one was aware of the control her late husband used to exert over her. She relayed to her new friend the conversation with Lizzy which put the issue to bed for all time.

Elizabeth liked her other grandparents, aunts, and uncles —the King, Queen, Princes, and Princesses—and cousins. However, given their positions in society there was always a formality that none of the others in the extended family had. Elizabeth was told the King had become ill some years earlier, but she never saw any evidence of sickness during the times she was in company with her royal grandfather.

Of all of her royal aunts, Elizabeth was closest to Princesses Elizabeth and Amelia. When with the royal family and her Aunt Elizabeth was present or not, the rest of the family called her Princess Beth—as the Queen had decreed—to differentiate between them.

Elizabeth put her book down as she had an epiphany. She loved William so very much that if Uncle Robert had been unwilling to accept elevation to the dukedom, or if there were no option of elevation, she would have renounced her royal title happily in order to be with William.

There was not a shred of a doubt in her mind that William was the right man for her, and the *only* man she would ever be willing to marry. Oh, how ardently she loved her William.

~~~~~~~/~~~~~~~

At Darcy House, a day before the Darcys were to return to Hertfordshire, William knocked on his father's study door. "Welcome, William," Robert Darcy said as his son took a seat in front of the huge oak desk. "Why the pensive look?"

"Lizzy will come out in a month, or little more, and I know she loves me as I love her, but I have remembered something about who can be allowed to marry a prince or princess," William reported.

"You mean that you must be a marquess or above to marry a Princess of the United Kingdom of Great Britain and Ireland?" Darcy surmised. "It was a rule the King instituted after the Prince of Wales and his so-called wife, and then Uncle Freddy marrying the daughter of an Earl."

William nodded. "We have an ancient and noble line, but you are not a duke, nor am I a marquess," William pointed out.

"You heard I, and my father before me, turned down a title from the crown, did you not?" Darcy asked.

"Yes Father, I heard that," William responded with a quizzical look.

"We were offered the Dukedom of Derbyshire. The last duke died without an heir some sixty years ago. You will be a Marquess, the Marquess of Derby, before asking the King for permission to court Lizzy," Darcy told his son.

"You would do that for me so I might be with my Lizzy?" William asked, in awe of his father.

"William, I would do *anything* I needed to in order to secure your and Gigi's happiness," Darcy returned, his voice gruff with emotion. "When we see the Prince at Netherfield, I will ask him to pass my acceptance on to the Crown."

CHAPTER 30

There was an air of excitement, for the family was anticipating the arrival of the Fitzwilliams, and as little Andy, almost three months old, was travelling for the first time with his parents, Fitzwilliam grandparents, aunt, and uncle.

Fanny and Bennet were excited. Fanny had the nursery aired out and cleaned from top to bottom, as it had not been occupied since Tommy was moved into his own bedchamber when he had turned ten.

At fifteen and fourteen, respectively, Kitty and Lydia were growing into estimable young ladies who were looking forward to their nephew's arrival. When they saw him on the way home from Pemberley at Christmas, he had slept almost the whole time they were there. Now, according to Jane's letters, little Andy was interested in the world around him and would gurgle happily when someone played with him.

The two youngest Bennet sisters were not quite as proficient as their older sisters on the pianoforte, although they were by no means deficient. Their true strength in the musical arts lay in singing. Both spent many hours with Mr. Mercury, who encouraged their talent. They now had the best voices among the five Bennet sisters. They sang a duet for the Queen during Little Season just past, not just as part of a larger group —as they were the first time they exhibited for the monarch.

In addition, Kitty excelled at drawing and spent almost as many hours with Mr. Lambert as she did with the singing master. Sketching was Kitty's strongest discipline, but she was also quite talented with both water colour and oil-based paints. She could not wait to sketch little Andy and wondered if he still had deep blue eyes, or if they had begun to change, as she had been told was possible. If Jane and Andrew agreed, Kitty planned to make a sketch of them with one of them holding Andy, and then she would use her oils to make a portrait for them as a gift.

~~~~~~~/~~~~~~~

Further exciting the level of anticipation at Netherfield, the Darcys and Wes were expected later in the day; the Fitzwilliams including Cassie and Richard on the following day; and Anne and Jamey Carrington the day after that. Everyone was expected to arrive before the upcoming assembly except the Carrington parents, who would arrive the following week along with Lady Sarah.

Elizabeth was looking forward to the upcoming assembly with glee; she could not wait to see William again. Although she was not out in society in London, she was out locally and had been for the last six months.

What really amused Elizabeth was considering how the harridan that was Miss Bingley might behave. The woman had alienated the local populace with her airs and graces. She had denigrated the 'country hoyden' who had the temerity to turn *her* Mr. Darcy's eye and had let it be known she would put the nobody in her place at the assembly.

The Bennets and the Prince quietly let it be known around Meryton not to correct the shrew, so she would be allowed to discover her own insignificance in a way she could not but accept. If Miss Bingley thought she would be able to cow her rival—a rival only in her mind as William cared not a whit for Miss Bingley—she would be sorely disappointed, as Elizabeth's courage always rose at every attempt to intimidate her.

The Bennets and the Prince hoped more than believed that the social climbing harpy with her pretentions and airs might behave herself rather than make it necessary that she be put in her place at the assembly. From reports of what the shrew had been saying, it seemed a vain hope.

"Did you ask to see me, Papa?" Elizabeth said, after being bade to enter the study.

"We did, Lizzy," Bennet replied. "We received an express from Darcy House. Before you worry, all three Darcys are well, but there is some unexpected business that will detain them for a day or two. They will still be here in time for the assembly."

"Do you know what detains them in London?" Elizabeth asked.

"No, Lizzy. Uncle Robert was not explicit in his express. I am sure if it were something of concern or if he needed our help, he would have been more specific," Bennet opined.

"Thank you for informing me, Papa," Elizabeth said over her shoulder after her father dismissed her from his study.

~~~~~~~/~~~~~~~

"William, you and your sister are to go with me to St. James Palace at two o'clock today," Darcy informed his son.

"Why, Father?" William asked, confused. "I thought you would talk to Uncle Freddy when we arrive at Netherfield Park."

"I sent an express to him after we spoke instead, and he in turn communicated with the King. Evidently our monarch believes I may change my mind again, so this morning a royal courier delivered a message summoning us to the palace," Darcy informed his son.

"I suppose I understand the King's thinking," William returned with amusement. "How many have turned down such an honour as many times as you and grandfather have between you? I am sure I would need a single finger on one hand to count them, and even then, it would be one finger too many."

"I dare say you have the right of it, William." Darcy clapped his son on the back. "Bennet sent me an express as well." Darcy did not miss the look of concern on William's face. "Lizzy is well; it is about that Bingley woman and her pretentions. The plan is to allow her enough rope to hang herself at the assembly. If she behaves as a lady should, then she will be safe. If not, social suicide will not begin to describe what she will commit."

"As much as I dislike seeing anyone suffer, after the way she tried to attach herself to me when I went to welcome Bingley to the neighbourhood, she deserves whatever she brings down on her own head," William said with distaste as he remembered the cloying woman and shuddered. "I told Bingley that even should she be found naked in my bed with all of London as witnesses, I would not offer for her."

"And I would support you completely. I could not imagine consigning my son to such a fate as to be aligned with that harpy," Darcy stated emphatically.

"It is bad enough she was the reason Bingley felt we could never form a closer friendship—or any friendship at all—the woman must be delusional to think she has anything to offer me. Even were I not irrevocably in love with Lizzy, I would not look at her twice," William stated firmly.

"Please make sure Gigi is ready to depart. I do not understand why a girl not yet twelve needs so much time to prepare." Darcy shook his head. His little girl was growing up, and each day she looked more and more like his beloved late wife.

~~~~~~~/~~~~~~~

Miss Bingley entered Longbourn's drawing room with a sniff, her nose high in the air. "Why did you summon me, Charles?" Miss Bingley asked disdainfully.

"Although we are not sure you will hear what we are about to tell you, it is our duty to do so," Bingley began. Seeing his sister was about to interject, Bingley held up his hand. "Not a word until we are done."

Miss Bingley's look was venomous as she glared at her brother, sister, and brother-in-law. When they did not relent, she sat on a sofa with a huff.

"Your pretentions concerning the younger Mr. Darcy must stop." Bingley gave his sister a quelling look as she saw her about to object, so she held her peace—for now. "The man told me in no uncertain terms that even were you to sink so low as to try to compromise him, regardless of how many witnesses, he will not offer for you—he will *never* offer for you, Caroline."

"What would induce you to think a man from the top of the first circles, who has connections to peers of the realm and royalty, would even consider the daughter of a tradesman as his future wife is beyond me," Hurst stated as he shook his head at his sister's wilful blindness.

"I have been educated at the *best* seminary and have ten thousand pounds!" Miss Bingley retorted.

"You were told to be silent until we were done, or would you prefer I send you back to Uncle Paul this very day?" Bingley threatened. "Did you learn nothing at that school you attended? It is *birth* which sets your position in society. Not only that, compared to most in the *Ton*, your dowry is insignificant."

"Caroline," Louisa tried a gentler approach to attempt to reach her sister. "I have heard talk that there are many of the very top of the first circles who visit this neighbourhood, including peers and even royalty. Would you really like to expose yourself in front of some of the leading members of society? If you walk the path you have started, your dreams of being accepted in *any* circle of high society will turn to dust. Is that what you want for yourself?"

Miss Bingley silently seethed; she would not give her brother cause to send her away before she was able secure *her* Mr. Darcy, then she would show them all. Once she was a leading member of the *Ton*, she would shun them.

"You may respond if you care to now, Sister," Bingley allowed.

"High society in this neighbourhood?" Miss Bingley derided. "If you think thusly, you have no idea what constitutes high society. Hereabouts there are none but a bunch of country bumpkins who are far below me."

Bingley shook his head. He, Louisa, and Hurst had tried.

As was her wont, Caroline would not hear or see anything which did not fit her presumptions. He only prayed that he would not be ruined along with his sister when she brought ruination down on her own head, but he could not see another way for her to learn the truth of their station. She was nineteen, almost twenty, and so would have to face the consequences of her actions.

"As I can see you will not relent, you will not attend the assembly. We will not allow you to sully the Bingley name with your behaviour." Bingley held up his hand to stay the vitriol his younger sister was about to launch. "One word and you will be on your way back to Uncle Paul before your feet touch the ground. You may have fooled him, but we see the truth. Your delusions will be your ruin, sister."

Miss Bingley stomped out of the drawing room in a decidedly unladylike fashion. Not long afterwards, sound of her bedchamber door being slammed reverberated around the manor house.

~~~~~~~/~~~~~~~

It was done. Darcy was His Grace, the Duke of Derbyshire; William was the Marquess of Derby; Georgiana had the honorific title of Lady. The Darcys returned to their house a little after four. The newly minted Duke sent a copy of the patents the Lord Chamberlain had presented him with to the firm of barristers and solicitors at Norman and James who represented his family.

The estate of Rivington, in the Darcys' opinion the second-best estate in their home county, four satellite estates, and substantial additional liquid assets came with the titles.

According to the Lord Chamberlain, the notice of the Darcy elevation would appear in the evening edition that same day as well as in the morning papers on the morrow. Their plan was to depart for Hertfordshire in the morning. With the decree appearing in the evening broadsheets, their elevation would not be a secret to their friends, family, and everyone else by the time they arrived at Netherfield Park.

That evening, before the papers were delivered to Holder House, the three Darcys arrived for an impromptu family dinner and informed their relatives of the day's happenings. After many congratulations and much 'your gracing', it was decided the Carringtons would join the Darcys for their journey into Hertfordshire in the morning.

William hoped he would be able to come to an understanding with his Lizzy soon as if he had thought he had been hunted by fortune hunters before, it would be nothing in comparison to what it would be like after the elevation was made public.

~~~~~~~/~~~~~~~

When the three Darcys walked into the largest drawing room, followed by the Carringtons, all of those present rose as one and gave the newly elevated Darcys the deepest of bows and curtsies they were able to—including the Prince and Princess.

As William expected, Richard engaged in a bout of heavy teasing of the newly elevated Marquess. Luckily for William, one look from Cassie ended the teasing long before Richard would have preferred.

"Very droll," Darcy exclaimed as Georgiana made a beeline for her best friends.

"My Lord," Elizabeth intoned as she approached William, her eyes shining with humour.

"Your Royal Highness," William gave his beloved a deep bow.

"*Touché*, William," Elizabeth conceded. "It is good to see you again."

"It is *very* good to see you, Lizzy." William took her hand and bestowed a kiss on her wrist. As she always did when he touched her, Elizabeth felt a fluttering of joy. "I would like to reserve the first, middle, and final sets, if you please."

"I do please, William; they are yours," Elizabeth granted immediately. "I do want to warn you, my Lord, the woman claiming you as her future husband will not be happy to see

SHANA GRANDERSON A LADY

you dance those sets with me."

"*Your* happiness is everything to *me*; she matters not," William stated with meaning.

"All we can pray for is that Miss Bingley has a modicum of common sense so there will not be a scene," Elizabeth shared. "Somehow I doubt it, though."

"Let us discuss more pleasant topics, please. I have no interest thinking about—wasting my time with you on—that woman." He led her to a corner to ask about her and her family.

"I have news on that front," Bennet informed the group. "Hill sent me a note. Mr. Bingley has denied his sister permission to attend the assembly, so we should have a harpy-free night." Everyone approved of Mr. Bingley's stand against the social climbing, fortune hunting virago.

~~~~~~~/~~~~~~~

"I am to be a *Duchess*!" Caroline Bingley exclaimed after she saw the decree in the papers when she finally joined her family to break her fast. Her brother refused to keep Town hours in the country, and after she missed breaking her fast three days in a row, Miss Bingley had learnt she would be required to follow suit when Mrs. Hill had refused to provide her with a plate, referring her to Mr. Bingley. Now she flounced in at the limit of her brother's forbearance for her to join the meal and eat with them.

"What are you babbling about?" Hurst asked frustratedly.

"Did you not see? Mr. Darcy is the Duke of Derbyshire, and his son, who I will marry, is the Marquess of Derby," Miss Bingley gushed.

Her family held their breath to cool their porridge, knowing they would be wasting time and would only destroy their own equanimity, as she would not hear that which she did not desire to hear.

"Do not forget Caroline, you *will not* be accompanying us to the assembly," Bingley reiterated. His sister gave a disinterested wave of her hand.

After a bit of toast with a little butter and jam, Miss Bing-

310

ley pushed her chair back and left the dining parlour without a word. *'I must go prepare to impress my marquess!'* Miss Bingley was off to her bedchamber to plan her outfit, coiffure, and jewellery to make sure she would stand out at the assembly. She had determined she would ignore her brother's edict, even if she had to walk to the assembly hall. Nothing would stop her winning her marquess, especially not her weak-willed family!

She would have been gratified to know that her family in the dining parlour were under the impression she would not defy her brother.

CHAPTER 31

By the Friday, the day of the assembly, the level of teasing Richard visited on William regarding the Darcy elevation had reduced to perhaps one witticism per day. Again after the first night, his wife made her opinion known that enough was enough, so Richard desisted —almost.

William was gratified that so much attention shifted to little Andy, just now three months old. He was blond like his mother and—at this stage of his life—had the deep blue Fitzwilliam eyes.

Little Andy was a pleasant and cheerful babe who would gurgle happily when anyone gave him attention—which was almost constantly when he was awake. The only time he would fuss was when he was tired, if he was hungry, or was wet or soiled—then he would display an impressive set of lungs for one so small.

After Andy drank hungrily from his mother, Nurse put him over her shoulder and he emitted an impressive belch, after which Nurse put him down for a nap in his cot. Although he let out one or two little whines to protest being put down, within a minute he was fast asleep.

"Jane, he is a delight," Elizabeth said quietly as she stood next to her sister in the nursery as they watched Jane's son sleep.

"It is my opinion as well, Lizzy, and of course I am not at all biased," Jane stated smiling.

"If you and my brother did not feel thusly, it would be scandalous," Elizabeth teased.

"He is so lucky to be surrounded by so much love, is he

not?" Jane stated with pride as she watched her babe sleep. "You have become close with your Grandmama Sarah, have you not, Lizzy?"

"All of the family has, but yes, I have as well. After her mourning period ended, she accompanied me to teas and to my other grandparents a few times, but she eschews society now," Elizabeth reported. "I think when she came to realise fully the cost of chasing the approval of society as her husband demanded, she decided to live her life quietly and enjoy her children and me as much as she is able. Despite multiple requests, she has refused to return as a patroness of Almack's. The rest of the patronesses stated they will hold her position open for the next Countess of Jersey—if she desires the position."

"Talking about the next Lady Jersey, does Wes still pay particular attention to Mary?" Jane asked.

"He does. As you know, Mary will be sixteen the day after the assembly, which is why Mama and Papa are allowing her to attend as 'out locally.' Wes wanted to have three sets with our Mary, but Papa will only allow two because of her age," Elizabeth informed her sister. "I am not sure who was more disappointed, Wes or Mary."

"Papa is allowing you three sets with William, is he not?" Jane asked with arched eyebrow.

"Mary brought up the same point, and Papa explained that I am weeks away from being eighteen and coming out, even though my coming out will be vastly different than my sister's," Elizabeth averred.

"Well do I know it. We only had to curtsy; you will have a full day with your royal grandmother and then your ball will be at St. James Palace," Jane enumerated. "Mama told me His Majesty will start the first with you, then your father and your Uncle George, and only then Papa will have the second dance of the first set with you."

"William and I spoke last night," Elizabeth stated shyly. "You know why Uncle Robert accepted the elevation, do you not?"

"Yes, we have been told," Jane replied. "Now that I am a parent, I understand Uncle Robert's actions much better." Elizabeth gave her sister a questioning look. "When you have your own child, Lizzy, you will understand the absolute unwavering love you will have for him or her. You will move heaven and earth to keep your child from sadness, even if that includes accepting a title you refused more than once so your son will be allowed to marry his beloved."

"Jane, I did not know I could love a man as much as I do William," Elizabeth stated dreamily. "My heart races whenever he is near, and when he is not with me it seems as if half of my heart is missing."

"That, sister dearest, is the epitome of love." Jane gave her sister a hug. The two looked into the cot one more time and then departed to prepare for the upcoming assembly.

~~~~~~~/~~~~~~~

The Prince was sitting in his study at Purvis Lodge prior to making the short journey to Netherfield Park so the whole group could travel to the assembly together. "Captain Tremaine, this Bingley woman is—I believe—unstable. You will have the Princess under guard the whole time, will you not?"

"We will, your Royal Highness," the Captain returned smartly. "There will be ten men in regular dress who will help even up the numbers of women to men at the assembly. At least two of them will be near her Royal Highness at all times. In addition to those selected for that duty, there will be a contingent of twenty uniformed guards around the perimeter of the assembly hall."

"Your plans are sound, Tremaine," the Prince approved. "If that shrew defies her brother and arrives and is aggressive in any way, I do not care what you have to do to her, as long as my daughter and the rest of the participants are unharmed," the Prince instructed.

Happy every precaution that could be taken would be implemented; the Prince dismissed the Captain charged with overseeing Elizabeth's security. In addition, both Biggs and Johns would be inside the hall, stationed in opposite corners. At his own peril would a man—or woman—believe them slow and lumbering.

~~~~~~~/~~~~~~~

Lucas Wickham was most impressed. Over the last two years, his son had become the man the father had always wished he would. George had become as honest as the day was long, and his work ethic was second to none.

He was as diligent in his studies as he was at work. George was close to completing his first year of school. His results at school were as impressive as his work. Now that he was applying his intelligence for good rather than in nefarious schemes, he had come close to full marks on each of his tests and exams.

It warmed his father's heart to see the man his son was now; he did not recognise him as the one who had stolen from the carpenter in York. Thankfully, any last vestiges of his mother's bad influence had been excised and had held no sway over George for some time now.

Mr. Darcy—His Grace—gave his steward an extra week's holiday to spend with his son. Even though George could afford to rent his own place, he chose to stay at Mr. Gardiner's house for the one pound per month. As he explained to his father, it allowed him to save as much as possible—which he turned over to Mr. Gardiner to invest for him—and he had society when he and others in the house wanted some company.

Another change was that George had friends, genuine and true friends. He had become close with two of the clerks who also resided at the house and like him had no local family. Before these two friends, George had an easy time making friends, but had never been able to retain them as it had been his wont to use them for his own selfish or avaricious purposes. He had learnt to give more than what he took.

Some months earlier, George visited his father at Pemberley for the first time since he departed for his ill-fated apprenticeship. Not only was he welcomed at the estate, he and his father were invited to the manor house for a meal. His Grace told George how proud he was of the man he had become.

Even after the elevation, George felt no envy. It did not take long for George to see—even though it was not what he was looking for—the advantages of being a friend of the Darcys.

While he was at Pemberley, he finally met the blond who he had obsessed about when he was younger. Even though they would never have known, he sought an audience with His Grace and the Viscount. They had allowed him to make his amends to the Viscountess. He admitted his former obsession and begged the lady's pardon, which she granted without reservation.

Mr. Wickham senior would return to Pemberley in a few days, but meanwhile he intended to enjoy his time with his son. He took every opportunity he could to tell George just how proud he was of him.

~~~~~~~/~~~~~~~

Like the rest of the inhabitants of the area, the Netherfield Park party arrived before the first set was called, as none in the area believed in being fashionably late—or as some called it, *unfashionably* rude. Elizabeth accepted William's hand with pleasure as he led her to the line forming for the first dance of the first set.

At Longbourn, Bingley and the Hursts departed at the time they desired, not having to wait for Caroline to make her entrance. His younger sister believed the fallacy about being fashionably late.

Just before they departed, Miss Bingley glided into drawing room in an awful burnt orange creation.

"Caroline! Why are you dressed so? I told you, you are not to attend tonight!" Bingley stated angrily.

"It was my hope you would relent, but I see you are not in a mood to be reasonable," Miss Bingley sniffed.

"No Caroline, I was perfectly serious," Bingley stated forcefully. "There will be no carriage here if you try to defy me, and I do not see you walking more than a few steps."

"Do you take me for that harridan, Eliza Bennet, who is known for being a great walker? I will never walk," Miss Bingley sniffed.

"Then you will remain at the estate as I instructed." Miss Bingley looked away from her brother but nodded her head. "Do you not understand that we will be lower than anyone there? Regardless of your delusions, the offspring of tradesmen are not, nor will they ever be, above a landed gentleman." If Bingley had told his sister the same once, he had done it a hundred times. As she always did when reminded of her antecedents, Caroline looked away in fury.

Even after the confrontation with his sister, the Longbourn party arrived at the assembly hall in time for the first dance. Bingley requested the older Long niece's hand for the first set and was granted it.

~~~~~~~/~~~~~~~

Miss Bingley, already fuming after her brother took her to task before he departed and stood by his refusal to take her, realised the Hills were keeping an eye on her. After a little while she left the drawing room and made a show of climbing the stairs.

She first made sure the pillows she had placed under the covers on her bed were still there, and then slammed her bedchamber door—not an uncommon occurrence in the house.

Then she donned her outerwear and waited in the hall above the stairs for ten minutes. She had considered climbing down the trellises outside her window but rejected that idea as too much even for her. When she heard no more noise from below stairs, she carefully descended the stairs, making sure none of them creaked under her weight.

Not seeing anyone about, she slipped out the front door and closed it without a sound. She was sure her brother and sister would never suspect she would walk the mile to the assembly, as they knew how much she detested walking like a commoner—or the hated Eliza Bennet.

~~~~~~~/~~~~~~~

After arriving at the assembly hall, she stood in a corner near some huge brute so her family would not see her. Not one person, not even these country mushrooms, had noted her arrival. She sneered at those who snickered giggled when they caught sight of her fashionable outfit. She should have remained unobtrusive, but she could not help herself.

Her plan was simple; as soon as she had an opportunity, she would compromise the Marquess. She was sure her brother was wrong. In front of all of Meryton, there was only one option he would have, to marry her.

She did not see the way the huge man next to her was looking at her or that he seemed to signal others to make them aware of her presence. It was mere minutes before all of the guards were aware of her. Not long after, the Prince and Lord Thomas were informed as well.

To rub salt in the wound of having to walk, her Marquess was dancing with that Eliza Bennet chit. She conveniently forgot the older sister was a Viscountess and the parents were titled. They were Bennets, therefore they were beneath her notice.

When the set ended, Miss Bingley positioned herself where she could watch her prey. Once her Marquess returned Miss Eliza to her family, Miss Bingley, still hidden in the corner, made as if she was talking to someone though no one was close by.

"I agree, she is tolerable I suppose, but not handsome enough to tempt *any* man. I wonder what the harridan did to cause the Marquess to give consequence to a young lady who should be slighted by all men. I am sure it could only be pity, and she will be the wallflower she deserves to be the rest of the night." Miss Bingley smiled to herself; sure she had degraded the woman in the eyes of the Marquess.

Now she just had to make her move towards the Marquess. Each time she tried to approach him, someone seemed to be in her way. Across the hall, Bingley was sure he had heard his younger sister's cutting voice but could not see her. He prayed she was not so far gone that she would have disobey him thusly.

Miss Bingley did not notice the quick shake of the Prince's head—not that she knew who the man was—when two of the guards in regular clothing gave him a questioning look to see if they should remove the objectionable woman.

Not one man requested her hand for a set as she waited for her chance to approach the Marquess, even though many men waited for the next dance, and the one after. It was evident to her that she was the only lady present who no one would ask to dance. Miss Bingley attempted to approach the Marquess between sets, but he always seemed to be surrounded by other men who looked at her pointedly but did not ask her to dance.

The pressure reached the point of no return when she saw the Marquess lead the hated Bennet chit out for a second set. She found a knife on the refreshment table that had been used to cut cakes and hid it within the folds of her orange monstrosity. She noted which way the line was moving, then started towards her mortal enemy purposefully.

If possible, Elizabeth and Darcy were enjoying their second set together even more than the first. If it were a private ball, the set they were dancing would have been the supper set, but there was no supper at local assemblies.

William and Elizabeth saw the woman in the orange gown—who they believed would not be at the assembly—approach them. She was hard to miss given her outrageously flamboyant garment, and neither missed the malevolent look on her countenance. As she approached, time seemed to slow as they watched her reach into her gown and withdraw a knife. As she drew her hand back, many things happened at the same time.

William put his body in front of Elizabeth, which only seemed to provoke the insane woman more. As her arm reached its apex, Biggs arrived just ahead of two of the royal guards who had been dancing nearby and caught Miss Bingley's wrist in his enormously powerful grip, causing the knife to fall to the floor.

"Unhand me, you damned brute," Miss Bingley unleashed a most unladylike invective. The other two guards reached Miss Bingley; one stood behind her and the other grabbed her left arm—none too gently.

"Why did you stop me? She is the one who is importuning my Marquess!" Miss Bingley screeched maniacally.

"Do you know who I am, Miss Bingley?" Elizabeth asked evenly.

"Your Royal Highness, please excuse my sister, she obviously belongs in Bedlam," Bingley bowed low. "She was not supposed to be here at all." Bingley looked at his sister with distaste.

"I belong in Bedlam? Here you are addressing this country hoyden thusly, that is rich," Miss Bingley cackled.

"Do you know the penalty for attacking my daughter, you shrewish harpy?" The Prince stepped forward with a thunderous visage.

"If I had been allowed to dispatch one so low, I would have been rewarded," Miss Bingley allowed her delusion full reign.

"As I am the granddaughter of the King and Queen, somehow I doubt that, Miss Bingley," Elizabeth stepped forward. For the first time Miss Bingley really looked at the woman she had wanted to dispatch. Her clothing was far finer than anything Miss Bingley owned, and her jewels were flawless gems and the pieces they fit in were far finer than those Miss Bingley had even dreamed about.

As reality began to set in, Miss Bingley's expression changed to one of absolute horror. She did not fail to notice that the man her brother called 'Your Royal Highness' was looking at Elizabeth to ascertain if she was well. Neither Elizabeth nor those watching missed the moment realisation of the truth hit her.

"When I asked if you knew who I was, you did not

answer, so allow me to oblige you now," Elizabeth stated assertively, in absolute control of the moment. "I am her Royal Highness Elizabeth Priscilla Francine Bennet, Princess of the United Kingdom of Great Britain and Ireland. This gentleman you insulted so recently is my birthfather, Prince Frederick, second son of his Majesty King George III, the Duke of York and Albany, Earl of Ulster. My late birthmother was Princess Priscilla."

By now, Miss Bingley, stricken with fear, would have collapsed were it not for Biggs and a second guard holding her up by her arms. As she looked from one face to the next, all she saw was disgust and she knew none would speak in favour of clemency for her.

"Your Royal Highness, I know what she attempted was treason, but she is insane. If you allow it, we will have her admitted to a secure facility where she will remain under guard for the rest of her natural days," Bingley beseeched the Prince.

The Prince looked to his daughter, as she was, after all, the one the woman had attempted to murder. Elizabeth gave a curt nod of agreement. "We shall see, Mr. Bingley. I want to question your sister first." It was not a request.

"Of course, your Royal Highness," Bingley backed away a little.

"Miss Bingley, why did you become so frightened when you realised who my daughter is?" the Prince asked easily.

"She was supposed to be a nobody, not a Princess," Miss Bingley explained.

"Were you not warned, Caroline? I told you but you refused to hear me," Bingley interjected. "By disobeying me and not staying at Longbourn, you have ruined your life and ours along with you."

"Why did you ignore your family when they tried to warn you of my and my daughter's presence here?" the Prince followed up.

"I thought they were lying to me," was her short explanation.

"One more thing—why did you, the daughter of a trades-man, think Mr. Darcy, the Marquess of Derby, would look at you with an eye to matrimony?" the Prince demanded.

Miss Bingley did not answer, she just dropped her head and closed her eyes. "Caroline, do you know what the penalty for treason is if his Royal Highness does not recommend the King grant my request?" Bingley asked, and Miss Bingley just shook her head. "It is death by beheading! That is what you are facing, Sister. Either way, your days in society are over. It is either an asylum for life or you will have a date with the execu-tioner at the tower."

"She will have a minimum of six months in Bedlam, and then—only then—will you be allowed to move her to a facility of your choice," the Prince decreed. "Know, however, that there will be a contingent of guards there at all times. If she attempts to escape and survives the attempt, she will be taken to the tower."

"We will withdraw from society, as we are now tainted by the actions of my sister," Bingley stated sadly.

The Prince nodded and Miss Bingley was led away, fol-lowed by her family. Before Bingley and the Hursts could exit the hall, Elizabeth walked up to them. "My father, my birth-father, my family, and I do not hold you responsible for your sister's actions, and I will be pleased to get to know you once this unpleasant business is completed. We will be happy to re-ceive you for tea at Netherfield Park."

Bingley and the Hurts departed, greatly relieved their reputations had been rescued by Princess Elizabeth, in spite of Caroline's actions. Thankfully, the rest of the assembly passed without drama. By the end of the evening, the insane attack was forgotten—almost.

CHAPTER 32

The following day, there was a meeting in Bennets' study among Mr. Bennet, Fanny, the Prince, and the new Duke. "Yesterday highlighted a problem Lizzy will experience in society," the Prince stated. "I do not believe there will be another insane attack such as we witnessed last night; however, word that she is fabulously wealthy has been spread abroad."

"You are concerned our girl will be the target of compromises by unscrupulous fortune hunters?" Fanny asked worriedly.

"As you requested this meeting, obviously you have a solution to propose, York," the Duke surmised.

"Yes, I do. Because Lizzy needs royal sanction to marry, she has a level of protection other debutantes do not have. That being said, I do not believe any of us here would like to see her suffer even one more attempt to harm her in any way." The other three nodded their agreement vigorously. "None of us is blind, and we have all seen the mutual attraction, love, esteem, and respect between Lizzy and William," the Prince stated.

"It is impossible not to recognise they are besotted with one another," the Duke pointed out. "It is, after all, the reason I accepted elevation to the dukedom."

"What are you suggesting?" Fanny asked, although she already had a good idea where the Prince was going.

"I think we should go to my parents and seek permission for William and Lizzy to marry. However, there is a critical step we must take before we do that," the Prince pointed out. "We need to consult them and give them a choice. Neither would appreciate us making a decision for them as momentous as this one—regardless of how in love they may be—and ignoring their thoughts on the subject."

"I agree with York," William's father stated succinctly.

"As much as I would love Lizzy to remain with us for many more years, I recognise this is the only way, Thomas," Fanny conceded. "We must put our own desires aside and do what is best for our girl."

"Like you, I will find it difficult to let her go, but if Lizzy and William approve, this will be the most effective way of protecting her from being hunted by all of the fortune hunters waiting for her to come out into society and salivating over it. I wish there were another way, but to my chagrin, I do not see one," Bennet accepted. He rang for Nichols and instructed him to inform William and Lizzy they were required in the study.

A few minutes later, William and Elizabeth were bade enter and were told to sit. They had a good idea it was related to the insane woman's aborted attack. It was not difficult to see the serious looks on the four who were present when they arrived.

"Lizzy and William, we asked you to join us here as we have been discussing potential issues that will affect you both after Lizzy comes out into society," Bennet began.

The four explained the problems as they saw them, and the fact that Miss Bingley's ineffectual attack had necessitated a discussion held prior to the two being called for.

"Lizzy," Fanny said gently, "there is one way for you to be protected and remove you as an object for the circling vultures."

"If I were already betrothed, or even better married," Elizabeth stated perceptively.

"We did not want to make a decision about either of your futures without your input. If you *both* agree, then we will journey to London and request the King's permission for his granddaughter to marry," Lord Robert informed the two.

"It is *your* decision," the Prince assured them. "If you are not ready, or if one of you is not inclined to choose the other as their partner for life, we will devise other ways to protect you, Lizzy. We are not saying this is the *only* choice, just the one we believed you both would prefer, and the one that would be the most effective."

"We will withdraw to allow you two to talk," Fanny stated as she stood. "The door will be partially open." Fanny led the other three out of the study.

Once they were alone, William and Elizabeth did not speak for a few minutes as they assimilated what they had been told. If they could have read each other's mind, they would have seen their thoughts were similar.

Far from being opposed to moving forward, each one felt their heart's desire was being fulfilled; however, although they knew they loved each other, they were not sure if the other was ready for the step they would have to take.

They both started to speak at the exact same moment. "You speak first, William," Elizabeth stated.

"If you are sure, Lizzy," William verified and received confirmation in the form of a nod from Elizabeth. "For my part, I have no objection to moving forward now. It has been my heart's desire for some years to have you as my partner in life. I will admit, right after we discovered your true parentage and rank, I believed you were out of reach for me until my father set me to rights. As you know, thanks to my father's accepting the elevation, I am of an appropriate rank for the King to accept me as a suitor for his granddaughter, unless…" William felt a chill throughout his being as he verbalised his greatest fear. "Unless the King wants to marry you to some Prince of Europe to make an alliance, as he did with your birthfather."

"Let me put that worry to rest first," Elizabeth replied as she felt joy at his words about his desire to have her as his helpmeet. "Father has assured me, as I have been removed from the line of succession, coupled with the King's desire to make amends for forcing the divorce, my grandfather will not attempt to arrange a marriage of convenience for me."

"That is the best news I have heard for a long time, Lizzy,"

William replied as he visibly relaxed.

"As to the first point you made, like you, being tied to you for the rest of my life is my absolute wish. I thought we would have to endure the season before we were allowed to begin a courtship, so I find that, like you, I have no objection whatsoever to beginning our road together now, William. You are the one I love, the *only* man I could ever be prevailed upon to marry." Elizabeth beamed at him and William saw her love for him shining from her.

In but a moment, he was on his knee in front of her as she was still seated on her chair. "Elizabeth Priscilla Francine Bennet, Lizzy, as far as I am concerned, we have been courting for a few years now. From my perspective—unless you disagree—there is no need for a courtship."

"In that we also agree, William," Elizabeth returned as she felt fluttering in her belly as though butterflies were flapping their wings inside of her; at the same time her heart sped up in anticipation.

"To say I love you ardently is an understatement. You are my everything, Lizzy. You are my world, my heart, and my soulmate. There is none other in the known world I could imagine spending the rest of my life with. I not only love you, but my respect for you runs deeper than the deepest ocean. You will always challenge me and you have never agreed with me when I was wrong as so many fawning women do. In you I will have a partner, not a socialite interested in perception rather than reality. My dearest, loveliest Elizabeth, will you grant me your hand in marriage?"

"Yes, William, *absolutely* yes. I want to marry you. I love you more than I have words to describe and I cannot wait for us to begin our married life together." William thought he would float off the ground as he heard the words he most wanted to hear. He stood and pulled his betrothed up with him.

He gently drew her to himself and she came without any resistance or hesitation. Elizabeth lifted her head and closed her eyes in anticipation as the distance between them closed. As their lips met, her feelings caused a warmth to spread throughout her body such as she had never before felt. Untutored though she was, Elizabeth responded eagerly, winding her arms around his neck, and pressing herself close to him. For a brief moment, which felt like an eternity, their lips were connected as one of their mutual desires was accomplished. Their first kiss had been long, but chaste.

Elizabeth was sure William could hear the beating of her heart; she could hear it beating loudly. It sounded as though a host of drummers were beating a steady rhythm. Even though they had been restrained, the effect was electric. Elizabeth's grip around his neck tightened and she pulled him even closer. At the same time his hands snaked around her waist, pulling her so close that their bodies touched on all plains. William did not need further invitation. Their second kiss was deeper and released their pent-up passions. All too soon, William pulled back slightly as they both took shuddering breaths. They could not know it, but their hearts were almost beating in sync.

William did not miss her look of disappointment as he created a little distance between them, and his expression gentled when Elizabeth kept her hold around his neck. "Lizzy, we must step back before someone enters. We do not have unlimited time, my love," William rasped as he tried to bring his breathing and heartbeat back to normal.

As if to make his point, there was a knock on the door, causing Elizabeth to release him, reluctantly. After a slight pause, the door opened and the four adults returned.

"Given the joy I see radiating from you both, I assume you have reached an understanding?" Fanny asked as she looked from one to the other. Lizzy was not one to blush easily, but at this moment she was deep scarlet all the way down to her day dress.

"Bennet, Uncle Freddy, I—we—request your consent and blessing to marry. I proposed to Lizzy, and she accepted me," William managed to relay in his dreamlike state.

All four parents looked to Elizbeth who nodded emphatically. "We did not doubt you William, we just needed to hear from Lizzy as well." Bennet teased, "She who is never at a loss for words, seems to have been robbed of the power of speech, however."

"Papa!" If possible, Elizabeth blushed even deeper than she had before.

"As her birthfather, I bestow my hearty consent and blessing," the Prince granted.

"And from her adopted father, you have the same," Bennet stated. "We will enjoy having you as a son, William."

"For my part, I cannot imagine gaining a better daughter than Lizzy here," the Duke said as he hugged his soon to be daughter-in-law.

"If my father approves—and I see no reason he will not —I suggest that we plan the wedding near Lizzy's eighteenth birthday. It is six weeks away, a respectable length of betrothal. That way, anything planned to capture Lizzy and her fortune will be moot."

"For my part I agree with Freddy, but it is up to you two," Fanny declared.

Elizabeth and William looked at one another and each gave a slight nod of their head. "Will we be able to marry from Longbourn Church?" Elizabeth asked.

"I am afraid not, Lizzy," her birthfather averred. "Yours will be a royal wedding, so my mother will want the ceremony performed in her church by none other than the Archbishop of Canterbury." All those present all understood the reference to Westminster Abbey.

"For my part, as long as I am able to marry Lizzy, I do not care where," William indicated.

"As much as I would have liked to marry in our church, I understand and accept that, in this, I will have to bend to my grandmother's will," Elizabeth qualified.

"In that case, I will send an express to my parents and request an audience with them on Monday coming." Bennet indicated his desk and the Prince sat to write a note to be sent to the King and Queen.

~~~~~~~/~~~~~~~

They received an affirmative response from Buckingham House by Saturday evening, so Monday morning found the six on their way to London. The betrothal would become official only after the King's consent had been bestowed, so no one was to be told before the group returned from Town.

The Lord Chamberlain showed the group into the receiving room at the designated time. After announcing the group, he withdrew and closed the doors after his exit.

"You look well, Frederick," the Queen said, "Granddaughter, Lords Robert and William, Lord Thomas and Lady Francine, we welcome you all to our home."

"Father," the Prince turned to the King after bestowing a kiss on his mother's cheek. "I am here to request your royal sanction for Princess Beth, my daughter, to marry the Marquess of Derby."

The King cogitated for a minute. "We assume you approve of young Darcy, Son?"

"Yes, Father, I most certainly do. There is no other man I believe I would willingly give her hand to than William here," the Prince assured his father.

The King looked to his Queen, who nodded almost imperceptibly. "Lord William, Marquess of Derby, you have our unreserved consent and blessing to marry our granddaughter." The King granted.

"You have my heartfelt thanks, Grandfather," Elizabeth approached the King and kissed both his cheeks. The King kissed his granddaughter on the top of her head.

"We will place a royal decree in the newspapers this evening and tomorrow morning," the King informed them. He looked to William. "We welcome you as our Grandson, Lord William." William inclined his head in thanks toward the monarch.

"You will marry at our church, will you not?" the Queen

asked, though no one present mistook it for a request.

"Of course, my Royal Grandmother, we will be happy to marry in your church," Elizabeth bowed her head to the Queen.

"Our parson will officiate," the Queen added. No one misunderstood to whom she referred. "We will hold a betrothal ball befitting a princess at St James."

"Mother, could we have the ball *after* Lizzy and William are married?" the Prince requested. He enumerated his fears and the reasons for his request.

"Yes, my Son; we will hold a wedding ball for our granddaughter and new grandson," the Queen granted easily, appreciating the measures all were going to in order to protect their Princess Beth.

Until that moment, William had not thought about the fact he would be gaining some rather highly placed grandparents, aunts, and uncles. He schooled his features. He had royal sanction to marry his Lizzy and that was all he cared about.

There was a discussion about wedding dates, and, in the end, Elizabeth's birthday on Saturday, the fifth day of March, was selected. As much as Fanny would have liked to be the one to organise the events, she was not put out. Lizzy being a Princess of the United Kingdom of Great Britain and Ireland, the wedding breakfast would be held at Buckingham House. The Queen, displaying great sensitivity towards her granddaughter's adoptive mother, invited Fanny to be an active participant in the plans for the wedding and following breakfast.

Not long after, the Bennets, Darcys, and Prince Frederick departed for Hertfordshire.

~~~~~~~/~~~~~~~

There had been much speculation at Netherfield Park about their unscheduled trip to London, so when they arrived home, the six did not make their family and friends wait long before sharing the good news with them.

Prior to informing the others, Elizabeth took her Grandmama Sarah aside and told her of her betrothal, and more importantly of the King's sanction, so Lady Sarah had no need to worry her granddaughter and William would suffer the same fate as her daughter and Prince Frederick.

No one was surprised by the news, as the families had expected this for some years. When the reasoning behind not waiting until after Elizabeth came out into society was revealed, besides indignation that any would want to use their Lizzy so ill, there was universal agreement the correct course of action had been taken.

By seven that day, the evening editions of the London papers were delivered, and on the front page was the royal announcement of the betrothal of Princess Elizabeth Priscilla Francine Bennet to Lord William Darcy, Marquess of Derby.

It was not heard in Meryton, but in London there were sounds of gnashing of teeth of many men, those who planned attempt to capture the country-raised Princess for their wife, most of whom were in desperate need of an infusion of cash.

One or two of the more desperate men shifted plans to act at the Princess' coming out ball as if she were not married at that point—at least that was what they believed.

CHAPTER 33

By mid-February plans were finalised for their departure to London. Fanny had been communicating with the Queen's principal Lady in Waiting, the Duchess of Wolverhampton, to make sure the wedding would reflect Elizabeth's and William's tastes as much as possible.

During February, Cassie felt the quickening and informed the family she was with child. She had shared her suspicions with Richard in January; she had not been surprised when he—very much attuned to his wife—told her he suspected it beforehand.

To Elizabeth's and William's chagrin, the weather over the last month had not been cooperative; they were forced to spend many a day inside the house. In addition to reading and the subsequent discussions, hours had been devoted to card games—vingt-un, lottery tickets, whist, and loo.

On the first cloudless day for some time, Elizabeth and William rode to Oakham Mount. Elizabeth wanted to watch the sun rise from the mount—merely a glorified hill—once more before she left, but the particularly cold weather meant they, and their escorts, departed after ten that morning.

Fortunately, the ground had dried sufficiently so they were not covered in too much mud by the time the horses stopped at the base of Oakham Mount. Leaving four guards with the horses, Biggs and Johns followed the betrothed couple at a respectful distance. Johns stopped just below the summit, while Biggs placed himself on the path where he could see the flattened surface of the top and still allow the couple the illusion of privacy.

"In little more than two weeks, we will never be separated again," William pointed out as they looked out over the familiar view. Elizabeth stood in front of William; he wrapped his arms around her, holding her in tight against his body and resting his chin on the top of her head. Both would have liked to have stolen a kiss—as they had on a few occasions when they had snatched a minute of complete privacy during the last month— but knowing the ever-observant Biggs could see them on the summit kept them in check, despite their desires for a more passionate embrace.

"I am counting the days as well. Time cannot pass quickly enough, although it does remind me of a conversation I had with Jane on the eve of her wedding about a woman's lot of leaving home," Elizabeth said as she looked across the plain to Netherfield Park. "Before you ask, no, I do not require that we live within an easy distance of my parents, but I will miss them very much nevertheless."

"There is no need to feel maudlin, Lizzy. You know we will see them many times during the year," William assured his beloved. "Have you thought more about where we *will* live after the wedding? At Derby Springs or Pemberley? Rivington, the main estate of the dukedom, is an option, but I am not sure we need an estate which rivals—or exceeds—Pemberley in size."

"We have many options, but I would like to live at Pemberley for at least the first year. For myself, I know I will always be happy at Pemberley, so as far as I am concerned it can become our permanent residence, but I will leave it up to you. I do not like the idea of Uncle Robert, I mean *Father* Robert, alone for much of the year while Gigi is at Netherfield with the masters and my siblings," Elizabeth informed her betrothed of her preference.

"As I love Pemberley, it will be no hardship for me to continue living there. I believe you are correct; Father will love having us with him. Also, remember we will be almost half of the year with the family between Hertfordshire, Kent, and

London," William reminded her. "I cannot hide a Royal Princess away in the wilds of Derbyshire forever, no matter how much I would like to have her to myself alone."

Elizabeth blushed becomingly at the allusion to soon having time alone. She had read enough books, and she had grown up on a farm, so she had a very good idea what the marriage bed entailed—physically. She thought herself wanton that she was so keen to experience marital relations with her William, rather than having trepidations, which she had heard was appropriate for a new bride.

The wind starting to pick up was cold and biting, so they reluctantly separated and started walking down the hill, with Biggs and Johns following at a distance.

~~~~~~~/~~~~~~~

Elizabeth knew she and the Bennets would not stay at Darcy House; she thought they would be hosted at Matlock, Hilldale, or Holder House. Instead, the day before departure, Fanny received a missive from the Duchess of Wolverhampton *inviting* Princess Beth, her adoptive parents, and her siblings to be hosted at Buckingham House.

As with other invitations from the Queen, this could not be refused. Wednesday was cold with occasional light flurries visible from the windows of the Bennet coaches as they drove past the royal guard members on duty in front of Buckingham House.

The Duchess of Wolverhampton met them on behalf of Her Majesty the Queen and had one of the housekeepers show the Bennets and the Princess to their apartments. Everything there, from the décor to the furnishings, was gilded and ostentatious, as was the rest of the house. Thankfully, the furniture, including gigantic beds in their bedchambers, were comfortable in spite of being ostentatious.

Tommy had been wondering what he would do in the enormous house. Uncle Freddy took them on a tour and pointed out St. James Park across from the house, telling them that behind it was Green Park, which ended at Hyde Park.

Uncle Freddy promised he would organise riding parties when the weather allowed, and that he was sure that a few of his nieces and nephews were in residence who would love to join them.

Before the end of the tour, he pointed out Westminster Abbey, where the wedding would take place in less than ten days, as well as the houses of Parliament, all visible from the upper floors of the house.

That evening at dinner, the Bennets were announced by a major-domo and joined the King, Queen, Prince of Wales, Prince Frederick, Prince Edward, and Princess Amelia. The latter was one of her father's favourites. Kitty and Lydia had been moved to Darcy House that afternoon; they would be more comfortable staying where they could be themselves with Georgiana, without having to worry about royal protocol. Tommy, even though he liked the idea of riding in the parks, missed Eddy, so Fanny sent him to stay with the Gardiners vastly pleasing the youngest Bennet.

Luckily, the Bennets at Buckingham House had been schooled in protocol, so they knew not to begin eating until the King had, and to cease once the King had completed the course in front of him. The King, conscious others took their lead from him, ate slowly so no one left food on their plate they preferred to eat.

~~~~~~~/~~~~~~~

Three days before the wedding, those involved in the ceremony met at the Abbey to go over the order of service. However, they would meet his Grace, Charles Manners-Sutton, The Most Reverend Willowmere, by Divine Providence Lord Archbishop of Canterbury, only on the day of the wedding. The meeting on this day was held with one of the bishops who assisted the Archbishop.

Young May and Peter Gardiner, seven and five respectively, were excited that they would have a role in the wedding. May was to be the flower girl and Peter was to act as page and carry his cousin's train. Jane and Mary were to stand up with

Elizabeth, while Andrew and Richard would do the honours for William.

The Bishop explained that the congregation would stand until the royal family was seated, the congregants would bow and curtsy to the royals, and then they would be seated. Each participant would bow or curtsy to the King and Queen and their children in attendance as they entered the abbey from the vestibule.

Elizabeth would be walked up the aisle between her papa and her father. After the service, the bride and groom would return to Buckingham House in a royal coach pulled by eight white horses and escorted by a contingent of royal guards.

~~~~~~~/~~~~~~~

The next day, the betrothed couple went for a walk in St. James Park, escorted by Biggs, Johns, and a cadre of royal guards. Jane and Andrew, Cassie and Richard, Wes, and Mary walked with them.

None of them realized they were being watched. Lord Harrington Hamstead was desperate. He had no way of paying his debts of honour. He had been so confident his luck was changing that he had put his estate in Shropshire and his town house in London up as collateral. He had lost, and if he did not make a substantial payment in the next few days, the man holding his vowels would foreclose on the properties that had been in his family for generations—they were not protected by an entail.

He watched Buckingham House for a chance to get near the countrified Princess. Desperate men are rarely smart men, and he needed funds desperately. Deciding his only option was to compromise the Princess before she was lost to him by marriage, he watched as the four couples entered the park.

There was a major flaw in his plan; he did not know which lady was the Princess. He knew who the Fitzwilliams were, but he had no idea who the other two men were. All of the ladies were similarly dressed which did not help the hapless lord decide which was the princess. He calculated that it was one of those two not accompanied by a Fitzwilliam—he had a one on two chance of selecting the correct lady. He started running—as fast as he was able with his corpulent body—toward the last couple, Mary and Wes. Before he was within twenty yards of the group of walkers, he found himself flat on his back staring up at the angry visage of one of the biggest men he had ever seen.

As Lord Hamstead attempted to rise, the man growled at him to stay down and, to make his point even more clearly, Johns placed the sole of his boot on the wheezing man's chest. Two of the royal guard were assisted Johns within moments and dragged the sputtering man to his feet.

The only one of the walkers who noticed anything amiss was Richard. His military training helped him identify threats, but almost as soon as he saw the man, he knew the escorts would never allow him close enough to disturb them. Once he saw the man was subdued, he nodded to the captain of the guard, conveying his approval of their swift actions. Cassie looked at her husband quizzically when she saw the grin on his face. "Later my love, I will tell you all," Richard told his wife as he watched the guards dragging the hapless man away.

The rest of their walk was undisturbed and, after enjoying tea in one of the large parlours in the house, the six visitors took their leave. Elizabeth and Mary walked them out to the courtyard.

"You will be my husband in less than two days, William," Elizabeth said softly as they approached the waiting coach.

"When you become my wife, my love, it will be the greatest day of my life," William stated quietly as he squeezed her hand.

"For me it will be my best birthday ever," Elizabeth told her betrothed. "I will never have an excuse to forget the date of our anniversary."

"Even though it is not my birthday on Saturday, as I am marrying you, my dearest, loveliest Elizabeth, I feel I am the one being given the gift, one which I will treasure for the rest of my life," William returned quietly, his voice laden with certainty.

"We will see you later at Darcy House for a family dinner, William." Elizabeth would feel bereft of his company until she and her parents arrived at Darcy House.

After the sisters saw their extended family off they returned to the parlour, where their parents were waiting for them with Prince Frederick and the captain of the guards. "Did you notice the disturbance while you were walking in St. James Park?" Bennet asked.

Elizabeth and Mary looked at one another questioningly; both shook their heads. "No Papa, we did not notice anything out of the ordinary," Elizabeth reported.

"Then I commend you, captain, as you and your men were beyond efficient," Bennet stated as he turned to the commander of the guards.

"As much as I appreciate your words, Lord Longbourn," the captain bowed, "it was your man, Johns, who neutralised the threat before any of the walkers became aware of the issue, other than former Captain Fitzwilliam."

"Where is the dastard now?" the Prince asked.

"In the dungeon, your Royal Highness," the Captain averred.

"Thank you, captain, please hold him until you hear from me. You are dismissed," the Prince commanded. The captain broke off a smart salute and left the parlour.

"What happened?" Mary asked.

"A desperate fortune hunter tried to compromise Lizzy, except he did not know who she was so it seems he was aiming at you, Mary, before Johns brought him down," the Prince explained. "The closest he got to you was little more than twenty yards."

"What will happen to him?" Elizabeth asked.

"He will be held until after the wedding," Bennet replied. "Evidently, he has gambled his birth right away and was trying to save it by acquiring your fortune. We have been informed his debts will be called in and he will lose everything by next week."

"Even though he did not know who you were, he will still be charged with treason. I will recommend transportation for him," the Prince explained.

Elizabeth and Mary retired to prepare for dinner with the family that evening. When they joined their parents in the courtyard before climbing in their coach, Bennet informed his daughters that the King had accepted his son's recommendation, and the now ex-Lord would be on the first ship sailing to Botany Bay after the wedding.

~~~~~~~/~~~~~~~

"Did that gambler, Hamstead, not notice the escorts?" Lord Holder asked. He shook his head at the man's folly while the men sat enjoying their libations and cigars after dinner.

"He was desperate enough that he threw caution to the wind," Richard reported. "I watched as he made his ill-advised charge—if one can call it that. It was barely above walking speed. The only question was who would stop him first. Unfortunately for Hamstead, he was closest to Johns, who had the hapless man flat on his back in an instant."

"After today, the rectitude of our decision to allow Lizzy and William to marry now has proven to be for the best." The Prince raised his glass of port to Bennet. "The man is lucky Johns took him down when he did. Had he gotten closer, the guards would not have hesitated to run him through."

"There is nothing the man could have done that would have deterred me from marrying Lizzy in two days," William stated definitively as he blew cigar smoke out.

"He is lucky he did not lay a finger on her, as then nothing would have saved him from the tower," the Prince informed them.

~~~~~~~/~~~~~~~

"You know how happy your mother would have been if she were still with us to witness you marrying, Lizzy," Darcy said wistfully as he looked to the heavens. "Your use of Seaview would have pleased her as well. It may not be warm enough for sea bathing yet, though."

"It will be much warmer than when Jane and I were there during December and January after our wedding in '07," Andrew stated and then took a sip of his cognac.

"We will still have four children at home, but I suspect we will lose one more in the next two years," Bennet stated as he looked towards Wes.

Wes had a faraway look on his face, which slowly transformed to a grin as he thought about Mary, with whom he was well on his way to falling in love. *'Yes, Bennet, you have the right of it. If Mary and I have any say in the matter, she will be leaving your protection in about two years,'* Wes told himself with anticipation. He and Mary had made no verbal declarations to each other as yet, but they spent as much time together as propriety allowed.

<center>~~~~~~~/~~~~~~~</center>

The ladies drank tea in the music room while Anne played softly in the background. Catherine, whose playing had improved somewhat under the tutelage of *Signore* da Funti, still marvelled at how well her daughter played the instrument. Thankfully, she had ceased berating herself about the past and was able to look to the present, and the future, rather than being caught up worrying about that which she could not change.

Lady Sarah was thankful every day that her children and granddaughter had accepted her back into their lives. For almost her full year of mourning, she had blamed herself for not finding a way to contact Priscilla. It took her son, daughter, and granddaughter some time to convince her none of them held her responsible for the actions of her late husband, and that she should leave the past where it belonged.

Because their circumstances were similar and coupled with the fact they were often in company with their shared family, Lady Sarah and Catherine had become good friends. The former found it helpful to talk to the latter about the changes she had made in her life. In addition, Lady Sarah forged an extremely close relationship with Priscilla's daughter—her granddaughter. It was balm to her soul to be with Elizabeth; she saw Priscilla's eyes looking back at her when they were together.

Fanny watched her second daughter as she sat with her sisters, Gigi, and Cassie. How she would miss Lizzy when she left home in two days! She knew she would see her daughter often during the year, but for Fanny it was as though she were losing Priscilla again.

Watching the gathering, Fanny thought about Lizzy's generous spirit. Before they all departed for Town, Lizzy asked Uncle Phillips to draft a document which gifted Netherfield to the Bennets effective on her marriage, as the bequest from her mother would be hers when she and William married. Elizabeth also wanted to augment her sister's dowries. She was told that, thanks to Uncle Gardiner's management and because money had been added each year to the amount bequeathed by her birthmother, the amount had grown to more than thirty thousand pounds each. None of the younger Bennet girls lacked for a dowry.

"Are you ready to marry your William, Lizzy?" Jane asked, though she already knew the answer to her question.

"Yes. In fact, I have been ready for some time now. I believe William and I will be as happy in our marriage as you and Andrew, Anne and Jamey, and Cassie and Richard. It seems members of this family have chosen good life mates," Elizabeth opined.

"It is because none of us have ignored our hearts," Jane stated. "It looks like Mary has been listening to her heart, too, have you not, Sister?"

"It is still two years before I come out—well, a little less than—so it is premature to talk of my future." Mary's pleasurable blush belied her words, proving that her connubial future was something she thought about often.

"I am very happy I will be the last of my sisters to marry,"

Lydia stated meaningfully. "Until I meet a man who excites a love in me like I see in my sisters, our parents, and our relatives, I have no interest in thinking about matrimony."

"You are not fourteen yet, Lyddie, so it is only right you should think so. You have years to go before you come out," Cassie pointed out.

"It is so exciting," Georgiana enthused. "In less than two days we will all be sisters and brothers." She looked to Tommy as she said the last.

Tommy no longer thought girls the strangest creatures in the world, but he still preferred the company of boys. He and Eddy Gardiner, almost eleven, were sitting in a corner of the room planning a game with their toy soldiers for the morrow.

The men joined the ladies and were served tea and coffee. A little over an hour later, the Bennets and the Prince departed for Buckingham House. The next time Elizabeth and William would see one another, she would be walking to him up the aisle at Westminster Abbey.

CHAPTER 34

Friday, the day before the wedding, Jane arrived at Buckingham House to be with her sister on her last day as an unmarried woman. They stood together looking at the wedding gown Elizabeth was to wear on the morrow. It was white satin, puffy sleeves slightly off the shoulder, with a gossamer overlay embellished with diamond chips. The long train would flow behind her as she walked up the aisle. Thankfully, Peter would be helping with her train as she walked.

Elizabeth would have preferred a simple dress like the one Jane wore at her wedding, but since hers was a royal wedding, that was not possible. Her trousseau had been ordered during a trip to Town before they arrived at Buckingham House. Being poked, prodded, and measured by London's premier modiste, Madam Chambourg, was not her favourite thing to do. Madam Chambourg, who only accepted new clients occasionally—and then with a long waiting period—made an exception for the Queen's granddaughter. Her shop had been closed to the public for a little more than a week to accommodate Princess Beth's huge order. Elizabeth and others in the family had completed their final fittings since arriving at Buckingham House.

Dinner was a formal affair—as it always was when dining with the King and Queen. Much to Queen Charlotte's delight, her granddaughter thrilled them with an exhibition of playing and singing once the men re-joined the ladies in a music room after the separation of the sexes.

Lady Sarah marvelled anew each time she heard Priscilla's daughter—her granddaughter—play and sing. Her daughter had been accomplished, but not to the level of Elizabeth or her sisters. Listening to Elizabeth sing, she was convinced she could feel Priscilla's presence shining down on them from heaven.

For their final performance of the night, Jane played on the harp, Mary played the pianoforte, and Elizabeth sang an aria in German as a special treat for her royal grandmother. Much to the Queen's delight, whenever she and Elizabeth conversed in private, it was in German.

Everyone retired relatively early that night, given the momentous occasion occurring on the morrow.

~~~~~~~/~~~~~~~

Once Elizabeth was ready for bed, there was a knock on her door. When bade to enter, Fanny sat on the bed with her second daughter and held Lizzy's hand. She intended to talk to her daughter about the wedding night.

"This is the last night we have sole claim on you as a daughter living under our roof—even though we are certainly not in our own home tonight. Cilla, Priscilla, would have loved to be the one giving you this information, Lizzy, so it is my task to do it for the both of us," Fanny told her daughter.

"Mama, I never met my birthmother, but I feel her love in everything she did to protect me; she left me with the best person other than herself in the world. In my mind, I have always had the love of two mothers," Elizabeth imparted to her mother as she squeezed her hands.

"From tomorrow your William will have the honour, and I dare say pleasure, of your protection, though you must know that all of us will protect and love you all of your days," Fanny began. "He understands you, Lizzy, and your father, Papa, and I are equally happy and relieved that your marriage will be a true partnership, which is the only kind of marriage in which we knew you would find your own happiness. William respects you as much as he loves you.

"Tomorrow night is your wedding night, and I need to talk to you about what to expect in the marriage bed," Fanny offered softly. With a blush rising in her cheeks, Lizzy nodded for her mother to proceed. "The intimacies of the marriage bed are not something to be feared, especially not with someone who loves you the way that your William clearly loves you. When there is love like the two of you share, the marriage bed will be a wonderful and pleasurable experience for both of you.

"Anyone that advises a daughter to 'lie back and tolerate' the relations between man and woman has no idea of what they speak. Do not be afraid to tell William what you like and do not like and let him know that you want to know the same from him. Just as you want your marriage to be a true partnership, Lizzy, the same is true of the marriage bed. My wish for you is that you will discover that it is as pleasurable to give as to receive. Never be ashamed of the relations that you will have in private with your husband. A good relationship in the marriage bed enhances your marriage as a whole and gives a depth of joy that cannot be harmed by anyone.

"I will not lie to you; there will be some pain and more than likely a few drops of blood the first time, but it is only the first time that this should happen. The pain will be but a moment and marks your becoming a wife in every sense of the word. William likely expects that he will need to stop for a moment at that point, so if you need him to, tell him and I am sure that he will. He is a man that will never force you to do that which is unacceptable to you. That is why telling each other what you enjoy, and do not enjoy, is so very important.

"If you never think of your relations with your husband as a chore, they will never be so. No matter what anyone else may say, both husband and wife deriving pleasure from the marriage bed is a good thing and does not make you a wanton, nor is it a sin to love your husband as only a wife can. You and William are passionate people, so I believe that both of you will take pleasure in your marriage, and in the many ways it can be enjoyed. Never be afraid to be spontaneous. Regardless of what society professes, night-time is not the only acceptable time for conjugal relations with your beloved husband. Whenever the two of you have privacy and you both desire the same thing, it is never wrong.

"I pray you both will be able to keep your stubborn streaks under good regulation. There will be disagreements and arguments at times, but no matter what, never go to bed angry one with the other. Do you understand this, Lizzy? It is critically important to the health of your marriage.

"Yes Mama, I do understand what you are saying," Elizabeth returned, looking anywhere but directly at her mother.

"I am now jumping ahead, but when you are with child, there is no reason to stop having relations with your husband until you feel it is too uncomfortable for you as you near your confinement. Remember, it will be a partnership, and like any good and equal partnership, the shared experience of love, passion, and pleasure will be very fulfilling. Do you have any questions for me, Lizzy? If you feel the need, I can summon Jane to see you and talk to you as well." Fanny gently squeezed her daughter's hand.

After she calmed down at the thought of the pleasure and experiences that she would start to share with William starting on the morrow, Elizabeth shook her head. "No, Mama, I have no questions. I always love to talk to Jane, but your talk was very thorough, so I have no need for more information at this time. Thank you, Mama; you have helped me look forward to the marriage bed with pleasure and not fear." Lizzy drew her mother in for a hug and kissed both of Fanny's cheeks.

After her mother left, Elizabeth felt warm all over as she imagined seeing William undressed for the first time on the morrow. She had seen plates of nude men in a book she had discovered in her father's library, and sculptures at museums, so she had a rough idea what she would see. She fell asleep with a smile on her lips as she imagined William and herself intertwined in their bed together.

~~~~~~~/~~~~~~~

William, unlike most young men of his age, had not experienced the pleasures of the flesh; he sat with his father in

Darcy House having the most uncomfortable—if informative—conversation of his life.

There were some similarities to the talk Elizabeth received from her mother in the information Robert Darcy passed onto his son, but also many differences. By the time the mortifying conversation was completed, William was sure he was the colour of an overripe tomato.

Robert gave his son some *informative* books after the betrothal was made official, but he felt William needed additional information. As hard as it had been for father and son, the former had not shirked his duty and made sure his son was aware how to give his wife pleasure as well as receiving his own.

When William finally fell asleep in the bed he would be sharing with his Elizabeth on the morrow sleep finally claimed him after the final stroke of midnight. As he fell asleep he wished she was with him that night ever more impatient to have her in his arms.

~~~~~~~/~~~~~~~

The fifth day of March dawned clear, with hardly any wind. Elizabeth was awake when her maid entered her bedchamber, followed by her mother. "Happy birthday, Lizzy; it looks like a good day to get married. With little or no wind, it will be warmer than the last few days," Fanny hugged and kissed her daughter. "The maid there," Fanny indicated one of the Buckingham House maids, "has tea, toast, scones, butter, jam, and cream. You need to eat and drink, as it will be some hours before the wedding breakfast."

"Mama, you know full well I can never pass up having warm scones with jam and cream—especially as I see strawberry jam." Elizabeth had thought herself too excited to eat, but she could not pass up scones. Once she had one and realised how hungry she was, she had a second, followed by toast and butter. She washed it down with two cups of tea.

"I will leave you to Jacqui now, Lizzy," Fanny kissed her daughter on the top of her head. "Jane, Mary, and I will return to help you dress after your bath," Fanny told her daughter, pulling the bedchamber door closed.

Shortly after her mother left, Elizabeth luxuriated in a steaming tub while her maid washed her mahogany tresses. '*I wonder what my William is doing now*,' Elizabeth thought as she relaxed while Jacqui massaged her scalp.

~~~~~~~/~~~~~~~

The morning of his wedding, William made his way to the breakfast parlour to break his fast, following the advice of his father and others. He normally ate a large breakfast, but today he took one egg, a piece of sausage, and some toast. His drink of choice in the morning was coffee, and he savoured a steaming cup. His father, Gigi, Kitty, and Lydia joined him just as he was about to leave the parlour. He was about to ask where his soon-to-be little brother, Tommy, was when he remembered the lad was still being hosted at the Gardiners.

Thinking about the Gardiners made William remember the time when he and his father signed the settlement. Phillips and his wife were being hosted by the Gardiners; they were there to represent Priscilla's interests, and by extension, Elizabeth's. Elizabeth, Bennet, Gardiner, and the Prince were present.

There was no disagreement about Netherfield being transferred to the Bennets. Her marriage would release her inheritance, so Elizabeth did not need to wait for her majority; the property would be the Bennets' after the wedding.

William had been prepared for Elizabeth's massive fortune, bequeathed to her by her mother. What he had not known was she was her birthfather's sole heir, which would add another massive fortune—larger than her current one—when the Prince passed on.

He grinned as he remembered how vociferously his Lizzy had argued against any Darcy money being settled on her, as her fortune would remain hers to do with as she wished. Even though he felt a man should settle money on his wife, William had not fought Lizzy on that point. Once an acceptable settlement was drafted, it was signed.

After this reminiscence, William thought about his Lizzy as he bathed. As he reclined with his eyes closed in his—soon to be their—oversized tub, William snapped out of his reverie when Carstens informed him it was time to get dressed.

~~~~~~~/~~~~~~~

Both Jane and Mary assisted Elizabeth with her dress's train as she came down one of the grand staircases at Buckingham House. Both her papa and father were waiting for her in the foyer at the base of the stairs. The diamond chips caught the early morning sun shining through the large windows, creating prisms that reflected onto the walls.

Fanny kissed her daughter before she lowered her gossamer veil. Both Bennet and the Prince were stunned by the vision Elizabeth made as she walked down the stairs.

Recovering from his trance, the Prince led his daughter to the foremost coach, a gilded royal viewing coach drawn by four pair of white horses; it was the same one that would bear the newlyweds back to Buckingham House for the wedding breakfast.

Bennet, Fanny, Jane, and Mary rode in an only *slightly* less ostentatious royal carriage, pulled by three pairs of matched bays. As the conveyances began to move, twenty mounted royal guards took up their stations, half in front of the lead vehicle and the rest behind the second carriage.

Elizabeth waved to the people lining the route. When the coaches halted at the Abbey and Elizabeth was helped to alight, a rousing cheer rose from the considerable crowd.

The congregants were already seated, and all rose before the King, Queen, and some of their children, led by the Prince of Wales, took their seats. After they accepted curtsies and bows, the King nodded and everyone resumed their seats.

William had been introduced to the Archbishop before the royal party arrived. He was standing with his cousins —soon-to-be brothers—when they heard the cheering of the crowd outside, alerting them to the bride's arrival.

Fanny was escorted to her seat by Lord Matlock. She curt-
seyed and he bowed to the royals before they took their seats.
First up the aisle was May Gardiner, who remembered to curtsey.

Mary made her way up the aisle next; Wes could not take
his eyes off her in her light blue satin gown. Jane was the last
attendant before the bride. Andrew's eyes followed his wife
from the instant she walked through the vestibule door, made
her curtsey, and took her place opposite him.

There were a number of friends from Meryton seated
together with the Gardiners and Phillipses, including the
Lucases, Collinses, Gouldings, and Longs. Sir William had
never seen so many highly ranked and royal individuals in one
place before, not even at his investiture at St. James.

When the Archbishop gave the signal for the congregation to stand, all did, except for the King and Queen. The organ
at the choir's entrance behind the central screen started to play
as the doors from the narthex were opened. With her birthfather on her right, her adoptive father on her left, and Peter
behind her helping with her train, Elizabeth started to walk up
the long aisle towards her beloved William, whose eyes locked
with hers.

After the acknowledgment to the King and Queen, Prince
Frederick lifted his daughter's veil and kissed her cheek, and
then stepped back. Lord Longbourn kissed her other cheek and
then, after lowering the veil, placed Elizabeth's arm on William's forearm. The Prince joined his parents and siblings as
the Baron joined his Baroness and children.

The bride and groom climbed the three steps until they
were standing in front of His Grace the Archbishop and the
two bishops concelebrating with him. Peter joined his parents
as he had been instructed to do. The Archbishop nodded to the
Princess in greeting, opened the Book of Common Prayer, and
began. "Dearly beloved…"

For both Elizabeth and William, time seemed to pass in
the blink of an eye. There were no objections—even had some-

one had one, they would not have dared make it given the bride was a granddaughter of the King and Queen, both present. Then they were reciting their vows. William did not miss the arched eyebrow when Elizabeth recited the part of the vow where she promised to *obey* him.

William allowed himself a small smile; he had no doubt that if any of their vows would be bent, it would be that one. A few minutes later, he slid a diamond-encrusted wedding band onto her ring finger, next to his mother's engagement ring.

It was done. The Archbishop announced that "...they be Man and Wife together, In the Name of the Father, and of the Son, and of the Holy Ghost. Amen." He intoned the final benediction, and the marriage ritual was complete.

The King and Queen stood and clapped, which allowed those in the congregation to do the same. A bishop led the newlyweds to the register, on a stand to the side of the altar. Elizabeth and William signed, as did their four attendants as witnesses. By the time the register was signed, the King, Queen, and their children, except for Frederick, had exited the Abbey through a side door, after which most of the congregants began to file out of the main doors.

The new Duke of Derbyshire was the first to hug Elizabeth. "You are perfect for William, Lizzy, and I know you will continue to be a good sister to Gigi. I only wish my Anne could have been here today," Robert Darcy said quietly with his mouth close to Elizabeth's ear.

"She is here, Father Robert. She and my birthmother are watching over us," Elizabeth returned as she kissed her father-in-law on both cheeks.

After much hugging, kissing, and well-wishing, friends and family entered their conveyances to take them the short distance to Buckingham House. A few minutes after the last of the coaches departed, Elizabeth and William made their way toward the exit. Elizabeth and William exited into the bright sunlight, walking between lines of royal guard members lining the steps of the Abbey. A rousing cheer rose from the crowd which had grown larger since the ceremony began. William handed two bags of coins to two guards, who tossed them into the crowd, causing the cheering to grow even louder.

William handed his wife into the coach, and then followed her inside. The cheering from the crowd reached a crescendo as the new husband gave his wife a chaste kiss as the conveyance pulled away.

CHAPTER 35

As the carriage with the newlyweds arrived at Buckingham House, Elizabeth turned to her husband and said, "You know we will always have a contingent of the Royal Guard with us? Not to mention Mr. Taylor, do you not William?" You are a grandson of the King and Queen now, so this will become a part of our lives."

"Well, we will never be a target for highwaymen," William jested as he kissed his wife again.

"William! We are at Buckingham House; there are guards and footmen all over the place who can see us," Elizabeth scolded with mock indignation.

"If I must accustom myself to the guards and other personnel who will be around us from now on, they must accustom themselves to my kissing my royal wife when I need to," William replied impertinently.

"You are incorrigible, husband," Elizabeth returned, "which is one of the many things I love about you."

The two did not notice a footman in royal livery had opened the door of the ornate coach and was waiting for them to alight. Elizabeth had her husband make sure all of her hairpins were in place in her hair, then William turned and handed his wife out.

A major-domo led them to a large ballroom, where the breakfast was being held. Two footmen opened the huge doors as a butler announced them. "Your Royal Majesties, Your Royal Highnesses, Your Graces, Lords, Ladies, and gentlemen, I present to you Lord Fitzwilliam Darcy, Marquess of Derby, and Princess Elizabeth Pricilla Francine Darcy, her Royal Highness, Princess of the United Kingdom of Great Britain and Ireland,

Marchioness of Derby."

"My, that is a mouthful," William whispered to his wife and was rewarded with one of her tinkling laughs.

The newlyweds brought themselves under regulation and bowed and curtsied to the King and Queen. The King took a sip from a goblet, thereby signalling the commencement of the feast. William and Elizabeth made their way around the ballroom to thank those who had come to celebrate with them.

When they reached the tables where the people of Meryton were seated, they took a bit longer to speak to each one. "Please allow me to wish you much joy and happiness, my royal cousin," Collins bowed over Elizabeth's hand.

"Thank you, Cousin. As long as you keep my friend happy, we will be friends," Elizabeth returned smilingly.

"You know Charlotte's happiness is, and will always be, my priority, Cousin Elizabeth," Collins averred.

"Yes, I am aware that you make my friend and cousin very happy," Elizabeth owned.

Sir William, normally a voluble and ebullient man, was awestruck. He had been in a receiving room at St. James when he was granted his knighthood, but never inside the King's and Queen's primary residence in London. Everywhere he looked, his eyes fell on another member of royalty or a peer.

Next, the couple stopped to speak with Mr. Bingley and the Hursts. The three would be forever in their debt for what the Princess did at the assembly to rehabilitate their family names and hold that they should not be held responsible for Miss Bingley's actions, and as such they had not been tainted by those actions.

"Your Highness and Your Lordship, on behalf of my sister, brother, and myself I wish you both joy and happiness for the future. We thank you for including us in the celebration of your wedding day and inviting us to your ball tonight after what my sister attempted to do in Meryton," Bingley stated thankfully.

"As I told you at the assembly, Mr. Bingley, you are no

more responsible for your sister's actions than you are for the sun rising in the east. We are happy all of you are here to celebrate with us," Elizabeth told Bingley sincerely.

After the couple spent time with each of the neighbours from Meryton, they continued around the room for about an hour, when they arrived where the family was seated. As would be expected, their first stop there was the King and Queen.

"You look exquisite today, Granddaughter," the Queen complimented after Elizabeth kissed her grandmother's cheek. "You have caught a very handsome husband there."

"Grandmother!" Elizabeth exclaimed as she blushed deeply. "I do not disagree, but this is not a discussion I would have thought to have with the Queen."

"Are we not a flesh and blood woman?" the Queen asked.

"Yes, you are, Grandmother," Elizabeth replied.

"I agree with her Majesty," added Lady Sarah who had been talking to the Queen.

"Thank you, Grandmama," Elizabeth smiled. "We have to be careful not to give my husband a swollen head," Elizabeth teased.

Throughout the teasing, William tried to keep a straight face, but it was a losing battle as the corners of his mouth turned up. "Just accept their words graciously, Grandson," the King advised.

"I will endeavour to do so, your Majesty," William replied.

After accepting good wishes from the Prince of Wales and some other royal aunts and uncles, Elizabeth sat down at the table with their non-royal extended family.

"You two need to eat; there is a long day and longer night ahead of us," Lady Elaine advised. "Balls at St. James seldom end before the sun rises, and as you two are the guests of honour, you will not be able to slip away until a few sets after supper."

"When will it be polite to depart the wedding breakfast?" Elizabeth asked.

"You want to be away from us already, Lizzy?" Fanny teased her second daughter.

"No, Mama, not at all. I did not get much sleep last night, and I would like to rest before tonight," Elizabeth stated.

"Indeed, Sister," Richard drawled, "I am sure you and William want to *rest*."

"Richard do not tease them on their wedding day," Cassie told her husband, swatting his arm playfully.

"Yes, dear," Richard replied as he waggled his eyebrows at his wife.

After the newlyweds ate and drank, they circulated among those they had not yet greeted, those seated in the other half of the ballroom. Just after that, the King decided he needed to rest. Everyone stood and acknowledged the King with a bow or curtsey. Once the monarch exited the room, the celebration resumed.

It was another hour and a half before Elizabeth and William were satisfied they had spoken personally to all of the well-wishers. Jane and Mary accompanied Elizabeth to the apartment she had been occupying during her stay at Buckingham House.

They assisted her to remove her intricate wedding gown and to change into her travel attire, although they were crossing only through Hyde Park to Grosvenor Square—a ride that would take less than twenty minutes.

"Lizzy, I am sure you and William will be happy. I am so glad for you, little sister," Jane told her as they fell into one another's arms.

"That we will have a felicitous marriage is not in doubt, Janie. With our living at Pemberley in the summer, we will be much closer to your estate. William told me Hilldale is less than five hours away by carriage," Elizabeth hugged her older sister tightly in return.

She drew Mary into their hug. "Mary, I will miss you, and my other sisters and brother."

"The house will seem empty without you there every day,

Lizzy," Mary stated stoically. "However, I have a feeling Tommy will make sure we do not have too much peace."

"Until Tommy goes to Eton in two years," Jane pointed out. "You will love Seaview, Lizzy; Andrew and I have many warm memories of it. We would have liked to bathe in the sea at the private cove, but it was far too cold when we were there in December."

"It has been warmer lately; mayhap you and our new brother will be able to venture into the seawater," Mary surmised.

"Just wait, Mary, it is less than two years until you come out and Wes will at last be able to declare himself," Elizabeth told her younger sister with arched eyebrow.

"There is no guarantee he will wait for me, Lizzy," Mary demurred.

"Mary Rose Bennet! Do not talk drivel. You know very well Wes is besotted with you, and were he allowed to declare himself today, he would," Jane stated firmly. "A blind man could see how in love you two are."

After final hugs, the three sisters joined William and the rest of the family near the doors leading to the portico, where a Darcy coach awaited them. There were long hugs with everyone, including Kitty, Lydia, Georgiana, and Tommy.

"Will I see you at Darcy House after your rest, Lizzy?" Tommy asked innocently.

"If Lizzy and William are not too tired, it is possible you may see them before dinner, otherwise we will see them then," Fanny told her son.

"William," his father said quietly as he pulled him aside, "This is from your mother. She asked me to give it to you on your wedding day so you can read it with your wife if you so choose. As you married Lizzy, having her read it will not be the problem it would have been had you married another." Darcy handed his son a sealed letter with his name written in his late mother's neat script.

William placed the precious letter in his inside pocket,

and soon the new husband and wife were on their way to Darcy House.

~~~~~~~/~~~~~~~

The Killions welcomed the Marquess and his Princess to Darcy House with warm wishes for their future felicity. The couple made for William's suite, the one he had moved into after he had become betrothed. It was the farthest one from the Duke's and Gigi's suites.

Once they dismissed their personal servants, the couple sat on a settee in their shared sitting room. William held his mother's missive for a while, just looking at his mother's flowing, neat handwriting. Elizabeth gave his free hand a squeeze and he broke the seal. It did not take long to discover why his father had made the comment about reading the letter with his wife.

July 1, 1803

To my dearest darling son, William:

I asked your father to give my letter to you on your wedding day. If my Robert has joined me in heaven already, he will have arranged beforehand to have someone deliver this in his stead, though I pray you have received this from his hands.

If a mother's intuition is correct, then Lizzy is the one sitting next to you as you read this, my son. From the day I watched the little mite kick your shins, I had a feeling she would be the one for you. If I was incorrect and it not Lizzy who is your wife, I apologise to your wife for my presumption, should you allow her to read this.

Whether it is Lizzy or another, please welcome her to the family on my behalf. It saddens me greatly I was unable to be with you today, but I will be watching with pleasure from heaven.

You were told this while I was alive, William. You are the best son a parent could wish for. As long as you have followed your heart when choosing your wife, you both love one another, and you have mutual respect, you cannot go wrong.

It does not mean there will never be disagreements, but if you do have them, once you have children, make sure it is not in front of them. You never knew about any disagreements your father and I had. They were few and far between, but they were ours.

Never hold back from your wife, William. Give her the whole of your heart and allow her to see your true self at all times. It is my great regret that I will never know my grandchildren, but I am sure you will be wonderful parents. Never follow the Ton's *mores of hiding children in the nursery for most of the day with nursemaids and governesses. Follow the example we—and all the parents you know in our extended family—set with you and Gigi.*

Have a good life with your new wife, William. Always be open and honest and, especially if it is Lizzy, make sure you never make unilateral or arbitrary decisions without consulting with her. I pray you have what your father and I had, a true and equal partnership.

It is tiring me to write so I will end here, William.

With all my love and best wishes for your marriage,

Mother.

William read the precious letter a second time before handing it to his wife. "What a wonderful letter to receive on our wedding day, and what perspicacity Aunt Anne had! I would have loved to her as my mother-in-law as much as I loved her as an aunt," Elizabeth stated as she returned the letter to her husband.

Knowing that, in her final days, his mother told them to carry on, love each other, and live life to the fullest was a precious gift. After a few minutes, William stood and led his wife into his—their—bedchamber. They had decided to share a bed, so the second bedchamber of their suite would become another dressing room for Elizabeth.

Wordlessly, they set about undressing one another. Both had imagined the other in an undressed state, but the reality was far better than their imagination. "Make me your wife in every way," Elizabeth managed in a breathy voice, heavy with passion.

William picked her up, carried her to their bed, and proceeded to obey her command diligently.

~~~~~~~/~~~~~~~

The newlyweds joined their family in the drawing room an hour before dinner. "Did you have a good rest, Lizzy and William?" Lydia asked guilelessly.

"We did, Lyddie, thank you," Elizabeth replied, unsuccessfully attempting to stop her blush.

"Before we left Buckingham House, Prince Frederick pointed out an omission in the properties listed as part of the Derbyshire dukedom. Derbyshire House is across the square, two doors down from Matlock House. The crown had it leased out and the lease has expired. I will move into that house after it has been inspected to see if changes are needed, Robert Darcy said," turning to Fanny. "Fanny, you will help me if new décor is needed, will you not?"

"Do you really need to ask me that, Robert? Of course, I will help, as will Elaine and Edith," Fanny averred.

"Once I have moved in, then you two will have the use of Darcy House, and you can move into the master suite. Evidently, there is a second house, Derby House on Portman Square; you could move into that one if you prefer," Darcy told his son and new daughter.

They looked at one another and Elizabeth nodded. "We thank you Father, but I think we prefer to remain at Darcy House," William informed his father.

"Will I be able to reside with William and Lizzy part of the time when we are in London, father?" Georgiana asked.

"That goes without saying, Gigi," her father informed her. "Unless Lizzy and William object."

"Which we never will, not for *any* of our siblings," Elizabeth stated for them both.

After a light dinner, those who would attend the ball at ten o'clock went to rest until it was time to dress. Mary and the younger girls understood that no one who was not out would be allowed to attend. Mary would miss dancing with Wes, but she knew there would be many future opportunities.

~~~~~~~/~~~~~~~

There were considerably people attended the ball than the wedding breakfast that morning. Elizabeth and William were part of the receiving line, along with Elizabeth's birth-father, adoptive parents, and William's father.

The Prince filled a dual role, as the representative of the King and Queen and one of the bride's fathers. It seemed that the stream of humanity was never ending. It took about an hour and a half, but eventually the line dwindled to a trickle and then ended.

As it would have been at her coming out ball, Elizabeth opened the ball with the King, the Prince of Wales, her birth-father, and then her adoptive father for the first dance of the first set. William opened with the Queen, followed by Princesses Amelia, Augusta Sophia, and Elizabeth.

When the newlyweds were able to dance together for the second dance of the first set, Elizabeth thought it amusing William had completed the first half of the set with her aunt, Princess Elizabeth and then danced the second half with another Princess Elizabeth. William corrected his wife gently, pointing out when she was with the royals she was to be addressed as Princess Beth.

The King, Queen, and the Prince of Wales withdrew after supper, at one o'clock in the morning. Although they would have preferred to be alone at Darcy House, Elizabeth and William did not leave their wedding ball early.

~~~~~~~/~~~~~~~

The next morning, everyone met for breakfast at eleven. The younger group who had not attended the ball had hot chocolate, toast, and pastries to break their fasts at the time they would have normally had the morning meal.

By midday, the coach arrived in front of the house. The extended family, including the Prince, were all present to see the newlyweds off on their way to Seaview Cottage.

After the two departed, the younger set drifted off towards the music room, except for Tommy. He returned to the

Gardiners' house to be with Eddy when the Gardiners and Phillipes departed for Gracechurch Street. Lady Sarah and Catherine de Bourgh were with the new Lord Jersey at Jersey House. That left the elder set who had been through so much alone in the drawing room.

The gathering consisted of Lord Thomas and Lady Francine Bennet, Lord Paul and Lady Edith Carrington, Lord Reggie and Lady Elaine Fitzwilliam, Prince Frederick, and his Grace, Lord Robert Darcy.

"Do you think Cilla imagined the waves that would be created by the vows she asked of you, Fanny?" the Prince asked reflectively.

"I am not sure, Freddy," Fanny stated thoughtfully. "My belief is there is little she would have regretted, other than being unaware it was not her mother's choice to cut her. I am sure if she had known that, it would have lifted her spirits, as she felt most betrayed by her mother."

"Do you think she would have been stronger when she birthed Lizzy had she known her mother did not choose to abandon her?" Elaine asked.

"According to what the midwife said at the time, I do not think anything would have changed the outcome," Fanny informed them. "We have not discussed this before, but the midwife told us that something tore inside of Cilla and the bleeding could not be stemmed; that is what took her, not melancholy."

"Have you told Sarah?" Edith asked. "I know she felt guilt over what was done, fearing that being cut by her parents contributed to Priscilla's death.

"Yes, Sarah knows. Knowing that made the burden she carried that much easier for her to bear," Fanny reported.

"I am sure Cilla knows we all protected her daughter and that she was raised in a loving home with a family far larger than she had when she was born," the Prince opined. "She would have loved the young woman Lizzy become, and that they would have looked so similar would have been a source of pleasure to my Cilla."

"York, I hope this question is not impolitic, but do you ever see Princess Frederica?" Bennet asked. "I know your separation is amicable, but I never thought to ask before."

"I have no objection to your question. We do not spend time together, but we communicate by letter if and when we need to. Yes, it is amicable, but we have nothing in common, so it is better for both of us to live separate lives," the Prince informed the group. "She is loved by the populace of Weybridge as she is heavily involved in charitable works there, much like Catherine is at Hunsford."

"Lizzy may be a Princess of the United Kingdom of Great Britain and Ireland, but she will always be my little Lizzy, my second daughter," Fanny stated wistfully.

"As she will always be to me," Bennet stated as he took his wife's hand in his own.

"She has been, and I am sure she will continue to be, the light in my life. I was lost in my sorrow after Cilla was taken, but that changed the day you told me I had a child," the Prince related in a gruff voice heavy with emotion. "She has the best parts of both Cilla and me."

~~~~~~~/~~~~~~~

Elizabeth and William enjoyed their time at Seaview cottage, and their love deepened day by day. March was one of the warmest in recent memory, so they spent time at the private cove, and discovered the wonders of other activities in the sea other than sea bathing.

They spent a month complete at Seaview Cottage, exploring the area and each other until it was time to leave their magical wedding trip and return to London and then to Pemberley.

EPILOGUE

"Mama, when will grandmother and grand-father arrive from Longbourn?" Lady Sarah Darcy asked, not for the first time. At eight, she was the baby of the Darcy family. She was named for her mother's late Grandmama who passed away in October of 1824, two years after her namesake was born.

"Sarah Anne Darcy, you asked Mama that ten minutes ago," Lady Olivia, who was fourteen, remonstrated with her youngest sister.

"Olivia, I do not object if Sarah asks me," the Duchess of Derbyshire, Princess Elizabeth Darcy, soothed her youngest while redirecting Olivia. "They will be here within the hour. Uncle Tommy and Aunt Gigi went to collect them and your cousins.

"The sooner Tom returns the better; we are going to model the battle of Waterloo, Mama," his Grace, Lord Frederick Darcy, twelve, informed his mother. He and Tom, who was nine, were the closest of friends, just like Tom's mother Lady Georgiana was with Kitty—Catherine now—and Lydia.

"When will Papa, Ben, and Robert return from their ride?" Lady Anne Darcy asked. Anne, at sixteen, was the third of the six Darcy children. Ben, the Marquess of Derby, was twenty and in his final year at Cambridge. and Robert, the Duke of York, was almost eighteen, in his first year at the same university.

~~~~~~~/~~~~~~~

Elizabeth was as happy and as in love as she had ever

been in her marriage, notwithstanding all of the deaths in her extended royal families. First Princess Amelia, the youngest of the King's and Queen's daughters and favourite of her father's died in November of 1810. The King had started displaying some of the mental issues which led to an attempt to impose a Regency in 1789. After the death of his favourite daughter, he was pushed over the precipice and a Regency was established —this one with the full support of her birthfather.

Eight years later, also in November, her beloved grandmother, Queen Charlotte, died. The only blessing arising from the King's maladies was that he was unaware his wife was no more. In January of 1820, Elizabeth's grandfather, King George III, passed away. He was succeeded by the Prince of Wales, who ended the Regency when he became King George IV

In August of the year King George III died, Princess Frederica died at Oatlands Park near Weybridge in Surrey. To commemorate her good works, the populace of the area erected a monument on the green in Weybridge to honour her. The Prince, his daughter, and her husband all attended her funeral.

The next blow came seven years later. Elizabeth's birthfather, whom she loved dearly, died from what the doctors said was a bad heart. He was four and sixty when he died and Elizabeth was his sole heir. Not only did she inherit a fortune far greater than what she already had, but a number of estates, including Oatlands Park in Surrey.

To honour his late brother, King George IV bestowed his brother's two dukedoms on Elizabeth's and William's second and third sons. Robert became the Duke of York, while Frederick became the Duke of Albany.

In June of that year, King George IV died and was succeeded by the oldest person to assume the monarchy—King William IV. Elizabeth was beyond thankful she had been removed from the line of succession. If not, she would have succeeded her Uncle George and became Queen Elizabeth of the United Kingdom of Great Britain and Ireland and she much preferred her—in her own words—simple life.

~~~~~~~/~~~~~~~

There had been a few other deaths in her non-royal family as well. Catherine de Bourgh and her two brothers passed away in November of 1827. All three contracted pneumonia and were called home to heaven within weeks of each other.

Robert Darcy lived to see nine of his grandchildren born —Elizabeth and William's six, and Gigi and Tommy's three— Tom, Franny, and Annabeth.

It had been a heavy blow when the three had passed so close to one another, following the passing of Frederick in January of that year. Their consolation was in knowing that all of them had led full and happy lives.

Reggie Fitzwilliam lived to see ten grandchildren, five each from Jane and Andrew, and Cassie and Richard. In addition, Anne and Jamey had added three, which were counted as surrogate grandchildren by Elaine and Reggie.

Catherine lived with Anne and Jamey until she drew her last breath; she had lived a happy and fulfilled life. She spent her time overseeing her charities in Hunsford each year and keeping a close eye on them whenever her son and daughter were in residence at Rosings Park.

Elaine missed her husband, and three years later still wore half mourning. She lived four months each with her son's families and two months with Anne's. Jamey and Cassie were grateful that their parents were still spry and in excellent health.

Wes proposed to Mary three months after she came out, which surprised no one. They had married in 1810, and the new Countess of Jersey respectfully declined an offer to become a patroness of Almack's. They had four children, two of each gender ranging from Thomas at seventeen to Sarah-Jane at five.

Kitty waited for both Lydia and Gigi before she came out. So, it was in 1813 when Kitty, who a year earlier had asked to be called Catherine, came out at twenty. Lydia, nineteen, and Gigi, seventeen, came out at the same time.

Georgiana had already decided Tommy was the one she wanted to marry but waited until he completed Cambridge and his grand tour. They married in late 1817. She was a few months older than Tommy, but that was never an issue for them.

During her first season, Catherine caught the eye of Mark Creighton, the heir of the Duke of Devonshire. They were married before the year was out, and after the old duke passed, she lived at Chatsworth with her husband and four children when not in Town for the season or visiting family. For her parents, having three daughters living close one to the other was ideal.

Lydia did not find a man she could truly love and esteem until 1816, when she met Harry Smythe-Jones. He had inherited an estate in Surrey a year earlier when his father passed. They married that year, and now had four children.

William Collins had remained the rector at Longbourn and was awarded the living at St. Alfred's in Meryton some fifteen years previously when the incumbent suddenly passed away. He and Charlotte were as happy, but had only two children, a son born five years after they married and a daughter three years later.

Charlotte was happily married to the man she loved. Whenever her friend Eliza visited the area the two would catch up in person; the rest of the time they relied on the post.

~~~~~~~/~~~~~~~

After his lease of Longbourn ended, Charles Bingley decided he preferred a life in trade and returned to Scarborough. His good friend's sister, Karen Jamison, was seventeen and had caught his fancy. He returned after she was eighteen to court her; they were married in 1812, had five children, and lived happily near the Bingley Carriage Works.

Harold and Louisa Hurst were blessed with three children, two boys and a girl, and were happily ensconced at the Hurst estate, Winsdale in Yorkshire, inherited by Hurst in 1811 after his father passed.

Of Caroline Bingley there is little to tell. She was never

moved from Bedlam and passed from injuries inflicted by another inmate she had upset with her pretentions two years
after she was committed to the institution. She was mourned
by her brother and sister, but after the mourning period was
done, they very rarely thought of her again.

~~~~~~~/~~~~~~~

George Wickham never reverted to his previous bad
behaviour and completed his schooling. As he had always
dreamed of doing, George read the law and, as he had during
his years of schooling, he did exceptionally well.

After thanking Mr. Gardiner for taking a chance on him
when he resigned his position, the young Wickham started
a clerkship at Norman and James after Lord Robert and Mr.
Gardiner vouched for him. Within five years George Wickham
—who had always had the gift of the gab—was a sought-after
barrister. A few years later he earned a partnership in Norman
and James.

In 1814 George met the love of his life, the daughter of
one of the solicitors at Norman and James. The couple lived
happily in London and were blessed with three children, two
sons and a daughter.

Mr. Lucas Wickham retired as the steward of Pemberley
in 1816 and came to live with his son and daughter-in-law. He
passed away in 1823, a happy man with a successful and honourable son.

~~~~~~~/~~~~~~~

Baron and Baroness Longbourn were almost ready to
depart with their son, daughter, and three grandchildren for
Netherfield. Fanny just needed to impart some information to
Mrs. Hill. No not the original Hills, however. Mr. and Mrs. Hill's
son and daughter-in-law filled the roles the parents had retired
from some fourteen years previously.

To accommodate the growing family, in 1814 the original house was torn down, and a new manor house built,
more than double in size. Between the two estates the Bennets owned, they had enough room for their extended family,

which included some of Lizzy's royal cousins who visited from time to time.

"Mother Fanny and Father Thomas, are you ready?" Georgiana asked her parents-in-law, the only living parents she had left.

"Yes Gigi, we are. Are the children in the coach?" Fanny asked.

"They are, Mother Fanny. Tommy is waiting with them," Lady Georgiana Bennet confirmed.

"In that case, let us return to your home," Lord Longbourn said as he followed the two women out of the house.

When Gigi became with child a few months after marrying Tommy, Fanny and Bennet moved back to Longbourn, leaving Netherfield Park to their son and new daughter. Since Elizabeth gifted Netherfield to the Bennets, Bennet had his brother Phillips deed the estate to his son—he would inherit it one day anyway.

The two estates became one large estate with two manor houses, each with its own name. To honour the late Priscilla, Netherfield Park's name would never be changed.

As they traversed the three miles to Netherfield, Fanny's mind fixed on thoughts of her sister of the heart and the changes her love, friendship, and generosity had wrought on the Bennets' lives.

'Cilla, my dearest Cilla. I pray you are happy in heaven with your Frederick, your mother, Robert and Anne, Catherine, and Reggie. Things were disclosed earlier than you wished in some cases, but in the end, we protected your daughter—the Bennet of Royal Blood—just as you desired.

'She was raised in love, as a normal young girl, never in a gilded cage. Thank you, Cilla, for your generosity to me and my daughters. You took all of my anxiety about the future away.

"I miss you every day. Each time I see my—our—Lizzy, I see your eyes and face looking back at me. Thank you for the gift you gave me. You thought we were helping you, but the truth is, in Lizzy, you gifted us with the most precious thing in the world.

SHANA GRANDERSON A LADY

Thank you, thank you, thank you, Cilla.' Fanny looked to the heavens through the coach's window and saw a beam of light break through the clouds. She was sure it was Priscilla answering her.

As the carriage made the last turn towards Netherfield, she saw her son, her daughter, and their children waiting for them. The rest of their extended family would arrive in the next few days and they would be—as they always were—be wrapped in the love of all their large, caring family.

The End

BOOKS BY THIS AUTHOR

A Change Of Fortunes

What if, unlike canon, the Bennets had sons? Could it be, if both father and mother prayed to God and begged for a son that their prayers would be answered? If the prayers were granted how would the parents be different and what kind of life would the family have? What will the consequences of their decisions be?

In many Pride and Prejudice variations the Bennet parents are portrayed as borderline neglectful with Mr. Bennet caring only about making fun of others, reading and drinking his port while shutting himself away in his study. Mrs. Bennet is often shown as flighty, unintelligent and a character to make sport of. The Bennet parent's marriage is often shown as a mistake where there is no love; could there be love there that has been stifled due to circumstances?

In this book, some of those traits are present, but we see what a different set of circumstances and decisions do to the parents and the family as a whole. Most of the characters from canon are here along with some new characters to help broaden the story. The normal villains are present with one added who is not normally a villain per se and I trust that you, my dear reader, will like the way that they are all 'rewarded' in my story.

We find a much stronger and more resolute Bingley. Jane Bennet is serene, but not without a steely resolve. I feel that both need to be portrayed with more strength of character for the purposes of this book. Sit back, relax and enjoy and my hope is that you will be suitably entertained.

The Hypocrite

The Hypocrite is a low angst, sweet and clean tale about the relationship dynamics between Fitzwilliam Darcy and Elizabeth Bennet after his disastrous and insult laden proposal at Hunsford. How does our heroine react to his proposal and the behaviour that she has witnessed from Darcy up to that point in the story?

The traditional villains from Pride and Prejudice that we all love to hate make an appearance in my story BUT they are not the focus. Other than Miss Bingley, whose character provides the small amount of angst in this tale, they play a small role and are dealt with quickly. If dear reader you are looking for an angst filled tale rife with dastardly attempts to disrupt ODC then I am sorry to say, you will not find that in my book.

This story is about the consequences of the decisions made by the characters portrayed within. Along with Darcy and Elizabeth, we examine the trajectory of the supporting character's lives around them. How are they affected by decisions taken by ODC coupled with the decisions that they make themselves? How do the decisions taken by members of the Bingley/Hurst family affect them and their lives?

The Bennets are assumed to be extremely wealthy for the purposes of my tale, the source of that wealth is explained during the telling of this story. The wealth, like so much in this story is a consequence of decisions made Thomas Bennet and Edward Gardiner.

If you like a sweet and clean, low angst story, then dear reader, sit back, pour yourself a glass of your favourite drink and read, because this book is for you.

The Duke's Daughter: Omnibus Edition

All three parts of the series are available individually.

Part 1: Lady Elizbeth Bennet is the Daughter of Lord Thomas and Lady Sarah Bennet, the Duke and Duchess of Hertfordshire. She is quick to judge and anger and very slow to forgive. Fitzwilliam Darcy has learnt to rely on his own judgement above all others. Once he believes that something is a certain way, he does not allow anyone to change his mind. He ignored his mother and the result was the Ramsgate debacle, but he had not learnt his lesson yet.
He mistakes information that her heard from his Aunt about her parson's relatives and with assumptions and his failure to listen to his friends the Bingleys, he makes a huge mistake and faces a very angry Lady Elizabeth Bennet.

Part 2: At the end of Part 1, William Darcy saved Lady Elizabeth Bennet's life, but at what cost? After a short look into the future, part 2 picks up from the point that Part 1 ended. We find out very soon what William's fate is. We also follow the villains as they plot their revenge and try to find new ways to get money that they do not deserve.
Elizabeth finally admitted that she loved William the morning that he was shot, is it too late or will love find a way? As there always are in life, there are highs and lows and this second part of three gives us a window into the ups and downs that affect our couple and their extended family.

Part 3: In part 2, the Duke's Daughter became a Duchess. We follow ODC as they continue their married life as they deal with the vagaries of life. We left the villains preparing to sail from Bundoran to execute their dastardly plan. We find out if they are successful or if they fail.

In this final part of the Duke's Daughter series, we get a good idea what the future holds for the characters that we have followed through the first two books in the series.

The Discarded Daughter - Omnibus Edition:

All 4 books in the Discarded Daughter series are combined into a single book. They are available individually, in both Kindle and paperback format.

The story is about the life of Elizabeth Bennet who is kidnapped and discarded at an exceedingly early age. It tells the tale of her life with the family that takes her in and loved her as a true daughter.

We follow not only Elizbeth's life, her trials and tribulations, but that of the family that lost her and all of those around her, immediate and extended family, and the effect that she has on their lives. There is love, villains, hurt, and happiness as we watch Elizabeth grow into an exceptional young woman.

If you are looking for a story that only concentrates on our heroine, then this is not for you.

Surviving Thomas Bennet

Warning: This book contains violence, although not graphically portrayed.

There are Bennet twins born to James Bennet, his heir, James Junior and second born Thomas. They boys start out as the best of friends until Thomas starts to get resentful of his older brother's status as heir.

The younger Bennet turns to gambling, drink, and carousing. In order to protect Longbourn, unbeknownst to Thomas, James Bennet senior places and entail on the estate so none of his son's creditors are able to make demands against the family estate.

Thomas Bennet was given his legacy of thirty thousand pounds when he reached his majority. He marries Fanny the daughter of a local solicitor in Oxford where Thomas is teaching. He is fired for being drunk at work. He manages to gamble away all of his legacy while going into serious debt to a dangerous man in not too many years.

When James Senior dies, Thomas and Fanny Bennet arrive at Longbourn demanding an imagined inheritance. They find out there is no more for them and leave after abusing one an all roundly swearing revenge.

James Junior, the master of Longbourn, and his wife Priscilla have a son, Jamie, and daughters Jane, Elizabeth, and Mary. Thinking he can sell Longbourn if his brother and son are out of the way, Thomas Bennet murders them and James' wife by causing a carriage accident.

The story reveals how the three surviving daughters are protected by their friends and how they survive the man who murdered their beloved parents and brother. Netherfield belongs to the Darcy's second son, William. There are many of the characters that are both loved and hated from the canon in this story, some similar to canon, a good number of them hugely different, there are also some new characters not from canon.

Unknown Family Connections

This is a book of two volumes, but all in one book. It is a one off, standalone story.

Over 150 years in the past an Evil Duke plotted to separate his first and second sons. He was a man who had two interests: money and status. Lord Sedgewick Rhys-Davies, the 3rd Duke of Bedford sets off a chain of events that ultimately ends up doing the exact opposite of what his original evil intent was in the far future.

Mr. Thomas Bennet lives with his second wife and family on his estate Longbourn in Hertfordshire. As far as he knows, he is an indirect descendant of the last Earl of Meryton whose line died out with him over 150 years ago. The family has owned Longbourn and Netherfield Park for as long as anyone remembers. There is an entail on Longbourn, but not the one we are used to. As in the canon, this Bennet dislikes London, and the Ton and he and his family keep away from London society. His second wife is the daughter of an Earl but just goes as Mrs. Bennet.

The Bennet's new tenants at Netherfield Park are the Bingleys. One of the major deviations from canon in this tale, Jane Bennet has more than a little backbone while Bingley has little or none. How will Darcy behave, will he make assumptions and act on them? Will Elizabeth allow her prejudices to rule? When Wickham slithers onto the scene will he cause havoc?

The 7th Duke of Bedford is ill, and he will be the end of the line as there are no living relatives to inherit the dukedom and vast Bedford holdings. He removes an old letter from a safe in his study written by the 4th Duke. Witten on the outside of the letter is: 'Open ONLY if there are no more Rhys-Davies heirs.'

The Duke opens the letter and learns of the 3rd Duke's evil and there is in fact an heir, although a direct descendant, he is not a Rhys-Davies.

This is the story of different families and what happens when their lives intersect and are changed for ever. There is quite a bit about Lizzy & Darcy, but there are not always the main focus of the story as the title infers.

Cinder-Liza

No fairy godmother or magic in the story although there is some imagery we would expect to see in a Cinderella story – my apologies to those who thought there would be magic based on the title.

Mr. Thomas Bennet married the love of his life: Miss Fanny Gardiner. She gave him three children, Jane, Elizabeth and Tommy. 2 years after Tommy, Fanny was taken from her loving family birthing a second son, who was stillborn.

Another branch of the Bennet family, cousins to the Long-bourn Bennets, are titled, the Earl and Countess of Holder, who live in Staffordshire with their 5 children. The two families are extremely close and after Fanny dies Bennet's cousins, at his request, keep and raise Tommy. In his grief Thomas Bennet doesn't think he can raise a 2-year-old at the same time as his two daughters. He also feels Tommy needs a mother figure in his life.

Martha Bingley is the widow of an honourable tradesman, Mr. Arthur Bingley, who had died of a heart attack. Bingley senior was a minor partner of Edward Gardiner in Gardiner and Associates. They had three children, Charles, Louisa, and Caroline. Unlike canon, the Bingleys are not very wealthy, and the girls have small dowries of £2,000 each.

Bennet is introduced to Martha at his brother-in-law's house. The Bingleys live in a leased house a few houses down from the Gardiners on Gracechurch street. Martha has always dreamed of climbing up the social ladder, raising her family above their roots in trade, so she compromises Bennet as he is a landed gentleman with an estate. Being an honourable man, and against advice of friends and family, he marries her.

Our 'prince' in the story is of course none other than His Grace Fitzwilliam Darcy, Duke of Derbyshire, Earl of Lambton. Like canon his parents have already passed away. Dear old Lady Catherine de Bourgh will do anything to make her sickly daughter with a nasty disposition a Duchess. At some point the Duke purchases Netherfield to be closer to London so his sister, Lady Georgiana, will have her preferred music master close by.

Bennet never reveals the existence of his son or his relations, who are peers of the realm, to his new wife, who he dislikes intensely. The neighbours, none of whom like the new Mrs. Bennet or her children, keep the Bennet's secrets without question. Bennet allows his new wife to believe the entail on Longbourn is away from female line giving her the impression that on his death, she and her three spawn will be evicted from the estate by a distant unnamed cousin.

Sometime after sending Jane to live with his cousins, for reasons that will be revealed in the story, with Lizzy refusing to leave her father's side, Bennet has an accident which kills him. When no heir presents himself to throw her and her children, still at Longbourn, into the hedgerows, the stepmother feels more secure at the estate.

Several the usual suspects are present as well as some other characters. This is a story of hope and survival and the eventual triumph of good over evil.

Book 1 Of The Take Charge Series: Charlotte Lucas Takes Charge

None of the books in this series are purely about the title character, but how their taking charge affects those around them.

Fanny Bennet dies of an apoplexy two years prior to the start of this story.

As in canon, the Bingleys, Hursts, and Darcy arrive in the area residing in the leased Netherfield Park. Up until the Reverend William Collins arrival, things are close to canon. Collins is the sycophant we all love to hate and sets his sights on Jane. Bennet, who by necessity takes a little more of an active role in his daughter's lives tells him in no uncertain terms he will not consent to such a man marrying ANY of his daughters.

Charlotte Lucas overhears Collins ranting to himself about how he will evict the Bennets from Longbourn the day Bennet passes. He then tried to woo Charlotte hours later and she too rejects him. He is derisive when she rejects him out of hand, he tells her that no man would ever offer for one on the shelf, without fortune, and as homely as her.

Collins then proposes to Matilda Dudley, Lizzy's friend and Longbourn's widowered parson's daughter. Matilda accepts him much to Elizabeth and Charlotte's surprise.

Collins's words to her spur Charlotte to take charge, the story tells the tale of what she does and how it affects the lives of not a few people. The book examines how Charlotte actions change the trajectories of some of our favourite (to love and hate) characters from Pride and Prejudice.

COMING SOON

The Take Charge series Book 2:
Lady Catherine Takes Charge

The great lady is very much like she is in canon until in a horrific accident in 1804 both her husband Lewis and her daughter Anne die.

For a lady who believed she could control all by force of will and desire, the deaths of her family rock her world down to the foundations. She revaluates all of her priorities and becomes a surrogate mother to both surviving Darcys.

The story is close to canon with regards to the interactions between the Netherfield and Longbourn inhabitants with the dastardly George Wickham pouring poison on our Lizzy's ear.

Jane Bennet after losing more than one suitor to her mother's vulgar and inappropriate behaviour has had the blinders removed and Lizzy is no longer in awe of her father as she has had her eyes opened to his indolence and abrogation of his parental responsibility.

Things are not as in canon at Hunsford except for the horrendous proposal of marriage Darcy makes to Elizabeth. Lady Catherine has taken a back seat so far, but she sees too much happening that needs correcting, so she takes charge.

This story looks at how this version of Lady Catherine changes the trajectory of a number of character we all love, and some we dislike intensely.

Made in the USA
Monee, IL
31 July 2023